The
VIOLIN
MAKER

Dear Jill,

Glenn J Hill

I hope you enjoy

GLENN J HILL

This novel is dedicated to the memory of my hidden Jewish Mother, Katherine Kiel/Kyle, who always encouraged and inspired my creativity. And to our ancestors who at times and for generations, had to hide who they were, sometimes on pain of death.

And to my loving wife Laurie, who is my muse, and loving supporter in all things. Laurie, you are my love for all time.

This novel would not have been possible without the fabulous critique and support from all my friends in The Ashland Novelist Group. I am grateful for my various Beta readers, the amazing editing of Karen Sanders, and the beautiful cover design by Fiona Jayde.

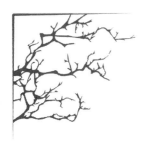

Return Again

RETURN AGAIN, RETURN again, return to the land of your soul.

> *Return to who you are, return to what you are,*
> *return to where you are. Born and reborn, again and again...*
> Jewish Song-Prayer

Copyright © 2019 Glenn J. Hill

First Printing, 2019

Cover Design Copyright © 2019 Fiona Jayde http://fionajaydemedia.com/

EBOOK ISBN 978-1-7338749-0-8

PRINT ISBN 978-1-7338749-1-5

Mountain Glen Publishing

809 W. 1st Street

Phoenix, Oregon 97535

mountainglenpublishing@gmail.com

The Jewish mystical prayers, songs, legends, and practices in this novel are based on traditional Jewish, Kabbalistic, mystical practices, and beliefs.

Portions of the 'Third Secret of Fatima', as well as descriptions of the events that occurred at some of the visions of the 'Shepard Children' used in this novel are accurate, as recorded by witnesses. Other parts of 'The Third

Secret of Fatima' in this novel are fictional. The debate regarding the complete content of the 'Third Secret' is ongoing among various Catholic groups.

'The Circle of Fatima' is a fictional group invented for this novel. However, it is based on real groups with similar outlooks and philosophies that have existed in the 20th century and in some cases are still very active today in 2019. These groups are fringe organizations that, in most cases, exist outside the mainstream Catholic Church.

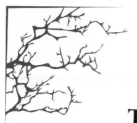

Prologue
The Angel of Death

CALIFORNIA, DONNER Summit Highway 40
February 1967

Blinding snow pelted the windshield piling up fast with only a tiny space kept clear by the laboring wiper blades. Two tire ruts ahead barely showed as streaks of gray in white. Beyond the pavement, the sheer cliff edge vanished in a swirl of white-out and black night. He could see his target now. A slow moving station wagon wallowing through the deep snow just entering a sharp curve ahead.

The endless bitter-white-cold and the deep snow reminded him of Stalingrad. Franco had called for volunteers from Portugal to fight with the Germans, so he went to war in the name of the Lady. They had killed many Russians, but there were always more. His Blue Battalion had fought stubborn rearguard actions, retreating to Germany with the loss of many friends captured, shot dead, or left frozen in the snow. He survived the defeat of Germany in nineteen-fifty-five, coming home to Fatima to join the Blessed Lady's Circle to continue fighting all enemies of the Church.

With this last mission in Her name, I will have a final victory.

"Hail Mary, full of Grace... pray for us sinners now and at the hour of our death. Amen." Reciting the Rosary to himself he shifted the semi-tractor into third gear, gaining speed as the tire-chains dug into the snow. Faster into fourth, and then, with increasing speed and momentum, the diesel engine roared into the highest gear he could manage in the short stretch of road left to him. Plunging down the steep twisting road like a massive sleigh it was all he could do to keep the semi-tractor and its heavy gasoline tanker-trailer on the pavement.

But that didn't matter. His mission would soon be complete with these enemies of the Lady destroyed.

My confession has been heard. My sins absolved. Soon, I will be in the arms of the Blessed Virgin.

The last things the two adults and the young child saw or heard before everything changed were the bright beams of light that pierced the car and the roaring sound of the accelerating metal-mass that enveloped and crushed it.

No one witnessed the mingled terror of three souls or the twisted cry of triumph of a fourth. No one else heard or saw the ear-rending crash, exploding fuel, crumbling cliff face, or the careening mass of twisted metal and flame. Flesh, blood, metal, and snow combined as it all crashed down the mountainside into the dark, jagged canyon.

And at first, no one saw the bright blue bundle with its halo of flames thrown clear as the combined wreckage went over the cliff.

Archbishop's Palace, Circle of Fatima, Fatima, Portugal
February 1986

"Perdonami. Forgive me, Monsignor. We al-most had it, but we m-missed him. He g-got away," mumbled the priest as he fell to his knees and then went belly-flat, stretched out on the floor at the feet of his much taller superior. As the priest lay there, he failed to notice the vibrantly colored silk Persian rug beneath him, feeling only his trembling limbs and the rapid beating of his heart.

The face of his superior, Monsignor DeSilva, had grown still and unreadable as the trembling priest spoke. "It was a simple task. Nothing difficult," the Monsignor quietly spoke. "To overpower an old man and claim the object he carried. And you say that somehow, he eluded you? And you do not know where he is now, or where he hid what I am seeking?"

DeSilva, with a rising wave of anger, pondered his options.

Who else can I send worthy of accomplishing this task for our Blessed Lady? Does this one deserve another chance?

Turning back to the prone figure quaking on the carpet he spoke calmly but coldly, his anger now an icy dagger, though not yet unsheathed. "You may yet save yourself from the fire."

"P-lease..."

"Is there word on our other problem? Is it true the child lives? That he survived?"

"No. He must be dead. It has b-been nineteen years. The records show the mission was c-completed as ordered," quivered the desperate voice from the depths of the floor. "One of our finest soldiers, a veteran of the Blue Legion, per-formed the task."

"So, you believe the original reports and have found nothing at all? No trace, despite the rumors?"

The wretched man on the floor croaked in despair. "No-thing at all. The wreckage b-burned so hotly no bodies were found. E-ven the bones were burnt to almost nothing. So, nothing. He is dead, like his parents."

"You do understand the prophesied object is said to be possessed by a golem, a Jewish demon with a power to disrupt all our plans? We must find it as soon as possible for if these two are the ones the Third Secret foretold; they can never be allowed to unite."

"Yes, Monsignor," said the miserable priest.

"It could threaten the supreme authority of the Church. It must be brought to me here. The boy, if he lives, has to be captured and dealt with. He must be turned to the service of the Lady or eliminated. When we find this object, its power will become our power to use to destroy all of our enemies."

I will extinguish this ancient heresy, these Jews if it is the last thing I do. Victory is close. Just a few left but all must be found and turned or purified in the fire. I will avenge you, Mother.

In a voice as hard as frozen steel, the Monsignor's words sliced through the air. "I have new intelligence the child may have survived. You will go and find him. Do not alert him to your presence. Our members within the government will confirm if his work number has been activated and direct you to his location." Picking up his long-handled whip, he added, "Proceed with care, and if you find him, report back for instructions. Otherwise, that is what your fate may be. As you said, 'no-thing' at all. Now, prepare to receive my gift to you."

"Wait. Please, wait. I have an idea. A way to find out if he is the one, we seek."

DeSilva paused, with his vicious whip held aloft ready to strike the prone figure. "Yes. Tell me now. What?"

He dared to raise his face from the floor and look at the Monsignor. "The agent in Chicago. Is their mission finished?"

"Yes."

"Monsignor, send that one to find the boy to verify or not his connection to the Third Secret."

"Yes. Very clever thinking. That one would indeed be perfect for this job. You may have saved yourself, young man. For such a fine idea, I will give you a gift."

With excitement, the young priest started to rise from the floor, smiling and exclaiming in relief, "Father, Monsignor, thank you. Thank you."

DeSilva raised the whip back over his head, saying, "A gift of your life."

"No, Father! Don't!"

The leather whip thongs with their heavy pointed lead balls rose high into the air above the priest, descending with force, tearing the black wool robe, now red with fresh blood, forcing him back to the floor. Again, and again, spots of bright red were added to the color of the luminous rug. The priest's cries of pain were swallowed by the dense silk fibers of the carpet of Paradise.

Villa Vista Per Sempre, Portofino, Italy
March 1986

Deep in the cellars of the ancient villa among the Roman brickwork and bedrock limestone, the sound of stone on stone echoed. With a strength that belied his aged look, the old man lifted the limestone blocks one by one, setting them into the fresh mortar.

His work this day was to reseal the hidden cavity in the ancient wall where she had been hidden at the back of the wine cellar. He had uncovered the first treasure and awakened it to consciousness, placing her where she needed to be. Now her power would unfold and grow as she called out to the other one.

The enemy had pursued him from Italy to America, but he had lost them there in the maze of new, New York City. Despite their long reach, money, and power, they had not yet discovered the villa or the real power that the two vessels contained. That had to remain so.

They knew now of this one but not its true nature and what it was capable of, nor were they yet aware that the other one lived. He would finish there and then would resume his journey to aid the other on his challenging path.

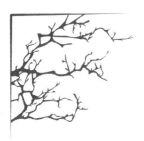

One
Joseph

HE KNEW THE PLACE EVEN with his eyes closed. There was the familiar scent of hot sun on stone, fragrant flowers, and salty sea air. It was the same dream that came to him almost every night now. Though that night there was a strange new smell. A strong, sickly sweet smell of burned meat and wood smoke that hung in the air. He kept his eyes squeezed shut.

It can't be happening again. Please, no... Wake up... Please, dear God, wake me up...

Opening his eyes, Joseph knew it had captured him once again, the nightmare that haunted him leaving him bleary-eyed and exhausted in the morning. Looking down at his feet, he saw he was wearing the same worn, dusty leather sandals, and a long black woolen robe.

Everything's so clear this time; more solid, less hazy. Somehow more real, more... I'm not sure...

He was standing on a scorching hot cobblestone pavement with white plastered stone buildings all around him. There were red tiled roofs, balconies hung with colorful flowering vines, and citrus trees showing their blossoms over the tops of the courtyard walls. The sky overhead was a bright sapphire blue with a few tiny white clouds. While awake, he had never seen this kind of beauty; a sky that was so blue, endless masses of colorful flowers, and such bright sunlight, in his entire life. His world was nothing like this. It was never hot, with few flowers, dull-colored trees, and a sky that was almost always cloudy and gray.

In the distance, he could hear a low roar of many voices faint at first but now louder. Ugly, angry, shouting voices were moving closer. Clouds of smoke were beginning to rise from far off scattered buildings. He knew it was merely a dream, but he felt a growing fear.

An enormous crowd was coming. Hundreds of feet pounding on the cobblestones running towards him. Some were carrying lit torches. They were closing in, almost upon him now. Streaming into the open square where he stood, the sound of hundreds of screaming and yelling voices overwhelmed him like a crashing wave.

He couldn't make out the words at first. But one voice heard above the others cried out, "Matar os Judeus. Kill the Jews. Find the swine where they are hiding. Kill the Jews. Kill the pigs."

Joseph knew this was a different tongue, yet he somehow understood it. He stood frozen in fear as the crowd surged forward, rushing directly at him. Dream or not, now he was truly terrified. The mob broke upon him flowing past and around the spot where he stood, yelling and screaming very close, but seeming not to see him standing there.

Some were running for their lives with their hair and clothing partially burned, sometimes stumbling, then being overrun and swallowed by the crowd. In absolute horror, Joseph saw these victims caught and torn apart in front of him. The shrieks of their death agonies rose above the roar of the mob. Brilliant red blood flowed on the pavement. The hunters were pursuing and catching their prey.

Some in the crowd carried wood. The broken bodies were piled on top of it, covered with oil and lit with torches. Joseph cried out in terror, but no one seemed to hear him.

Paralyzed with horror and fear, he now understood the burned meat smell. He was an invisible witness to all of this... he thought. But then one set of dark eyes focused on him with a chilling stare. Their black robed owner turned, blood dripping from knives held in both his hands and shouted, "Obtenha ele. Get him." With outstretched arms and the lethal knives pointed at Joseph, the figure lunged directly at him.

Salt Lake City Utah
March 26, 1986
Year Thirty-one of the 'Jewish' Nuclear Winter
Joseph inhaled sharply. Holding his breath and shaking uncontrollably, he awoke in his bed, a foam pad on the concrete floor in the simple basement

space he rented. Despite the icy cold outside and the chilly room, he was sweating as if with a fever. Pushing the tangled old sleeping bag and blankets off his legs he quickly backed onto the edge of the pad against two walls. He folded his slim, lanky body into the sharp space, his heart beating wildly panicked by the nightmare horror he had just experienced. The burn scars on his back grated against the rough wall plaster, but still, he pressed himself harder into the corner.

Where am I? What just happened? Am I losing my mind?

He could still see the enraged faces and hear the frenzied voices. The smell of the burning wood, oil, and human flesh. The screams of the dying. The blood and burning bodies. Those dark eyes and the knives in bloody hands were reaching for him. It was all vividly imprinted in his memory. He had dreamt of that place before and had always felt some fear along with the beauty. But this time all the charm had been smothered with unspeakable horror.

Can I ever sleep again?

The dream was so vivid it took him some time to feel grounded in what he knew was real. Feeling the cold, rough concrete floor under his bare feet and gripping the old sleeping bag and coarse blankets of his bed with his hands, Joseph spoke out loud, trying to calm his nerves and to remind himself of what was real. "I'm Joseph Davidson. I'm almost twenty-one. I'm studying Italian violin building at the American Violin Making School in Salt Lake City. It's March 26th, 1986. Thirty-one years since the end of the war and the start of the long winter."

After a while, finally catching his breath and slowing his heart, he sat upon his pillow with crossed legs and tried to meditate. Meditation often worked for him to find a calm center after his usual dreams. But that morning, after a few minutes, with those new, frightening images still filling his mind, he knew it was not going to work. He got up and threw cold water on his face and neck. Looking in a broken piece of mirror hanging on the concrete wall, he could see a wet and wild looking face with deep blue eyes staring back. Drying his face with its two day old beard on an old torn piece of towel he ran his fingers through and tried to smooth his unruly brown hair, saying to himself, "A dream. It was only a dream."

Still shaken by the nightmare, he realized he was late for school. Sitting at his small chair and table, he ate a cold breakfast of granola with water, downed with yesterday's cold coffee, and set out on foot to make his way to school. A cold winter wind fiercely bit into him as it funneled between the buildings. The wind poured down from the high, snow-covered peaks, blowing the fresh-fallen powder against his back and neck.

He was run-walking in an awkward rolling gait with every step painfully pulling at the old scar tissue on his arms, back, and legs. In the wind whipped snow, he was carefully trying to not slip on the icy sidewalk. Joseph's steps were helping to warm him, though not nearly enough. His winter coat was thin, cheaply made, and cheaply bought. A good coat for an orphan.

Attempting to lighten his mind after his disturbing night he hummed to himself the opening bars of the Mendelssohn Violin Concerto in E Minor. As the melody ran through his mind, the glove covered fingers of his left hand started automatically fingering the notes in the air as he walked. The opening theme that ran through and haunted Mendelssohn's mind now helped to soothe Joseph's troubled thoughts.

Not fully awake and still shaken by the nightmare visions. He hadn't noticed that someone was taking the same route, gaining on him and now keeping just twenty feet or so behind. It was not unusual for another pedestrian to follow in ones footsteps broken in the newly fallen snow, but this man had followed him for some blocks almost from the front door of Joseph's building.

When he reached the last corner in the sheltered entranceway near the front door of his school, Joseph turned and looked at the man who was following him. The man was walking vigorously against the increasing wind belying his apparent age. He approached Joseph, stopping just two feet in front of him, and calmly stared. The man was well bundled against the cold but in layers of mismatched, ragged clothing. Despite the morning chill and gathering snowstorm, a strong repellent scent of dirt and sweat hung over the figure. He looked like so many of the hundreds of homeless men on the cold streets. Joseph wondered if the man needed help.

Mostly hidden by a hood and hat just a bit of his deeply creased and wrinkled face could be seen. Some strands of wild, white hair peeked out. Around the figure's neck—an odd shape in bright gold—something that looked so out of place on him was partially visible. The man's brilliant blue eyes pierced the morning gloom. They focused intensely on Joseph, staring into his eyes with a look, Joseph would not soon forget. There was something about this old man that felt powerful and perhaps dangerous, a mysterious hidden presence, though on the surface he seemed harmless enough. Was Joseph thrilled, or a bit scared, or some of each? He wasn't sure.

Then, without a word, the stranger turned and started to walk away.

"Wait! Who are you? What do you want of me?" Joseph called after him.

Stopping for a moment twenty feet away and partly obscured from view in the blowing snow, the stranger turned speaking just loud enough for Joseph to hear. "Tikun Olam." He turned once more and walked away.

"What do you mean, ticome? Who or what is olume?" Joseph shouted into the swirling snow. The only answer was the whistle of the wind as the receding figure faded into the gathering storm.

Joseph paused on the threshold of the violin making school, leaning against the wall, sheltered from the icy wind and blowing snow. Shaken by that look, he was somehow pierced to his core with a deep feeling of something strange and not of his world. Oddly, he now had a sense of significant loss, a tearing in his heart, as if a death had just somehow occurred a moment ago. He wanted to scream into the storm, *"Wait. Don't go. Who are you? Come back,"*. But the words wouldn't come, and it was no use as the stranger was gone.

Who was that and what is he to me? What does he want? What's happening to me? The dreams and last night's nightmare, and now this? It's crazy. How can an old bum affect me like this? What did he say? What did it mean?

And then there was that shape, the golden form he had seen hanging at the man's neck. It looked somehow like an open hand, and it seemed welcoming to him.

I have seen something like it before, but I'm not sure where or when. Then, in a flash, it came to him. *Maybe something my mother wore?*

He could barely remember his parents. Just the touch of warm, loving hands and a woman's voice sweetly humming, and a lower man's voice singing strange words he could not recall.

And that shape. Like an open hand bright and shining, inviting me closer. That's it. It would catch my eye when I nursed at her breast. She wore it around her neck. Always. But that was a faint memory, so long ago. Nineteen years now, when his parents were killed in a traffic accident when he was only two. *They told me my scars came from the fire and crash, though I cannot remember any of it.*

Quite chilled from standing outside so long and trying to shake off the strange encounter and nightmare Joseph opened the front door and entered the school. He settled into his seat at the end of the long workbench, by the window overlooking the sidewalk. In front of him lay the violin he was building, in its cradle, with the top plate sitting on the rib structure, not yet glued into place. The warmth of the large overhead gas heater started to thaw his face and hands. Trying to relax, he inhaled deeply, drawing in the comforting smell of hot coffee from the many small desktop coffee makers mixed with the scent of spruce and maple shavings.

The two high ceiling workrooms, former old-fashioned retail shops with their sidewalk facing large glass windows, felt comfortable and safe after the events of his nightmare, and the strange encounter just outside. The other students were already at their workbenches, intensely focused on the detailed tasks in front of them. This included Rachel, the attractive young woman Joseph sometimes daydreamed of.

Rachel had just transferred to the school two weeks before. She was from a school back east as a third year student, the same as Joseph. Her infectious laugh, relaxed, natural smile, and radiant beauty had delighted him the first moment he saw her. She had long curly dark brown hair, a shape that was both slim and curved at the same time, emerald green eyes, and skin the color of warm honey.

"Morning, Joe. You all right?" his friend, Charlie whose workbench was next to Joseph's, said. Adding, "You look frozen stiff."

"I'm just a bit cold. Maybe I need a better coat. Thought I could get by through the winter with this one, but I need to go by Goodwill to see if they have more. It seems like winter is not getting any shorter like they said it would, even after all these years."

"Yeah, it sure is cold. And the frigging snow is getting deeper out there. But, Joe, you look more than cold. You're looking spooked like you've just seen a ghost or something. What's happening, man?"

Joseph thought that even though his recent experiences were so strange and sometimes frightening, he still needed to tell someone, to maybe get some perspective. So, he moved his chair closer to his friend, the wheels squeaking on the old wood floor. He bent close and lowered his voice. "Charlie, I don't know. It's crazy stuff. I'm not sure if I can talk about it, or if I even want to. You'll think I'm going off the deep end."

"What do you mean, crazy stuff? Like what?"

"Some strange things have been happening to me. Weird, bizarre stuff. Like I had another strange super vivid dream last night. I've had a bunch of them just this week, almost every night now. It used to be I'd have an odd one sort of like this once a week or so, but now..."

"Wow. Every night?"

"Yeah. I'm not getting much sleep. In these dreams, I'm somewhere hot and sunny, with buildings that look like something from the Mediterranean area, like maybe Spain. It's somewhere with bright colored flowers and a sky that's blue. I mean, really blue, like in the colored pictures in old National Geographic's, or color films from before the war. They're so real, and somehow, they're more than real. But these dreams are now turning into real freaking nightmares with people chasing others and killing them. Tearing them apart right in front of me. It's terrible. I can see it inside my mind, happening right now, like I'm still there."

Charlie's expression had gone through changes from brighter to darker as he registered what Joseph was saying, his brown eyes growing larger as his friend spoke.

"And, last night someone in my dream seemed to see me. It was a guy dressed all in black with bloody knives in his hands. He saw me and then tried to grab me. Oh man, I'm not getting enough sleep. I'm getting scared just to close my eyes."

"That's wild, Joe." Charlie leaned back in his chair, stretching his back and taking a deep breath. "That sounds bad like some real nightmares. Jesus. People chasing and killing each other and tearing people apart in front of you?" A slight smile had formed on his face as he laughed and added, "are you sure it isn't something bad you're eating that's causing them?"

"Something I ate?" Joseph replied with a sharp tone as he gave his friend a dirty look, and turned to look away from Charlie.

With an apologetic expression, Charlie said, "Hey, hey, take it easy, Joe. I'm sorry. I was just messing with you a bit. It really does sound pretty scary."

"Okay, but this is serious, Charlie. I wouldn't have told you if I knew you'd laugh at me."

"Sorry, I laughed. It's just that I don't know much about dreams 'cause I don't have any. Or any I remember. Though some of it does sounds pretty good. Blue sky, you say? That would be very cool to see."

"It's amazing, and it's so beautiful. I wish I could somehow show you what it looks like for real."

"I read in school about how the sky used to be blue all the time before the bombs fell. New York, London, Berlin, and the rest. They were all such beautiful cities. Man, what a waste. All gone. All destroyed. The nukes ended the war, but they almost ended us too. And they still might if the weather doesn't warm up pretty soon."

They both paused, each taking a deep breath. Charlie's words caused them to remember the history that dominated their lives. The cool summers and long winters, and sometimes, a shortage of certain foods. A long silence ensued filled with the cold reality of their present day world that had caused them to grow up faster than earlier generations. The other students were carving and scraping away with their tools unaware of the serious silence between the two young men.

"And here we are building violins instead of saving the world," added Charlie.

"Yeah, but we have to keep on living. And violins, music, art, and other things of beauty are important too." Joseph said as he looked across the room to where the new transfer student Rachel, had her workbench. He could see the amber color of her neck showing where her long curly brown hair parted into two, as she hunched her shoulders, concentrating on some intense detail of the viola she was carving.

He didn't know what it was but the first moment he had seen her he knew there was something, some connection between them. He had never been with a woman, but he daydreamed about Rachel every day. He wanted to ask her out, to kiss her lips, touch her hair, and maybe even be with her as a lover. *But what if she said no? He couldn't take that. No, he wouldn't risk it.*

Charlie could see where Joseph was looking and said, "Maybe Rachel can help you with that kind of thing; figuring out the dreams? She's into dreams, what they mean, and that reincarnation stuff too. Like who you were in a past life."

Joseph lost concentration on his work at Charlie's mention of Rachel. How did he even know what she was into? As he tensed, it caused his burn scars to pull sharply, adding to his cross mood.

With Joseph glaring at him, Charlie said, "Hey, Joe, lighten up a bit. I don't know anything about that stuff. But maybe I can help you with the cold." Taking his down jacket off the back of his chair, he held it out to Joseph. "I have my old coat here you can have. It's as good as new and warm as toast. My mother just sent me a new heavy down jacket."

"That's okay. I'll buy a warmer one this week. Just leave it, I'll be fine."

"Hey, don't be dense. Here, put it on so you can warm up." Charlie handed Joseph his coat. "I have the new one next door in my apartment. I'll go get it at lunch."

Joseph, though poor, had fierce pride. But he was cold. Charlie was an okay guy though a bit of a snot. A rich kid. And, sometimes, a real ass.

Joseph held the unwanted gift for a while, looking at Charlie while inwardly fuming. Then, slowly and painfully, he stood up, the scars on his back and legs pulling on him as he did so. He knew if he warmed up the wounds wouldn't hurt so much, so he pulled his arms into the jacket, and zipped it up. Sitting down again, he started to feel better as the thick, soft coat helped to comfort his damaged body.

"Thank you, Charlie. It feels good."

"Hey, man. You're welcome."

Joseph was still mad at Charlie but continued the story of his strange morning.

"But, to tell you more, this morning I had some guy follow me to school. He looked like a homeless guy and smelled like one too. He got almost right in my face, and his eyes were so freaking blue, like pools of dark blue water. But it was weird 'cause he scared me in some way, but in some way, he was maybe all right. I don't know."

Charlie leaned in towards Joseph. "What do you mean, he scared you, but it was all right? Are you sure you're okay?"

"Well, he was wearing something odd. It looked like it was real gold, shaped like an open hand. It resembled something I had seen before a long time ago."

"Hey. Now you're really freaking me out with all this stuff. A homeless guy wearing something made of gold? No way!" Charlie turned to stare at Joseph. "Joe, why don't you find a warmer place to live? That school apartment is still open next door. I think you're getting sick from this cold, damp weather. The rent is pretty cheap, and the heat works. And then nobody can follow you to school 'cause you'll be right here all the time."

"I don't have enough money, Charlie! I only make eight bucks an hour at the store, and my savings need to stretch until I finish school."

Seeing them huddled in the conversation for so long the school shop teacher, who sat at the end of their row of workbenches, was now looking at them. They both saw this and started back to work on their respective instruments. After a while, they resumed the conversation, but at a much lower tone.

"But, Joe, aren't you getting an inheritance or something? You mentioned it last week, and you're about to turn twenty-one, right? That's so cool! I can take you out to get drunk at one of the private clubs when you do." Charlie had raised his voice in his excitement, "You need to quit that stupid grocery job and move in next door before you freeze to death. And if you took more time in the workshop and worked less, you could also graduate early."

He just doesn't give up once he gets started.

"Keep your voice down. All I have is an odd package from some lawyers in California. I'm not even sure it's real. So, until I know I have some money or find out it's some stupid scam, I need to be careful of what I spend. I don't know where I would get an inheritance from anyway. I don't even know who my family was."

"Maybe you're an heir to some exotic kingdom somewhere. And rich as a king to boot!"

Joseph ignored him, and cutting into the hard rock maple of his violin's scroll with the razor-sharp gouge, worked on refining the narrow V-shaped curves of the spiral shape. Joseph then changed the subject. "That field trip to the Shrine to Music collection... are you going? You know it's this weekend?"

"For sure. It's one of the best violin collections in the world."

"I was maybe going to skip it to work some extra hours at the store."

"Are you crazy? It's a chance of a lifetime. You have to go. You'll get to see some totally cool violins that you might never have a chance to see again. They're going to let us handle and examine each instrument, including the Strads and Amati's. You can't miss this trip."

"Okay, okay. I guess I should go, though it's a long drive to Vermillion. I looked it up in the road atlas. Plus, the motel and food costs. I don't know. It's going to cost a lot. But I need to finish school with the best appraisal possible from the director. I have to get a good job so I can have that surgery I told you about. My scars hurt so much, and the pain seems to be getting worse. So, I need to see and learn everything I can to build my resume, to land a job in a good violin shop."

"You need to go see that collection if you're serious about getting a good job when you graduate."

"Yeah, you're right. I guess I need to go," Joseph said, surrendering to his friend's arguments.

"And you know, Rachel`s going. I think she likes you a lot and you might get a chance to spend some time with her."

Joseph raised his voice in reply." Just leave it, Charlie!" Other students and the shop teacher turned and looked at them. He added in a fierce whisper, "Enough with Rachel, and the field trip. You're pissing me off." Joseph turned back to his work; his whole body tensed.

"You should go on the trip, and you need to talk to Rachel," Charlie said as he pulled on Joseph's old hooded coat. "Do you want to go out and play some hacky-sack during the break?"

"Where? Out in that blizzard? Are you nuts?"

"Out on the street where the snow`s been plowed. Come on. Take a break and have some fun. It's even more fun in the snow. Especially with an orange and blue sack."

"Nah, I'm still chilly. I'll stay here. And I still have a lot to carve on this scroll."

"Okay. See you in a bit," Charlie said as he stepped through the door of the workshop, followed by several other students.

Joseph turned back to his workbench and thought about his next steps to complete the violin, first matching the two sides of the scroll, so the carving on one side perfectly mirrored the other. Then the fine scraping of the inside arching of the spruce top plate, and the preparations for gluing the bass bar into place.

And he thought about Rachel. The way she moved her body like a dancer when she chiseled the maple of a viola's back. First leaning in with her back arched, bracing her long legs against the floor then cutting into the hard maple with the razor-sharp tool, peeling each long curl of maple free to fly into the air while her long, dark brown hair bounced back and forth.

Because of my scars, I've never had a girlfriend. Never touched a woman's body. And probably never will.

His eyes were becoming wet with longing and loss for what could never be.

And that dream last night. Those hands that were reaching for me. Wow, what freaky shit.

A deep chill moved through his body, causing him to shiver. And this time, it wasn't from the cold.

Joseph was startled from his thoughts by a loud crashing sound just outside, a car spinning its tires and moving away at high speed on the snowy street as yelling voices came through the now opened front door.

"Someone call an ambulance. Charlie's been hit by a car."

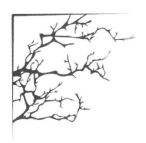

Two
Marcus

LISBON, PORTUGAL

March 29, 1522

His body curled in a tight ball; Marcus awoke to the screaming in his mind. He was four years old again, and his mother was being murdered just outside his hiding place. In his dreams, it was Lisbon 1506, as it would always be for him. It was a living nightmare that plagued his dreams most every night.

Drenched in sweat, he opened his eyes. He had crammed himself into a dark, dusty corner under the bed in his small bedroom workshop. A spider on the underside of the bed seemed to stare back at him, and he moved to smash it, but stopped, and instead said very softly, "Life is a rare and precious thing, my little friend."

In a whisper, he said his morning prayers. "Master and Holy God, who are beyond our understanding... you gave us rest through night-long sleep and raised us up to glorify your goodness, your exalted and blessed Name. Father, Son, and Holy Spirit, always, now and forever. Amen."

He stiffly stood up and dusted himself off. Through the thin walls, he could hear his landlady saying her rosary.

I wonder if she hears me cry out in my dreams.

He had tried to distance himself from the memories, but they were embedded in the deepest recesses of his mind, stuck like something dead, dried and horrible smashed on the paving stones of his memory. He found the dreams both terrifying and confusing. His memory of the mob crying, "Christ-killers," and "Death to the Jews," made no sense to him as neither he nor his family was Jewish.

He could not reconcile this with what little he remembered of his childhood. And lately, the dreams had become more vivid in detail, gradually becoming an ongoing, ever-present horror. A horror that he could not shake off even in the full light of day.

Knocking on his door, his landlady called out, "Marcus, are you awake? Are you hungry?"

"Yes, I am. I would love some food."

"Is it today that you are to become a priest? I am so proud of you. My son, who is in heaven with the angels; if he had lived, I would have wished that he would have become one."

"Yes, Marie. Today is the day. At the cathedral."

"Do you want some hot food?"

"Whatever you have is fine." Marcus opened the door and stepped into the main room. Smiling at his landlady, he added with a warm laugh, "Your cooking keeps me going."

She continued in a teasing voice, "Have you finished those boxes you're building? Or are you building your viols again? Can you pay the rent today? Or do you expect a poor widow like me to give a free roof and food to such an excuse for a priest-to-be?"

Marcus knew her gentle nagging meant well. "I will be able to pay you when I sell what I made this week."

"Marcus Antonius, I am concerned about you. I heard you screaming something again last night. Do nightmare creatures plague you? I cannot sleep with the noise you make. You need to ask the Virgin to intercede for you to drive them away."

"Something like that." Marcus thought he knew who the nightmare's creatures were. Voices he seemed to recognize. Neighbors to his family. Two men. His father's closest friends, part of the mob who butchered his family. The ones who had so viciously taken his mother's virtue and then her life.

I can still hear them, as I did then from my hiding place. They were taunting my mother with insults as they violated her and my sisters. "Jewish bitches. Christ-killers. You never got it so good."

None of it made any sense to him, as his family had all been good Catholics, not cursed Jews.

Someday, I will send those who murdered my family straight to Hell, along with their entire families. If I can find them, I will destroy and extinguish them all for the crimes they committed. 'An eye for an eye, and a tooth for a tooth.'

His landlady was sweet and helpful to him, treating him like a son, having lost her own in the plague. But he could not risk her finding out about his confusing background and his family, and his plans for revenge. His nightly terrors might give him away or lead to dangerous questions. For the work that was ahead of him and for the mission of revenge he was on, he must soon find a safer home.

After four years of study in Lisbon, Marcus was about to be consecrated as a Catholic priest. He would be sent to the city of Evora, where his uncle lived. As he ate the food, his landlady had prepared —boiled pork and barley gruel—she tried to get him to talk.

"Marcus or I should now say, Father Antonius? Where are you going to be sent? What town or village will be your home? Do you have any family after all? Where was your family from to have such a name as Marcus Antonius? Where they foreigners? Italians?"

He had never told her that he had an uncle. He had just said he was an orphan who knew his name but did not know who his people were. He told her that he was left with no family by the plague that had swept the land in 1505. That was true in a way, though it was a different sort of plague that had taken his family.

Marcus replied, "I do not know yet. Most likely, far away from Lisbon, in the south, near the sea. In time, they will tell me."

"You must tell me where you go, so I can maybe come to visit. You have become like my son."

His uncle had seen him when he could during Marcus' stay in Lisbon, though they always met outside the city in private. After he had obtained revenge against those who had murdered his family, he would need to cover his trail. No one could know where he went.

"Marie, you can give my wood stock and pieces to the next lodger, and here, you may have these boxes as payment for what I owe you. Then take the two viols to the market and sell them for yourself as I now need to travel lightly. You have been most kind to me and provided me with a good home while I have studied, but now I must move on."

With tears in her eyes, she touched him on one shoulder. "Marcus, thank you for the boxes and viols. You are a good man. Go with God and the Virgin's blessings."

Dressed in his ankle-length black robe, with a rough wooden cross around his neck and his small travel bag in one hand, he stepped out into the warm spring morning on his way to the Cathedral of Santa Maria. The air sounded with the roaring sounds of the great city. The shouts of donkey drivers urging their stubborn charges to keep moving. The complaining of cattle, as men drove them to market and the squealing of pigs as they were herded down the street to slaughter. All of these sounds and more, made up the enormous din of a sizable commercial capital at work with its mixed aromas. The smells of baking bread and roasting pork from ten thousand ovens mixed with the scents of a multitude of flowers filled the air. And in the background, the ever-present background smell of urine and dung.

That day, Marcus did not see the beauty of the white-caped green sea, the colorful flowers falling over the rooftops, or the blue sky, as his thoughts focused in determination.

I am on my way now. I will avenge my family.

As he walked, the blue sky seemed to change to a deep, dark gray. He started to lose feeling in his arms and legs as his body now felt heavy and sluggish.

He felt like he was almost part of the stones, stuck and dizzy, spinning in place as something alien, an extraordinary presence, was overtaking and possessing him.

... Holy Mother of God, save me. Save... me ...

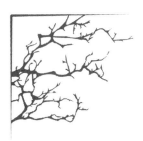

Three
Joseph

VERMILLION, SOUTH DAKOTA, The Shrine to Music Museum
   March 29, 1986

She had been waiting in the dark many long years for him to come back to her, for him to caress her again, to awaken her once more into her full power. She was ready. *Come to me, my Master. I am here.*

"Your dreams remind me of ones I've had of a place much like that." Rachel paused, looking thoughtful. "It almost sounds like we're dreaming the same dreams. How can that be?"

They had sat next to each other on the long drive from Salt Lake City to the Shrine to Music Museum in South Dakota, and Joseph had told her about his dreams. He kept his telling to just the beautiful aspects, unsure if he could talk any more of the frightening parts.

I just told Charlie about it, and now he's in the ICU on life support.

Joseph was feeling spooked by the last few days' events.

"I have no idea how we could, but it sure sounds like we're somehow dreaming about the same places or something similar."

As they traveled, he began to relax around her. He had no expertise with the opposite sex, as the self-conciseness he felt about his injuries had always kept him from getting too close to any young women. His lack of confidence did not seem to matter to her, as she continued the conversation with him for all the many miles they traveled on the trip.

They had both just sat down in their chairs with the other students, at a series of long tables in the museum. They were getting ready for a full day of examining and handling the violins and other stringed instruments at the museum, some of the rarest in the world.

Bringing his focus back to Rachel, he said, "Tell me more about your dreams. Are they really like mine?"

"Yes, they are like what I've seen in mine so many times. The same type of landscape and bright sun, and all the blooming flowers in color. How odd that we might have similar ones."

"Yeah, that's pretty weird." He was distracted, thinking about Charlie. Seeing him lying in that hospital bed hooked up to those machines.

It could have been me in that bed, or worse if I had been out on the street with him. He was wearing my old hooded jacket... So, was the car aiming for Charlie, or was it just a freak accident? They said the car drove straight at Charlie, dead-on.

He had been torn and felt guilty that his friend was hurt so severely after he had felt so cranky towards him. But Joseph decided he had to make the trip to further his education.

I have to have the surgery to repair the scars. They hurt so much every single day.

"What do you think they mean, and do you have them often?"

With a deep sigh, he said, "I'm not sure, but I have them almost every night now."

"That often? Wow. Mine happen just now and then. But I keep dreaming of a house with carved stone archways, white plaster walls, a courtyard filled with flowers and palm trees, and fountains with colored tiles. The sound of the water, and seeing it sparkling in the sun, it's so gorgeous, amazing, and so unlike our world today. I would go and stay there if I could."

"Sounds wonderful. I'd sure love to see the world the way it used to be before the war. It sounds like you're dreaming of how it used to be."

"Yes, maybe so."

He looked around the old 1920 Carnegie library the museum occupied with its wood-paneled walls and floor and high wood-beamed ceiling. The building interior had an almost timeless look, with a lingering smell of musty old books blended with lemon-oil wood polish. The lighting was soft with rows of high windows, admitting the dull late winter sunlight. Long rows of wood-framed glass cases lined the walls, housing famous violins, looking like two long lines of beautiful feminine forms. He felt that, in the presence of the antique violins, he could have been in almost any year and any century in time.

He was brought back from his reverie by Rachel asking, "I think it might be of a past life coming through my dreams for me. Do you think that's possible? Maybe yours are something like that too."

The rest of the twenty-five students had now settled into their chairs and were still talking with each other when the head curator of the museum indicated by clearing her throat that they were about to begin. "Ahem..."

Joseph whispered to Rachel, "I will tell you more about my dreams after dinner, later tonight."

The students were sitting against one side of three long wooden tables. Their arms rested on layers of thick quilts that covered the tabletops, with their hands wearing clean white cotton gloves. A student curator stood guard behind each one of their twenty-five chairs, poised and ready to reach out and arrest any careless touch to the valuable instruments.

The hours rolled by as one famous violin after another was brought out of the glass cases for them to hold and examine. It was a long day of immersion into the world of antique instruments. Antonio Stradivari and Guarneri del Gesù built a number of the violins, and there were other instruments by members of the Amati family, the inventors of the modern violin and teachers of Stradivari.

Rare, fragile lutes with their bodies made entirely from ebony and ivory came forth, and finally, late in the day, the head curator appeared with the last violin. By now, Joseph had started to feel quite sleepy with his eye's half shut and his mind feeling numb from all the beauty he had seen.

But with the sight of this last instrument, his fading energy quickly came alive. He startled, sitting upright from the slump his body had assumed.

The head curator spoke. "This last instrument was recently loaned to the museum by its owner. It is unique, with what we believe to be a fused amber varnish, and with very sophisticated lines and curves. We do not know who made it, except that it appears to be of the very early sixteen-hundreds, possibly Italian. There is a strange set of marks carved on the top of the scroll." At this point, the curator's voice changed to a tone that conveyed distaste. "They appear to be Hebrew letters, which make up the word emet, which translates as 'truth' in Hebrew. No one has any idea what a Hebrew word is doing carved on this instrument. It is possible that, in the past, this disfigurement was perpetrated by a previous owner."

Distracting Joseph for a moment from his intoxication with the violin, Rachel softly exclaimed in response to this new information. "What did she say? How could that be?" She then whispered to him, "How can she say that? Disfigurement!"

Joseph did not seem to hear her, as he was mesmerized by the sight of the instrument. Flashes of fire sparkled in the golden varnish and the illuminated gem-like wood as the old violin was slowly passed from hand to hand down the long set of tables so each student could examine it. Time seemed to stretch and crawl for Joseph. It felt like it was taking so very long to reach him. The sunlight hitting the varnish continued to produce magnified sparks of fire-light that caught his eyes, almost blinding him as it grew closer and closer.

There was something about this violin that was so very strange and so different from the others that Joseph did not understand. He felt that it was calling out to him, almost like the sirens of Greek mythology. *But where are the rocks? Am I about to be dashed apart?*

Was it just the glowing radiance of the varnish and sensual curves of its back and belly, or what? It felt to him like some powerful presence had just entered the room when it had been brought in. His heart beat faster, his breathing becoming shallow, and he was filled with keen, prickly anticipation as he waited to examine it.

With his gloved hands, Joseph received the violin that was at long last handed to him by Rachel. As she gave it to him, she looked at his face and said, "Joseph, are you okay? You're pale, and you're sweating."

"I'm all right, I think. I don't know. *"All I can see is this violin and nothing more.*

Rachel`s eyes grew larger as she looked intensely at him, "Are you ill? Do you have a fever?"

"I'm fine. Don't worry."

He was struck at first by what seemed to be almost an aura, a glow of strange light that surrounded the violin. It somehow radiated from the depths of the honey-colored varnish covering the wood. The finish seemed able to capture and hold the dull sunlight that streamed into the large room, somehow magnifying it. It was as if it possessed the capacity to store the light and re-radiate it in concentrated form.

The violin looked to be quite old, though still in excellent shape with no severe damage to the wood or the surface finish. There were just a few tiny cracks in the spruce top that needed repairing. The flowing contours of the upper and lower bouts, the curve of the waist, and the finely carved spirals of the scroll were all close to those of the Amati family violins, though shaped with a much finer delicacy of line and curve than any Amati ever possessed. It was somehow unique and very different from any of the dozens of valuable violins he had been privileged to hold and examine while at the violin making school. It somewhat resembled a Stradivarius violin but was, as the curator said, much older by at least a century.

Even though this instrument was not playable as it was missing its bridge, tuning pegs, saddle, and strings, Joseph thought he could almost hear it quietly humming and vibrating in his gloved hands, somehow with a life of its own. It seemed to possess a warmth that was strange and animal-like, almost moving as if with a quiet and very slow heartbeat.

Carefully turning the violin around in his hands, he looked into the first 'F' sound hole and could see a faded paper label. Holding the violin close to his eyes to read it better, he could smell a strong scent from within it of old wood, but also something spicy; a smell like incense, like Frankincense?

On the label, he could barely make out what might be the maker's name scrawled in what looked like Italian. Looking closely, he could see a few letters; Ma, or, us. An, fto, s, maybe, very faintly. There were other shapes of a different type as well, drawn in black ink on the wood close to the label, which might have been lettering in another language. But the strange marks which could barely be made out in black ink on the darkly aged inside wood were like nothing he had ever seen before.

Turning the head of the violin, the scroll, around in his hands, he looked at what the curator said were Hebrew letters carved into the middle three grooves of the scroll. A strange, tingling feeling was striking him hard in his belly.

What is this to me? How can looking at this word make me feel this way? "Emet, truth"?

The head curator was continuing to lecture about the violin, but Joseph did not hear a word as he gazed into the brilliant amber waves of the luminous finish. He held onto it much longer than he had any of the other instruments. He could not, or did not want to, let it go. He was mesmerized with all the world closing in around him and coalescing into just the violin and nothing more.

He had felt this way before, once, during his daily meditations, when a radiant white light had penetrated his inner eye, blinding him with ecstatic brilliance. What this instrument did to him was similar though different. His body started to feel almost transparent, as it did when he saw that inner light. He felt as if a crack was opening and breaking apart what he knew to be real, tearing the space beneath his feet. But, this time, Joseph was not meditating.

He saw intense light reflected in its deep iridescence. The glowing amber varnish, the waves of gem-like fiddle-back maple, and his reflection all blended in the bright surface. Joseph was in a trance, drawn to do what was forbidden. To dare to touch the varnish with his bare skin.

I want to feel it just one time. To see if it is as warm to my skin as it looks to my eyes.

Risking reprimands from his school director and the student curator hovering behind his chair, he could not resist any longer. He moved his right arm just a bit, exposing a little of his wrist between his shirt cuff and the glove and pressed his bare skin into the varnish-covered wood.

It felt so warm and soft to the touch. So excellent and intoxicating, almost hot, like it had an inner fire. It was somehow erotic, but spiritual and sacred at the same time.

Is this what it feels like to touch a woman, to feel like this? It's amazing.

In awe, Joseph felt like he was caressing and pressing against the warm flesh of a divine feminine presence.

Without warning, his wrist sank into the varnish, and he felt himself falling. Arm first, then shoulder and head. Joseph's whole body was melting and curving over into a wisp of cloud, of vapor. Out of control, he was spinning with dizzy vertigo. Panic rose into his throat as the room around him vanished in a swirl. His entire world resolved into a spiraling vortex of golden light and darkness. A searing pain pierced his brain as he plunged into the unknown.

What's happening? Am I dying? Is this what it's like to be dead? I've never felt so un-tethered, so completely weightless, so far gone.

Joseph was dropping faster and faster as if falling from a great height into the varnish, melting as spinning energy, both deep black, and brilliant white-golden-hot, plunging deeper and deeper into forgotten time, and sinking into lost forsaken memory.

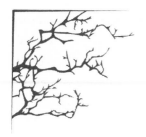

Four
Joseph

LISBON, PORTUGAL

   March 29, 1522

The sun was so bright; his eyes hurt. Blinking rapidly, Joseph was dazzled and staggered as he drew a stifling breath of dusty, super-heated air. Almost overwhelmed by a gust of hot wind pushing against his back, the wooden floor had vanished, and he could not find his footing on what felt like uneven stones underfoot. Looking down, he saw he was wearing sandals on his feet, and heavy black clothing that dragged on the ground, trying to trip his footing. He was carrying a brown cloth bag in one hand. Feeling dizzy, he struggled to not fall on his face.

A strong odor of animal dung rose from the dirty pavement blending with an array of other aromas, both rank and sweet, blowing on the wind that swirled around him. Wiping fine red dust from his eyes, he looked around.

Where am I? In a dream but waking? This place can't be a dream. But is it real? Where is the violin? The museum? My friends? My teacher?

They had all vanished into a stiflingly hot space of glaring white plaster, bright red and multi-colored flowers, with lush green vines and a deep blue sky cast with a dusty red haze.

And that wind. It was blowing hard, pushing him forward toward a deep shadow. He saw as if in a fog a bench in the deep shade of some large trees, with a gurgling fountain. Barely able to walk, he stumbled over and sat down with his field of vision, swinging crazily back and forth in front of him.

He was Joseph Davidson. But another name floated to the surface of his mind; *I am Marcus. Marcus Antonius, soon to be consecrated a priest.* His head hurt, with a loud buzzing in his ears.

Who are you? Who are you? One voice asked another within his mind.

He felt crowded inside. Like being layered and smashed with another person, tossed and blended in confusion. He had become two radically different minds and feelings, not knowing which was alien and which was his. Whoever he was, wherever he was, he felt like a fly caught in tree sap. Everything he saw with those different eyes, seen through a hazy yellow-gold cast, with his limbs moving as slowly as against glue.

An elderly woman, dressed all in black, who had stopped in the street and saw Joseph's stumbling steps, waddled over to him and asked, "Pai, posso ajudar? Você está doente? Father, can I help you? Are you sick? Do you need water?"

Father? She said strange words, but I understand her. He looked at his black robe-covered arms, belly and legs, his feet in their dusty sandals, and he saw the rough wooden cross around his neck. *What am I?*

"Eu, eu penso que eu estou bem. I... I think I am fine." Joseph hoarsely spoke. "But I am not yet a priest. I was on my way to the cathedral to receive my blessing, and, I... I just started feeling faint."

"The hot wind, the Devil's Vento, the Xaroco. It is the Devil's wind itself," the old woman replied. "Blowing from those Muslim heathens in the south, in Africa. May they be cursed to burn in Hell." She then waddled over and brought him a gourd of water from the fountain, spilling some of it as she approached him.

"Thank you, Grandmother. May Mary and Jesus bless you for your kindness," Joseph managed to mumble, making the sign of the cross with his right fingers pushed together.

He drank deeply from the cooling water as his parched throat started to revive. *How do I know those words and that hand movement?* It was like a part of him was watching another part as he spoke. In confusion, he attempted to mentally unravel who he was, or who he thought he was. *How can I be both a stranger to myself and myself at the same time?* His head ached with the competing voices in his mind.

Sitting for a time as the white-haired woman stood looking at him, he felt more stable and spoke to her. "I will be fine now. Thank you for your concern." Somehow, he knew the words, as it was his tongue, though he felt he heard two simultaneous voices in his head. After a bit, he thought he had succeeded in reassuring the woman who now sat in the shade with him, looking his way now and again.

Joseph sat resting, maybe only a short time. Minutes? Did time mean anything there at all? And just where or when was he? He then became aware he did know the year.

It's the year of Our Lord 1522. King Manuel the First is sitting on the throne of Portugal in Glory, controlling the world's spice trade. I am Marcus Antonius, twenty years old. My body is healthy, strong, and un-scarred. It is so wonderful to feel this body; arms and legs with no injuries, and no constant pain.

But yet, at the same time, this Marcus, who he now was, was gravely wounded with the pain of some hidden horror, his heart torn nearly in half with a deep, burning hatred filling the gaps. There was a secret. A profound mystery, buried in the darkest recesses of his mind, of who he truly was. What was it? A deep, piercing fear. This secret was hidden, buried, locked in a mental cell of stone and iron. A smell of blood and fire haunted this 'other' life he was now sharing.

Fearful memories began flooding into Joseph's mind in a headlong deluge of images and sensations, overwhelming him with their intensity and sharpness. The nightmare that haunted his other self, Marcus, now unfolded like a horror movie in his mind.

The sound... the mob... front door beat in, crashing open. I'm crying. I'm afraid. My mother is taking me to a hiding place ...

"Put Marcus in the secret cupboard." I hear my father's voice. "Marcus, make no sound. I will come and free you when it's safe."

A place I've never seen inside, I tightly squeeze in with books, pieces of cloth, a cup, candle holders... the cabinet swings shut... muffling sounds outside... voices louder... howling, shrieking. I hear terror approaching... desperate fighting in the next room ... cries, pleas for mercy... my mother, sister, calling the Virgin Mary... their screams cut off. I was crammed, in the cupboard for days, arms and legs cramped. A nightmare, darkness, terror, waiting for my father to free me... smoke choking me. Thirsty, cramped, hungry, afraid to move, to make a sound. Uncle finally came... pried opened the door to see me. I was, barely alive, a terrified child.

Joseph/Marcus had sat frozen on the stone bench for what had seemed like hours. But it was just a moment in this time. He felt like his head was about to explode. And just when he thought he could take no more, it ended.

When the flood of images, sights, and sounds had subsided, and he was starting to feel that he could breathe once more, he looked around and found everything as it had been in that strange place, that dream world. Or was it all just a prolonged nightmare?

He was shaking inside but still was able to smile at the old woman, who looked at him rather intently with alarmed and questioning eyes. Joseph realized he had better fit in and not stand out in this place where he had been thrust. He felt the danger he could be in was intense, very present, and deadly. He turned to his benefactor and gave her a reassuring smile.

"I am feeling so much better now, Grandmother. I was overheated and thirsty."

The woman seemed to accept that. "I am very glad, Father."

Resting now, in the healthy body he was experiencing, but with his mind reeling, tugged one way and then another, he felt good but also lost in this strange, dangerous though beautiful place.

He had dreamed of something like it, and this must be it. It was just the other night. It was a good dream at first. But in that dream, he had become afraid and threatened. Now he understood just why he had felt so scared.

Just what is real? Is anything 'real'? And what is a dream?

The old woman settled once more into the shade and leaning back into her seat as if to take a nap, closed her eyes.

Joseph noticed a change in the weather with the hot, dusty wind easing off, replaced by a gentler sea breeze. Remembering where he, Marcus, had been headed, Joseph stood up and prepared to step back out into the summer morning to walk to the cathedral.

The silver-green of the olive trees, the blue-green of the distant sea, the red tiles of the rooftops, and the now gentle morning salt-sea breeze all caressed his senses. The great city of Lisbon sang with the hum of thousands of people, with all of its smells of roses, orange and lemon blossoms, jasmine, lavender, and dung. Of roasting meats and baking bread, and the sharp memory of blood and smoke. It drew him onward on his way to the Cathedral of Santa Maria. All of this carried him forward to an unknown future.

As he began to turn, to walk away from her, the old woman opened her eyes and spoke one last time to him, softly saying, "Tikkun O`lam."

Startled by this, Joseph turned to stare at her, and for the first time, noticed a small, bright golden shape around her neck. It looked like an open hand. It was the same shape he had seen on the man in the snowstorm.

In the next second, the sky seemed to darken, and his vision clouded. He felt as though he was about to step through the paving stones, their solid surfaces of a moment before becoming liquid and glassy, cloud-like, almost transparent, and then he was falling through them, dizzy, spinning... and he was gone...

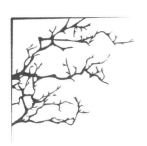

Five
Marcus

LISBON, PORTUGAL
March 29, 1522

Marcus staggered, his sandals sliding on the smooth cobblestones, his knees weak from what he had just experienced. He was dizzy and unsure if he was losing his mind.

Am I sick with the fever? Or am I possessed?

It felt like some other being had overtaken him and then let him go. He could still hear strange sounds in his mind, maybe words, but nothing he had ever heard before. His soul overflowed with frightening images of places that were dark, gray, cold, and wet. The lingering shadow that had filled him was so strange, but somehow not strange, almost familiar.

But how could it be familiar to me? And what was it?

Standing with more stability, he turned to see an older woman sitting in the shade by a fountain. She looked up at him and smiled. Marcus tentatively smiled in return while still rocking from side to side.

Feeling slightly more stable, he turned back and started to walk down the cobblestone lane. He was still high up on one of the city's eleven hills, and the road was quite steep. In the distance, he could see the towers of the cathedral, and farther away, the ships in the harbor. On the far horizon was the white-capped sea with more vessels moving away and approaching the port.

The dizziness was passing, but the feeling that something extraordinary had visited him persisted. He was sure that something powerful had taken control of him for a time, forcing him to observe passively what it had done to him.

Not knowing what to think of the experience, he shook his head in an attempt to free his mind and body from its lingering hold.

It must be the sun, the heat. I'm getting too much of it. The cathedral will be cool, fresh, and dark. It will feel good, better there.

Setting off at a faster walk, his mind calmer and becoming focused, Marcus headed down the street to his appointment at the cathedral to be blessed and consecrated.

He made his way through the busy marketplaces, the narrow-twisted streets, and crowded squares, until, at last, he arrived at the cathedral. The spires reached to the sky and were the tallest things he had ever seen. Shaking his head again, he tried to forget it, whatever it had been but found he could not do so.

He entered the cathedral, stumbling over the threshold into the dark shade, breathing in deeply the scent of burning incense and beeswax candles.

I will be safe here. What possessed me is now gone. I must pray hard to keep it from attacking me again.

As his eyes adjusted, to the relative darkness inside, he breathed a deep sigh of relief, feeling that his Mother church would offer protection from whatever dark forces had tried to possess him.

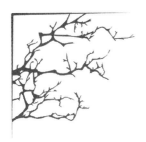

Six
Joseph

VERMILLION, SOUTH DAKOTA

March 29, 1986

"Joseph. What are you doing with that violin? Why are you standing? Sit down now!" demanded the school director.

He was startled by the words, causing him to lift his bare wrist from the violin varnish. Finding he was standing, Joseph looked around, puzzled by what he saw.

Severed from the vision or dream, or whatever it had been, he was reeling, dizzy, and not entirely stable. In shock with the flood of images that had assaulted him, the horror and the beauty, he found he could not get his eyes to focus. The hot sun and brilliant colors had been so bright and shocking. So utterly different from this gray, damp, and dark world of his.

"Joseph, pass that instrument on; you have been holding it for ten minutes now." The student curator behind him had lunged forward as he suddenly stood and reached out to seize the violin from his hands. As always, the director's voice had sliced through the air and caught Joseph's attention.

He opened his eyes and found the room was moving before him, insubstantial as if in a haze. Gradually, his eyes cleared. "So sorry. I'm not feeling well. I'm dizzy, tired, or something. Maybe catching something."

"Well, sit down. Now. And pass that violin to Peter. You must take better care of yourself if you want to graduate," the director retorted.

As he sat and passed the violin, the student curator behind him relaxed her stance. She had been poised just above his shoulders, about to pounce on him. She stepped back from Joseph with a look of relieved embarrassment on her face.

It was good that he was sitting down as he slowly regained his vision and focus.

Oh my, I might have fallen with that violin, maybe crushing it.

Feeling insubstantial and almost transparent with the lingering feeling of the dream or hallucinations he had just experienced, he was shaking inside, his heart still racing faster than usual.

The touch of that violin is still there. It's burning like a brand on my wrist like I touched a red-hot iron skillet. But, oh, I have to touch it again...

He was in pain, torn inside from the loss of contact with it. He felt like an addict who had just taken such a drug as no one had ever dreamed of or experienced before. A drug that was both terrible beyond imagining and yet still unbelievably intoxicating.

I have to have more of it, but what was that? What did I see, where was I? Like being in an awakened dream.

He felt like he might never be the same again.

As the students rode in the vans to their motel for the night, Joseph was lost in thought, recalling what he had just experienced. It was as it had been in the repetitive dreams; a beautiful land of hot sun, scorching winds, and fresh sea breezes — a place of lush trees and flowers, but also hidden horror. The edge of the terror burned into his mind. What had he seen through another set of eyes?

And with the sights, smells, and the frightening images he had seen, there was the intoxicating beauty of that violin.

I have to go back. I must. To see it, somehow touch it again. I must have it for my own.

As they drove, Rachel, who was sitting next to him, kept looking over at the quiet, intense face of her new friend. He seemed distant now, after opening up to her on the long drive to the museum. He was closed down. She slid closer to him, her thigh touching his, causing him to start from the contact. "Joseph, are you all right? What happened to you back there in the museum?"

He found the contact with her body, a touch that he had never experienced before, was stirring his body to the core. He glanced over at the attractive young woman, catching her eyes with his. He found himself pressing his thigh back against hers, and she did not move away, but pressed her entire leg against his, subtly moving it back and forth against him. Kicking her right shoe off, she caressed his lower leg with her stocking-covered toes.

Feeling her touch is almost as exciting as the violin.

Rachel placed her hand into his lap, clasping his hand in hers. Her fingers reached around his hand to gently touch him. With her toes rubbing against his calf, her fingers stroking him through his jeans, and her mischievous smile beaming his way, he was fast approaching a point of no return.

Finding it hard to speak, he tried to tame the roaring in his body and mind. With everything, he had experienced that day, and now the exciting touch of this so desirable woman, he tried to calm himself by looking out the window at the bleak, wintry landscape rolling by.

"Joseph, are you okay?" Rachel asked, with a twinkle in her eyes.

Saved from needing to answer her question by their arrival at the motel, he said, "I'll see you at dinner." as he rapidly slid past her, his back brushing against her breasts as he headed for the open door of the van.

Both vans full of students unloaded, with everyone grabbing their overnight bags and getting their room keys for the night.

"Joseph, here's yours. It's single, so you don't have a roommate tonight," spoke the school director, Herr Shrouder.

Joseph settled in, turned up the heater, and unpacked in his room. Bundled against the cold, he then walked across the snow- and ice-covered parking lot to the small cafe. After he was seated, Rachel joined him at his booth, squeezing in next to him and joining four other students there.

He had calmed himself since his reaction to her contact with him in the van. But feeling the warmth of her whole body pressed against him, while wedged in from the other side by another of the female students, Joseph found himself out of his depth with no choice but to surrender to the lovely soft contact of the two women.

Alice, on his left, was not paying attention to the tight fit between them, even though he could feel her every curve. But Rachel, on his right side, certainly was. Once more, she started to rub her lower leg against his while turning to smile at him, causing his resistance to begin melting, despite his hesitation. Several times she reached for condiments on the table while extending her left arm behind his shoulders, brushing her left breast against him. Joseph could feel his body responding to this intimate contact.

Oh, jeez. I can feel her through the sweater. I don't know what to do; I've got to get out of here.

The conversation of the other students was lively, discussing the series of ancient instruments they had been able to handle and examine that day. But Joseph was silent, with no comments to offer.

Peter jokingly asked him, "Hey, Joe, what were you doing standing up with that fiddle? Were you thinking of walking off with it?"

"Nah, ah, I was feeling a little dizzy. Not-not, myself," He managed to stammer.

I can't tell anyone what happened; they'll think I'm nuts. But I would have liked to walk off with it. It feels like it's mine, somehow.

"It's a pretty righteous violin, totally out of the accepted timeline for that style and shape. Remember the curator said it was found just last month, like buried treasure, hidden in a villa in Italy. Does anyone know any more about it?" Diane asked.

Peter replied in his precise British accent, "Yes, it is very early, but somehow in the style of later ones, which is quite odd. It also has a fused amber varnish, a quite rare thing. It is said to be an extremely difficult varnish to make. The amber has to be cooked at a high enough temperature to melt it, but not too hot, because it will catch on fire."

Rachel added, "But how did they know the date? When it was made?"

Diane answered, "The curator said there was some different type of date written inside it on the label. She said it translated to 1623."

As they ate their hamburgers and fries, the conversation continued, devolving into friendly arguments about varnishes, other violin details, and debating the history of the violin they had started to call, 'Joe's violin.' All the while, Rachel was leaning against Joseph's right side, joining in the animated conversation as he soaked up her body warmth.

I can't stand this. Oh god, she feels so warm, so hot. I've got to get out of here.

"Sorry, guys, I'm going to bed now. I don't feel good." Joseph suddenly stood up, forcing Alice and Peter on his left to quickly half-stand and slide out of their seats.

He threw on his coat and walked out into the cold night across the parking lot to his room.

"Wait," called Rachel as she struggled into her coat and ran after him. "What's wrong?" She caught up to him, lacing her arm into his. "Can we talk? Can I come into your room for a bit to warm up?"

Both yes and no formed together on his lips, tearing him between the two.

He finally got out, "Okay. Just for a bit."

As he unlocked the door, she reached out and gently took his face in her warm hands. Her soft lips molded to his, her tongue caressed his, and Joseph's knees turned weak. As they stumble-stepped through the doorway into the warm room, he felt his fear start to let go.

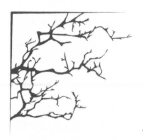

Seven

VERMILLION, SOUTH DAKOTA
March 29, 1986

The couple fell through the doorway as they continued kissing passionately, tongues dancing together, their arms holding each other up.

She pushed the door closed with one foot, and while still kissing him, let her coat slide off one arm and then the other. The small, musty-smelling room had seen better days, with its thin carpet, faded wallpaper, and cracked mirror facing the narrow bed. But the two young people didn't notice any of that.

With her hands at her waist, Rachel broke the kiss for a moment and lifted the thick sweater and long-sleeve pullover she was wearing over her head. Not wearing a bra, her nude upper body revealed itself. He saw before him a gorgeous young woman who was tall and slim with long, flowing, curly dark brown hair falling freely, framing her flawless warm honey-colored skin.

Stepping back from the door and away from her, he stammered, "Rachel, I... I've never been with a woman. I don't know how to... or what to... if I can do this. But also, how can we not, you know, get...?"

She replied by unbuttoning her pants and pushing them to her shoes. Despite Joseph`s fears, his entire body trembled, responding to the vision of this near-naked woman.

With a loving smile, while caressing his curly brown hair with both hands, she said, "Do you mean, how do you not get me pregnant? It`s okay; I'm taking a pill to prevent it. Some of my old friends get it for me from Canada, where they're legal. So, no worries. We won`t create a baby when we make love tonight." Kicking off her shoes and pants, she slid off the small piece of blue lace that had remained and reached out for him.

Placing her hands on his shoulders, she said, "Come to me, lover. I want you. 'Let him kiss me with the kisses of his mouth: for thy love is better than wine.' Do you know that poem?"

Nervously, with his resistance fading, he quoted in reply, "'Your two breasts are like two fawns, twins of a gazelle, that feed among the lilies.' Yes, I know it. I learned it as a child. The woman who raised me told me it's the greatest love poem ever written, the *Song of Songs* by King Solomon. 'I have come into thy garden, my sister, my spouse: I have gathered my myrrh with thy spice; I have eaten my honeycomb with thy honey; I have drunk my wine with thy milk...'"

"Oh, sweet man, my lover has the heart of a poet," she softly murmured, stretching out her naked arms to encircle him, bringing her body and lips to embrace him once more.

As she reached around him, he could feel the warmth radiating from her body like a furnace as she pressed close, her lips about to contact him.

He stopped her with his hands, placing them on her warm, smooth arms. "Rachel, wait. I never have. I don't know how to do this. I... I've never even seen anyone like you. But I need to tell you. My back, arms, legs... I'm badly scarred, scaly like a reptile. I was burned in a fire as a baby. I'm afraid you won't want me."

I'm ugly; I'll scare her away.

"I know. Charlie told me you had injuries from a fire, but I don't care. I love you, and I want to see all of you."

"Charlie told you? What did he say?" He stepped back from her, hesitating from her embrace.

"He was explaining to me why you walked and moved a bit oddly. I asked him if he knew why, if you were injured, and that was all he said. I was worried about you. I have been falling in love with you ever since the first day I saw you at school. You looked so lost to me, lonely because you were entirely by yourself all the time. But you were so kind and helpful to everyone, always ready with a friendly word. And I felt like I knew you as I've always known your heart somehow. I don't see how it's possible, but I feel like, in some strange way, I've held you in my arms before."

"Rachel, I think I'm falling for you too. I felt something like that too the first time I saw you. It makes no sense. I don't know you, but I want you. I've daydreamed about you, but I can't do this yet. Please, can we go more slow-ly?"

She replied by pulling back his coat to drop it off his shoulders and lifting his sweater and shirt in one swift pull over his arms and shoulders. The scars on his back and arms stung sharply with this quick action as the cloth pulled across his rough, furrowed skin.

He quickly stepped back from her, crying out in pain, tears forming in his eyes, "Ow that hurt! Damn it; you hurt me! I can't do this. It's why I never could before, could never even think of being with anyone. My body is just not flexible. I'm no good for you. We have to stop and forget this. It's not possible for me."

Bending down, he picked up his shirt and sweater to try to put them back on to cover his body.

She reached around with her arms to try to embrace him once more, and could now see his back and the undersides of his upper-arms with the deep red furrows of rough skin there. She kissed his neck and shoulders. "I'm so sorry I hurt you. Please forgive me. I didn't realize how badly you were injured."

Joseph, with tears streaming down his cheeks, dropped his arms and pulled away from her once more. "You see, I'm a monster. I'm not human. I know you don't want me now. You can't want me."

Her face had fallen, and she also started to cry, stretching out her arms to him once more. "No. I do want you. I'm so sorry I hurt you. I want to love you. All of you."

Pushing away from her, he started pulling on his shirt to cover his scars. "Rachel, just get dressed and go. Please leave me alone from now on. I'm supposed to be alone. I'm used to it."

Reaching out and holding the struggling man, crying and matching his tears with hers, she softly said, "Joseph, you`re not meant to be alone. We`re meant for each other. Let me show you everything I know. I will be gentle; so gentle, my love. And I will try never to hurt you again."

"This is so new to me. It's happening so fast. You're so pretty, so beautiful. I know what I want to do, but I never have. Can you show me? I don't know how."

Embracing him once more, she said, "I will. Now relax and let me make love to you."

After a while, she leaned over him, kissing his lips and face, her brilliant green eyes brimming with tears. "I love you, Joseph Davidson, just as you are. You`re a strong, handsome man to me."

"And I love to touch you, Rachel." He replied. "You're so soft and warm, so beautiful. You take my breath away."

She carefully traced the edge of the scars with one gentle finger. "Oh, sweetheart, for your first time, you're doing so well.

His scars hurt some, but he was past caring. All he knew and saw was this amazing sight: a beautiful woman making love to him. "You feel so good. How have I lived without you?"

As she rested, wrapped around him, she said, "Joseph, I want to share something very special with you. I know what your body wants to do, but for now, rest quietly and feel me as part of you. We can share our love in so many ways with our bodies, our hearts, and souls by meditating this in this way together.

She lifted his hands to her breasts and said, "Hold me. Just rest your hands and feel my heartbeat and breathe with me now. I will match my breath to yours." She placed her hands on his chest, and closed her eyes, slowly breathing in and out, matching her inhalations and exhalations with his.

He stayed still and gazed up at his lady, softly holding her, while her hair hung down, tickling his chest. She was quiet, meditating, holding still except for her breath, warmly but gently embracing him. He closed his eyes and following his breath in and out, slowly merged his with hers, feeling her embracing warm love, hearing and feeling her heart beating with his. They stayed in this embrace, blending their hearts, breaths, and bodies, for extended minutes.

She quietly said, "Now, my love, I want you to feel my life force moving through you, following my breath flowing into yours. When I breathe out, you breathe in and follow my energy flowing into and through you, from the crown of your head flowing down along your spine to where we are together, and back into my body. I will carry it through my spine and back into yours again. This way, we can blend our souls, life force, and bodies as one."

"This is all so new to me, but yes, I'm all yours."

Softly, in her melodious voice, she started to chant, "God is love, God is the lover, God is the Beloved. God is love; God is the lover; God is the Beloved. God is love; God is the lover ..."

With his eyes closed, he breathed deeply and slowly, visualizing her energy flowing into his spine, and his into hers. After a few moments, a deep, violet light filled his field of vision. He found he could see with his inner eyes, a circular stream of brilliant warm-golden light flowing through his body and on into hers.

She continued chanting, "Only one, only one of us here. Only one, only one of us here. Only one, only one of us ..."

The light he saw was like a chain of luminous amber-golden beads. This vision was forming the shape of an illuminated tree within each of their bodies, linking their energies together. His concentration was wholly engrossed in this marvelous dance of light and color. Then a thought interrupted his concentration. *The light flowing between us is so bright. If I open my eyes, will I still see it?*

But when he opened his eyes, instead of Rachel, he saw a similar but different woman, wearing a ruffled silken chemise. The rose-colored ribbons at the top were untied, exposing her breasts to his hands. She was gazing down at him, her sea-green eyes filled with love, breathing just as Rachel had been. The room was no longer the simple motel room, but a richly appointed bedroom with a high gilded ceiling lit with many candles and decorated with tapestries hanging from the walls.

"Rebeca, eu te amo. You are so beautiful," he blurted out.

As Joseph said this, his vision went dark then flashed with a bright light. When he could see again, he once more was being tightly held by Rachel in his motel room.

Snapping out of her meditation, she asked, "Why did you call me Rebeca? That's my middle name. I used it in my childhood, but how could you know? Since I transferred to the school last month, I've told no one. How did you know? And what was it that you said? It sounded like you were speaking another language just now."

He paused, completely stunned by what he had just seen, felt, heard, and said. It was as real as anything could be. *Like a tear in something has been opened up by our lovemaking, shifting space. Or time? What is happening to me? The violin, and now this. What has it done to me?*

"How did you know? Did someone tell you?

"No. I'm not sure. I just saw something so strange, someone, somehow..."

How can I explain to her what I just saw and what I experienced? Will she believe me?

"Tell me what happened, and what was that strange look in your eyes just now? You looked like how you did earlier today. When you were standing there with that violin. Are you all right? Are you having a seizure or something?"'

"I don't know. Something, somehow just happened. Yes, it was like with the violin, but it was here with you. It was you, but it was also not you. But it felt like you, and that's how I knew the name, your other name, I guess. It's crazy, but you were both you and another woman who looked a lot like you. Both of you, with me at the same time."

"I want to be jealous of who you just saw. Though how can I be jealous of myself, or another version of me, if that's who it was? Maybe we caused something to happen. We both have had similar dreams of places that are alike, from what seems to be another world or time. Maybe we have been together in the past, and you just experienced that?"

"It does feel like we have been together, and it sure feels good to me. But it was so strange. I felt how I did when the violin affected me earlier today."

Laughing, she replied, "I have heard of lovemaking being described as, 'causing the Earth to move,' but we have been keeping still and haven't even gotten to the best part. Well, my sweet man, you have had a full day. I'm not sure what you saw, but I know you are here and that you are mine, so I won't be jealous. You can tell me all about the violin and what you just saw later. Now, before you fall asleep, are you ready to melt in my arms?"

"I love you so much. Yes." He ran his hands gently over the curve of her breasts, around her back, and down her legs, kissing everywhere he could reach.

She smells so good, like violets. Her skin tastes like salt and flowers.

A similar, untethered feeling was starting to engulf him, as all he could see in front of him appeared soft in outline, almost transparent. As he gazed at her luminous skin, his experiences of Rachel and the violin were beginning to merge and converge on this day of strange new wonders, as he again sat on the edge of the bed and gazed at the beautiful woman before him now.

Touching and caressing her skin feels like touching that violin. The warmth of her body... as the violin felt, warm, alive, vibrating... humming. The amber-gold shade of her skin is like the color of the violin. Oh my...

"Being with you, Rachel... wow. I feel like I'm a new person. This day is like a new life for me. Being with you, I feel almost whole."

HIS VISION BLACKED out momentarily with the explosion of sensations, and when it cleared, he once again was looking at the half-naked Rebeca in her silken chemise, by candlelight as she loudly cried out and moaned, "Oh, Deus. Oh God, Marcus, I love you so."

He was having the strangely disorienting but indescribably delicious and overwhelming experience of making love to two similar-looking women, in two places at the same time, feeling the sensations of both women's bodies embracing him. His eyelids flickered, and he could barely stay conscious with the waves of intense, ecstatic feelings engulfing him. He inhaled with a gasping, "Oh my God, Rachel, Rebeca. Oh my... "

Gradually the presence of Rebeca faded, with just the incredible warmth of Rachel embracing him still.

LATER, THEY LAY TOGETHER breathing deep drawn-out breaths, inhaling the shared joy of their lovemaking, their hearts beating fiercely.

Reaching around his back, she carefully caressed him and held him to her breasts, smoothly running her fingertips over his scars, kissing him and saying, "Joseph, it just happened to me as well. I was there, in that room with the sound of the sea outside, making love to you and Marcus, as Rebeca."

"So, I'm not crazy? But Marcus. I wonder if that`s the person I was part of, or in today when I touched that violin? So, you were making love to me, and to this Marcus?"

"Yes, lover. We are, as far as I can tell, making love to each other here, and in our dreams and maybe across space and time. Joseph Davidson, I am your lover. 'I am love, I am my beloved, and my beloved is mine.' And no, you're not crazy. Unless we`re both crazy together."

Yawning, he murmured into her ear, "Rachel, I think we are."

Continuing gently to caress each other, they drifted off to sleep, with his head cradled in her arms.

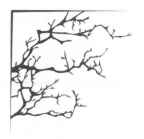

Eight

CIRCLE OF FATIMA, FATIMA, Portugal
March 30, 1986, Easter Sunday

Showing Archbishop Arturo to his chair in the place of honor, at the head of the table, Monsignor DeSilva pulled out the ornately carved walnut chair and said, "Welcome, Your Grace, to my humble quarters. My secretary, Father Servino, has prepared for our Easter supper, an old recipe for us that his family has cherished for generations. Wild mushroom soup. His mother and grandmother before her would gather certain special varieties in the hills of Sicily to make this dish."

Settling comfortably into the plush cushion on the chair, Arturo said, "How did you know I cannot resist anything with mushrooms? I love mushroom soup."

"I have my sources, Your Grace. But I cannot divulge them. One must have some secrets."

With a full laugh that made his ample belly quiver, Arturo replied, "Well, I do understand full well the need for secrecy concerning the serious matter of family recipes." His tone turned more serious. "But, Diego, my old friend, let me be frank on another subject. I wish to ask you a difficult question before we eat. And I wish to do so here, informally, as a friend and fellow seminary student."

"Certainly, Your Grace. You have my full attention. You are one of my oldest friends. You can ask me anything at all."

"Well, this is a very delicate subject. Can you ask Father Servino to leave the room?"

"Yes, of course." Turning towards Servino, who was standing ready to serve them at the kitchen door, DeSilva said, "Father Servino, can you please leave us for a bit?"

Servino, seemingly startled by this, looked at his master for a moment, before stepping out and closing the door leading to the outer rooms.

Arturo said, "Well, this is very difficult for me to say, but we need to discuss certain allegations that have come to my attention. I'm sure that there have been some misunderstandings involving this matter."

DeSilva listening intently to his old friend, checked his posture, sitting up straighter in response to this. "What allegations would those be, Your Grace?"

Clearing his throat, Arturo continued. "Ah, allegations to do with the young novices under your supervision. Now, Diego, I am sure it is just the overactive imaginations of a few young girls. But there are rumors of you have had, shall I say; inappropriate contact with at least one of them."

DeSilva startled at this, tried to keep his expression as innocent as he could. "Your Grace, I'm not sure I understand. Who has been saying such a scandalous thing about me? I can assure you that there must be some misunderstandings here. Perhaps when I placed my healing hands on one of the novices who was suffering after hearing distressing news of her family? I assure you, Juan, that nothing untoward has ever occurred. I would never violate my vows. And I certainly would never touch one of the novices in an improper manner."

" Now, take it easy, Diego. This type of thing has to be taken very seriously. And I had to ask you. Your assurances have satisfied me completely. Let's move on and enjoy our meal together. The smell of this soup is making my stomach growl."

With a nod to his secretary, who had slipped back into the dining room, DeSilva said, "Father Servino, will you please serve His Grace first?"

"Certainly. Your Grace," said Servino as he carried in a large cut crystal bowl of steaming soup with small brown mushrooms floating on the top. "Archbishop Arturo, this crystal bowl is reserved for our special guests."

"Well, thank you, Father. I am indeed honored." As the sparkling bowl was placed before him, he bent his face closer to the table, deeply inhaling the aromatic dish. "My, that smells simply divine. Father Servino, your cooking is transporting me to heaven."

"Thank you, Your Grace. My family's recipes have a reputation for doing so."

Climbing the stairs to the top floor of the Arch Bishop's palace, Arturo was puffing his breath in and out at the unaccustomed exercise.

"Diego, I have never been up here. It... is a lot of... steps... to get up... this high."

"We're almost there, Juan. I wanted you to have the very best view of the plaza." Reaching the top of the narrow stairs and finally stepping out onto the balcony projecting high above the large stone-paved plaza, DeSilva held the French doors open for his friend. "Come, Juan. Let me show you my ideas for the improvements I mentioned earlier."

"View is... magnificent, but... I do not... feel...so good... anymore."

"I wanted you to see from this height my plans for the plaza here at Fatima. Come over here to the railing. I will point out the changes I'm proposing."

"Diego, I'm not sure I can see... where you... are... pointing." Slurring his words, the Archbishop staggered off-balance closer to the low railing and looked over the edge at the darkened plaza far below.

"Diego, why are the stones... why are they... moving... so fast? Did you change the colors already to blue, to water?"

Beckoning with his hand, Diego urged, "Yes. And if you come a bit closer, you will see them better. Look over here."

"Are you floating too, Diego? In the water? I... I'm so hot. So... hot. Going to... dive in... and cool off."

"Yes, Your Grace. The water is very cool and very deep. It`s so refreshing. Dive in, my dear old friend. It's quite heavenly. You first." Stepping slowly backwards to the glass door, DeSilva said, before he closed it behind himself, "Juan, please. You first. I'll join you in a bit."

"Father Servino, can you please notify the Holy Father that there has been an unfortunate accident? Archbishop Arturo has somehow fallen to his death."

With a small laugh, his secretary replied, "Yes, Monsignor. I mean, pardon me, Your Grace. I will be happy to do so."

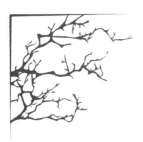

Nine

VERMILLION SOUTH DAKOTA

March 30, 1986

After a while, Rachel awoke, and whispered in Joseph's ear, "'I slept, but my heart was awake. Listen. My beloved is knocking.' Are you awake?"

Opening his eyes and yawning, he replied, "Oh, you've made me believe. I couldn't dream I would be holding you and making love with you. 'Open to me, my sister, my love, my dove, my perfect one...'"

Reaching to him again and taking his hand in hers, she whispered, "Please, touch me again. 'My beloved thrust his hand into the opening, and my inmost being yearned for him. I arose to open to my beloved ...'"

Now fully awakening from his light doze, he quoted, "'How fair and pleasant you are, O loved one, delectable maiden. You are stately as a palm tree, and your breasts are like its clusters. Your kisses are like the best wine that goes down smoothly...'"

He proceeded to kiss and embrace her, this time feeling very confident and taking the lead in realizing the poetry with her, making slow, sweet love to her once again. And, this time, it was just the two of them, sharing the present moment.

Later in the night, as the icy bright full moonlight shone through the thin curtains, fast-moving clouds were flitting by, casting shadows that traced over their sleeping forms. Once more awakening from sleep, she cuddled him in her arms, gently waking him. "Joseph, please tell me about your dreams. Remember, you promised to?"

He breathed out a long, relaxed sigh, "Well, sweetheart, you are my dreams come true."

Laughing, she gently punched his shoulder. "No, silly! The dreams you told me about the sunny place with all the flowers — the ones like mine. Please tell me more about them? And tell me what happened to you with the violin."

"Well, you asked me about the 'look' you saw on my face tonight and to-day at the museum. It's so strange, but I think I was there, in reality. In another place and, I think, at another time. I was someone else, and I was making love to both you and another version of you somehow."

She laughed lightly. "I promised I wouldn't be jealous, but don't push it. That other woman has to go."

Gently caressing her hair by twirling his fingers in the dark brown waves to reassure her, he said, "You are the only woman I see and want. This might be a past life recall or something, and you could be right about that. Maybe a doorway or whatever it is into this place or time has now opened up, triggered by us being together and me with the violin."

She reached out to him, pushing her pillow closer and pulling the top of the warm quilt up to cover their necks. As she settled next to him, she said, "Please tell me more of everything that's been happening to you. You told me some about your dreams on the drive here, but now tell me more."

He replied by carefully stretching his legs and arms, brushing his hands over nearly all of Rachel's naked body. His fingers lingered on her breasts, and he began to tickle her there, as one of his toes traced a line up one leg towards the junction of her thighs.

With a laugh, she gently swatted his hands and foot away. "Stop that. You don't get any more candy 'til you 'fess up, and tell me everything that happened today."

Propping up his head with one hand, he said, "Well, it's hard to describe, and it's all still a mystery to me. I've have had strange, vivid dreams all my life. At least once or twice a month. But lately, they have been more often."

"Are they always the same?" she asked as she traced a line down his chest with one finger, twirling it through his curly brown chest hair.

"I'm most often dreaming of a place that's warm and dry, with colorful flowers, blue sky, and hot, bright sunshine. Like I mentioned before, there are plaster-covered buildings with carved stonework, red tile roofs, and balconies hung with flowers. It's all so wonderful, and there are fountains with cascades of flowing water, decorated with colored tiles. And the sea, sometimes I'm on a balcony overlooking it, and it is such a deep blue-green color."

"It sure does sound like we're dreaming of the same place or time or whatever it is."

"I've heard that most people don't remember dreaming in color. But all my dreams are in full, bright colors."

She caressed his head, tracing small circles on his forehead with one fingertip as he gazed out the curtains at the cloud shadows flitting by in the moonlight.

"As I told you before, I have had many dreams like yours, and in color too. Most often, I am standing in a sheltered courtyard with tiled fountains. There are what I think to be palm and olive trees and many flowers. And sometimes I'm inside a house, decorated like a palace. It's so beautiful, so richly furnished. Then there's an elegant bedroom, with a large bed, tapestries on the walls, and a gilded, carved ceiling. And just outside the bedroom is a balcony overlooking the sea, high above the shoreline. I can hear the ebb and flow of the waves down below. I do wonder if I remember a past life experience and a real place, as it just seems so real. What do you think? Do you know anything about that type of thing?"

He softly touched her neck and shoulders, gently stroking her arm. "I don't. I never went to church growing up. So, if they talked about it there, I wouldn't know."

"Oh, the Church doesn't tolerate anything like that to be discussed. That type of thing, like reincarnation, is considered heresy and can get you sent before the priests of the Holy Office."

"Well, I guess it's good I've never told anyone, except for Charlie, and now you. I trust you both completely."

"You can trust me with anything. I love you so much."

"Thank you for that." He squeezed her hand in his and continued, "The bedroom you just described... the tapestries on the walls, what did they look like? Was there one between two windows, a woodland scene, with cupids?"

"Yes, there was one like that. There were little cupids, all playing different musical instruments. A harp, horns, and stringed ones too. How did you know?"

He sat up, the quilt falling to his waist, startled by this information. "My God, Rachel. You've dreamed of the same room I saw when I was making love to you. I was there, and I could see that tapestry on the wall behind Rebeca, or you, making love to me. What the hell is going on? This is getting so weird."

She stared at him with her mouth held open in amazement as she set up next to him and took his words in. "We're dreaming, or living, the same dreams. Was it me somehow, somewhere, with you tonight in two places, in two different times? And I was with you there too, making love with both you and Marcus. We were each making love to each other, and with another, you with Rebecca, and me with Marcus. And it was somewhere else, apparently in our dreams. How can that be? No wonder you think you`re going crazy."

Reaching an arm around her shoulders to hold her warm body closer to him, he said, "I have no idea of what's happening to me, except that now it`s happening to us both. It's connecting us in a strange kind of scary, though delightful, way."

With the clouds gone, the moonlight flooded into the room, brightly illuminating her green eyes, brown hair, and amber-gold skin. He was gazing at her, in wonderment at this new information that connected them further and profoundly enjoying the sight of her.

"I'm sure it was enjoyable for you to make love to me twice at the same time, wasn't it?" She laughed while, again, playfully punching him on his shoulder.

"It was, but it's still weird. I don't know what's happening to me. This is all too hard to understand." Joseph shook his head in puzzlement. Laughing, he added, "But did you enjoy making love to me and, I guess, my other self, Marcus?"

Giggling, she said. "I did enjoy you both, feeling you loving me twice over."

Joining in with her merriment, laughing, he ran his fingers through her long curls, saying, "Well I`m glad you enjoyed it, as strange as the experience is. But let me try to answer your other questions." In a more serious voice, he said, "The dreams starting this last month have now been happening to me almost every night. And just this week have begun changing to horrible nightmares, with people chased-down and murdered right in front of me."

She reached out to pull him closer to her, hugging him, and kissing his neck and face "I'm so sorry, lover. That sounds terrifying."

"It is. Then today, that violin. When I touched it with my skin... I can't describe it. It felt like the Earth opened up beneath me, and I was spinning and falling a long way into the dreams. But this time it was real, not like a dream. I was somehow physically there. I found myself inside someone else, another body, my mind blended with their mind. I had my memories and thoughts, but I also remembered another person's life, hearing and sharing their thoughts. It seemed like I was there for hours. But to everyone else in the museum, it was just for a moment or two, right?"

"Yes, that's right. You were only standing up with that violin for a few seconds."

"Well, it felt ancient there. Very old but with bright sunshine and a sky that was deep blue instead of cloudy and dark. I have never in my life seen a sky like that." Now he was talking faster, his voice getting louder as he spoke. "The body I was in was healthy, with no burn scars. Or anything wrong. Except for the memories. They were frightening, so terrible; I can still see them now."

"What memories? What do you mean?" Rachel reached to touch his arm.

His voice now was suddenly quite loud, close to shouting, "The person I was, he had memories of his family, murdered right outside his hiding place!"

Joseph, his eyes wide, staring into space, cried out, "I was just a small child. My family! They murdered my family. I have to find and kill them! Punish them! They will now suffer like my father, my mother, and my sisters! They will taste justice, and I will kill them all! I will not be merciful! Vou matá-las todas. Não vou ser misericordioso!"

As he yelled, she abruptly moved away from him to the edge of the bed. "Joseph, what do you mean you have to kill someone? And what language are you speaking?" She was crying, her tears nearly blinding her. "What are you saying? You're scaring me. Stop it. Stop it now!" She jumped off the bed, pulling the quilt off and wrapping herself in it while stepping quickly away from her lover, looking at him with apprehension.

Catching himself, he found his fists were clenching the blankets as his entire body shook convulsively. He had sat up, his body stiffly held against the wall behind the bed, but now he collapsed, exhaling, releasing the tension. "Oh, God. What am I saying? Rachel, I'm sorry. I'm so sorry. It's a nightmare; It's not real. It's not my childhood, but Marcus`s. This person I was blended with." He spoke forcefully. "That damn violin! What did it do to me? I never want to see it again as long as I live."

She stepped back towards the bed, having gotten chilled with just the top quilt as a cover. "Joseph, are you all right, now?" She wiped tears from her eyes and sniffled. "Please don't scare me like that again. I can't handle that type of thing."

Calmer now, his voice soft and gentle, he said, "Oh, Rachel, I'm so sorry. Please come back to bed. I love you so much. I'm sorry. I didn't mean to frighten you like that. I could never hurt anyone, much less kill them. I don't think I could ever do that. I'm afraid I'm going crazy with all this nightmare stuff, and that violin. I want it to all go away. Everything but you. You're the best thing, that`s ever happened to me."

She returned and sat down on the bed, covering them both with the quilt as she climbed back under the covers. She reached out her arms to surround the distressed man, holding him tightly against her. "Sweetheart, I'm here with you now, and you're okay. You're safe with me."

"I'm so sorry to have frightened you like that. Please forgive me. My life has changed so much in one day. Everything has changed. It's all happening so fast. Please don't run away from me again. Please don't be scared.

"Please try not to say things like that ever again? Please don't frighten me with these nightmares. Try to step back from them, and I will try to help you feel safe."

"I have you, and I feel reborn. I'm like a new man. But I feel as if I'm floating, untethered, and I have no idea where I`m going. It's like my shell has been cracked open, but with no clue as to what is emerging, what I'm becoming."

"You are a new man, a handsome, strong, brave man. I will not stop holding you in my arms, ever."

The first early light of dawn shining through the clouds danced on his face, waking Joseph. He could hear the shower running as steam poured from the half-open bathroom door. He stretched and rubbed his eyes, greeting his lover. "Morning, beautiful girl. Did you have sweet dreams?"

The shower turned off, and a steaming, naked Rachel stepped into the room, rubbing her long, wet hair with a towel. She smiled at him and then started laughing, pointing to the tangle of coats, clothes, and shoes that stretched from the door to the bed. "I think someone had a good time last night. And yes, I had wonderful, very normal dreams."

"You smell so good. Is that lavender?" he asked as he reached out for her.

She softly laughed. "Wait a sec. You need a shower. You smell a bit ripe, rather than sweet. And we need to get ready to leave for home, so no more of what you're thinking of right now." Laughing, she added, "We can continue with that where we left off after we get back."

Still lying in bed, he continued, "I didn't dream at all last night. What a relief; the first time in weeks. Maybe you're a good influence on me."

His voice now turning thoughtful, he asked, "I was thinking, can you tell me how you know *Solomon's Song*? Where did you learn it? Was it in church, or from school with the nuns?"

She wrapped herself in a towel and reached for another one, tying it around her hair with a chuckle. "No. The nuns, you've got to be kidding? That's a laugh. They never went near the *Song of Songs*. It's in the Catholic Bible, but they say it's a poem of Christ's love for us. The translation the Church uses is dull, not sexy at all. The original version is erotic, Jewish, and celebrates sexual love between a bride and groom. It also is part of Kabbalah." She reached out to him on the bed and kissed him deeply.

Feeling the warmth of her still damp body, he reached out and started to caress her through the towel. She kissed him again, but then removed his hands. "We have to start getting ready to go. Time for your shower."

He ignored this and asked, "But how do you and I know the same translation since I learned it at home? And what makes it Jewish, and how would my family know it too? And what is Kabbalah?"

"That's a lot of questions all at once, but I'll try to answer them. I don't know about your family, but it is indeed Jewish. Anything not in the New Testament is of Jewish origin. The Kabbalah part is regarding the merging of the divine feminine and masculine aspects of God within each of us." She paused, hesitating, then added, "And where I learned it, well, I learned it in a secret synagogue."

"Where? What kind of place is that?

Sitting on the bed, caressing his head with her fingers and running them through his hair, she softly said, "A Jewish place."

"I don't know what that is. What is a Jewish place? What do you mean by that? How can there be such a place when all the Jews are gone?"

"Well, first of all, all the Jews are not gone. They're in hiding. You really don't know, do you?"

"I know almost nothing about them."

"Well, many years ago, there were lots of people known as Jews who lived all over the world. Hitler, the Nazis, and his allies murdered almost all of them. Millions and millions were killed in all the countries they conquered, in all of Europe, England, most of Russia, North Africa, and the entire Middle East. Even in the ancient homeland of the Jewish people, the land of Israel, they were hunted down and all murdered. Jews in the past had dreamed about reviving the ancient Jewish state in Palestine, but now that will never happen. As for the rest of the world and even here in America, with England defeated, almost no one would help, until President Lindbergh was assassinated." Tears formed in her eyes and rolled down both of her cheeks as she sat on the bed wrapped in the bath towel.

Seeing her distress, he reached out and gently placed a hand on her shoulders. "I remember reading in my great aunt's library about some of this, but I don't remember too much about the Jews, except in the church history books where they said how awful the Jews were. I read how the Church said that the Jews murdered Jesus, and were also the bankers who plotted all the wars and stuff like that. They say that for thousands of years; Jews have been the root of all evil. The books even said Jews murder, Christian babies, to use the blood in their rituals. Though, that I don't believe."

"Those are all lies. Total lies. The same lies the Spanish Inquisition told five hundred years ago when they burned Jews at the stake."

"Sounds like I need to unlearn a lot of false stuff."

"You and a lot of the world. How did you avoid church schools?"

"I was raised Quaker and homeschooled out in the countryside in rural California, away from the Catholic Church, but I read their history books."

"Yes, indeed. They tell their lies very, very well."

"Though, even with them, Jews, supposedly being so bad... what you've just told me sounds unbelievable. So many murdered like that."

Placing her hand on his and firmly clasping it, she intertwined her fingers in his, gripping his hand tightly. Tears continued flowing down her cheeks as her voice became louder. "It is hard to believe, but it happened. And the history of it has been suppressed. The Jews were unjustly accused and blamed for everything. All that has happened, blamed for everything bad. None of it was true. Murdered in the millions." She sobbed, louder now, as her tears splashed on Joseph's arms and hands.

"Rachel, it's so sad and terrible. I understand why you're crying now. But wasn't that a long time ago? Here's my handkerchief." He tried to pry his fingers from her tight grasp. "Can you loosen your grip? My fingers are getting crunched."

"Oh, sorry. It's just so awful, and I can't stand it. But it's still happening. Jews are still being arrested and pursued by the Priests of the Holy Office, the Inquisition from Fatima. The Circle of Fatima wants to bring back the horrors of the Spanish Inquisition. Even burning alive so-called heretics once more. They have been gradually taking over the Catholic Church, worldwide now." She released his hand, wiped her eyes, and blew her nose as he gently rubbed her shoulders.

"I never knew anything about this. I'm so sorry. I didn't understand how terrible it was. Mostly my home-schooling was ancient history, math, science, art, and music. The woman who raised me was a retired school teacher. She had old textbooks I read, and a big library too."

Somewhat recovered, she continued her story. "In 1945 Hitler decided that the Italian fascists were not anti-Semitic enough for him, and the Germans occupied the Vatican after they took Italy. They sent almost all the Church officials and the pope to the camps in Poland where they were all put to death as punishment for aiding and hiding Jews in Church properties."

"So, some of the Catholic Church officials were not so bad?"

"Yes. There were many priests and nuns, and high officials who helped to protect Jews and escaped prisoners of war. There were many good catholic men and women, who paid with their life's, for their heroic acts of loving-kindness. Because of the Nazi attack on the Vatican, the new president, Father Coughlin, a former Catholic Priest, declared war on the Axis. In the nuclear exchange that followed between America and Germany, Hitler was finally defeated and killed in 1955.

But it was a young Jewish man who had assassinated Lindbergh, and with the restored Catholic church in New Rome now dominating America via President Coughlin, most American Jews were rounded up, imprisoned or exiled. A wandering people were now even more scattered and lost. Jews have been shunned ever since, in most places as a threat to so-called 'Christian Civilization.' They were blamed for the rise of Hitler, the war, and the destruction of the Vatican. And now they're being hunted by the Holy Office. They even blamed the nuclear war on the Jews since most of the scientists who designed the bombs were Jewish. That's why it's called the 'Jewish Winter,' 'cause of the bombs."

"I had heard this cold, wet weather we've grown up with called that, but I never thought about what it meant." Joseph caressed her long brown hair as it spilled out of the towel and over her body, tracing strands to their ends here and there with his fingers. "It's a sad history. So sad and terrible. But what do you have to do with these hunted and murdered people? These Jews."

She paused, gazing into his blue eyes. Finally, she closed her eyes and gently took both of his hands in hers, gripped them tightly again, and speaking softly, said, "Joseph, I have a confession to make to you. I wasn't going to tell you this. But with the dreams, we've shared, and after last night, I've decided that I will."

"Sweetheart, what could you possibly need to confess to me?"

"That I am a Jew. And today, we are still a hunted people. It's still happening. Even now. I am trusting you with my greatest treasure, my life."

He bent his face to hers, kissing her gently and pulling her firmly to him, holding her tightly. "It doesn't matter to me if you're wanted in fifty states and forty countries, I will never let anyone harm you. Your life is safe in my hands, Rachel."

They sat together in silence for a time, holding each other as this confession sank in. Rachel noticing the time on the bedside alarm clock, broke the spell with a lighter expression and a small laugh, as she said, "And you, my stinky sweet, had better get into the shower. We need to eat, and get ready to head home to Salt Lake."

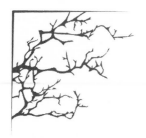

Ten

HIGHWAY 42, SOMEWHERE in Nebraska
March 30, 1986

Rachel was whispering in Joseph's ear so the others in the school van couldn't hear, grinning and quietly laughing. "I think our neighbors heard us last night. Oops."

"Yeah, I guess we were kind of noisy." He softly chuckled.

"There were some knowing looks this morning at breakfast. My room-mate, Anne, was grinning as she asked a few pointed questions, like where I'd spent the night and did, I have fun."

A black Suburban had come up behind the two school vans, passing the back one at high speed. It collided with the back corner of the first van with tremendous force, shoving it off the narrow road. Plowing into the barbed wire fence, the damaged vehicle came to rest in the snow-covered grass and sand of the road cut. Joseph was thrown hard into Rachel, despite their shoulder belts having been fastened, and she was slammed sideways against the window. The Suburban sped off down the road without stopping or slowing.

She was stunned by the impact of her head hitting the glass. As her vision cleared, she stuttered, "Wh... what was that?"

"Are you all right?" Joseph helped her out of her seat-belt and softly touched the large lump forming on the side of her forehead. He was not feeling well himself with his stomach gripped tightly in a thick knot as shattered images from his past flooded his mind.

Glaring lights... screams... flames... pain... voices. "My God, a baby, burned ... C.B... state patrol..."

He was reeling from both this crash and from the suddenly remembered fragments of memory.

"Is anybody hurt?" the school director called out. "Please, everyone, carefully get out of the van. Let me know if you have any bumps or scrapes."

Joseph helped her to her feet and out the door. The cold air outside hit them hard in their faces. He made a place for them to sit on a tarp and blanket he spread out on the snowbank. "Here, let's sit and rest. How's your head?"

"It hurts. I don't feel so good. That maniac could have killed us all. What were they thinking, driving like that?"

"I don't know, but it's kind of freaky; first Charlie hit by a car, and now this." Joseph held her in his arms, cradling her bruised head on his shoulder, and whispered in her ear, "If I ever lost you, Rachel." He picked up a small handful of snow and gently held it on the growing lump on her head.

Whispering, she said, "Hmm... sweet man. That helps. Thank you, lover."

After fifteen minutes of checking over the van, and with no way to call for help, they decided to see what could be done to get the van back on the road. After the director checked everyone, it was clear that the van was the chief victim, though Rachel's head was quite sore, and others had bangs and bruises.

The drivers and the school director decided, if they could back the van out of the sand and snow, they might be able to make it to the next town. After a few tries, and with almost all the students pushing, the driver was able to get the van back onto the road. Testing the steering, he found the damage was confined mostly to the back corner.

Shaken by the encounter, the group was extremely subdued as they drove into the next town with a gas station. The trip home was delayed, while the mechanic checked out various parts of the van and banged out the bent-in rear end.

While everyone was buying soft drinks, several of the group slipped out to the payphone at the back of the gas station to call family back in Salt Lake City. One waited until everyone was finished and placed a collect call.

"Damn it, Servino! Was that your scum in the SUV? Are you trying to kill us all?"

"Maybe it was, and maybe it wasn't. But if we did do something, it might be just to get your attention. Have you made any progress? Where the hell are you calling from anyway?"

"Fuck you! I think it was one of your so-called 'priests.' Just back off, do you hear me? Give me some space. And we're somewhere in the Sand Hills of Nebraska, as you well know."

"We'll back off if you get some results. What have you found out? Do you have any idea what the object is? It will be something connected to him."

"Not much. You've got to give me more time. I'm just getting started. At this point, I don't think he knows anything. I think this time you're on a dead-end."

"Honey, we do know who he is, and we're pretty sure he's the one we've been looking for. His work number came up active in the records."

"Well, I think your information is screwed up. There is no object, and he doesn't know anything."

"No, you are screwed if you don't get some results for us, and soon. The boss is not a patient type."

"Tell me the truth. Was that your car in Salt Lake that hit the kid?"

"Now why would we do that, except to run down some kid playing hacky-sack?"

"You monster! You didn't!"

"It would be one solution to our little problem. But, yeah, so what? One of our operatives got a little eager is all. But the boss wants the kid alive. He wants him to see the light and maybe join us. Can't do that if he's gone to Hell first. But, if he doesn't want to join us, then a place in Hell is available for sure."

"Leave him alone."

"Are you getting sweet on him? Ah, that's so fucking cute. Just remember, it's just like the other jobs we've had you do for us. You should literally be a fucking pro by now."

"Fuck off. You can't push me on this. This is hard. And you should be ashamed of yourself, being a priest, forcing me to do this."

"Stop complaining. I'm sure you're enjoying it. You're just a slutty little Jewish harlot, and we own you. Don't forget we know all about the rest of your family, and where to find them. Might be time pretty soon for a nice little family barbecue."

"You bastard! Back off!"

"We know your baby sister is a novice at the Marian Convent in Fatima. She changed her last name, but we found her. The boss likes them young and pretty like her, as you well know."

"Fuck you! Leave my sister alone!"

"You do still have your mother, and another sister, is that correct? Maybe we should put them all to work for us as well. Do you think they're as good at it as you are?"

"Goddammit, leave my family alone!"

"Of course, your father's already dead. Unfortunate indeed. Have you ever wondered just how it happened?"

"You didn't. You couldn't have..."

"And your grandfather? He was one of the Jews that helped build the bombs, but he got what was coming to him. Too bad we don't burn heretics anymore, though there are other options. And the boss does want to bring back the old ways."

"Really? You're going to start burning people again?"

"Or we could always let your family know what you've been doing for us."

"You wouldn't."

"Have a pleasant drive home."

"Goddammit! Fuck you to hell!" shouted Rachel as she violently slammed the phone back on its hook.

I'm not telling them anything ever again. This whole thing is bigger than I know. I've got to protect Joseph. But my sister... how did they find out? I have to get her out of there.

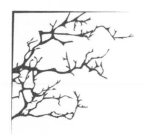

Eleven

ON THE ROAD TO SALT Lake City
March 30, 1986

After the crash, most of the students crowded into the first van, leaving the damaged one nearly empty except for the driver.

"Joseph, I'd like to rest for a while. Can we ride in the damaged van so I can have room to lie down?"

With his arm protectively around her shoulders, he looked closely at her. "Sure, as long as you're alright with being in the one that was hit."

"It's okay, and there's lots more room. Plus, our bags are still there under our seats."

"All right. I'll try to make you comfortable, and I'll seat-belt you in so you'll be safe."

The couple settled on one of the long bench seats in the back of the van, with Rachel lying down to rest. He covered her with his warm new coat Charlie had given him and firmly belted her in. Three of their classmates settled in the front seats.

The rest of the drive back to Salt Lake City was, thankfully, uneventful with no further excitement. To Joseph, the long trip on the two-lane highway across the snow-covered rolling hills of northern Nebraska passed in a blur that blended with the cloudy sky and snow-covered countryside. After taking some aspirin, she had fallen asleep with her head in his lap, her lustrous, soft dark brown curls spilling across his thighs and onto the seat. Eventually, they joined the interstate, heading south-west towards Utah. They were now driving through rolling sagebrush-covered hills and rocky plains with fresh snow blowing in from the north.

As the seemingly endless miles stretched across the frozen wastes of Wyoming, Joseph thought about the events of the previous day and night, and still could not grasp exactly what had happened to him.

That freaking violin - what did it do to me? Where, when, what was I? Somehow, I was inside someone else, in an entirely different world, with someone else's thoughts.

And being a young man of almost twenty-one, the night's events were very present in his mind.

Sex. Oh my God, I love it. I can't get enough of it. I love being with her. The feel of her skin, lips, of everything. Wow. I had no idea what it was like to be with a woman. Rachel is so smart and funny, so beautiful.

He thought of what she had told him, the secret that could endanger her life, that she is Jewish. He didn't know what that meant. The history she had told him was so frightening. He didn't know what to do, how to help or protect her.

He bent his lips down and kissed her head.

A flashing image of fire and pain moved like a violent wave through his mind and body for a moment. What had happened to him as a baby now blended into the accident, he had just experienced. He shivered. He was mulling over this and more; his mind almost overwhelmed with all of his new experiences as he nodded off, soothed into sleep by the motion of the van.

After she had slept for more than two hours, Rachel stirred, her head twisting sharply from one side to the other. She loudly cried out, "No! No! I don't... I won't do it. I won't tell you ... can't make me ... leave him... alone!"

Joseph could see their three classmates in the front, and the driver suddenly turn to look at them to see what was occurring. He reached out to hold her head while softly rubbing her temples.

"Rachel, I'm here. You're okay now. What are you dreaming about?"

Her green eyes opened as she woke. "Joseph! Oh, thank God you're here with me. The dream... oh... it was nothing, some weird nightmare. Nothing real."

He gently caressed her neck and shoulders. "I was scared that you were hurt badly, with a concussion or something. How are you feeling now? Is your head better?"

"Ow, my head still hurts, but not so much now. I think I'm starting to feel better." He continued softly massaging her arms and shoulders. "Thanks, that feels so nice. Keep rubbing like that. You're helping me relax."

"I'm glad. It's hard to see you hurt like that."

With a sudden thought, she turned to him and crossly said, "That jerk who nearly killed us. What were they thinking? And they just took off after running us off the road!"

"It happened so fast that I didn't get a look at it, but some of our group did get some info. But the weird thing is the ones who saw it all said the back-license plate was covered up with something, like black tape. It was like the driver wanted to make sure no one could see it. But they said it had an odd-looking frame around the plate, where some of the tape had peeled off, with some gold letters and what looked to be something like a gold-colored curved shape, as part of a circle, showing a bit on the top. Peter said he'd seen one something like it on an official Church vehicle from the Circle of Fatima Ministry. What do you think about that? Why would a Church SUV hit us and run off like that? And what is the Circle of Fatima? You told me last night that they were trying to bring back the Spanish Inquisition or something. If it was them, why would they intentionally run us off the road like that?"

Her face froze for a moment, her eyes suddenly fixed, staring into space.

"Sweetheart, are you sure you're, all right? You've got a strange look in your eyes. Is the pain worse? Do we need to stop and try to find a doctor for you?"

She gave him a weak smile, shaking her head. "Oh, no. Sorry, it's nothing. It'll be okay. Hmm... can we try to forget about this now and talk about something else? I'll tell you more about The Circle when we get home."

"Sure. Then what do you want to talk about?"

"Can you tell me about your family and where you grew up? I realize that I really don't know much about you." She whispered so the driver and fellow students couldn't hear, with a small giggle in her voice. "About the man who made love to me all last night."

He blushed, as he was doing a lot of lately, and laughed, something he was starting to enjoy immensely. "I will if it helps you feel better and takes your mind off the pain."

As they talked, the school van finally started to climb up into the high Uinta Mountains with thick forest cover on the rising slopes. They were gradually getting closer to home.

"Yes, please tell me your story. Do you have any brothers or sisters?"

"No. I'm an orphan with no one left at all." Wiping the tears that began to form in the corners of his eyes, he continued. "As far as I know, I was an only child. After my parents died, I was raised by an older couple, friends of my family. I called them my great aunt and uncle, but we weren't related. They told me my parents were killed in a car crash and that I only survived by being thrown clear of the wreck."

She reached out to take his hand in hers, squeezing and kissing it as her eyes filled with tears as well. "Joseph, I'm so sorry to hear that. How terrible to lose your family that way."

"Well, I was only two years old and, lucky for me, a passing car saw me, I was told. I was found wrapped in a burned blue blanket. They said my rescuers could see it half-hidden in the white snow. They were able to get me to a hospital in Truckee just in time to save my life. That's how I was burned, on the entire back of my body."

With tears rolling down her face, and despite her pain, she put her arms around him and gently caressed the scars on his back, kissing his cheek.

"I was so young that I can barely recall my parents, though I do get a flash of a memory of them from time to time. I know them mostly from a few stories the folks who raised me told me. I don't actually know anything about my family, what they did for work, or where they were from. And I never saw any pictures of them, either. The couple who raised me would always just say, 'when you're older, we will tell you more.' But before they could tell me anything more, just last year, they both passed away, within a week of each other."

"Oh, Joseph. So, you never had a chance to learn more about your family? That's so sad."

"No, I never did. But, as for the car crash, I don't remember it. Though, lately, I've just started to recall some tiny flashes or images and sounds that I think are from it. I only recall a bit of being in the hospital. They told me I was there for about nine months. They had to do repeated skin grafts from my legs and arms to try to repair my back."

She reached out to him and again stroked his shoulders and back.

The scar-tissue on his body pulsed with pain as he changed his position in the seat. He grimaced and continued, "I'm hoping to be able to afford the newest surgeries to repair some of the deepest scars when I graduate from school and get a good job."

Rachel stroked his arm once more. "That would be so wonderful. Hopefully, it will help you a lot."

"Yes. It's one of the things that's driving me so hard to finish my degree early. That hope, and now being with you. You are giving me more hope that one day, I will feel human and have a full life. Hopefully with you?"

She wound her arms around his neck and pulled his lips to hers, kissing him deeply. And then, without a word, still very close, she just gazed into his blue eyes with her emerald green ones for a long time.

He gazed back, enjoying the beautiful woman before him.

When he had recovered from this sharing with his lady, he continued with a long sigh. "Hmm, the crash." He looked out at the cold blowing snow, now surrounding the van like a white curtain as they barreled through it homewards. "It was in a storm like this one, they said. When I was older, they told me that a semi gasoline-tanker truck lost control on the snow and ice-covered road, and ran into the back of the car. But the driver was killed as well, so no one knows what happened. The gasoline-fueled fire was so hot that my parents' bodies were, just gone."

"Oh, God. I`m so sorry."

"There was nothing left to bury. So, a stone was set just off the road at the curve where they died, as a memorial." He paused for a time. "But, early last year, I asked my aunt to tell me exactly where, the milepost, where the wreck had happened, and I drove to the spot. I saw the stone. It was engraved with their names, just, 'In loving memory, David and Leah.' There were still parts of the twisted, burned, and rusted wreckage, scattered down the rocky cliffs, more than two thousand feet to the bottom of the canyon. I wanted to honor and remember them where they died, where they are... buried." His voice caught in his throat, as his tears flowed freely at the memory of his loss.

She reached out and hugged Joseph, pulling him close. "I'm so sorry for you, darling. If it was me, I don't think I could stand to go to a place where something that terrible had happened."

He took a deep breath and sighed. "I felt like I could almost sense my parents' presence. I couldn't stay very long. When I got home, I just lay on my bed for a couple of days and didn't eat or speak. I felt so empty. My aunt finally threatened to call the doctor if I didn't get up."

"Oh, my. That must have been so hard."

He silently gazed out at the flying snowflakes, holding her tightly in his arms. After a while, he sighed again. "Yes, it still is."

The two lovers held each other tightly as Joseph, with tears flowing from his eyes, buried his face in her hair. After a while, they both drifted off to sleep once more, leaning against and holding each other up on the seat.

With a rare end of the day sunbeam breaking through the storm clouds, the bright light awoke the two from their rest. They were nearly home to Salt Lake City now, with only about an hour to go.

"I feel so much better after sleeping. Now, will you tell me more about your childhood? Where did you grow up?"

He resumed his story. "My grandfather's neighbor and her husband informally adopted me, taking the place of any living relatives. She was a retired teacher, from the state schools, not the Church ones, and she taught me at home using her library and textbook collection. I grew up working on their olive ranch, spending all of my time with them, and with a few of their close friends and neighbors."

"You didn't have any friends your age?"

"No, not that I can recall. The place was way out in the country, almost to the foothills on the far edge of the valley. It was so far out that they still had old Aladdin oil lamps in parts of the house, with just a single on and off again power line and a generator to keep the fridge going. And no television, just a radio with lots of reading by lamplight when the power was out. When we had power, they turned the radio to classical music all the time, avoiding the news whenever it came on."

"Is that how you came to love classical music?"

Gazing out at the passing landscape, he could see by the fading twilight that the snow had stopped falling. They were traveling through a deep snow-covered forested canyon on the final approach to the Salt Lake valley. "Yes.

I've always loved all kinds, especially the violin concertos. They seem to be able to carry me to a peaceful place, away from all the pain."

"I love them, too; do you know many of the parts to play?"

"I know some of the great solo parts and a lot of complete pieces. I especially love the Mendelssohn Concerto in E Minor; it's so haunting. Somehow, it stirs my heart like no other music."

She turned to him and whispered into his ear, "Did you know that Mendelssohn was Jewish? I mean, he was a convert to be outwardly Christian, but he was a Jew in his soul, nonetheless."

"I didn't know that when I read about him. That was no mention in his bio."

"Yeah, there's a lot of history that`s 'not mentioned' nowadays."

Looking thoughtful, he softly replied, "So it seems from what you told me last night." He barely whispered into her ear, "Your secret is safe with me. I won't even whisper it here, even though we are almost alone."

"Thank you. I would not have told you if I had not sensed I could trust you."

Keeping his voice low, he asked, "But sometimes, I want you to tell me your story. About your family, and how you learned the things you know, including..." He added with a broad smile while softly stroking her hair and kissing the soft skin of her neck. "...What you taught me last night."

"I promise I will. There is so much I can share with you. But your story, please tell me more. How did you get here to this school?"

"Well, I passed the GE high school test when I was fifteen and never went to any school, Church, or state. I stayed there, living and working with them for a while after that point. And then, when I was sixteen, I saw an old violin, a friend of my uncle was playing at the house one day. I just looked at it and said, 'I'm going to build one of these.' And I did, from memory, having seen just that one violin, using a neighbor's woodworking shop. Somehow, and it`s so strange, I was able to do that, with no training at all."

"That's incredible. How did it turn out?"

He laughed and said, "It was sort of playable, and looked like a violin... mostly. I got some of the parts from my uncle's friend, who had messed around with fixing and making violins, or 'fiddles,' as he called them in his earlier years. And between the friend and my adopted parents, they all encouraged me to pursue the craft, considering my injuries, like something I might be able to do for my living."

"Wow, that's pretty amazing. It sounds like your family and friends were very supportive of you."

"Yeah, they were, and so I built a dozen or so, working from some books and plans the family friend gave me, and each one got better and better. And then I started to learn how to play them, and that was so wonderful, and it seemed natural as well.

"My aunt and uncle and a few of their friends all pitched in to help me move here and to pay for school, though I`ve still had to work a full-time job as well."

"Well, about your need to work. Can you tell me about that letter you received?"

What letter?"

"The one from an attorney's office somewhere? Charlie told me about it. He said that it looked like it might be something important, maybe about an inheritance?"

"Charlie has a big mouth, but I don't mind you knowing about it. I don't want to keep any secrets from you."

"Sweetheart, thank you for trusting me. But it sure would be wonderful if you had an inheritance, so you could stop working at that job, and fully concentrate on your studies... and on me."

"That would be good. I think I need to have more faith in the universe. Maybe something good is happening to me. I mean, something good is, indeed, happening. You are the best thing to ever happen in my life."

She gently kissed his cheek. "And you are for me too."

"My aunt was an unusual woman, as she also taught me a lot about Buddhism, and how to meditate. That's why even though what we did last night was all entirely new for me ..." Whispering, he continued, "...being a virgin and all. I did understand that you were teaching me some sort of meditation when you were... you know... doing what you were doing and saying what you were saying."

She giggled, and reaching her face to his, softly kissed his ear and began gently tickling the inner lobe with her tongue.

Joseph's face grew hot, and he blushed a bright scarlet. His heart beat faster as he whispered, "Rachel, you'd better stop that. We're in public."

Continuing to laugh, she replied, "They already know everything. Among our classmates, news travels fast. Plus, right now, we're practically sitting in each other's laps anyway, fully in public. So, I'm sure that our new 'thing' is no secret. But what about that letter? Can you show it to me when we get back home?"

"I can do better than that. Here it is." He reached into his small day pack and handed her a large crumpled envelope. "I brought it with me to try to puzzle it out while on this trip. It's made out to me with my address here in Salt Lake, but inside is another strange-looking envelope."

She took the large envelope as he handed it to her, and said, "It looks like it was forwarded from a California address. Joseph, is that where you grew up?"

"Yes."

"The return address is from a law office in Sacramento, California: Hart, Rose, and Goldman, Attorneys of Law. Does that sound familiar?"

"I`ve never heard of them. That`s why I wasn`t sure if it was real, or some scam."

Opening the outer part, she reached in and unfolded a piece of thick old stationary, softly reading it out loud. "January 10th, 1966. Joseph Davidson, as the only son of David Davidson and Leah Hartman, receive this legacy at your ascent into adulthood. With all the obligations and responsibilities herein attached."

He reached into the outer envelope and pulled out an unusual-looking inner parcel made of what looked like thick parchment. The material was faded, crinkled, and fastened shut with what looked like several blobs of old sealing wax. The impressions from the seal used, showed two lions facing each other with additional shapes that were not entirely clear to him. Written across the front was a string of different letters, ones that caused Rachel's eyes to grow large as she looked at them. "Oh, god, it can't be."

He leaned closer to her. "These letters look like those on the top of that violin's scroll. Do you think they might be the same type? Can you read it?"

"Wow, this envelope is addressed in Hebrew, or I should say that these are Hebrew letters. But the letters are an odd combination. They don't seem to spell any words that I know of."

Turning the package over in his hands, feeling how bulky it was, he said, "I hadn't thought much about what might be inside it, but now I'm quite curious to see." He pulled at the sealing wax and heavy parchment but couldn't get it to budge or tear.

"I have an idea. Here, let me try." She pulled out a nail file from her bag and started to saw at the envelope flap and pry under the wax seals. After a few minutes, the file was able to cut the wax from the parchment with audible snaps. They both looked up to see that their three classmates in front of the van were still fast asleep, and the driver showed no sign of having heard the sound.

Opening the inner envelope, she pulled out a small cloth bundle. The cloth was white wool with black stripes running through it. The fabric was finely woven but had a look of great age, worn and frail in places. The four corners appeared to be each edged with long-knotted cords that wrapped around the bundle.

"What's this?" He asked, holding it up at shoulder level.

She moved the bundle lower, down into their laps to make sure it wasn't visible to those in front. "Joseph, you need to make sure to never, show this to anyone else."

"Why? What do you mean? Is there something dangerous about a piece of cloth like this?"

"It's Jewish," Rachel whispered into his ear. "It looks like a prayer shawl; a Tallit. Jewish men and some women wear them when they pray."

"What is such a thing doing in a parcel addressed to me? I don't understand."

"I don't know, but I have goose flesh all over my body right now." She shivered and moved closer, huddling against him.

He gently unfolded the soft wool material, and as it opened, he could see the bright gleam of gold in the darkened van.

He gasped as another memory came back to him. "My mother wore a shape like that around her neck. I remember seeing it when I was a baby. But who would send me something like that?"

"Your mother wore this? Joseph, it`s not a Christian symbol. It's a Jewish or Muslim one, and it's called a Hamsa, like a hand. Oh my, could you be ...?"

He looked at her with an increasing tingling in his body. "So that's what it's called. I've also seen this same shape twice before. An old homeless man in Salt Lake City who followed me to school one day was wearing one. And then when I was dreaming or whatever, while I held that violin, the old woman I met in that experience was wearing one too."

"That is so very strange, to have seen it that way. It is a rare thing to see even one these days."

With a small laugh, he said, "Wow. Just another strange new thing in my life."

"Yes, you are right about that. Well, let me tell you what it means. It represents the open right hand as a sign of protection for the person wearing it. It's supposed to provide blessings of power and strength and to deflect the evil eye. It's an ancient symbol of the Goddess. In Judaism, she is called the Shekeniah, the feminine presence of God on the earth. It was often worn in the past... as a Jewish symbol. And your mother wore one?"

As the van entered the city, he stared out into the black night. The city lights reflecting off the dense cloud cover caused the clouds to glow with an eerie light. The strange light matched how he was now feeling; fully extraordinary. "Yes, I believe she did, and here is one in a package addressed to me. But, what could this possibly... What does this mean for me? I'm not Jewish. Why would someone send me things like these?"

"Joseph, I have an idea that your family may have been Jewish. And that would make you Jewish as well. I'll try to help you figure this out."

"Really? I have no clue, but that would explain some of this or all of it? I guess."

She unrolled the cloth the rest of the way, exposing the smooth linen top neck lining cloth of the Tallit. They could both see, and she could read, the Hebrew blessing that was said before putting it on one's shoulders, where it was embroidered into the cloth. In addition to the usual prayer, there was a string of additional letters.

"This is the prayer that`s said before putting it on, and there`s a person's name here. I'm guessing that it must be the name of the man who once owned this Tallit. I read it as Daveed ben Daveed, David, son of David. Does that mean anything to you?"

"I think my grandfather was maybe named David, along with my father, but the rest of it means nothing to me."

With rising excitement, she said, "Oh my god, this may have been your father`s Tallit." As she looked more closely at the name, something small and shiny dropped out of the last fold of the cloth to the floor of the van, the light of a passing car catching it for an instant as it fell.

"What was that? I think it's by your left shoe."

Reaching down to the floor mat, Rachel felt around until she could barely reach the object. Bringing it into the scattered light of passing cars, they could both see that it was a small silver key. Looking closely at it, she said, "It has letters on it. C.V. N. B. Do you have any idea what they could stand for?

"I don't know what it could mean, though the valley in California where I grew up is called the Central Valley. If this is all somehow connected to an attorney my family knew, maybe C.V. is initials for the valley."

Rachel's excitement was rising, along with her voice. "I think I may have seen something like this once when I was young. Before my father died, he took me to our bank and showed me what he had in a safety deposit box. The box had a key like this, about the same size if I remember right, and it had initials on it too. I think this is a key to a similar box."

Joseph was looking anxiously upfront to their classmates who were apparently now awake. "Rachel, shush. Keep your voice down. I don't want the others to hear. But I'm sorry to know your father is gone. Do you have other family?"

"I do. I'll tell you more when we're home and somewhere more private."

Holding the inner envelope in her lap and whispering once more, she pointed at it and said, "I think I may have an idea of what these letters might be."

"What do you mean? I thought you said that they don't spell anything, that they make no sense?"

Holding his hands in hers, she squeezed them tightly together, and speaking very quietly into his ear; she said, "My sweet, each letter in the Hebrew alphabet is also a number. I think it could just possibly be an account number. And maybe this is the key to a safety deposit box."

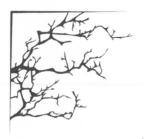

Twelve

SALT LAKE CITY UTAH, March 31, 1986

A tall, shadowy figure materialized out of the afternoon gloom, carrying an elongated object in each hand. Pushing the workshop door open with one foot, he raised his arms, brandishing a beautiful old violin in each hand, and called out, "I'm on my way to auction in L.A. I've got a Strad and a Del Gesu. You've got fifteen minutes." Charles Honeyman, the premier British violin expert, and father of one of the students stood just inside the doorway and large plate-glass windows of the old storefront space that made up the main part of the school. Hearing his words, the entire student body of twenty-five students eagerly clustered around to share in the special treat.

One student picked up the Stradivarius, grabbed a nearby bow, checked the fine-tuning, and started playing a lively, rhythmic bluegrass tune on it. Others were looking inside the Guarneri Del Gesu with small mirrors and penlights.

When it was his turn, Joseph picked up another bow and started to play the Bach Partita in E on the Del Gesu. The resulting musical blend filled the workshop with a slightly strange but exciting mix of sounds. Joseph was, instantly drawn into the waves of incredible music coming from within the violin he was playing. The quick notes of the piece cascaded up and down the scale as his fingers moved rapidly back and forth on the violin's neck. Filled with ecstatic joy, he was carried to another place. *I feel like when I was with Rachel making love... or touching that golden violin.*

While he was playing, Rachel stepped over behind him and whispered in his ear, "Come see me tonight at ten. Top floor, number twelve."

He turned to look towards the lovely young woman as she walked away from him. The sweet scent of the lavender oil she wore stayed with him, tickling his nose. His breath caught in his throat, and he stumbled over the notes he was playing as he watched her slim, curvy body swaying towards her chair. He thought about the incredibly sexy night they had just spent together.

Oh, yes. I'll be there.

After Charles had gone with the two violins, Joseph returned to his workbench by the large front window to look over the violin he had just finished building. As he picked it up to take it upstairs to the varnish room, he noticed a man standing on the sidewalk across the street in the afternoon gloom. The man almost appeared to be staring straight at him. As their eyes locked, the man suddenly turned and walked rapidly away.

What the hell was he doing looking at me like that?

Joseph realized that he might have seen him before, but wasn't sure where.

Shaking off the weird feelings that were twisting his stomach, his thoughts shifted to Rachel and what had happened on the trip. It was just the day before, though it felt like a long time in the past.

It actually happened, she made love to me. She shared her secret with me.

Standing up and carrying his finished unvarnished white violin by the neck with a clean rag, he walked by Rachel's chair at the far end of the room. He bent close with his face near her ear. "Okay, see you tonight." She turned a bit as he passed and gave him a quick, mischievous smile.

Upstairs at the varnish bench, Joseph joined another student, Rick, already at work, carefully brushing varnish onto his instrument.

As he placed his violin on the workbench and still standing while moving his chair into position, there was a brilliant flash of light outside the large windows that momentarily blinded him.

What the hell was that?

Joseph was now alone, with the other student vanished from sight. He was still standing with a white violin laying before him, but everything else inside and outside the room had changed in an instant. The workbench and room now looked old and rough. The varnishes and brushes were different as well, with what seemed to be hand-tied horsehair brushes. There were a clear blue sky and bright sunlight outside the windows. The glass was gone, replaced with open shutters, and the outside sounds of oxen pulling a cart with the driver cursing their slow pace, overlaying the background roar of a great city at work filled his ears. Mixed smells fiercely assaulted him; of blooming flowers, urine, freshly baked bread, and roasting meats. He saw a large, strange city spreading out over rolling hills to distant blue water dotted with white sails of small and larger vessels. Though, from his recent experience, the city was a familiar one, as he gazed out onto the cobblestones, white plastered walls, and red-tiled roofs that receded down a sloping street into the distance. Brilliant flowers cascaded from balconies on either side of the narrow road.

What the...? How? Where, am I? It was like this when I touched that violin at the museum. Oh no, maybe I'm losing my mind after all...

Blinking his eyes and rubbing them, the experience vanished before all of his senses. Once again, he was standing next to the other student, who was looking at him with a strange expression on his face. The familiar cold, dreary sky with dull sunlight could be seen again outside the large glass windows. Joseph slowly sat down and sighed an extended exhalation, realizing he had been holding his breath.

Rick turned to him. "Joe, are you alright? You look like you're catching something. You were standing there like a statue just staring out the window."

"I'm all right. Just tired after the trip."

"Oh, that's right." Rick chuckled softly. "I heard about you and Rachel. You're a lucky guy."

"Ah, how did you know? I thought we were discreet."

Rick started laughing. "You've got to be kidding? Everybody knows. You two lovebirds are pretty obvious. But everyone thinks it's wonderful for you both. Have you heard her play the cello yet? She's a brilliant musician, very smart, and as you know, beautiful as well."

"Thanks, she is. Ah, Rick, I think I'm done for the day. I'm going to stop a bit early and get my varnish started tomorrow."

"Okay, take it easy, Joe."

Still roiling from the flash of whatever had just happened to him, he made his way down the wooden stairs and quickly put on his coat and headed out into the chilly night towards his apartment. After a shower and a hot plate meal of instant noodles, he settled in to try to work on the violin he was building at home. He was excited, and a bit stressed by Rachel's invitation, and so he kept standing up to look at his clock that sat on the basement window sill.

At five minutes to ten, Joseph made his way up the four flights of stairs in the apartment building next to the school. He could hear overlapping waves of cello music coming from above him, as someone bowed deep repeating but ever-changing passages of combined higher and lower notes.

Who is making that beautiful music? They're playing the Bach prelude. It's so haunting. So mesmerizing...

Climbing to the top level, he could see her door in front of him, number twelve, one of only two larger apartments on that floor. The music was filling the space, echoing off the walls, the music he now knew was being played by Rachel. The door was painted with colorful flowering vines framing a deep blue sky, and he wondered if she had painted it.

With the soaring notes from inside the apartment surrounding him, he noticed a small handwritten note pinned to the door. It spelled out, with a large heart drawn around the letters, 'Come into my parlor, said the spider to the fly.' Chuckling to himself at this, he knocked quietly, and a musical voice that carried over the cello notes replied, "Come in if you dare."

He opened the unlocked door and saw such a sight as he had never seen before in his life. The apartment was stunning, with thick multicolored rugs on the floor and a wall painted like the front door with a realistic land and seascape mural with bright colored flowers, green trees, vines, and blue skies. It was warm inside, and there was even one of the new CD players he had heard of. There were soft plush chairs and a deep blue sofa. And sitting on the sofa was a sight that caused his body to respond eagerly.

"Come here, lover boy," spoke a near-naked Rachel, who was holding her cello between her bare thighs and still gently playing it. She was wearing an almost transparent rainbow-colored gown over her honey-colored skin. It was barely tied in front, revealing to him her rounded breasts on either side of the beautiful golden-brown cello.

As she stopped playing and set the cello down on a soft rug, she said in a low, sultry voice, "Well, don't just stand there, sweetheart. Come here and make love to me."

He kicked off his shoes and started to remove the several layers of warm clothing he was wearing, finally reaching out and joining with her on the couch.

Much later, the couple had migrated to her warm, soft bed, where they slept to recover from their vigorous exercise. Joseph awoke, holding her in his arms. He had dreamed again, but this time, not a nightmare, just an odd dream. There was only light, brilliant light, and a voice saying, 'Who are you? Where are you? What are you?', over and over again. Waking from the strange dream, he was more mystified than disturbed by it as he thought of those words and what they could mean.

The warmth of her naked body spooning against his chest and thighs was deeply soothing to him. He had taken the lead in their lovemaking this time and hoped he had satisfied her. He was so delighted by the deep, slow rhythm of her breathing while he softly stroked her flowing hair, that he let loose an involuntary sigh, awakening her from her sleep.

Seeing her eyes were open, he turned to face her and softly asked, "Rachel, you told me about your dreams on the trip, but did you dream anything tonight?"

Pulling the thick down quilt higher up on her soft shoulders, she sleepily said, "No. I don't think so. I was sleeping so deeply, enjoying you holding me like that. I feel so safe in your arms."

Kissing her in response, he said, "Well, I did have a dream I recall. But it was such a different one than any I've had before. Just now, I dreamed there was brilliant light with a voice coming out of it that said, 'Who are you? Where are you? What are you?' And it said that over and over again." He had been staring, looking away from her, up at the ceiling as he recalled this. Now looking into her green eyes, he asked, "What could that mean?"

"That sounds like a Jewish prayer-song, I know."

"Again, something Jewish? Maybe you're right about my family and me. But I don't know for sure."

"Joseph for you to dream that song, I think it means something powerful is occurring, unfolding for you. Something we can't understand yet. But maybe in time, we will?" She kissed him on his forehead and lips, and added,

"Lover, I`ll help you all I can. Maybe together we can find some firm answers for you."

With a long soft molding of his lips to hers, he answered, "Thank you, my beautiful woman. I love you, and maybe we will, in time. But that reminds me, this afternoon I had a strange experience at school. I went upstairs to the varnish room, and something happened. There was a flash of light, then suddenly I was looking out at a street from my dreams, or from my experience with that violin. I was there, wide awake, seeing, hearing, and smelling everything. And then, as suddenly, it all vanished, and I was back."

Running her fingers through his hair, she laughed softly, "Joseph, a dream while asleep is one thing, but a wide-awake one? That is something new, for sure."

"Yes, for sure."

"Lover, if I had not been so close to you the last few days, I would think from what you are experiencing and telling me that you were having some kind of brain disorder." Patting his head gently while saying this with a smile, she added, "But I experienced it with you the other night, when we both were somebody else and somewhere else, together."

"I've wondered if I'm going crazy. But that shared thing we experienced while lovemaking, plus my dreams matching yours. I think we're crazy together."

"Well, I do know I`m crazy about you lover, and you`re about me?"

"Yes, I am, no question about that." With a soft laugh, he reached his arms around her shoulders and embraced her closely.

Joining in with his mirth, she squeezed him back and gently caressed his arms and scarred back. "So maybe this is all okay?"

"Yes, but that's enough about my weird experiences for now. I want to know more about you, this beautiful woman I am holding in my arms. You said you would tell me more about your family when we were alone. Can you tell me now?

After a bit, with a sweet smile, and a deep, slow yawn, she stretched out her arms and legs, and replied, "Okay, I think I can. It's a lot of history wrapped up with my family story, and it`s pretty sad, so bear with me. My father and his father were both scientists in the US nuclear program under

President Lindbergh and VP Coughlin. And you do know that Lindbergh gave the Nazis the bomb?"

"Yes. I remember that in the history books."

"Well, Lindbergh was an anti-Semitic who generally agreed with Hitler that the world would be a better place with all the Jews gone. But my grandfather felt that he could best protect his family by working with the American Fascists, as part of the program."

"Wow, so he helped the U.S. Fascists despite being Jewish?"

"Yes, and eventually he was murdered by some of them. When the U.S. entered the war after Lindbergh was assassinated, by a young Jewish man, there were anti-Jewish riots. My grandfather was driving my grandmother to the opera one night in 1945 in Chicago when a mob attacked them and set their car afire. They were both burned to death."

Holding her tighter in his arms, he said, "Oh, darling, I never knew my grandparents. But for you to have lost yours that way... It's like how my parents died."

"Yes. And with my family, it didn't stop there. All of my remaining relatives in Europe were murdered by the Nazis there."

"Oh Rachel, I'm so sorry."

"And then I lost my father in a high-speed car wreck in the mountains of Colorado ten years ago. I still don't know what happened. But after my grandparents were murdered, my family decided to go into hiding and create new identities. Instead of being Jewish, we were now, to all appearances, devout Catholics. We went from being called Greenbaum, to being just the Green family. That was when I entered the convent as part of our cover, to try to blend in."

Caressing her hair as it spilled over her shoulders and onto his chest, he said, "I'm so sorry to hear about your grandparents and your father. We both have lost parents and more." Gently massaging her shoulder and neck, he added, "Rachel, I love you so much."

He held her as he continued to softly massage, her neck, and shoulders.

After a while, her face lost the sad intensity it had taken on, as she smiled and said to him, "I love you too. And I was wondering if you might want to move in with me and share my apartment with me? You would be much more comfortable here with me. We can make love every night, and I have a bathtub big enough for two."

"I'd love to, but let's take it a bit slower. We have plenty of time to get to know each other better. I'll need to think about it, to get used to the idea. I've lived alone for so many years."

Caressing his chest and face, she smiled. "Okay, that sounds good. I'm just excited to be with you as much as I can now. And now that you know I'm Jewish I can say this to you. To most Jews, sex is always sacred and spiritual; an extraordinary thing for a man and woman to share. When we join our ecstasy together, we are joining with God as the divine feminine and masculine powers of creation. And the meditation I taught you the other night is part of that. To me, it's Jewish Tantric Yoga, East and West together as sacred sexuality." With this, she started gently caressing him, re-awakening his passion.

He gave a long relaxing sigh and holding himself perfectly still. He said, "I want to do what you showed me the first time, what you just called Jewish Tantric, with us breathing together and moving the energy between us."

Gazing into his blue eyes, so filled with love for her, she said, "Yes me too. I'm so glad you enjoy our meditative lovemaking."

Breathing deeply, he placed his hands over and around her firm, rounded breasts, closed his eyes, and started visualizing the brilliant energy moving with his breath up his spine, out the top of his head, to then flow into her. As they both lay together, breathing as one, with their bodies warmly connected, her hands on his chest, and his on hers, they both started to feel again, similar energies as they had the night before. As their breathing deepened, and the light within them moved faster and faster, something new began to occur.

He thought, *There's a rushing sound like the wind. And that light piercing my eyelids. It's so bright...*

"Can you feel that? Can you see it?" Joseph whispered.

"Yes, I can see it, hear it..."

As the sound, they heard increased in volume, and the light grew so intense, it seemed to somehow crescendo and explode all around and through them as they both almost blacked out. They were ecstatically molded to each other, wholly joined in love.

Later Rachel held him, with his back cradled against her breasts as he slept, gently caressing his soft brown curls with her mind in turmoil.

What was that? What does it mean? He is in my soul, part of my heart, and I'm in him, part of his soul. This is like nothing I have ever felt before. I cannot betray him or lie to him. I must protect him and protect my family somehow. But I don't know how I can do both.

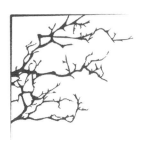

Thirteen

FATIMA, PORTUGAL
April 1, 1986

The trim, athletic-looking older man coasted down the sharp, twisted road along the mountainside on his lightweight road bike. *It is a blessing to rest after that strenuous climb.*

Picking up speed, coasting faster in his exhilaration at being free from his heavy robes of office and out in the cold, fresh open air, he did not see the black Sedan moving at high speed, quickly gaining on him.

Feeling so completely happy and free, he shouted out a quick prayer of thanks to the Virgin. "Mother Mary, thank-you for this joy!" As he finished his prayer, he pedaled some more to pick up even more speed. As he did so, he suddenly startled at a louder sound he could hear over that of the wind in his ears. It was so loud, roaring just behind him, that he quickly turned to look at the source of the last sound, and the last sight, he would ever hear or see.

Walking into his office, Archbishop DeSilva gravely addressed his secretary. "Servino, there has been an accident on the mountain road out of the city."

"Yes, Your Grace. What has happened?"

"His Grace, the Cardinal, went off the road on a sharp curve. He has apparently not survived. Can you please notify New Rome?"

With a long laugh, Servino replied, "Certainly, Your Grace. I will happily do so. He was a weak man. Unfit to be a Cardinal, and much too soft to be head of the Holy Office."

"Father Servino, you do know that it is not polite to laugh at such a tragic death? I know your upbringing in Sicily was rather rough, but do try to show some decorum."

Startled by the reprimand, Servino replied, forcing himself to control his voice, "Yes. Your Grace." *Don't push it, boss. Remember, I know everything.*

"And how is the Holy Father's health?"

Relaxing his face and smiling once more, he replied, "Precarious. Very precarious, Your Grace."

"And the College of Cardinals... have the funds been distributed?"

"Yes. All is in readiness for your elevation. Can I now say, Your Holiness?" *As long as you make me Cardinal, all will be well.*

"In private, yes for now. For the later, everyone will say it."

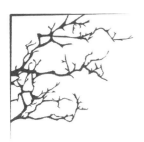

Fourteen

SALT LAKE CITY UTAH
April 12, 1986

The next week and a half blossomed with the first hints of a cool spring in the air, as the snow gradually turned to rain, with an occasional weak hour of sunlight shining through the gloom. Joseph hardly noticed, as he was feeling his inner warmth, a warmth he was sharing with his lover.

When they returned home, Joseph at first went back to his chilly old basement apartment, with Rachel urging him to move into hers. Laughing, she kissed his neck and whispered into his ear one day when they were sitting alone outside during lunch, enjoying a moment of sunlight. "Lover, are you ready to move in with me? You've been with me almost every night anyway, so let's make it full time. What do you say?"

He took another bite of his sandwich, and after a thoughtful pause, said, "I'm still thinking about it. I`ve had so much happen to me, so quickly. Everything is becoming so different and new in my life."

"Lover, I will not push you into it. But I love you so much. I want you to be with me every moment of the day and night."

"Ok, I`ll give notice on my apartment. So, in a couple of weeks?"

Kissing him on the cheek, and hugging him, with excitement in her voice, she said, "Okay. Oh, I`m so excited, sweetheart. I`ll have you every night."

The two new lovers had spent as much time together as they could that his job and school hours would allow. They had started going out for dinner, and he had spent the night in her apartment many times since returning home.

They often met in the school tool sharpening room where they were expected to sharpen their tools at least every half hour, to be able to cleanly cut the rock-hard fiddle-back maple wood they worked with. Usually, they could talk privately for a few moments there during school hours, standing side by side at the grinding wheels or sharpening stones, continuing to get to know each other.

When they were at their workbenches, working on their instruments, they sat on opposite ends of the workroom with Rachel seated near the back. They weren't close enough to each other to be continually talking but still tried to do so. The other students were starting to get annoyed at the 'cross room action' disturbing their concentration, and so Joseph, who had a prime spot in the natural light by a front window finally asked to trade workbenches with a student who was next to Rachel. The other student was pleased to not sit by her with the ongoing distraction of the conversations, but also to take possession of the prime window location.

There was another reason Joseph wanted to move away from the window. And once he had moved to work next to Rachel, he finally told her about it. Leaning in close to her to keep the conversation quiet, he spoke with a serious tone to his voice. "I haven't told you about this, but just last month before the field trip I started to have the odd feeling that someone was watching me. That the same person was always around, following me."

"That doesn't sound good."

"On the Tuesday of the week, before we left, I looked up from my workbench just before school was out to see this guy. He was standing across the street in the evening dark, looking at me through the windows. The next day, he appeared again, walking past the windows several times. And again, later in the week with changes of clothing and hats. But still the same dark eyes. The same intense stare."

She was listening to him intently, with a strange look of shock and perhaps recognition in her eyes. "How creepy."

"Are you alright? You look like you're not feeling well."

"I'm fine. It's just so scary to hear you describe seeing someone like that watching you that way."

"Yeah, seeing him there, it felt like a chill or a cold draft, like ice water poured into my gut. For the first time in my life since the crash, or what I was told about it since my parents died, I thought that maybe I wasn't safe anymore."

Leaning closer to him, she took his hand in hers and said quietly into his ear, Joseph, you're scaring me."

"Seeing him again and again like that made me feel like some threat was circling me, coming closer and closer. I'll remember that face for sure. Those dark, staring eyes. After this experience, I will always watch out for anyone who seems to give me too long of a look."

"I'm getting chilled just listening to you talk about it. That's disturbing.

"And I just remembered ... oh no. The first time I saw the guy was the day, Charlie was run down."

She startled at those words. "Maybe we need to get out of town for the summer. Did you see the posting for the internship at the Shrine to Music Museum, to work on their collection all summer? They're looking for two students to go, and they'll provide room and board and a stipend."

"Wow, I'm not sure. I don't know if I want ever to see, or touch that weird violin again."

"Sweetheart, it won't bite you. I would think you would want to check it out to try to figure out just what happened when you picked it up."

"Well, maybe. Let's talk about it later. Money is a problem for me, though. I was planning on working here all summer to save up for next year, and ..."

"Well, we have more time until the sign-up deadline so we can talk about it later. Hey, speaking of Charlie, how is he doing? Have you gone to see him since we got back?"

"Nah, I've been so busy catching up with work and then school. But I should go. I feel pretty bad about being so mad at him that day, and then him ending up in the ER. I remember he wanted to take me out for my first legal drink at one of the private clubs since I'm turning twenty-one this week. The director did say that Charlie is doing well and will be released soon."

"Well, I think we should both go to see him together this weekend. What do you say? Do we have a date at the hospital on Sunday? And you can tell him he was probably right about you receiving an inheritance,"

"I'm still not sure what that letter and the key is all about. It could mean nothing." He started laughing. "But, you know, I could try to smuggle a drink in to share with him."

"Well, be careful. It's a Mormon hospital, and they don't like booze. But what's the harm of telling him what we found? That is just the key part, not the cloth and the rest. He might be able to help you figure out what it is. He does know about banks and such, 'cause he told me his father works for one."

"Yeah, I think we could. I guess there would be no harm in asking him to check with his dad. He was maybe guessing right about it all the time."

Taking his hand in hers once more, she said, "Well, I have a little confession to make. I went to see him twice last week, and he is mending quite well with physical therapy, helping him walk. And, please don't be angry at me, but I told him about the key. Charlie thought it did sound like a safety deposit key. And he asked his father what C.V.N.B. could stand for."

"You did that without asking me?" Joseph stood up from his chair and stepped away from her, anger in his voice. "Rachel, we need to talk about things before you do something like that. This is my family stuff, whatever it might be."

Reaching out to him, as to try to calm him and quiet his voice, she said, "I'm so sorry. But we need to lower our voices." She said as she looked at their classmates who had noticed his raised voice. "But I just knew you were curious and maybe excited to see what it might be. I didn't mean to make you angry. Will you forgive me?"

"Yes. But this is the kind of thing that makes me think we're moving too fast in moving in together. Please, you need to slow down and check with me on something important like this."

She reached out to encircle him with her arms. "I'm sorry. Please sit down? I stepped out of bounds by not checking with you first. Please forgive me?"

His body relaxed, and he allowed her to hug him. "Okay. It's alright." He sat back down and smiled at the other students who had been distracted by the argument.

In a whisper now, she said, "I'm so excited to tell you the news I have. On my second visit, Charlie said his dad checked his bank's listings of other banks in California and said there used to be one called the 'Central Valley National Bank' in Northern California. It had branches in various small towns there."

"Really? Wow. So, it might still be there, in a bank in one of the towns?"

"Yes, and there may be something from your family in a safety deposit box in that bank that's been waiting for you. Waiting for you to turn twenty-one years old. Or else it's a weird coincidence that it arrived just before your birthday."

"I wonder, maybe it will tell me what these things are that were wrapped up with the key? What they mean to me."

"Didn't you tell me that the town near where you grew up was called Palermo? That the family that raised you were olive farmers?"

"Yeah, that's right."

"Well, spring break is coming up. Do you want to drive to California and see what we can find out? My little car is one of those Japanese ones that get good mileage."

"Yeah. Better than my old pickup, that's for sure."

"Okay. Road trip. It'll be our first adventure together with no one around to watch us! We can have so much fun. A week on our own. Just the two of us. I can pay for most of it from my trust fund. So, don't worry about the cost."

"I do have a week paid vacation that I can use. And we can share the costs. Alright. Let's do it!"

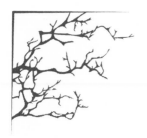

Fifteen

CIRCLE OF FATIMA, FATIMA Portugal
   April 12, 1986

"Cardinal, ah, Archbishop DeSilva, the Jesuit scientist is here with his progress report." The voice of Servino, Diego's secretary, called over the intercom.

"Send him in, please."

A tall, bespectacled priest dressed all in black rushed into the office, carrying a briefcase. He quickly knelt and kissed the ring on the outstretched hand of DeSilva

As he was about to speak, DeSilva stopped him with an upraised hand. "Father Lee, before you give me your report, I wish to ask your opinion on a subject."

"Of course, Your Grace. How may I be of service to you?"

"Father, what is your thought on the legend of the golem, from Jewish folklore? Can such a thing be created, or is it pure fiction?"

The Jesuit priest gave a start, staring at the archbishop for a moment before answering, "Your Grace, surely you know that such a thing is just a folk tale, told by the Jews to each other to help them feel better in their benighted and cursed state. We Jesuits deal with science, not with nonsense mystic mumble-jumble that is believed by ignorant simpletons."

"Hum, very interesting, Father. It's good to know where the Jesuits stand on such matters of import. Well, pray, do continue with your report."

"Archbishop DeSilva, thank you for seeing me. I have important news regarding our project to repair the climate. As you know, we are preparing to start launching church satellites. All the engine tests have been successful, and with your approval and blessing as the about to be confirmed new Head of the Holy Office and Cardinal, we can proceed within two months to begin placing the satellites into orbit."

He continued speaking rapidly, cutting off DeSilva when he attempted to interject.

"Yes, I am awa..."

"I'm sure you know from reading our past reports which we sent to Archbishop Arturo, your predecessor, how they are supposed to work. They will collect and concentrate the sun's light and heat far above the cloud cover to reflect it, to warm and dry out different parts of the Earth. As you must know, Archbishop Arturo was the moving force behind this effort to help all of humanity. The remaining great powers are still arguing about what to do to try to turn the cooling around and save the planet. But with their inaction, the Church is poised to be the savior of humankind. You understand that we Jesuits honor both God and scien ..."

DeSilva, with his forceful voice, cut off the rapid-fire speech. "I know that you so-called Jesuit 'priests' worship science as your other god. But may I remind you of the Third Prophecy of the Virgin? That speaks of the destruction of the Vatican, and the thousands of priests, church officials, nuns, and the Holy Father, not to mention the civilians who perished in the fall of the Jewish bombs, in a great hellish fire all created by science."

DeSilva reached into his desk and withdrew a sheet of parchment. The Priest attempted to interject, "But science is not ..."

Cutting off the priest, DeSilva continued, "I read to you here the exact words of the Holy witnesses, the shepherd children, as they described the death of the pope and the destruction of Rome. 'The Third Secret, a vision of the death of the pope and other religious figures, was transcribed by the Bishop of Leiria and reads: After the two parts which I have already explained, at the left of Our Lady and a little above, we saw an angel with a flaming sword in his left hand, flashing. It gave out flames that looked as though they would set the world on fire, but they died out in contact with the splendor that Our Lady radiated towards him from her right hand. Pointing to the Earth with his right hand, the angel cried out in a loud voice, 'Penance, penance, penance.' And we saw in an immense light that is God 'something similar to how people appear in a mirror when they pass in front of it' a bishop dressed in white. 'We had the impression that it was the Holy Father.' Other bishops, priests, religious men and women going up a steep mountain, at the top of which there was a big cross of rough-hewn trunks as of a cork-tree with the bark. Before reaching there, the Holy Father passed through a big city half in ruins and half trembling with halting step, afflicted with pain and sorrow, he prayed for the souls of the corpses he met on his way. Having reached the top of the mountain, on his knees at the foot of the big cross, he was killed by a group of soldiers who fired bullets and arrows at him, and in the same way there died one after another the other bishops, priests, religious men and women, and various lay people of different ranks and positions. Beneath the two arms of the cross, there were two angels, each with a crystal aspersorium in his hand, in which they gathered up the blood of the martyrs and with it sprinkled the souls that were making their way to God.'"

DeSilva had raised his voice even louder in reciting the Third Secret and now paused for a second, once more cutting off the Jesuit before he could complete a sentence. "But, Your Grace, it ..."

"Science in the hands of the Jews almost destroyed the Church and the entire world. The cold and the wet, the hiding of the sun; it is all God's punishment for our worship of science. Only when repentance has been fully made, and enough sinners have perished, and the false gods of science and modern technology are thrown into the pit of hell, will God forgive his children. Only then will the Virgin return and cause the Miracle of the Sun to warm the entire world once more. Not a day sooner."

The Jesuit scientist stood fixed in place, seemingly shocked by what he was hearing. "But, Your Grace, you cannot reject all science. Are you serious? Do you want to take us back to the darkness of the middle ages?"

"Yes, actually, I do. And yes, I can. In the middle ages, the Church was all-powerful, and no one could or would dare question us. I now will very soon have the power to reject and condemn all heresy. My agents are at work this very day, seeking out heretical books and writings to destroy them. And they are seeking any dark 'science' magicians, or Jewish science sorcerers to eliminate as well. We are bringing back, as I speak, the Act of Faith, the Auto da Fae."

"But there has not been one since 1850! You are mad..."

"No, you are mad. You are in love with ungodly science. You Jesuits will need to bring any new publications or project proposals to my office to be reviewed and approved. Any found to be heresy will be banned or burned. There will be no satellites launched at this time. Many, many more sinners must be purged from the ranks of the unwashed masses so the survivors will be grateful and obedient to the Church when the sun returns. When the Virgin gives us her personal blessing, then, and only then, may you proceed to launch your rockets. "

The Jesuit scientist straightened his back and strongly spoke. "You will not get away with this. I will go to the Holy Father himself when I am back in New Rome and complain of your words and actions. You cannot stop us!"

"You really do not understand, do you? I have the blessing of the Holy Father to do whatever is needed to save our Church. Anything at all. The people need a simple faith, they can follow in this growing darkness, and if they are afraid, then so much the better. And the more afraid they are, the more devout they will be. And then they will obey the Church without question." DeSilva continued, in a different tone, "By the way, I would not advise such rash action, to complain of me to the Holy Father. You do understand that travel can be occasionally hazardous?"

The priest stepped closer to DeSilva, his body taut with tension, stopping almost in his face, and softly said, "Are you threatening me, Your Grace?"

Now, in a soothing, gentle voice, DeSilva responded, "No, no, my son. Not at all. I just wished you a safe journey to New Rome, that no harm might befall you in your travels."

The archbishop reached out his hand for the priest to kiss his ring. The Jesuit hesitated for a moment before he slowly knelt to one knee. As the priest knelt, DeSilva made the sign of the cross over his head, saying, "May the Holy Virgin of Fatima bless you with safe travel on your way. Amen."

After the priest left, DeSilva called his secretary back into the room. "Servino, can you be sure to help our Jesuit friend with his travel arrangements? Make sure he is... relaxed on his journey?"

With a broad smile, Servino replied, "Yes, Your Grace. I understand completely."

"You know what I am speaking of? Good, good. Quickly then. I believe that an act of faith is needed right now. It is time. And the sheep are ready."

"I understand. With pleasure, Your Grace. It will be taken care of. I will arrange everything."

"And as for our other problem, has there been any progress to report yet on the boy?"

"Nothing new, Your Grace. We have not heard any news from the agent since the call she made from Nebraska."

"That is not like her at all. What is different this time? She has always been a very productive agent, always willing and reliable in the past. One of our best. Until now. Servino, you must apply more pressure. Remind her of our power and abilities, and if necessary, apprehend the rest of her family."

"Consider it done, Your Grace, with pleasure. Our other field operatives who keep their eyes on our agents have plans in place to pursue various options. They are watching her and the boy as we speak, and the reports have them spending much time together."

"Good, good. I know you will accomplish what I need from you. Your dedication and loyalty will be greatly rewarded when I have assumed my rightful place here in Fatima, the real New Rome. And as for the prophesied 'vessel,' are there any new developments in that department?"

"Your Grace, we have reason to believe it was hidden near Portofino, Italy. We do not know what it is, and as you know, our agent there failed in his mission to obtain it."

"Yes. An unforgivable mistake on his part, and likely the last one he will ever make. I have yet to decide on his fate, though an act of faith may yet be in order for him as well."

With a quick, thin smile, Servino replied, "Yes, Your Grace. Just give me the word, and it will be arranged."

"Your eagerness to follow my desires is commendable for one with your background, Servino. You were taught well by The Family in Sicily. I trust you with all my secrets, and so only the pope, you, and I know of the contents of the last page of the Third Secret." He added, with a deep, hearty laugh, "And the sad excuse we have right now for a pope doesn't know that we know."

He pulled out a small key and unlocked a lower drawer in his desk. He unrolled a small scroll, and even though he knew it by heart, he silently read it to himself. '*Now I will reveal the final part of the secret; The Holy Vessel of healing, made by the hand of one of the House of the Palmist must be awakened. The lineage of the Prophets to be linked in love with the lineage of the Apostles, a circle of healing, of Sister Faiths through all time. And the angel cried out in a loud voice: Teshuvah, Teshuvah, Teshuvah.'*

This must never be known, especially the Hebrew at the end of the vision. As pope, I will destroy both copies. Along with any descendants of the House of David the Palmist I can find, and the 'vessel,' whatever it turns out to be.'

"Servino, have you learned any more about this so-called vessel? What it might be, and what power it might possess?"

"Your Grace, no more at this time. Though, if it is some sort of a golem, then the traditions say it would have been made from, or partially made of clay or mud. It could also be an object with a coating of clay. The traditional stories tell us that, to be activated, the Hebrew word for truth must be inscribed on its forehead. Your Grace, I don't think it is real. It's just a pathetic story used to scare ignorant, disobedient children."

"No. I disagree with you, Servino. I do believe it's real. And it may well be extremely dangerous to us. Anything created by Jews is a danger to us and must be at all costs destroyed or turned to our use. Along with the boy, if he is who I think he is. The last male descendant of the Nassi family. The last prince of the House of David."

After Servino left, Diego thought about the other, secret final ending of the Third Secret; a warning that he had not shared with Servino. He once again reached into the lower drawer and took out a second, smaller scroll, reading it to himself out loud. "Our Lady showed us a vision of someone who I describe as the pope, standing in front of a praising multitude. But there was a difference with a real pope; the evil look. This one had eyes of evil."

This has got to be our current weak old man who thinks he is the pope. It has to be.

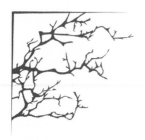

Sixteen

CIRCLE OF FATIMA, FATIMA, Portugal
   April 12-13, 1986

Strains of Wagner's *Siegfried Death* and *Funeral March* from Gotterdäm-merung echoed and reverberated through the marble halls of the Basilica of the Rosary. Archbishop Diego DeSilva, dressed all in white silk, made his way down the long corridor paved with multicolored marble on the floors and walls. He walked from the bishop's palace to the Chapel of the Appari-tions at the very heart of the Basilica. He had requested his favorite music, this Wagner opera, to be played over the Basilica sound system, and was hum-ming along as he walked. His thoughts turned to Berlin when he was still a young teen. *How I love this glorious music, the last I heard with my mother, my true love, in Berlin... before I lost her forever.*

He was alone for the entire night after ordering all his attendants to leave him. To allow him to pray in private at this, the holiest heart of Fatima. This was the sacred night just before he was to be confirmed a cardinal and as the Head of the Holy Office of the Inquisition. His predecessor had died in an unfortunate accident while out riding his racing bike, leaving the posts of car-dinal and high inquisitor both open and available to a newly appointed and ambitious archbishop.

His thoughts were not of prayer, however, but of power and revenge.

"In the morning, I will be made a cardinal. Cardinal Diego DeSilva. My ancestral family member, Bishop Diego DeSilva, who I was named after, the first Grand Inquisitor of Portugal, would be so proud. Me, Diego, command-ing The Holy Office of the Inquisition ... for the entire world. Soon, I will make Fatima the real New Rome and assume my rightful place on the throne of Peter. But first, I must punish those who murdered my beautiful mother. Those heretic makers of the bombs, the cursed scientists and Jews. They destroyed everything good; my mother, Germany, the Church, and plunged the entire world into cold and darkness."

When in Berlin, with his father as the Portuguese ambassador, he was too distracted with the city's delights to know what the Nazi Party was doing to solve the Jewish problem, but now, understanding the full history, he firmly approved. Starting tomorrow, with the power of his new office, he would seek to complete that great work of global cleansing.

Entering the vestment room adjoined to the chapel, he felt along the back corner of the space, behind a row of rich clerical robes, and pressed an unremarkable spot under the molding. A panel opened, and with a golden key, he unlocked a small closet door. Shoving the priceless vestments roughly aside, he opened the door, unfolding its several sections entirely to create a three-part mirror.

Reaching into the opening, he withdrew a sort of hat, but one like no other anywhere except in New Rome where one somewhat like it was sometimes seen on the head of the frail old man who was supposedly the Pope.

Diego loved the design of the papal miter he had secretly made, as it depicted the Virgin Mary standing upon a celestial orb with a crown above her head, ruling the entire world. The people were bowing before Mary on it, and rays of light emanated from her, the promise of the Miracle of the Sun.

Next, he pulled off its heavy hanger a stiffly brocaded robe that sparkled in the low light in the small room. Slipping it on and gazing at the magnificent vision of himself in the triple mirrors, he admired the double rows of images of the Virgin Mary made of finely worked multicolored silk, gold, silver, and precious gems. It had cost a fortune, but Fatima could afford it.

I will bring you endless glory, my Lady of the Rosary. Your place will be as ruler of both Heaven and Earth through my hands and my power.

He felt the weight of the miter of Saint Peter on his head, and the heavy bejeweled gold and silver threaded robe of office on his shoulders, and he felt a remarkable surge of overwhelming passion and energy.

I will be the most potent pope of all time when I am crowned. And I will smite all the heathens with my sword of justice. They will bow down and grovel at my feet, or they will die the heretics death, burned in the cleansing fire of the auto-da-fe.

Waking up, with rough wood against his cheek and a gag made of coarse cloth filling his mouth, the Jesuit Father Lee struggled against the tight bonds holding his hands behind the thick timber and his feet tightly bound together below him. A black hood blocked all light to his eyes.

A chilling voice nearby answered his attempts to struggle. "It is no use. There is no escape for a heretic like you. Pray to whatever gods you follow. Maybe they will save you."

What? You can't do this! You can't... Wait. WAIT!

Cardinal DeSilva's stern, authoritative, and richly commanding voice echoed across the enormous stone-paved plaza to a crowd that stretched as far as he could see under the gray, wet, cloudy sky.

"My children, you have been naughty and have been led astray. Will you be punished? Or cared for? The choice is yours. Damnation or the Glory of Heaven." Waiting for this to sink in, he paused for a moment. "We are at the beginning of a fierce and bloody conflict. In which, if all of you in this Holy place and all the people of the Holy Church, do not bind together and together form the Reborn Church Militant and the Triumphant, then Our Lady's message to us and all the world will be lost. And we will all be lost to the fires of Hell."

The voices of many thousands roared their approval. "Marie! Marie! Mother Mary! Holy Virgin ..."

He stood, in his scarlet cardinal's robes, gazing at the several hundred thousand pilgrims gathered in the drizzle on the limestone steps and huge stone-paved plaza. As every year had grown a bit cooler and darker, the pilgrims had increased in number, praying fervently for a miracle, for a re-occurrence of the Miracle of the Sun.

Diego knew what they were praying for as he remembered the history.

A miracle as in 1917, with seventy thousand persons present. After a period of rain, the dark clouds broke, and the sun appeared as a spinning disc in the sky. The sun cast multicolored lights across the landscape, the people, and the surrounding clouds. The sun then careened towards the earth before zig-zag-

ging back to its normal position. Many that day reported that their previously wet clothes became 'suddenly and completely dry,' as well as the wet and muddy ground that had been previously soaked because of the rain that had been falling.

Now speaking softly to himself with his head bent as if in prayer, he said, "I will bring this miracle back to the entire world, in time to cement my power and glory, in the name of you, my lady. The darkness will end, the sun will return, and together, we will rule overall."

Drawing a deep breath, he again spoke into the microphone, his voice now gentle and kindly, amplified and reverberating off the distant curving colonnades. "Now, my children, kneel with me. Kneel in penitent prayer before the Virgin, and ask her forgiveness for all of our many sins. Pray for me, and with me. The Virgin is merciful and will save us all from the fires."

The new cardinal humbly knelt at the microphone, and with an enormous rustle, the crowd of several hundred thousand knelt as one on the wet stone, joining their voices to say the Virgin's prayer. "O, Most Holy Virgin Mary, Queen of the holiest Rosary, you were pleased to appear to the children of Fatima and reveal a glorious message. We implore you, inspire in our hearts..."

When the sound of the multitude of voices had stilled, at last, Diego spoke once more, this time firmly with a stern command. "We are at war. A Holy War. And we must fight for our beliefs against this age-old barbarity that's strangling our world. " He paused for effect before continuing, gazing out at the adoring crowd. A chant began, and in a short time, spread through the entire congregation. "Father, Father, save us. Save us, Father DeSilva. Save us, Father DeSilva."

Holding up his hands as the crowd gradually quieted once more, Diego continued, "A barbarity of unbelief that could eradicate everything we've been bequeathed over the last two thousand years."

"Yes, yes, yes!" roared the crowd.

"We need to return to the Being, to the Logos, to the fundamentals, to the Sacred, to the New Middle Ages. Our only hope is with our Holy Mother Church, the Blessed Virgin, and the institutions of traditional society. All content of Modernity is Satanism and degeneration. Nothing is of worth. Everything is to be cleaned off. As the new head of your Holy Office, I will lead the cleansing of our globe."

The enormous crowd roared with cheers and loud cries of approval echoed across the vast plaza.

"Modernity is wrong—science, so-called values, philosophy, art, society, modes, patterns, 'truths,' understanding of being, time and space, have all led us astray. All that is Holy is dead with Modernity. And so, it should all end."

The roaring of the crowd swelled in volume.

Raising his voice to a roar of his own, he shouted in a deep bass voice, "And together, we are going to stamp it out and end it."

He waited, as the cheering and shouts rose and fell, and then raising his hands once more for silence, he added, "Your Virgin of Fatima will bring back the sun to her people. The Miracle of the Sun will bath the entire world in the light once more, if, and only if, all of you, and the entire world repents of their sins, and returns to the Holy Mother Church." Thunderous cheers filled the plaza as DeSilva once again held up his hands for silence." And now to usher in this new beginning for our Holy Church, we will celebrate a traditional act of faith."

The crowd roared their approval; applause and rapturous cheering echoed into the distance. "DeSilva, DeSilva, Papa DeSilva! DeSilva, Papa DeSilva..." Mixed in with loud cries to the Virgin, to "Save the people," and, "Bring back the sun. Holy Mother of God, shed your light upon us once more."

Cardinal Diego DeSilva, the new and powerful Grand Inquisitor of the Holy Office, stood for a long time, basking in his glory. Rising like a prophet of old in the flame-red scarlet robes of his office, while fingering the golden chain and cross that hung from his neck.

I have them now, like soft clay in my hands. And I can mold them into whatever I need, whenever I need it.

With his right arm, he reached out and signaled with to the red-clad Fatima civil enforcers bearing lit torches, to light the large pile of oil-soaked wood, books, and tree branches piled at the base of the large cross where a yellow-robed figure was firmly tied. The figure's face and head were hidden, covered with a heavy black hood painted with flames and devils.

DeSilva cried out, "Purifying flames will consume the heretics of ungodly science. I bring back to you my children, an Act of Faith, the Auto da fe!"

As the flames licked high around the robed figure, the enormous crowd resumed their cries of "DeSilva! Papa DeSilva! DeSilva save your people..."

The roar of the crowd drowned out the faint muffled screams coming from the now brightly burning figure.

After his sermon, the new cardinal was relaxing in his private quarters, his scarlet robes tossed on the back of a plush couch. His prized carpet of Paradise lay on the floor, covering most of the richly decorated room. He had only recently moved into the central part of the Archbishop's Palace and had, without delay, made himself at home there. The extensive remodeling was progressing well; he could see as he looked around at the newly gilded, carved wood paneling.

He held a large crystal goblet of deep blood-red wine in his hand while a very young nun with honey-colored skin untouched by the sun, brown hair, and small, firm teenager breasts, ministered to his needs. As her head bobbed up and down in his lap, he relaxed from the day's exertions, a sigh of bliss escaping his lips.

"Yes, my child, your rewards in heaven will be great for your service to me. Your confession is received, and your sins are now forgiven. Will you now recline and receive your Holy reward and penance?"

The nude young woman stretched out upon the couch, as the new cardinal eagerly embraced her.

She sighed a long purring sound. "Oooh... Your Grace," she said as she wrapped her arms around him. "I so love confessing to you. I had no idea confession was so pleasurable."

As he enjoyed her young body, his thoughts turned once again to his family, his beautiful mother Marie, who he had adored, and his stern father whom he had feared and hated. As a young teenager, he had desired his mother so very much, and the one day when she had finally surrendered to his advances and wholeheartedly welcomed him, his father had caught them, naked on her bed, fully joined in their sin.

The beatings he gave to both of them were brutal, but on reflection, well deserved, and Diego still had the scars. But being sent home to Lisbon far from the joys of Berlin, his mother, and his friends in the Hitler Youth was the hardest punishment to take. His anger was great, having lost his true love, and he had hoped to be with her once again someday when his father was dead. He had meticulously planned how to accomplish this deed, to kill his father and take his mother as his lover, but when the Jewish bomb fell on Berlin, and he had lost them both, his heart was broken, fully in two.

He knew then that it was his sin that had brought their deaths upon him, that it was all his fault in the end. So, he had found solace in the Church, and his passion transferred to the Virgin of Fatima. It was merely coincident that the newest statues of the Virgin in the Basilica resembled his mother.

Though he was never to have a chance to again be with his mother, and he had seduced a great number of young nuns who resembled her, it was never to be the same as it had been with her. He was still angry that he was interrupted before he had attained release with her. He had sought out many women who resembled her in body, face, and hair color. But no matter how many he seduced, and the punishments he had Servino administer to him, the empty pit in his heart was never filled or healed, and burned with unquenchable guilty lust.

The Marian Convent was conveniently located at the far end of the long, curving colonnade opposite from his palace, and was continuously supplied with new groups of innocent young novices, all of them seeking to serve the Virgin of Fatima, a fringe benefit for him that he was pleasantly surprised by and took full advantage of.

As he reached his release, his body shook, and he cried out as he always did with all his lovers, "Oh God... Mother, Marie... I'm yours, only yours..."

This new young one is perfect. I will keep her close with me as I arise to take my place on the Throne of Peter, here at Fatima, the real New Rome.

"My child, you must not tell anyone the details of our private prayers, as the Seal of the Confessional is absolute. This is my personal blessing and teaching for just you alone. Your confessions with me are a sacred secret."

The young nun, once more dressed in her modest blue Marian sister's habit with her lustrous brown hair covered by the novices' wimple, blushed as she knelt to kiss his ring, saying, "Your Grace, it is my pleasure to be of service to you and to have you as my confessor. May I come to see you again tomorrow?"

"Yes, of course, my child. Though, tomorrow, sister Mary Angela is coming. Am I sure you will have more sins to confess in a day or two? I will send for you then."

"Yes, Your Grace. Mother Superior says that it is a great honor for me to personally attend to you, Your Grace and that I should do whatever is asked of me."

"Yes, my child. Loving obedience is a blessing. Go now with God. And please ask my secretary to attend to me."

After his secretary had disciplined him, as Diego cleansed his body of blood and the reek of sex in his gold and silver tiled shower, he thought to himself, *Ah, Mother. You were so sweet, so young when I had you, and then lost you. Father, you are in hell for all I care. But, Mother, I will avenge your death. It was science and the cursed Jews who took you from me. I will always love you, Mother, though you had the taint of Jewish blood yourself.*

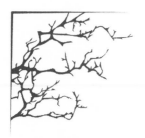

Seventeen

CIRCLE OF FATIMA, FATIMA, Portugal
   April 14, 1986

"What does our agent have to say in her latest report?" demanded Cardinal DeSilva to his secretary.

Entering the opulent office and closing the door behind him, Servino respectfully stood his distance just inside the door, knowing that the news he would give would not be to his master's liking.

"Your Grace, the agent has not reported in for over two weeks. Our last contact via a collect call was not to my satisfaction. Our other operative states that he has seen the young man extensively in the company of our agent. With such continuous contact, she must have learned some information of import to us. But we have had no reports from her. He has also seen them both leave in her vehicle, heading west on Interstate 80."

The Cardinal, his anger rising, felt a familiar stab of pain in his side.

With his voice rising to a crescendo, he shouted, "I have had enough of this Jewish bitch! Cut her off. Freeze her account. Stop her cards. Now, let's see how she does with zero funds. Fear of starvation might bring her to her senses and back to her service to Mother Church. She will pay for defying me, this Greenbaum! Servino, where did you say her younger sister was? In the Church?"

"Here, Your Grace. She is a novice, just down the colonnade from your quarters, at the Marian Convent. I'm sure that Reverend Mother will agree to send her to you for confession."

"Servino, yes. An excellent idea. And do have our other agent follow and track them to their destination."

"I already ordered him to do so. He installed a tracking device in the car last week, and he is following them as we speak. His last report had them in Northern California near the city of Oroville."

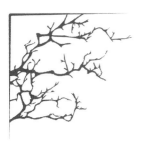

Eighteen

PALERMO, NORTHERN CALIFORNIA
April 14, 1986

They had just come from their motel in Oroville where they tried to check-in, Rachel was shocked to find her credit card rejected. "I'm sorry, Miss Green. But you have insufficient credit. I can't take your card."

"What do you mean I don't have any credit?" Her voice increased in volume as she began shaking with anger. "I have five thousand dollars available on this card! What the hell are you saying?"

"Rachel, calm down. I'll get this. I have cash." *Five thousand in credit? Wow.* He realized that he still just getting to know this girl.

As they drove into what little there was of Palermo, she drolly commented, "Wow. There is not much 'there' here. You described a town to me, but where is it?"

Stepping out of the car, they found they were standing on a muddy dirt street with mostly boarded-up buildings stretching for several blocks in the gloomy sunlight. It was a lot warmer in California than Salt Lake City, but still mostly cloudy, like it was everywhere due to the dust clouds that had been thrown up by the nuclear blasts of the last war. There were still olive groves, though the trees looked a bit straggly as they struggled in the low sunlight. The increased rains did show their results, though, with muddy ground, lush undergrowth, and grass under the trees.

A bit more sun was showing, and eager to have some sun on her bare skin, Rachel had worn an old-style summer dress, short above the knees with a deeply scooped back, neckline, and bare arms.

He was enjoying how she looked, on this, his first trip back in many years to his hometown. But he still had some questions, realizing that he did not know the girl very well.

He said, "Well, I seem to remember it being a bit livelier when I was a kid. Though we didn't come downtown very often."

"Downtown? You're kidding, right?" she replied, laughing merrily.

Smiling, he said, "Yes. Compared to the outlying areas, yep. Now, you wouldn't be making fun of my home town, would you?"

"Well, sweetheart, compared to my hometown of Chicago... yep, I am."

They noticed that the post office was still open, and was, in fact, the only place that appeared open, and so they went in to ask about the bank. Everything in the office was old and weathered with dull-colored tarnished brass mailboxes and deeply scratched dark wooden counters. A wrinkled, gray-haired woman behind the counter smiled as they entered. She looked them both up and down, eyeing Rachel's summer dress that did not wholly conceal her charms. "You folks don't look like you're from around here? Can I help ya?"

"Well, I grew up near here. I'm Joseph Davidson. I was raised by my great aunt and uncle, I mean, that is, my family's friends, about fifteen miles out in the sticks near here."

"Aw, now that I look at you, young man, I think I do remember you as a younger one. You used to play the fiddle when folks got together, didn't ya?"

"Yes, I did."

"Well, welcome home. Who you got here with ya? Is this here, your wife?"

"No, we're just good friends."

"Son, I can see more than most folks, even though my sight's almost gone. You two are more than just good friends. You're meant for each other."

Joseph blushed at this as he asked, "Mrs...?"

"Miller. Miriam, Miller." She cackled with a long laugh. "I'm a widow now, but I'm used to the old geezer's name."

"Mrs. Miller, is there still a bank here in town? Or was there one?"

"Yep, there was one. Closed up about ten years ago when the olive farming couldn't keep going with all the cold rain and lack of sun."

"Was it on this street? We didn't see much of anything that looked like a bank here."

"It was behind this office on the other street, over on Olive. It was an antique and junk store for a while, but now it's empty. Nothing in there. Just some trash and old junk. But I think the old vault's still in place."

They thanked the woman and promised to stop by again so Joseph could update her on his life since he had left town.

Making their way down the street and around the corner, they walked on the muddy half-visible sidewalk halfway down the block to find the most substantial building that they had yet seen in the old town. It looked to have been built in more prosperous times with dressed stone blocks and brickwork. The building had, at one time, apparently been quite impressive.

The old dusty plate glass windows showed traces of gold lettering half-hidden under the misspelled hand-painted sign that read, 'Bargains Galore. Reeally Great Stuff.'

Joseph looked closely and read the faded gold letters, "Central Valley..."

"National," She continued.

"Bank. Did we find it? Rachel, this could be it." They looked up to the top of the old building to see the carved stone archway on top where the date of 1890 was carved along with the name 'Central Valley National Bank.'

She tried the front door, and it creaked open a tiny bit.

"Here, let me try." Joseph stepped closer and pushed it hard, as the warped wood of the door bottom scraped over the old marble floor tiles.

Inside, they could see the old counter, and in the back, an old vault with the door half-open. Making their way inside and moving various pieces of junk and broken furniture out of the way, they approached the vault.

He asked, "What was the number you translated?"

"237."

"Okay, let's see if that box is in this bank. If not, we'll need to scout out all the other old branches to see if they still exist."

"Do you think something might still be here, in the box? If the box is even here?" They made their way to the back of the building through piles of junk, having to move various unidentifiable pieces of small machinery and cardboard boxes that were in the way.

"I think I see the vault in the back. And the door looks ajar." Clearing more boxes from in front of the door, she tried to open it further. As she pulled, it creaked and moved a tiny bit.

"I`ll help you," he said as he added his weight, to push against the open edge. As the door moved enough for them to enter, he could now see into the vault. Excited, he said, "I can see it in the back. It's there, number two, three seven."

Stepping carefully into the vault, she said, "Lets clear these boxes away. Have you got the key?" She asked with rising excitement in her voice. Not waiting for him, she rapidly shoved a pile of cardboard cartons aside to reveal the wall of safety deposit boxes in the vault.

Fumbling in his pocket, he pulled out the small key, and after brushing thick dust and cobwebs from the face of the box, tried to insert it in the keyhole. "Something's wrong. It won't fit."

Rachel looked into the small hole and said, "Here, let me see. It looks like something's stuck inside it..."

He picked up a piece of rusty steel wire from the floor of the vault and stuck it in the keyhole, wiggling it around. A small piece of wood came out and fell to the floor. "I'll try it again. Whatever was in there just fell out."

Joseph carefully inserted the key, turned it, and pulled on the door handle. "It won't budge."

"Here let me help you." She said.

They combined their efforts on the handle, pushing hard to turn it to open the door. Suddenly, with a loud creak, the handle turned, but the door was still stuck fast.

They both looked around to find something to use as a pry bar. He dug around in the debris for anything sharp and metal that could be wedged into the crack to try to pry it open.

But it was Rachel who stood up from the debris-covered floor with an old flat blade screwdriver. "This should do it." She stuck it into the crack, and with his hands over hers, they both pried as hard as they could. With a loud creak, it suddenly opened wide.

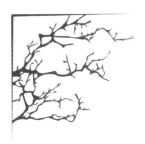

Nineteen

PALERMO, CALIFORNIA
April 14, 1986

A tall man with sharply chiseled Nordic features and close-cropped blond hair pulled up outside the old post office, parking his black Ford directly behind Rachel's red compact. Checking the clip to make sure it was full; he slipped his Luger into the holster hidden under his coat. Looking once more at the two photos, he replaced them in his shirt pocket and stepped out onto the dusty street. Opening the door to the post office, he went inside, intently looking for his prey.

Joseph excitedly looked into the deep narrow safety deposit box. The inside was hidden in the dark shadows of the abandoned bank. "I can't see anything. It looks empty."

"Here, let me see if I can feel anything," said Rachel, reaching into the narrow space and stretching her fingertips as far as she could. Feeling nothing, she exclaimed with deep disappointment in her voice, "There's nothing there."

"Let me try," Joseph said. He reached into the opening until he touched the far end. "Wow, nothing at all. Bummer. I was so hopeful." His high spirits of a moment before had fallen to a new low.

"Sweetheart, I'm so sorry. What a disappointment."

He moved his hand around in the box one last time to make sure there was indeed nothing inside. "Wait, I'm touching something. It feels like a piece of paper is stuck in the top edge of the box."

"What is it?"

Carefully pulling and wiggling the brittle paper free from where it was caught in a joint in the metal sections that made up the box, he brought the paper out into the dusty light. Holding it up, he carefully unfolded it and read, "'Contents of this box, number 237, transferred in receivership to The Agricultural Trust Bank, Sacramento California, March 10th, 1976.' That was about ten years ago."

"That must have been when the bank shut down. Let's go. It's still early. We can drive to Sacramento in an hour or so. We've got to go find out what was in that box."

"Okay. Let's head back to the motel and get going."

"Hello, anyone here?" The blond stranger called out, his deep voice echoing off the wooden surfaces in the old post office.

"Yep, I'm here. And who might you be?" The voice had a sharp edge to it. "And whadda ya want here, stranger? Ya woke me from my nap, so it better be important." The woman who had been out of sight, sitting down low behind the counter, rose up and stared at the stranger with her opaque eyes.

"I'm looking for two friends of mine. They came in the little red car there."

"Friends, ya say now?" She paused to look more closely at the man. "Well, I do believe that they connected with another old friend. Maybe you know 'em too? An' they went off driving in their friend's car to the west there to go see the big ol' mansion, Magnolia Manor, that old man Hearst built back in the day. Quite the palace it was all gilded and marble inside. Thought he could make a fortune with citrus and olives, 'til the citrus trees mostly froze out back in the thirties and lots of folks up and left."

"You're sure they went that way?"

"Yep. Wouldn't steer ya wrong, young man. Just keep on moving west on South Villa to Grubbs Road. It's a few miles out there, but you'll see it soon enough now."

"'Thanks,'" was all the stranger said as he stepped out the door that he had never completely closed and returned to his car. In a moment, he roared off in a cloud of dust.

"They only see what they want to see, an' that's just fine by me." The old woman said to herself as she sat back down to resume her nap.

Only a few minutes after the stranger's car had left, Joseph and Rachel came back around the corner from their visit to the bank. Joseph stuck his head in the door of the post office. "Goodbye, Mrs. Miller... Miriam. Thanks, so much for your help," he called out.

"Did ya find wha' y'all were looking for now?" The voice came from behind the counter.

"Not quite. But we have a clue now."

"Well, y'all had better move on where it's taking ya now, pretty quick, as ya got a feller following ya. He just left in that cloud of dust ya see lingering there."

Rachel, who had joined Joseph just inside the door, started at this news, "What did you say? Someone looking for us?"

"That's right, honey, and he didn't look like any 'friend' like he claimed to be. He had a nasty feeling about him. All tall and blond. German, I think. So, I sent him packing on a snipe hunt."

"A snipe hunt? What's she talking about?"

He laughed out loud at this. "A wild goose chase. Looking for something that isn't really there. A snipe is an imaginary creature. We used to send the little kids on them when I was a teenager here. Thanks again for your help, Miriam."

"Let's get out of here. I don't like the idea that someone is following us. And that guy sounds creepy."

"Yeah, what's with this? Why would someone even know where we are, much less be following us? That other guy in Salt Lake, looking in the windows at school, and at my apartment. And now this other guy? What the hell is going on?"

Rachel's eyes glazed over for a moment before she shook her head. "I don't know."

After packing, she left Joseph to place their bags in the car while she walked towards the motel office. She told him she needed to call her family attorney to straighten out what had happened to her bank accounts. Finding the payphone set against one of the white stucco faux Spanish pillars, Rachel placed a collect call to Fatima. When the call was accepted, she said, "Hello, Servino?"

"Rachel, how good to hear from you. Did you get the message we sent?"

"Yes, I did. Why did you cut off my accounts?"

"Well, you have not been fulfilling your side of our contract. So, we decided to cancel our end."

"You asshole. How do you expect me to do the job you want with no money? Are you stupid? And do you want him to get suspicious?"

"Well, do you have any information? Like what we asked you for? We know where you are. Tell me what you've found."

"Yeah, we know you have some goon following us. Call him off."

"Only if you have something of value to us to report."

"Okay, okay. So, this kid Joseph has some kind of inheritance. Maybe. I don't know yet what it is, or if it's anything at all. I still think you have the wrong kid. He is no threat to the Church that I can see."

"You're no expert, darling. You're just a Jewish whore, and that isn't much in our book." He laughed. "But you are good at what you do. I hear the cardinal enjoyed you very much when you were a bit younger. He does like his little girls young and juicy, as you know."

"You bastard. Don't you dare mention that ever again! I hate that asshole, and if I ever have a chance, I'll ki..."

"You'll what? Are you threatening the next pope? For a little Jewish girl, you've got some balls. Well, I'm not going to pass that last bit on to his Grace, if you straighten up and find out what we want to know. But I'll tell you what. If you start reporting in every day and tell us everything you find out about him and his family, and I mean everything, then I'll call off Rudolf. He'll be with you until I hear what I want to know. And I'll unblock your accounts today. But one more screw up by you... just remember where your little sister is living these days."

"Leave my sister alone."

"Aha, and I was going to watch her being introduced to the family business."

"You wouldn't dare! If you touch her ..."

"Okay, calm down, I`m just messing with you. Don't worry. She's safe, for now. As long as you keep reporting in and making progress, everything will be okay. And she'll never know what her big sister does for a living."

"All right. We're headed to Sacramento to try to find his safety deposit box."

"Ah, now that wasn't so hard, was it? You just keep calling and telling me everything you do and see. Don't leave any details out either, or you know what could happen."

She slammed down the phone and burst into tears, sliding her back down the rough stucco wall until she was sitting on the sidewalk. Her eyes were swelling, and her face covered with running tears. She sat there softly sobbing until Joseph came around the corner and rushed to her side. "Rachel, are you all right? Is there some bad news? Is your family okay?"

Sniffing, wiping her eyes, and trying to catch her breath, she thought fast about what she could say to him. "I just found out the estate is all messed up, and that's why my cards were frozen. The government claims some taxes were never paid. My family attorney is taking care of it. It's from my grandfather's work for the military. He was one of the scientists who developed the bombs."

"Wow, I'm so sorry. Is there anything I can do? Do you need to go somewhere to take care of it?"

"No. The best thing we can do is to go to Sacramento to find out about your family and what might be in that deposit box. That'll take my mind off this. Our attorney will take care of it pretty quickly, he said."

"Are you sure? So, it will be okay now?

Rachel, now recovering some from her meltdown, reached her arms around him and held him tightly. "Yes, it's okay. I know who I am, and who my people are. But let's go find out more about who you are, what you are, and where you belong."

Arriving in Sacramento, they checked the yellow pages to look for The Agricultural Trust Bank of California.

"Joseph, for some reason, it's not listed. What are we going to do?"

"Let's look up the state office that handles banks and see if they can tell us about that bank, and maybe where old safety box contents ended up."

Finding that the office was in a large building near the state capital, they drove downtown, parked out front, and went into the building. They found the right office, opened the oak and glass door, and walked in. An older woman with white hair briskly asked them, "May I help you?"

Startled by the woman's appearance and voice, Rachel asked, "Do we know you? Mary?"

"No, young lady, you are mistaken. I do not think we have met before. My name is Helen Garber. Perhaps I look like someone you know?"

Joseph looked from Rachel to the woman with a puzzled expression and quickly replied, "Yes, you can help us. We're inquiring about a bank that closed up years ago in Palermo. Apparently, the assets, including safety deposit box contents, were transferred to another bank. And that bank now also appears to be closed."

"What are the names of the two banks?"

"Central Valley National Bank, and the Agricultural Trust Bank of California." Rachel answered, adding anxiously, "We have a note that the safety deposit box contents were transferred to the second bank. But if it no longer exists, how can we find out what was in the box?"

"Are you the box holder?" The woman asked her.

"I am," said Joseph. "Here's my identification, plus the original key and the box number."

Looking over his ID and at the key, she said, "Well, this appears to be in order. I will look in the files to see what I can find out for you."

She sat at her computer and typed in the information. After some long minutes, she said, "Ah... young man, you need to go to this address. Today. In fact, right now. The contents from those boxes that were unclaimed are being auctioned off today to cover the storage costs for all those years. You're almost too late."

She wrote the address on a slip of paper, handed it to Joseph, who, grabbing Rachel's hand, rushed out of the office, saying, "Thank you," over his shoulder as they dashed off.

After a quick ten-block drive, they entered the county courthouse on Ninth Street. A parking place had just opened up at the back of the building, and Rachel almost ran up on the curb in her rush to park as a meter maid writing a ticket turned and scowled at them.

"Joseph, she almost looked like Miriam from the post office. Am I nuts to think so?"

"I don't know, but we need to run in there and see if you can find the box contents in the auction listing."

"I'll get the meter." She said.

He ran up the steps two at a time, ignoring the pain of the scars pulling on his back and legs as he did so. Entering the courthouse, he looked at the signs listing hearings and proceedings for the day. Seeing at last, 'Auction of unclaimed Assets, 3:00 PM, Third Floor, Room 309,' he ran to an open elevator. As Rachel came in; he held the door for her. The elevator seemed to take a very long time to travel up three floors. When at last the doors opened, she asked, "Which room did it say?"

"309."

Rachel pointed. "Down there at the end of the hall."

They ran even faster until they got to the door and pulled it open. The rush of their entry and pulling the door open so fast made such a sound that the room half full of people all turned to see what was occurring.

"Ah, sorry about that," Joseph said to a cross-looking man sitting at a table just inside the door.

"Are you bidding?" he gruffly asked them.

"Yes," Joseph replied. "I am."

"Sign here. Do you agree to pay for any winning bids in cash or credit card?"

"Yes, of course," answered Rachel.

Joseph turned to her with a question in his eyes. He thought she was broke.

"Here is your bidding number and paddle. If you wish to bid on a lot, raise the paddle and clearly state the amount."

"Okay, we've got it. Which lot is up next?" Rachel replied.

"The Agricultural Trust Bank of California unclaimed safety deposit box contents."

They rushed to seats in the second to back row.

"How much money do you have?" Rachel whispered.

"I've got two thousand three hundred and fifty dollars in my checking, and I will spend it all to find out whatever I can about my family."

The auctioneer proceeded to call out each box number in order. "Box number 139," he said as he held up a bundle of documents. "Do I have fifty dollars? No bids? Twenty-five dollars?" This time, one person bid and walked away with the papers.

"Box number 197." He held up a rough-looking cardboard box sealed with packing tape. Do I hear fifty dollars? Fifty to the man in back, fifty-five dollars upfront, sixty on the left, do I hear sixty-five? Sixty-five down in front. Do I hear seventy-five, seventy-five, yes, you in the front row, in the nice coat, madam? Seventy-five going once, going twice, fair notice, sold to the lady in the front row."

The door in the rear opened again, and a tall blond man entered, sitting down directly behind Rachel and Joseph. Rachel turned to see the man, and a chill ran down her back. A deep fear was rising to her throat, and she caught herself before she said anything to Joseph.

Turning back around, she saw the auctioneer was holding up another box. It looked to be made from some deeply figured wood, with darker colored inlays in a beautifully intricate pattern of circles and lines, and with what appeared to be inlay and fittings made of some gold-colored metal.

"I have box number 237. Now, folks, this is a lovely item, beautifully made, with some nice precision joinery." He hefted the box up in his hands. "And it's heavy as well. No way to know just what is in it. Could be pirate booty or the jewels of some former princess. Might be a real treasure, folks."

He has the small crowd full attention now, with people craning their necks to get a closer look.

As she saw the box, Rachel let out a gasp, "Joseph, look at that. That's your family's history."

"Wow! It's amazing."

"Do I have an opening bid for this beautiful box? Do I hear five hundred?"

"Six hundred."

Joseph turned to see who this was and saw the tall blond man for the first time, who had made the bid.

"Six hundred in the back. Do I hear seven hundred?"

Joseph stood and held his paddle high, shouting, "Seven fifty!"

"Seven fifty, do I hear eight fifty?"

From behind, Rachel and Joseph came, "Nine fifty."

"Well, folks, this item is an exciting one. Let's keep it going. Do I hear one thousand?"

Joseph stood up again and shouted, "One thousand."

He turned and glared at the blond stranger, who then stood up and shouted, "Two thousand!"

"We have two thousand on the floor. Do we have any other bids? Folks, this is the most excitement we have had all week with these auctions. Do we have any other bids? Do I hear two thousand two hundred?"

"Two thousand two hundred and fifty," Joseph countered.

"Two thousand five hundred," the blond responded.

Joseph slumped down in his chair in despair at losing all that might be in that box. The answers to questions he did not even know how to ask. Now he'd never know who his parents were. Who was he?

"Okay, folks, fair notice. Going once at two thousand five hundred. Going twi..."

"Five thousand!" cried Rachel as she stood and yelled at the top of her lungs. Joseph turned and stared at her.

"But, Rachel, you don't have any money. You were cut off."

"It's okay, it should be straightened out by now."

"The little lady in the back bids five thousand. Do I have any other bids? No bids? Going once, going twice..."

"Six thousand," shouted the tall blond behind them.

"Seven thousand," shouted Joseph while holding his paddle up, turning to the blond stranger and glaring at him, just daring him to counter.

The auctioneer whistled a long note through his teeth. "Ladies and gentlemen, we have a hot bidding war going here now. No telling what's in this box, but it's got to be something extraordinary to be worth seven thousand dollars."

While Joseph looked at the stranger, the man bared his teeth in a frightening smile as he abruptly stood and walked out.

"Okay, fair warning. Seven thousand once, seven thousand twice. Any final bids?" And with a sharp pound of his gavel, he said, "Sold. To the young gentleman in the back."

Joseph collapsed in his seat, letting out a long breath that he didn't know he was holding in. "Oh, my God ... Who was that guy, and why was he bidding against us?"

"I'm not sure, but I have a bad feeling about him. He made us spend a lot of our money, that's for sure. I sure hope it's worth seven thousand dollars, sweetheart," she said, laughing lightly with a note of gallows humor.

"So, do I. So, do I," Joseph replied, as the tension he had been holding in his body began ebbing away. "Thank you, Rachel, so much, for your help with this."

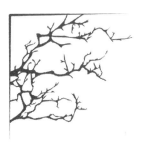

Twenty

SACRAMENTO, CALIFORNIA
April 14, 1986

The young auction assistant handed the inlaid wooden box to Joseph and Rachel with an impressed look in his eyes. "Ma'am, Sir, here is the item you won. You can pay for it at the desk in the back."

Rachel passed the inlaid box to Joseph, noting it was about six inches tall by seven inches wide, and about fourteen inches long. She could see the patterns of inlay in it, that was made up of circles within circles of different colored woods, with more circles and lines of some kind of gold metal that connected the rings, crisscrossing all around the box's six sides.

She hefted it in her hands, up and down. It was quite heavy. "I don't see any opening or latch. How do you think we can open it? I guess we can pry it open if we have to."

"No. It's too precious to me, and it's almost all I have from my family. I don't want to harm it by trying to force it. We'll just need to study it and figure it out."

"Okay, but first we need to pay for it. Do you have your card for the two thousand?"

"Yep, and you've really got five thousand?"

"Yes, more than that. My grandparents had left me a sizable trust, and it will be all straightened out now."

"This is turning into a real treasure hunt. Though, so far, all we've done is spend a treasure to get this box. It might just be my father's rock collection or something like that," he said with a laugh. "But I hope it has some value, 'cause I just blew almost my entire savings."

"Let's pay and get out of here," she said. "I don't like that guy who was bidding against us. I want to leave him far behind us if we can."

127

They took the box and went to pay in the back, while the auction kept going upfront. There was nothing as exciting as the box that Joseph saw. Though he did wonder if any of the other safety deposit boxes had belonged to friends of his family, or...?

As he walked out of the building, holding his inheritance in his hands, he shifted it from one hand to the other. He was also pressing on the circles of light wood inside the darker rings. He could see that there were ten in total, with a line of four that wrapped around the entire box, plus another six in three groups of two, on the long sides. The four linked in an extended running circle, except at one point where there was a gap, and then the two groups of three were also joined at two places each on the top of the box. More inlaid lines of gold metal connected the circles at angles as well.

Absently, as they walked out the front door of the building, he gently pressed the circles one after another in different combinations. As they reached the front lawn, she had noticed what he was doing. "Do those circles press in under your fingers?"

Joseph stopped and stood on the grass. "Yeah, they do. Do you think it's like a combination lock or something?"

"Try pressing them in this order," she said as she carefully examined the box, and pointed to one of the four in the middle at one end where it was not connected to the next circle.

He sat down on the grass and pressed the indicated circle, pushing harder than he had been, and with a click, the ring stayed depressed. "Now try this one and the next in line."

Both of these also stayed depressed with audible clicks.

She sat down next to him near a large shade tree, excited at what they were discovering.

"Now do this middle one here, and then hold down the two connected to it, all three at one time." There was a series of clicks as those three also stayed recessed into the surface.

"Wow, I think you've got something here. How did you guess?"

"Well, it looks to me like the Kabbalistic Tree of Life, with the ten Sephirot laid out wrapping around this box."

"This is another Jewish thing, along with the cloth you called it a Tallit? And that gold necklace thing, the Hamsa? So, it`s true that my family was maybe Jewish?"

"Well, I do believe that your family was Jewish at some point in the past. And maybe in the recent past."

"But my family were all Quakers. At least that was what I was told, by the folks who raised me."

"Well, they probably were Quakers to anyone who looked closely or who asked them. In my family, some of the first to arrive in the colonies in America had to pass as Quakers in early Virginia. It was not technically legal to live there as a Jew until Jefferson got the law changed in 1786."

"So, there is some Quaker, Jewish connection?"

"Yes. Jews have often had to pass as various types of Christians, Catholics, Church of England, and others, including Quaker, to avoid persecution or death. My family raised me to be Catholic on the outside. As I told you, I was in training to become a nun in Fatima." She added, with a different tone, "My little sister is there now."

"A nun?" he said, laughing. "Somehow, sweetheart, I can't imagine you as a nun." He reached out to her, trying to kiss her hair and started caressing her shoulders.

"Joseph, stop that!" She suddenly jerked away from him and moved his hands from her. "It's not funny. Something happened. Something horrible." She started to cry softly. "I was raped by a priest after he found out my family was secret Jews."

"Rachel, that's horrible. I'm so sorry."

"You need to understand that being Jewish is not something anyone would wish for these days. It's a dangerous thing. With the Church turning so reactionary, almost medieval, and the inquisition, the so-called 'Holy Office' gaining in power. So, it's true that you could be in genuine danger, as am I. I worry about my sister and if she's still safe."

A subdued Joseph replied, his hands in his lap, "Yes, from what you've told me, I'm starting to understand. But your sister, do they know about her as well?"

"She is there, safe at this point using a different name. So, they shouldn't know who she is."

Rachel's mood brightened as she then said, "But, in the past, it was a wonderful and sacred thing to be Jewish, to be part of the Jewish people. To be part of the 'healing of the worlds', Tikkun Olam."

With the inlaid box sitting between them, he looked up from the box, which he had been intensely gazing at while she spoke.

"What did you just say?"

"Tikkun Olam, the healing of the worlds."

"So that's what that means? I've heard what I think are those same words spoken to me a few times lately. By that old tramp, I told you about who I saw in Salt Lake City. And then I thought Miriam at the Palermo post office said it to me as well. And that old woman I saw in that vision or experience, in that hot sunny and beautiful place when I touched that old violin. She said the same thing to me too."

"Sweetheart, this is all getting stranger by the minute. Tikkun Olam is the central focus of the Jewish people, to focus on the healing of, the repair of, all of the worlds. As Jews, we are obligated to heal ourselves, inside our bodies, minds, and souls. As well as to seek healing between all peoples, and between ourselves and Yud Hay Vav Hay."

"What was that you just said?"

"It's the unpronounceable Hebrew name of God. It's four Hebrew letters. It can be translated to mean, 'Was, Is, Will be,' or in English from the King James Bible, 'I am that I am.'"

"Why wasn't I ever told this? That my family was Jewish?"

"The couple who raised you may have decided not to tell you to keep you safe. Especially after your parents died in that accident."

"But why would my parents' death have anything to do with them maybe being Jewish? They were killed in a car wreck, an accident. Are you saying that their deaths might not have been an accident? That's crazy."

"Yes, it would be crazy, but a lot of crazy, horrible things have been happening since the nineteen-thirties. And now it seems to be getting worse. The last fifty-five years have been unspeakable. So tragic. I... I just can't talk about it anymore right now."

"Okay, let's change the subject and look at the box again. Maybe we can figure this out and get it open."

"Try pushing the rest of the circles, here, in this order." She showed him what she had in mind, and he pushed two of the last three circles in with a satisfying click for each of them. Then with the final ring, a different sound was heard, as the flat lid of the entire box popped up out of the four sides, allowing them both to see inside the box around its edges.

He moved the box a bit, into the sunlight. "It's sparkling in the light." He lifted the lid, exposing the contents to the full strength of the dull sunlight.

"Joseph, it looks like... like gold, gold coins and something else, like bright crystals under the coins. You're rich. I can't believe it. You're going to be okay now."

"Wow, look at that. Could those crystals be diamonds?" Joseph said as they both looked into the box that sat open to the pale sunlight, brightly sparkling between them on the grass.

"Looks like what they are to me. Now, no sudden moves. Slowly hand over the box," said the tall blond stranger, looming over them, with his compact black Luger pointed at the back of Rachel's head.

"What the hell?" Joseph whipped his face around to stare up at the stranger. "Who do you think you are? I just got this box, and I'm not going to give it up." Joseph dropped the lid back onto the box, hiding the gleaming contents from view.

"If you want your girlfriend to keep her pretty head in one piece, you'll hand it over right now." The man moved the gun barrel closer to her head, pushing it firmly against her skull, with his finger on the trigger as his voice became harder. "Don't be a fool, boy. Hand it over. Now."

Rachel was visibly trembling, her eyes pleading and filled with terror, looking at Joseph.

Another voice cut through the air and carried over the three figures on the lawn in a commanding tone, "I would not pull that trigger if I were you. Carefully lower your weapon and place it on the ground."

Joseph looked beyond the tall stranger to see a uniformed courthouse security guard pointing a large handgun at the blond man.

All at once, Joseph dove for Rachel, pushing her away from the blond, covering her body with his. The blond spun around as if to fire at the guard, but before he could do so, the guard squeezed off three shots, piercing the stranger in the heart and chest, spattering blood over Joseph, Rachel, and the treasure box.

Rachel screamed, a piercing cry of terror that carried over the defeating blast of the shots. Joseph's ears were ringing as he continued to push her farther away. When the blond gunman was hit, he half spun and fell back towards the two of them and the box. His body halfway fell on the inlaid box, just missing Rachel. Thinking fast, Joseph pulled the box from under the still warm bloody body to hold it tight against his chest.

"Are you folks, okay? Are you hit?" the officer asked them.

Joseph, shaken by the events of the last few minutes, replied. "I think we're okay. Actually... we're not okay at all." He paused to wipe some of the blood off his face with the handkerchief he always carried. "Rachel, are you hurt?" Both of them were splattered with the gunman's blood.

"I... I think I'm all right." Rachel was shaking still and had trouble speaking as she cried, half choking as she tried to catch her breath.

"I'm Officer Delacruz, courthouse security. I was coming around the building to look for this guy when I saw him pull his gun on you two. The meter reader called me to check him out. She said he looked suspicious. Do you know who he is? And why he would pull a gun on you?"

Joseph answered, his ears still ringing. "We don't know. We came from the auction here, where he was bidding against us. He lost the bidding and left before us. And the next thing we knew when we came out front, he pulled a gun on us after we sat down on the grass here."

"Yeah, I saw him step from behind that black Ford. He was hidden from your view until he surprised you. Okay, you two sit tight for a bit. I've got to call this in and get some back-up here. And the coroner as well."

Joseph said, "Is it okay if we sit down over there, by that tree? And we need to get cleaned up, we're covered in blood."

"Please, can I clea-clean this blood off? I can't stand it," Rachel asked with a still quavering voice as she started to sob as the immensity of what had just happened sank deeply into her mind.

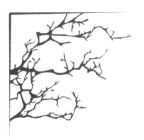

Twenty-one

SACRAMENTO, CALIFORNIA
April 14, 1986

The guard stood looking at the bloody body on the ground in front of him. His face grew ashen as the reality of his action sank in. "I've never shot anyone before... and now he's dead. Usually, I... I just deal with the drunks out here on the courthouse grounds." With shaking hands, he slipped his pistol back into its holster. "I've never even thought of killing anyone before... never thought I would need to."

"I'm sorry you had to shoot him," said Rachel as she rubbed at the spots of blood on her arms and face. "But we're so grateful that you did."

"You're welcome, Miss. I'm afraid he gave me no choice."

Joseph took his handkerchief and reached out to Rachel. "Here. Let me get some of that off you." Wetting the cloth by spitting on it, he wiped off some of the blood on her arms that had not already dried. "Can we go now?"

"I have to have you stay for higher authorities when they arrive. But I think... I think it would be okay to let you go to the restroom and get cleaned up."

"Thank you."

Pointing to the wooden box in Joseph's arms, Delacruz asked, "Is that what he was after?"

"Yeah," said Joseph. "He tried to outbid us inside at the auction but lost and then tried to steal it at gunpoint. He had his gun against my girlfriend's head. I was scared he actually would shoot her." He reached his arm around her shoulders as he spoke. "I was going to give the box to him to protect her, but then you stopped him. I'm grateful that you arrived when you did. You saved our lives."

"I'm glad you're both all right."

In the distance, sirens wailed. "Someone must have called the city police," said Joseph, then whispered into Rachel's ear, "Let's get to the car when we can and get going. We can clean up when we get to our room."

"It's all right. Okay, you folks get cleaned up but stick around for the police. I need to make some calls," Delacruz said as he started walking towards the courthouse entrance.

They waited until the guard was out of sight, then quickly walked around the building and got into her car. With relief at being able to get away, they buckled up and pulled away from the curb.

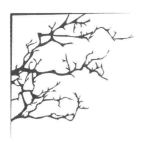

Twenty-Two

SACRAMENTO, CALIFORNIA
April 14, 1986

Arriving at their motel on the outskirts of the city and feeling much more cautious, Rachel parked in the back of the motel, so her car was out of sight from the street. They double-locked the door and closed the curtains tightly. Shedding their bloody clothing into the wastebaskets, they stood together in the shower for a very long time. Despite the hot water, she was shaking and shivering uncontrollably, almost falling in the tub before he reached out to steady her. "Hold onto me, sweetie. I won't let you fall." Gradually, her shaking stopped with his strong arms wrapped around her.

Joseph had dried off while she was still in the shower. "I feel the same way like I could not scrub hard enough to get the last bit of that guy's blood off me. But I'm afraid you're going to wear your skin off."

"I feel so dirty from that horrible man."

She finally turned off the hot water and stepped out of the shower. He handed her a dry towel, wrapping it gently around her shoulders.

"We're going to be all right now. It'll be okay," Joseph said, reaching out and wrapping his arms around her to gently hold her close.

"I know we will. I'll always feel safe with you."

"You have me, and you'll never lose me."

Changing into clean clothes, Rachel was mourning the loss of the dress she had been wearing. "That was one of my favorite summer dresses."

"I don't think we can clean it."

"No. Get rid of all of it."

Taking their bloody clothing, wrapped in plastic bags, from the wastebaskets, she watched from the window on the second floor as he placed them in the dumpster behind the motel.

He spent a long time cleaning the drops of dried blood off the treasure box with a wet washcloth. Some of the blood had penetrated the thin cracks between the inlay but finally seemed to disappear after he had worked on it for a while.

Hoping for no interruptions this time, they double-checked the room locks and again made sure the curtains were tightly closed. Sitting together on the queen bed, they once more went through the combination of buttons to open the box.

"This is the order of the prayers in a Friday night Shabbat service. The prayers move up the Tree of Life in our spine, in this pattern."

"You'll need to teach me more about this. It's so strange that I was left this box and the other things too."

Lifting the lid, the bright gleam of the two stacks of gold coins could once again be seen as they lay loosely wrapped in their richly colored red velvet covering. Lifting the velvet, he carefully moved the heavyweight of the gold coins out of the box and set them gently on the bed. The coins softly clinked together as they were moved.

Unfolding the cloth, he lifted one of the coins into the lamplight. "Look at the detail. You can read everything. All the letters and numbers are so clear they look like they're brand new."

"Are they real? I can't believe they look so perfect. It's like they're not worn at all. And they look like they're some kind of foreign coin."

Holding the coin in his hand, he hefted the weight on his palm. "This one sure feels like it could be gold or some heavy metal that's gold-covered. The numbers on it say fifteen twenty-five. That's four hundred and sixty-one years ago."

She took the coin as he passed it to her and said, "It looks like a fleur-de-lis on this side." She turned it over. "And on the other, a standing figure of someone. Maybe a saint? The lettering here is all in capitals. F, L, O, R, E, N, T, I, A. I think that means Florence. This must be a florin. It's an ancient coin from Florence, Italy. I've read about them somewhere. I think they're quite valuable."

Counting the coins carefully, he added up, "Ten, twelve, fourteen, twenty here in one row. Two stacks of twenty. There's forty of them." As he gazed at his newfound wealth, words failed him for a moment.

Looking at him in excitement, she said, "Joseph, all together they must be worth a fortune, and they appear to be in almost perfect condition. But how can that be if they're so old?"

After a long pause with him gazing intently at the coins, he said, "I don't know, but they sure look and feel real. We'll need to get an expert appraisal. We can take one of them to a rare coin shop to see what they can tell us. I'll look in the phone book for the closest one."

She reached into the box now that the coins were on the bedspread. "Oh, look under this other layer of cloth." Pulling aside a layer of purple velvet, she exclaimed, "They sure do look like diamonds!" A layer of bright, sparkling faceted crystals was revealed in all their shining light. When they had first opened the box on the lawn, they had only glimpsed a few of the stones before the gunman appeared. But now they could see that a solid layer of them was covering another layer of purple velvet.

"I don't think anything could be as clear and bright as this and not be real diamonds," he said.

"You know what this means, don't you? You can quit your job and fully concentrate on school."

"And I can afford the surgery I've dreamed of to repair the scars on my back and legs. As far as I'm concerned, Rachel, this is our fortune together. I want to share everything I have with you."

"That's very generous, but remember, I have my own money. So, this is all yours."

"I love you so much that I want to share it with you. We'll figure that out later. But now I want to see what other secrets are in this box." Joseph lifted the cloth covered with diamonds by the four corners holding them together, carefully laying it on the bedspread with the velvet covering the stones, now bunched in a small pile. As they touched each other, the stones made a musical tinkling sound.

"Look at this," he said as he reached down into the box and pulled out a flat fold of thick, yellowed paper wrapped in purple ribbon. Untying it, he unfolded a sheet of stiff parchment-like paper.

"What does it say?" She asked.

He started to read. "'December 21, 1966, Vina, California. To my son, Yosef ben Daveed on this, your twenty-first birthday.' What does this say,

Rachel? Is that my name? And here at the edge of the page, I see Hebrew letters."

"Yes. That is your Hebrew name. Joseph, son of David. And that is it in Hebrew lettering, reading from right to left. Joseph, you are Jewish. This proves it, from your father's own hand."

"Oh my. I would never have imagined this. Okay, I have to keep reading. 'I am so proud of you and the man you have become today, and of all that you have, I am sure, accomplished in your life so far.

As I am writing this to you when you are only two years old for you to read this day when you have turned twenty-one, I can only dream of your future growth.

All these long years, I hope we have enjoyed our loving father-son relationship with your mother helping both of us along our way. But in case you are reading this when we are no longer here with you to guide and protect you, if Adoni has seen fit to take us, or our enemies have found us, then I can only hope that those we have arranged to care for you will have guided and protected you well.'" He stopped reading as tears began running down his face. "I don't remember. I never knew him or my mother. I grew up with no father or mother, just the old couple, my parents' friends who I called my great aunt and uncle. Why? Why did they have to die and leave me? I was so young... just a baby. And enemies? Who do they mean? My father thought that someone, some enemy, would try to kill them."

"Lover, if you are indeed Jewish, then the Church would be my guess, but I don't know beyond that fact why they would target you and your parents. I'm so sorry, Joseph. Maybe that was what happened. The car wreck where you were burned. That for some reason, they targeted your family."

"There were a few things that my aunt and uncle let slip once in a while. I remember overhearing them talking about me when they thought I was sleeping. How I was somehow in danger?"

"I'm so sorry, lover. I've been lucky to at least have my mother with me all my life."

After a while, with his tears threatening to fall on the letter, recovering some, he kept on reading "'I will have taught you by now most all of our family secrets.'"

"Joseph, I have a bad feeling about all this. I think you need to find a place to deposit these stones and coins so you can draw on the funds. So, you can move freely and hide if need be."

"Hide? I suppose. But you guessed some of this already. The truth that I was born Jewish. That cloth that was in the package, the gold Hamsa, and now all of this? I'll need a lot more time to let this sink in."

"I'll help you all that I can, sweetheart."

"Okay. I'll read more now." He unfolded the stiff, brittle paper again, not seeing a piece of one-fold breaking off and falling to the floor, and started to read once more. "'Here is our family's precious Sperot puzzle box, which you will find has layers of mysteries. When you have solved them, one by one, you will discover some of your inheritance'".

He turned to Rachel and said, "Some of my inheritance?"

"Wow. Keep reading."

"'The rest is in the Swiss account I have told you of, and at our villa in Portofino.

I trust that by now, you will have spent many happy summers there with your mother and me. Your mother and I will continue to enjoy it with you as long as we both shall live.' Villa, Portofino, Swiss account? What the...?" Joseph shook his head. "How can this be true?"

Turning to him, she replied, "I don't know. It's so sad, your parents, but for your future now, it's wonderful. You'll be okay."

He resumed reading. "'But now, with your coming of age according to secular society, the villa is now yours along with all of its secrets that I will have shown you, and others that you will need to solve on your own.'" At this, he broke down again into flowing tears. "As long... as they both shall... live. I miss them so much. Even though I barely remember them."

Wiping his tears, he continued reading. "'You will find the key to unlock everything at the heart of our family, the center of all things. With the warmth of our love that you hold in your hands, all doors will open to you.'"

"JOSEPH, THAT IS SO sweet. Your father was a poet."

He read the last line. "'Your loving father, Daveed ben Yosef, David Davidson.'"

While he was speaking, Rachel had stood up and walked to the window. Moving the curtain aside, she looked out at the back parking lot, and said with a note of panic in her voice, "Joseph, we need to go. Now."

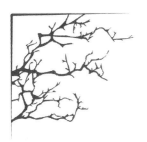

Twenty-Three

SACRAMENTO, CALIFORNIA
April 14, 1986

He looked up from the letter and could see that Rachel had a frightened look on her face as she said, "Grab the box and get everything back inside. We need to get out of here. A Church car has pulled up next to mine."

He dashed to the window and, looking out, saw the black Ford and two tall men dressed in dark suits. Quickly ducking his head back behind the curtain, he said, "One of them was looking up like he was checking out all the windows."

"Oh god. This is just what we need."

"How did they find us? How could they follow us? Do you think your car has a tracking thing on it?"

"I don't know, but it pisses me off 'cause I love that car. It was expensive."

"I'll buy you another one. I can afford to now. Quick, grab your clothes and stuff. "

"Okay, just give me a minute." She started cramming things into her large suitcase.

"No, not that one. Just take the small one. We're on foot 'til we buy a car."

"But I can't just leave all these clothes. They cost me a lot."

He placed his hands on her shoulders, stopping her packing. "No. You need to listen to me. I'll buy you more. We've got to go. Like you said. Now."

He rapidly packed his small shoulder bag. The inlaid box was already closed and tucked in the bottom. In his haste, he didn't notice the little piece of torn parchment paper fallen to the floor. As he turned to look for anything that might have fallen out of the box, his foot pushed the scrap just under the bed.

Holding two of the gold coins, he said, "This is your replacement car. I think there's a coin shop just down the frontage road. I remember seeing it when we first came to the motel."

With their small bags in hand, they headed for the far end of the central hallway. As fast as they could with Joseph's awkward gait, they made their way down the stairs. Looking out the glass door and seeing no one in the chilly afternoon gloom, they quickly left the building and crossed to the sidewalk along the street. They looked back, again and again, to see if anyone followed but saw no one who seemed to be paying attention to them. They briskly walked east along the frontage road but saw nothing like a coin shop while they kept walking for another twenty minutes.

"Where is this place? Joseph, are you sure you saw one? Are we even going in the right direction?"

"I think so."

Finally, after crossing two more side streets, Rachel said, "I think I see it. You were right. Good job. Is that the place, American Coins?"

"Yeah, that's the one I remember seeing when we first arrived."

"But these coins aren't American."

"But I'm pretty sure they're gold, and everyone loves gold."

Crossing another side street and a final long block, they arrived at the shop.

"Good, it's still open for another hour. We're in luck," Joseph said.

Before reaching the shop door, they caught their breath, calming their demeanor, and checked their appearance in the corner of one of the steel bar covered glass windows.

"We look a bit rough, but I'm not sure of what we can do now to fix that." Joseph patted down his unruly hair, tucked his shirttail in tighter and checked that all his buttons were in place. She touched up her lipstick, brushed off her coat and skirt, and smoothed her curly hair.

"Okay, ready?" she asked.

"Yes. Let's do this slowly and calmly."

Joseph walked through the door with his usual rolling limp, and Rachel smoothly followed. The door triggered a bell that softly chimed as they passed. The shop smelled to Joseph like a museum, with a pleasant smell of paste wax and cedarwood. Small bronze sculptures and delicate art glass vases and lamps sat on polished wooden pedestals scattered about the space. To the sides and all along the back, there were wood and glass cases filled with coins, all displayed on rotatable glass shelves.

"Can I help you?" asked a well-dressed middle-aged man sitting behind the counter.

"Yes, perhaps," Joseph answered. "Can we look around a bit?"

"Sure, though I close up pretty soon."

Joseph limped across the softly carpeted floor, approaching the man. In a softer, conspiratorial voice, he said, "Well, to tell you the truth, I'm looking for an engagement ring for my fiancée here."

"What? Joseph, are you serious?" She stopped and stared at him, eyes wide, her mouth hanging open for a beat.

"Of course, I am. I'm surprising my girl right here and right now."

"I can see that you're a romantic young man with a sophisticated flare about you." The man offered a broad salesman's smile that filled his face. "And I assume you have adequate funds?" he added, after looking more closely at their somewhat disheveled appearance.

"Oh, that's no problem at all. I have had a small inheritance, you see. Two old gold coins I would like to sell possibly. Can you tell me if they have enough value to allow me to buy a ring, and afford a trip to Reno to get married?"

"What did you say, Joseph? Are you out of your mind? You're nuts."

"I'm just crazy about you, Rachel." He clumsily went down on one knee, despite the pain of his scars. From the floor, he gazed up at her eyes and said, "Rachel Green, will you marry me?"

I hope she goes along with this. Though I really would love to marry this girl.

The shop owner had walked closer to the couple as he watched Rachel's stunned face and waited for her reaction. "Well, young lady, he certainly is a romantic one."

Looking down at Joseph, she saw him wink at her. The accumulated tension for the last half hour, and the last few minutes, went out of her body as she, at last, breathed out. "Yes. I will."

The shop owner shouted out, "Hallelujah, praise Jesus children! You, young people, have just brightened up my day. I can't thank you enough. Here, let me show you the diamond rings I've got. And when you're ready, you can show me those coins. We can see if we can make a deal that we'll both feel good about." He walked up behind the counter and brought out a velvet-covered tray of sparkling diamond wedding sets and engagement rings.

After she helped him to his feet, Joseph walked up to the counter and, one at a time, placed the gold florins onto the edge of the velvet.

"Young man, where did you say you got these from?" asked the man as he lifted each one and looked closely with a magnifying lens. He placed them one at a time on a scale and checked the weight. After a moment, he said, "Well, there is no doubt that they're solid gold and of high purity too. Is this all you have?"

"Yes. It's all my parents left me. Just these two."

Looking more closely at the two young people, seeing again that their appearance was more than a bit rough around the edges, he said, "Now... I have to be prudent, young man. You understand that, ah, I cannot buy anything that might not be legit. Are these coins indeed from your family? Do you have any documentation to prove that?"

Joseph thought for a moment and realized that he still had with him the original envelope he had received. Reaching into his bag, he fished among the things he had crammed into it. "Yes. I have here a letter from my family attorney that informs me of my twenty-first birthday inheritance. The coins were waiting for me in a safety deposit box here in town." He pulled out the original English cover letter from the attorney's office and showed it to the shop owner.

Reading through it carefully, the man, at last, said, "Well, this does appear to be in order. I'll tell you what; I'll take a chance on you. I can offer you two thousand dollars for each one. How does that sound?"

"Well, that's not too bad. But my dad told me that they were worth at least four thousand five hundred each."

"Ah, hum, maybe I can do a bit better for you kids. What about three thousand five hundred each? Seven thousand total. That's my early wedding present to you both."

Joseph looked at Rachel, and seeing agreement in her eyes, said, "Okay. I think we've got a deal. I can buy her a ring, pick up a cheap used car and we can get married in Reno. All that with some leftover too."

Joseph and the man shook hands, and he asked Rachel which ring she liked. Going along with the game her 'fiancé' was playing, she picked out a modest silver one with a single tiny diamond, for two hundred and fifty dollars. Looking at him, she enthusiastically said, with her eyes dancing, "This one looks good to me, sweetheart."

As the coin buyer went to his safe to get the balance in cash, Rachel whispered, "Smart thinking there. You got him distracted and sympathetic with your story."

"Story? I was serious. And you said yes.'" He started laughing at her once again shocked expression as he picked up the ring and slid it on her ring finger with a twinkle in his eye. "Just go along with it, honey."

The store owner returned. "You two lovebirds are pretty cute. Here's the cash." He counted off the remaining six thousand seven hundred and fifty in large bills. "Now, is there anything else I can do for you while you're here?"

"Well, I do need to buy a good used car that will take us to Reno. Are there any reliable car lots near here?"

"I'm about to close up, so I could drop you at my buddy's place. He's open 'til seven and has great clean cars. I'll ask him to give you a good deal for another wedding present."

"That would be wonderful," said Rachel "Thank you so much, Mr....?"

"I'm George. George Irwin. Pleased to meet both of you."

They waited just outside, hiding their faces and keeping their backs to the heavy rush hour traffic flowing past. Finally, George came out, locked the door, and closed the massive steel gate that clanged shut in front.

"Come on around the back, and I'll give you two a ride to my buddy's place. It's about four miles down the frontage road." Around the back, they could see a bright canary yellow Cadillac. "Got it from my friend. Runs like a charm."

As he was unlocking the car, Rachel whispered in Joseph's ear, "Just what we need to be less visible. What a piece of junk."

"I'm sure he's got other cars," whispered Joseph in reply.

"Okay. Hop in, you two, and I'll get you to the best car dealer in all of Sacramento. He'll get you a quick cash-buy turnaround."

As he got into the front seat, Joseph noticed two bulky radios installed under the dashboard, which cut into the available legroom.

"Sorry about that," said George, "I like to listen to the police scanner. And if I see or hear of something suspicious, I call it in on my CB radio."

After being dropped off near the office and with a quick introduction from George, the two young people found a cheap used Japanese Sedan much like Rachel's, though in blue rather than bright red. Joseph saw a Ford that he liked, but she said, "No. Never, never buy a Ford. Henry Ford supported Hitler."

"Okay, then let's buy the blue one we looked at."

Paying in cash, they tossed in their two small bags, and with the complimentary full tank of gas, hit the freeway, heading towards San Francisco.

After listening to forty minutes of his favorite country music station as he headed home up in the foothills, George turned on the police scanner under his dashboard. *All units. Possible 10-32. Description—two suspects, one male, one female, about twenty years of age. Wanted as material witnesses in murder of priest. Female, estimated five ten, dark brown curly hair, green eyes, gold-olive skin. Male, estimated five eleven, blue eyes, brown hair. Male injured, walks with shuffling gait. Report if seen.*

"Jesus, that sounds like those two kids. I just gave a lift to two murder suspects? Were those coins stolen? Oh my God!" Grabbing his CB mic, he said, "Breaker, breaker, this is gold49. Any bear with ears. Wanna report, seen two material witnesses. Repeat, just seen two suspects in the shooting of priest."

"Copy gold49, 10-4. This is smoky21. What's the 20?"

"Perp's last 20, location, forty-five minutes back. Honest Jon's Used Cars, 7256 Folsom Boulevard. Expected 10-8, destination, Reno Nevada."

"Copy gold49, 10-4, units en-route."

"Smoky21, 10-4, Gold49 out."

To himself, he added, "Go get 'em, boys. But those coins are mine." He had never seen gold coins that old in such perfect condition.

Another caller then jumped in. "Breaker, breaker, this is fatima900. Do not arrest suspects. Repeat, do not arrest. Hold for our agents and secure any articles in hand for office collection."

"Copy fatima900, 10-4, smoky21 here. By what authority? We have jurisdiction. Your agents have none."

"Copy smoky21, 10-4, Check with your chief. We're taking over this case. Priest a diplomat. Our jurisdiction."

"Copy fatima900, big 10-4, okay, they're all yours. If you can find 'em. Good luck, smoky21 out."

And they're gonna want those coins. Dammed if I'll give 'em up.

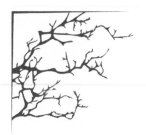

Twenty-Four

CARDINAL'S PALACE, Fatima, Portugal
April 14, 1986

Slamming his hand down hard on his enormous desk, Cardinal DeSilva shouted, "You're telling me that our agent was shot and killed by some lowly security guard? How did this happen? And where are that stupid girl and the boy?"

Father Servino stepped back a few paces, getting out of range of his boss' anger. "The guard confessed to our men, telling them everything. He described the two perfectly."

"So, I assume the guard will not talk to anyone else?"

"That is correct. We have him in custody, charged with interfering in a Holy Office operation. He told us everything, including that there was an inlaid wooden box in the boy's hands. The rep..."

Excitedly standing up and stepping closer to his assistant, DeSilva said, "A box. What did it look like? Did he describe it in any detail?"

With a patient voice, by now used to his boss' eccentricities, Servino continued, "As I was saying, Your Grace, the report says our men tracked her car to their motel."

"No, Servino. Tell me more about the box. This is very important. What more do you know?"

With an irritated sigh to himself, he answered, "Your Grace, it was described as being decorated with circles and lines all over it. But that is all the guard saw. At the motel, our men waited for the two to come out. But after a half-hour, they got the room number and persuaded the manager to let them in. Our agents could see they had left the room in a hurry, leaving many of their things."

"You must have the guard interrogated, to get more information about that box. It may be crucial to our efforts. It may well hold the golem I am seeking, the one that was foretold, along with the boy."

"Yes, Your Grace. I will so order our agents holding the guard to question him further. We can be quite successful in sparking forgotten memories."

The Cardinal returned to his plush velvet-covered chair, and continued, "Did the boy and girl leave anything behind in the room? Was there any trace of whatever he had inherited, of anything that was in the box?"

"Our agents went through everything in every part of the room. All they found besides some of her clothes was just a small piece of parchment under the bed."

"Was there any writing on it?"

"Yes, maybe. Though it didn't look like anything, it was just some meaningless squiggles."

"Did they fax a copy of it to you?"

"Yes, Your Grace. It's here somewhere."

He searched his desk for a while and finally walked over and handed the cardinal the sheet.

DeSilva translated the few Hebrew letters out loud. "'Dalet Vav Dalet.' Servino, this is it. We have proof of who this boy is. It is Hebrew, and it spells the Hebrew name Daveed, David. He is the one we are after. He must be apprehended as soon as possible. He is a serious threat to us all."

Servino, with a somewhat skeptical look on his face, said "Yes, Your Grace, if you're sure. I will so order it if you wish."

"I am more than sure he is the one."

"Yes, Your Grace."

"So, they're on foot, and our people there could not find them?"

"That is correct. We don't know where the two are now or which way they went. Our agents scoured the commercial neighborhood near the motel, but couldn't find anyone who had seen them. The footage from the motel cameras was not available since their camera system was broken."

"You told me that with this tracking thing you had installed that we could not lose them no matter where she went."

"I'm sorry, Your Grace, but she left her car behind."

"And once again she has not reported in for two days?"

"Yes, that's correct, Your Grace." Touching his earpiece, Servino held up his hand to pause the conversation. "Your Grace, just a moment." He listened carefully and then turned with a broad smile to say, "I have just heard a new development. The two were last seen in Sacramento at a car dealer. They were reportedly planning on buying a different car. The report says they were headed back towards Utah, via Reno, Nevada. Our agents will find out the model and plates of their new car and track them down."

"Are the local police being cooperative?"

"They are reluctant, but have no choice since this affair involves the murder of a priest holding a diplomatic passport."

"Very good. We need to apprehend them before they get back to Salt Lake City. For, as you know, the heretic Mormon authorities and police are, shall we say *reluctant* to cooperate with the Holy Office."

"Yes, Your Grace."

"We will bring the so-called Latter-Day Saints under our control in time, not to worry. Let me know when these two are in custody as I will wish to question the boy personally. Have our agents fly them under guard in my jet. Once we have them, you may do as you want to with the Jewish whore. You may enjoy her charms and dispose of her as you wish."

At this, Servino smiled and licked his lips.

"Oh, yes. Cancel her cards and freeze her account, this time for good. That should slow her down some. We are finished with this disobedient bitch."

"As you wish, Your Grace."

"And I want to see her sister for her confession on Monday."

"Yes, Your Grace. It will be my pleasure to ask the Revered Mother to send her to you."

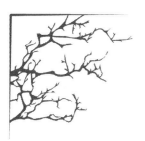

Twenty-Five

SAN FRANCISCO, CALIFORNIA
April 14, 1986

Driving across the bay bridge, Joseph and Rachel headed into San Francisco. Unlike those on the East Coast, the city had not been touched by the destruction of the Second World War and had continued to prosper. The many new skyscrapers pierced the ever-present spring fog high above the older buildings.

"I love this city," Rachel said. "SF`s a liberal city where folks live and let live. The Inquisition has not gained much ground here. In fact, they are distinctly unwelcome."

"Do you mean like Salt Lake City? How the Mormons are hostile to the Church?"

"No, way more than that. This is a city with lots of Buddhists, Hindus, and everyone else under the sun, including every variety of Christian and lots of atheists. There are even Jews safely living here still. Or I should say there were last I heard. It may have started to change with the expansion of Fatima's power and how they are infiltrating the American government."

"Sounds like our kind of town. At least I hope it is." Joseph reflected on this as he gazed out the window at the tall buildings. "We need to find a bank that will help me cash out the contents of this box. Someone that I can trust with a way for me to access the funds."

"Yes, and we will, tomorrow. But first we need to find a hotel, and we need to buy some new clothes. And I know just where we should stay. The Palace Hotel."

"That sounds expensive. Are you sure we can afford it?"

"Sweetheart, you can now afford it and a whole lot more with what you have in that box. You're going to need to get used to being very wealthy now you have your inheritance. And after what we've just experienced, I need to

151

be comfortable, with a hot bath, new clothes, a soft bed, and some good food and wine. I need to relax and feel safe."

"Okay. This is all new to me, so I'll follow your lead. It's hard to change how I think about money because I've never had any extra cash. This is a new thing to get used to. I don't feel any different, but in so many ways, I'm not who I was last week. I know now that my family was Jewish, and, apparently, so am I."

With a small laugh, she said, "Yes, my love. That is what it appears to be. Is it sinking in more fully now?"

"Yes, it is. And now I am—both of us are—being hunted by some nasty inquisition types willing to shoot us."

She took one hand off the steering wheel to give his hand a reassuring squeeze, "A lot of changes that's for sure, and at times this has been very frightening. What happened in Sacramento was bad. But let's try to relax now and take a break from all that. We should be safe here for a bit."

"Sounds good to me. Though I'm still wondering just how they tracked us. Was your car set up with some kind of a tracker? I've read about those being used now by the government. They connect to satellites."

"I think that, somehow, they know something about you, and about your family. And since you're with me now, they're trying to track where we go."

"So, we need to be careful. But does this mean we can`t go back to Salt Lake City?"

"Well, maybe. We`ll have to think about that. I'm guessing that you and I are in real danger if they catch us. I don't know why they're chasing us. But you've sure had some strange things happen lately, like your dreams, and that violin, and what you told me happened when you touched it. And what you said you saw that we both saw, the first time we made love. And then the next time too."

"Yeah, there has been some weird stuff happening to me. To us, both. Though finding you has been the best thing to happen to me in my entire life."

"Sweetheart, let's try to rest and forget about it today. We should be safe here."

Pulling up in front of the Palace Hotel, he saw the street in front was lined with lush trees in large stone pots and vintage lamp posts. On both sides, there were high-end retail shops with brilliantly lit window displays. As they stepped out of the car, he was amazed by the beauty of the hotel's massive building. Looking up, he admired the carved stonework that was accented by wrought-iron filigree, gold leaf embellishment, and carved angels presiding over every doorway.

It's like the dark history of the last thirty-five years has not touched this place at all.

Joseph got out their small bags, and Rachel handed the keys to the parking attendant. The attendant gave them and their small older car what Joseph thought was a skeptical look as if he expected no tip and for them to return to their car very shortly.

As they walked to the doors, Rachel remarked, "We must look pretty rough to that guy and the doorman too."

"We'll take care of that soon enough," Joseph replied, his confidence enhanced as he fingered the large roll of bills in his pocket.

"This hotel was built in 1909. Wait 'til you see the inside. It's incredible."

As they approached the front door, a ragged looking older man, dressed in layers of coats and sweaters, with long white hair and beard stepped out of a shadowed spot by the wall and walked towards the couple, saying, "You kids need a warm place to sleep? You look a bit travel-worn and all."

The two young people stopped at this, and Joseph turned to the old man and kindly said, "Thank you, sir, for your concern, but we're fine and staying here. Will you accept this from me?" He reached into his pocket and offered the man a hundred-dollar bill. The man, who had been looking down at the sidewalk as he spoke, now lifted his gaze to look at Joseph with piercing deep blue eyes. He smiled and said, "I will, and thank you, my son. Tikkun olam."

Joseph started at this, as Rachel stared after him with an open mouth. As the man turned and briskly walked away, Joseph said, "Wait. Do I know you?"

Over his shoulder, the man replied, "You know Tikkun olam. Which is all you need to know." He spritely crossed to the other side of the street and vanished into the growing darkness of the foggy evening.

Rachel turned to Joseph and said, "Did you hear what I heard?"

"Yes, and I wonder...?"

The doorman, observing this exchange, said with a smile, "Don't mind old Elijah. He thinks he's the neighborhood prophet. He's quite harmless."

He opened the front door for them, his face once again a professional mask, though seeming to betray some question regarding the couple.

Looking back at the man, Joseph whispered to Rachel, "Yep, I guess we do look a bit like refugees or something. But what was that with the old man? Like I told you, I've heard those words before. And he looked so much like an old man I saw in Salt Lake City, who said the same thing to me, that he could be his twin."

Rachel stopped and looked back the way the old man had gone. "Joseph, that old man, he must be a Jew.'"

"I don't know. Maybe Elijah just thought we were part of his crowd of homeless folks. We do look pretty ragged. But that was kind of him to be concerned about us."

Thoroughly startled now, she placed her hand on his shoulder, saying, "Wait a minute. Are you saying you've seen him before, or someone like him?"

"Yes. Why is that important?"

Now with both hands on his shoulders, she continued, "Joseph, I should tell you that Jews believe the prophet Elijah can appear on Earth to guide and help us. He is said to appear, usually as a ragged poor person or a tramp."

"What? Are you serious?"

"Yes. Very serious. It's a legend, but there may be some truth behind it. There are many mysteries that we do not fully understand, like the other stuff that has been happening to you, and now to me."

He gazed at her expression, one unlike any he had seen on her face until now — a look of stunned reverence.

Now noticing that the doorman was taking an interest in their conversation, she said, regaining her usual bright tone, "Okay, let's get settled here, and I will tell you more about this later in private."

Inside, they stepped onto soft Persian carpets laid over polished multicolored marble floors. Joseph stopped and looked around, stunned at the luxurious furnishings of the beautifully appointed lobby that surrounded him. He arched his head back and gazed at the gilded coved ceilings and soaring archways high overhead. "Wow!"

"Well, what do you think?" Rachel asked. "Pretty nice?"

"Amazing. I had no idea there was a place like this anywhere. It`s like nothing I`ve ever seen before."

"There's an amazing mural in the bar by Maxfield Parish. I'll have to show it to you tomorrow."

The carpets echoed the plum, charcoal, and dove gray paint on the walls as well as the richly upholstered furniture. Walking up to the guest reception desk, they set their small, slightly wet bags on the deep carpet. Joseph noticed that the desk and surrounding area was paneled with figured and deeply colored mahogany wood.

"May I help you with something?" the immaculately attired desk clerk inquired, as he looked closely at the two poorly dressed young people.

"Yes. We want a room for the night," said Joseph, his voice slightly louder than he intended as he stepped closer to the desk.

"Well, sir," said the clerk as his eyebrows ever so slightly raised while gazing at their motley appearance, "might I suggest that you may wish to try the Travelodge down near Fisherman's Wharf, as it might be a better choice for you."

As Rachel opened her mouth to speak, anger showing in the high color of her face, Joseph stopped her by gently extending his arm around her shoulders and placing the thick roll of hundred-dollar bills on the desk, saying. "No. We want to stay here. Do you accept cash? I will be happy to pre-pay for the night."

The clerk's face completely changed as if a stone mask had dropped from it, "Yes, sir. Of course, sir. We can certainly accommodate you. Would you like a top floor suite?"

"No, that won't be necessary. But do you have a honeymoon suite available?"

Rachel turned to him and blushed deeply; her green eyes bright with love as she lifted her hand with the small diamond ring.

Now, with a truly warm, welcoming smile, the clerk offered, "We do have a lovely eighth-floor corner honeymoon suite with a Jacuzzi tub set high by the window for a city lights view. It also has a king-sized bed. Would that be acceptable, sir?"

Looking to Rachel, who nodded in agreement, Joseph said, "Yes, that sounds fine. We'll take it."

"I will have the honeymoon basket and champagne we include brought up to your room before you get there. Is there anything else we can do for you right now?"

"Yes." said Rachel, "Can you direct us to the finest local clothing stores? We need to buy some new items."

"Of course. I will have your bags taken up for you. Right around the corner is Saks Fifth Avenue's San Francisco flagship store. Would that work for you?"

Now, with a warm glowing smile on her face, Rachel replied, "Yes. Thank you very much. That will be just fine."

Joseph reached into his backpack and pulled out a smaller cloth bag holding the wooden treasure box. "Can I secure this in the hotel's main safe?"

"Yes, sir. Can I take it for you?"

"I would like to place it inside the safe myself."

"Well, yes, sir. You can step this way and watch me secure it. Would that be acceptable?"

"Please understand it's not that I don't trust you. It's just that this bag is very precious to me."

"Of course, sir. Please follow me."

Stepping back outside onto the sidewalk, Joseph commented, "I feel better with the box secured like that. By the way, what is Saks Fifth Avenue?"

"Silly! Just one of the finest stores on the planet," She answered with a laugh. "Let me pick out your new wardrobe. Don't worry, and you'll love it."

But after an hour of shopping, when Rachel had acquired a full range of new clothing as well as new suitcases for them both, he had seen nothing that he wanted. She had insisted on new underclothes and socks for him, but he found the men's outerwear and shoes to be too fussy for his taste.

Stepping back out on the street dressed in her new brightly colored blue and a violet almost transparent silk blouse and skirt with a matching warm shawl, Rachel stopped to think. Looking at the next block of stores, she grabbed his arm and said, "The Banana Republic. That's where we need to shop for you."

"I have to say, that you look stunning," Joseph said as he admired his elegantly dressed partner, noting the hint of black lace that showed off the deep cleavage of her breasts.

She answered him with a mischievous grin. "If you like this outfit, wait until you see what I have to share with you in private later tonight."

With that, he stopped and kissed her deeply, stroking down her back to her upper thighs, holding her there until she broke the kiss with laughter and a smile. "Down boy. We're in public. Let's finish up here, have some dinner, and then we can play."

After another hour of shopping, Joseph was dressed in an array of finely made causal apparel, with many items being sent on to their room. This time, as they walked into the Palace Hotel, their appearance was strikingly different. The doorman's respectful movements and bearing seemed to reflect this as he quickly moved to open the door for this affluent young couple.

"Can we eat in our room? With room service? I'm pretty tired." Rachel turned and asked him.

"Ah, sure. Let's go up and get settled. But how do we do room service? What is it?"

"This really is all new to you, isn't it?"

"Well, yes. Remember, this is not my world."

She reached out to him and gave him a little hug and a kiss to reassure him. "It's okay, honey. I love you just as you are, and I'm so enjoying sharing all of this with you. This IS your new world."

"I feel a bit lost with all of this, that's all."

"Let me explain. There will be a menu in our room, and I'll order for us. They'll bring food up to us. Something delicious, don't worry."

When they entered the room, Joseph was once again stunned by the beauty and luxury that money could provide for them.

"Wow, this is amazing." He stopped in his tracks, looking around at the suite. "I've never seen anything like this."

"Welcome to your new world. You deserve it, lover." Joseph reached out for her, starting to undo her blouse buttons, partly exposing the new nearly transparent black lace bra she was wearing. A knock came at their door, and she said, "Wait for a second sweetheart." Closing the button, he had opened, she went to the door.

A deliveryman with the rest of their clothing purchases was admitted. After this, he started again on her buttons, getting three more open.

"Hold on again, sweetie. Let me order some food for us, and then we can relax." She gave a sweet smile while fluttering her eyelashes at him. "And with the other things I bought here, there is something I want to model for you."

"Hum, that sounds good."

Looking at the honeymoon basket on the table, she said, "Oh, look. Dom Perignon champagne on ice. It's my favorite." With a loud, pop she expertly opened the bottle and poured two flutes full, handing one to him and starting to sip from the other.

"I've never had this stuff before. How do I drink it?"

Stepping closer to him, she carefully clinked her glass with his and softly said, "A toast to us. You slip it very slowly. Let the bubbles tickle your nose and throat. Savor it, 'cause this stuff is costly nectar of the gods. And be careful as it goes down easily, and then it will float you gently out to sea."

"As long as I float out with you, that sounds fine to me."

Carefully and now more slowly sipping from his glass and stepping towards the in-room Jacuzzi tub, he exclaimed, "Wow, look at the view."

The lights of the city filled the windows of the corner room with a brightly lit-up Market Street stretching out into the distance before them.

Rachel had got off the phone after making their dinner order and came back over to stand next to him as he gazed out. "Joseph, we're going to be all right now. No one can hurt us, and nothing can tear us apart." She then added with a small laugh, "I'll be right back. Let me go get more comfortable."

When she stepped back into the room, she was wearing an all lace skimpy hot pink teddy with a large open 'V' in the middle that went all the way down to her waist where a small pink bow secured the filmy material. Seeing this invitation was all he needed to embrace her while running his hands along and down her bare back, kissing her through the lace.

"Oh, that feels so good." Rachel kissed his face and lips as she started to take off his shirt. "How about a bath before dinner? I'm going to fill the tub." And with a giggle, she said, "Do you want to join me?"

Almost speechless at the vision before him, he said, "Ah, yes... but if dinner comes while we're in the tub, what do we do?"

"Silly you. They'll wheel it in, while not looking. This is the honeymoon suite, after all. The staff is used to 'not looking' while serving guests here."

She turned to the tub and started to fill it. "How about some bubbles and bath oil?" she said as she poured in the provided bath salts, sandalwood oil, and bubbles.

Gazing with longing at her honey-colored skin and shapely curves, barely covered by the nearly transparent teddy, Joseph said, "That sounds so good." He took his shirt off the rest of the way and tossed it aside. Kicking off his shoes, he slid his pants down, stepped out of them, and reached out to her. Placing his hands on her shoulders, he slid open the front of the teddy, letting it fall from her shoulders to the white marble floor, caressing and kissing her, causing her knees to buckle and her entire body to gently sway and almost fall over.

Gasping, she managed to say, "Just a second sweetheart," as she stepped away to light the circle of scented candles that graced the edge of the tub. Then, with rising bubbles foaming up while they continued kissing, the lovers eased together into the steaming, scented water.

"God, I love you so much," He said

Their warm, soapy bodies slipped smoothly over and around, intertwining with each other as they caused small waves of water crested with bubbles to splash over the edge of the tub.

They both closed their eyes in response to the exquisite sensations filling their beings, as they moved as one. Feeling a strange sensation against his back, as if the bathtub had changed its form, Joseph opened his eyes and was startled by what he saw.

"Rachel, do you see what I see? Where are we?"

She kept her eyes closed, saying, "We're in paradise. Oh, God, don't stop, please." she urged him, her breath coming in rapid gasps.

But he stopped moving and holding her shoulders, softly said, "Open your eyes. Something's wrong. We're not where we were. We're not where we're supposed to be. Can you see it too? Please, stop and open your eyes."

Reluctantly, with a sigh of frustration, she stopped her movement, opened her eyes, and gasped in wonder. They were now intertwined in a large copper bathtub full of foaming water. Candle lights flickered on paint-ed plaster walls, and just outside the open French doors in the warm sunset light, the sound of soft sea waves lapping on a shoreline could be heard.

"Joseph, we're in my dream. In the bedroom, I've dreamed about. And we're both here, as ourselves."

"It's my dream too. See the tapestries on the wall? This happened when we first made love. You're Rachel and... Rebeca."

"And, darling, you are my Joseph and... my Marcus? When are we? Where are we?"

"I don't know Rachel. But I do know that whoever and wherever we are, I'm making love to you now. Just close your eyes, and maybe we'll be back."

He closed his eyes and resumed the motion of his body with hers. Their pace increased rapidly, splashing waves of water from the copper tub onto the stone floor until they both cried out.

Holding each other tightly, their eyes still closed, a knock came at the door. "Señor Marcus, Señora Rebeca, ¿puedo entrar?" a soft female voice called.

Softly caressing the scars on his back, made softer from the bath oil, she whispered to him, "Are we back?"

"I can't tell you." But as he opened his eyes, he could see that they were once again in the luxurious hotel room, intertwined together in the white marble tub with the hot foaming water still sloshing back and forth around them and flowing out onto the black marble floor.

The knock came once more. "Senor? Senora? Room service."

After a moment, Rachel called out, "Enter, please." And to Joseph, she said, "I think we're back now."

Somewhat shocked, Joseph turned to see the waitress with the food cart, wheel it in, while averting her gaze from the tub.

"Gracias, Senorita. Here you are," Rachel said as she stood up in the tub, her body partially covered with bubbles. Stepping out a few steps, she reached out with her bubble decorated arm and handed the woman a twenty she had left near the window. The young woman accepted the tip, made a slight curtsy, and silently left.

Afterward, as they spooned in warm, relaxed contentment in the soft bed after enjoying the delicious meal, Rachel turned to kiss him, saying, "You see what money can buy us? Luxury, privacy, and complete discretion."

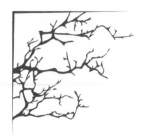

Twenty-Six

SAN FRANCISCO
April 15, 1986

The next morning, after they had enjoyed a sumptuous breakfast in the Garden Court under the magnificent stained-glass dome, the newly refreshed young couple approached the front desk. "Can you recommend a discreet private bank?" Joseph asked the clerk. "I need to open a new account."

"Yes, sir. There is a financial center right across the street that specializes in private full-service banking."

"Wonderful. Can you please bring me the bag I left in the safe last night?"

Crossing the street, they entered the main lobby of the bank and asked for directions to the private banking area. They were ushered to a separate elevator, tastefully appointed with gilded carved woods of several colors, and beautiful mirrors. They rapidly rose up to the twenty-fifth floor. The elevator opened directly onto a richly decorated foyer with an elegantly carved cherry wood desk.

An immaculately dressed receptionist was sitting behind it. "May I help you?" she asked them.

Joseph replied, holding the treasure box in its newly purchased finely-tooled leather carrying case. "Yes. I wish to open a private wealth management account."

Rachel had coached him as to the terms he should use to gain entry to this world. They were dressed for the part, and now he was speaking the language as well.

"Please follow me." The receptionist pressed a buzzer on the desk and led the way through a sizeable carved cherry wood door. Entering the richly decorated inner office, an elegantly dressed older woman was standing up to greet the two. "I am Ms. Anthony. How may I assist you?" she said as she pointed at two plush chairs. "Please sit down."

Joseph stopped in his tracks as he gazed at the woman. "Do I know you from somewhere? Miriam?"

"No, young man. I do not believe so. My first name is Mary. Perhaps I resemble someone else you've met."

I could swear that she's the same woman. Miriam. We met her at the old post office in Palermo. But how could she be?

Joseph placed the bag on the desk as he and Rachel sat in the chairs. Without a word, he lifted the inlaid box out of the bag, and laid it on top of the desk then went through the sequence of pushing the different wood circles in the correct order of the Sephirot in the Kabbalistic Tree of Life. When he had finished, and the top clicked open, he reached in and lifted out the velvet cloth holding the thirty-eight remaining gold Florin coins, setting them to one side. He then lifted out the second layer of velvet holding the sparkling diamonds. "This is an inheritance from my family, and I need a safe place to invest it," he finally said.

Ms. Anthony had quietly witnessed the treasure box being opened. She smiled broadly. "I do believe that you have come to the correct bank. I say this for several reasons. First of all, I can see that you're a member of our tribe; a Jew. And you are also an extremely wealthy Jew. We Jews always try to aid each other in times like these. And these are difficult and very perilous times."

"You're Jewish?" asked Rachel.

"Yes. Something that, even here in San Francisco, one of the freest cities in the world, is only said in private and only to others of our people. But yes, I am. And I guess you both are as well?"

"Yes, we are," Joseph replied. "I'm a Jew. And that is the first time I've ever actually said that out loud. Wow."

"You are one of the 'hidden ones'?"

Rachel answered, "He has only just found this out, quite recently, via his inheritance."

"Well, you are safe here. And your secret is safe with our bank, and with me. We specialize in complete discretion for our select clients. And please consider me your friend as well as your personal banker." Reaching across the desk, she warmly shook hands with both of them.

"So, I can open an account here, with these?" said Joseph, pointing at the gleaming array of gold and diamonds.

"Most certainly. We can have the gemstones and gold coins professionally evaluated and quietly sold at the highest prices for you. You will then have both a wealth investment fund that we can manage for you as well as a substantial liquid account to use in your daily life." Reaching towards the pile of diamonds, she added, "Did you happen to see that one of the stones is much larger than the rest? It looks to me like it's about five carats." Ms. Anthony handed a diamond of almost a half-inch across to set in front of Joseph.

"Wow, I hadn't noticed that one. We just received the box yesterday in Sacramento, and... events there did not allow us the time to examine them very closely," said Joseph.

Rachel picked up the stone. "Joseph, look at it and look at this place in this central circle on the top of the box. It's shaped just like the diamond." She placed the stone into the spot, a multi-faceted opening the same size as the stone in the center wood circle and firmly pushed on it. As the three watched, an audible click was heard, and a small side section at the base of the box sprang open.

He reached into the opening and lifted out a narrow slip of thick paper. "It has a long series of numbers running across it along with the initials C. S. What could that mean?"

"May I see it?" Ms. Anthony asked.

"Yes, certainly," he answered as he handed it to her.

She looked up something on her desktop computer, and after a few minutes, she said, "Sir, it is as I thought when I saw this set of numbers. You are the owner of a Swiss Bank account at Credit Suisse. And your reserves there are quite substantial, though the account has been dormant for eighteen years. I can link that account to the one I'm creating for you here. That way, you will be able to access your funds from either our branches or Credit Suisse anywhere in the world." She typed into her computer for a while, asking Joseph for his identification, as well as other questions. After about fifteen minutes, she looked up. "All done. Your accounts are created and linked to your Swiss holdings. Do you have an idea of how much you would like deposited into your liquid account?"

"I don't have any idea. How much would you suggest?"

"Most of my clients keep around two hundred thousand on hand to cover daily living costs."

"Ah, okay, that sounds good," Joseph replied with a stunned look on his face as Rachel reached out to massage his shoulders which had risen-up with tension at this stunning news.

"Very well. I will get you two copies printed of your new debit card that you can start using immediately. And both your names on the cards?"

"Ah, yes. Actually, can you issue one for me and one for my wife? She uses her maiden name. Green."

"Yes, I can do that." She rang the buzzer, and the receptionist came in. "Michele, will you serve our new clients some coffee while I have their cards printed?"

Looking around them at the beautiful office, and reflecting on his new great fortune, Joseph said, "I can't believe all of this is real. I had no idea. I never thought..."

"Sweetheart, you deserve it all. You're... *we're* going to be okay now."

After coffee was served from a silver coffee set, Ms. Anthony reappeared with the two new cards and two sets of checkbooks.

"There is something else I should also let you know now that we've concluded our business arrangements. As part of our service, we watch out for our clients, alerting them to any developments in the world that might affect their wealth or general affairs."

"That sounds like wonderful full service," Rachel remarked.

"And along this vein, I need to alert you to developments of concern. I recognized you both the moment you came into my office."

"How?" Joseph asked. "What do you mean you recognized us?"

"What are you talking about?" Rachel stood up suddenly and moved towards the office door as she looked pointedly at Joseph.

"Please don't be alarmed. You're safe here, in this office. It was from the TV news last night. The Church has your photos on the news wires. You're both wanted as material witnesses in Sacramento for the killing of a Holy Office Priest."

"Oh god, no. We've got to leave. Now," Rachel said. "Ms. Anthony, can you help us quietly slip out of the city? We need to fly back to Salt Lake City."

"Yes, certainly. As I said, we offer our clients full service and the utmost discretion."

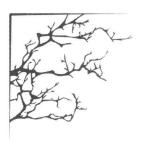

Twenty-Seven

IN-FLIGHT TO SALT LAKE City
April 15, 1986

Leaning back in her comfortably soft leather seat while sipping the provided champagne, Rachel said, "You sure picked the right bank to work with. Good job. 'Full service' indeed."

"Yes. She arranged everything. Our bags, the room charges, the limo with the smoked glass windows and then this private charter. I never thought I would fly anywhere in any plane, much less in a Learjet."

"That's right; it's your first time flying. Congrats, sweetheart." She turned to him and squeezed his hand in hers while bending over to kiss him on the cheek. "Joseph, what was that, again last night, when we were making love? When we opened our eyes, and we were both experiencing, we were other people, and actually someplace else? It was like we were making love across time and space."

He answered in a rush of words that spilled out like a flood as he looked out the window of the fast-moving plane. "I don't know. That is the third or fourth time it has happened to us? It seems to go back to my dreams, and that violin, I guess. The violin took me somewhere else, in another time, in the past. I didn't want to worry you, but lately, the dreams have been coming back, mainly the beautiful ones, but there's still an edge of fear around them. And the fear now seems to be growing stronger." He turned to look at his gorgeous companion.

"I noticed you waking up from a nightmare a couple of times this week."

He once again stared out the window, gazing into the passing clouds. "Yeah, it's started again. And I see a flash of the violin's varnish sometimes when I touch your skin. Almost every time I caress you, I think. Your skin is so warm and amber-gold colored, like that violin. Caressing you is like touching it. And when we make love, it's so incredible. It's like how I felt when I held the violin with my bare skin touching the varnish.

With the violin, my whole body was at first bursting and tingling from the top of my head to the base of my spine with a rush of dizzy pleasure I've never experienced before. It was like fireworks going off inside me, inside my spine.

But when you made love to me that first time, that same night after I touched the violin, it was so much more incredibly intense than anything I've ever felt. It was like a continuation of my contact with that violin. Now I want to touch you all the time, to caress and make love to you all the time, and I also want to touch that violin again. But I'm too scared of it. It feels like I'm on some kind of wild carnival ride at the county fair. Like being on the ghost train mashed together with the tunnel of love."

He had been staring out the window while this all poured out, but at last, he turned to look at her and saw her eyes were half-closed and her pupils were dilatated.

In a seductive whisper, she said, "Kiss me, touch me now and tell me what you see, what you feel. Tell me what happens."

Momentarily startled by this, he said, "Here? Now? But... there are other people on the plane. The pilots and the stewardess. What if they see?"

She chuckled, and said in the same low, sexy voice, "Oh, silly. This is a private flight. You don't think we're the first? Do you? They're well paid to not, ah, see anything..."

He hastily stood up and pulled shut the privacy curtains that closed off their seats in the spacious lounge in the back of the cabin.

Later, as they were enjoying the gourmet in-flight meal with more champagne, Rachel smiled broadly at Joseph and asked with a giggle, "So, sweetie, do you like the Thai food I ordered?"

"I've never had it before, but I like it a lot." Laughing, he added, "It's very spicy, just like you."

"So, tell me. Did anything happen to you, just now, when we were making love?" Continuing to giggle, she added, "Besides the normal extraordinary ordinary?"

He paused his eating and set his fork down to kiss her softly on her lips. "Actually, yes. I felt like I was, again, making love to both you and this Rebeca. And Rebeca was wearing some kind of a white woolen robe. We were in a stone-walled room or cell. She was a nun, and she called me Father Marcus."

"I should be jealous of this Rebeca, but I'm not, because I felt her this time in my body, twice over. Everything you did, every touch of yours felt doubled." She paused with a long sigh. "Ah, whatever we just shared, it was extraordinary. But you were a priest? And I was a nun? How extraordinary."

"Yes, but there was more than that. The violin, somehow at the same time, your and Rebeca`s curves were the violin's curves. When I was stroking your skin, your legs... it was again, all so close to what I saw and felt when the violin was in my hands. I felt like I was making love to the violin as well." Staring off into space and pausing, his voice faltered. "It's... it's in my mind now all the time, like it's calling out to me."

She replied by placing a chocolate-covered strawberry into his mouth as he tried to say more. "Hmmm. That's so good."

He chewed thoughtfully for a while and added, "But, all of this is so weird. Do you think I'm out of my mind?"

"No, you're not. Remember it's also happening to me sometimes when we've made love, like just now. That was the most powerful yet. I don't understand it, but I enjoyed it immensely." Adding with another giggle, "And I do think we need to keep practicing until we perfect it."

He laughed at this and picked up another strawberry. "Sounds good, even though loving you is a completely wild ride at times."

"I think we have been, and somehow are now experiencing a past life thing. That we were, or are, lovers in another time and place. When you first called out her name back in Vermillion that first time, I'll admit I was jealous. But now I wonder, and really think I am Rebeca."

"Sounds good to me. I'm delighted you're not jealous anymore."

"Seriously, though, I think that somehow, or somewhere, that she is me and I am her."

"It would make sense, with everything that's happened to us."

"I think we need to go back to the museum and try to figure out what the mystery is with that instrument. Maybe if you spend more time with it, you can figure out why it's having this effect on you. And maybe we can somehow break the spell it seems to have on you or find some clue inside it. You did see some writing inside. You told me when you were looking through the 'F' sound holes."

"Yes. I'm pretty sure from what I've seen of it that it's Hebrew writing inside. There was also that inscription carved on the head of the scroll. The museum curator said it was three Hebrew letters that spell Emet, truth. So, somehow, this violin has a Jewish connection?"

"Well, she did say something about it being vandalism, carved after the fact. But to me, it looked to be perfectly carved, and very much to be part of the original execution. So, yes, I think you're right. It is Jewish. I should know what those three letters mean if I could only remember."

"That would be great if you could. Can we look the word up somewhere? I copied them into my notebook before it did whatever it did to me when I touched the varnish."

"Joseph, you know what? I need to take you to your first Jewish service. We call it a Kabbalah Shabbat service. It's always on Friday evening starting just before sunset. Though, these days, in secret, likely not every Friday. It's so mystical, with the lighting of the candles, haunting prayers, and songs, and there should be other Jews there as well for you to meet. Maybe someone will be there who can tell us what those letters could mean, carved like that on the head of the violin."

"But where can we do that? I thought Jews were almost all gone."

"Well, there are small groups that meet in secret in some cities. Salt Lake City is a fairly safe place for our people as the Mormons do not like, or have any patience for the Circle of Fatima's so-called Holy Office agents. They know that the rising power of the Right-Wing Fatima Catholic Church would love to force them all to convert. And at the current rate, the Church may be able to try that someday. When the Mormons come to blows with Fatima, it will not be pretty. And we will not want to be in Salt Lake City then."

"Okay, I'm game to experience this. I guess it could be my Jewish coming-out party."

"Very funny. But, seriously, yes. We perhaps need to do it for your spiritual sanity. And if there is a rabbi, especially if they are a Kabbalist, then maybe we can ask him or her for help with what's happening to you. When we get home, I will try to get in contact with the community."

"A female rabbi? Can a woman be a rabbi? I know with the Quakers, the group my parent's friends, belonged to, there were or are woman leaders, but I didn't think there were female leaders in any other church. And just what is a Kabbalist?"

"Yes, my love, there are female rabbis. Also, Jews do not have churches. And a Kabbalist is a rabbi who has studied the ancient mystical traditions of Judaism. To help you figure out what is happening to you, a practical Kabbalist would be the most helpful. I've studied it myself, but I'm not that skilled."

"But can't you help me? If you know about this stuff?"

"My sweet, mystical Jewish women can be more powerful than you can imagine, but I'm just very much a beginner." She then added in a more subdued voice, "Though, centuries ago, I might have been burned as a witch. And maybe even today if things keep going the way they are, I could still be burned."

A musical chime then sounded, and the captain's voice on the intercom announced the beginning of their descent to Salt Lake City.

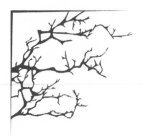

Twenty-Eight

SALT LAKE CITY, UTAH
April 18, 1986

Waiting. Waiting so long for you. And there you were, embracing me... connection... my master ... so brief... torn from your arms... but not forever. Now, all power, energy of centuries, will draw you back... We will again be one, one being, never to part with you...

It was hard for Joseph to settle down at his workbench and work on his violin after all that had occurred in the last few weeks.

I keep seeing it in my mind, that violin. Like it's calling to me, and Rachel too. They're both so under my skin.

He had moved into Rachel's apartment once they returned from San Francisco, and they were both warily watching every person they saw on the streets, wondering if Office agents were watching them. They only went out to the school that was directly next to the apartment building, not daring to go out to eat, to a store, or anywhere else. He ordered their groceries and take-out food on the phone and had it delivered, along with anything else they needed.

They had debated if it was safe to return home and to school, but Joseph still wanted to complete his education, and there was nowhere else they could think of to go.

Charlie had recovered from the car hitting him, and was back to his full good humor, teasing Joseph gently with a chuckle, "So, I was right about all the good fortune in your life, Joe, wasn't I?" He looked pointedly at Joseph's expensive new clothes. "You did have an inheritance. And you also got the girl too. I thought you and Rachel would be a great couple. You are one famously lucky guy now."

"She's a jewel, Charlie. Smart and pretty, with a great sense of humor. And she plays the cello beautifully. I'm fortunate to be sure. So, yes, I was able to quit the job, and I'm planning on the scar repair surgery in the summer when school is out."

"And you've moved in together. Nice. She has that apartment that the one guy remodeled and spent a lot on. And then he dropped out of school after one year. He wasn't serious, that's for sure. Oh, yeah, I almost forgot. While you were gone, there was someone who came by the apartment building asking for you both."

Joseph started at this news. "What? What did they say? Was it a guy, or...?'

"Hey now, chill a bit. Why are you so alarmed?"

"Well, before we left, someone followed me around town and was watching me through the school windows too."

"Wow, that's not cool. No wonder you're spooked. Well, this was just some older lady. She looked pretty harmless. Said her name was Miriam, and that you knew her. She said something about seeing you this Friday night." He laughed. "Do you have a date with her or something? Considering you're with Rachel, I don't think this one's your type."

"Miriam..." He then spoke softly, almost to himself, "The same name, but a different person. It can't be."

"Looks like class`s about to start, so I'll head back to my bench. And here comes your girlfriend, though I see that she has a diamond ring? Is she something more?"

"That's a long story, Charlie, but yes, she`s extraordinary and indeed something more to me."

"Hi, boys. Charlie, are you distracting my boyfriend from his work and keeping my chair warm?"

"Here you are, Rachel. I'm just getting back to my corner now."

Sitting down, she said, "He's doing so well healing up from that car hitting him. I'm so glad he's all right."

"Me too. I can't help thinking that the car was aiming for him. And he was wearing my coat. So, was that driver aiming for me?"

"Sweetie, I think you need to stop worrying about that now." In a whisper, she said, "Remember, you now have the means to travel anywhere you want and do anything you can dream of anywhere in the world. You're going to be okay now."

"It's sinking in, slowly. Though I still want to complete my education anyway. I do love building instruments. Violins, violas, and the one cello I made last year. And sometime I would like to build a harp."

"Oh, Joseph, I've got some news! I made contact via one of my cousins with someone who knows someone." In a low whisper, she spoke directly into his ear. "Tonight, we're invited to a gathering for Shabbat."

"Did you bring the note with the three letters?"

"Yes. I've got it here in my shirt pocket."

"Good. Hopefully, we can find out why they would be carved on that violin. I know that they spell Emet, or truth. But why would they be carved there? I know I've heard the answer, but I can't remember it now."

They had driven in Joseph's new car to a home in the Mount Olympus area of the city, high above the valley on one of the upper hillside terraces. As they were admitted through the high front gate, after an inspection of their identifications and the car by a grave-faced man, with several more standing alertly nearby in the shadows, Rachel told him, "This compound was built originally for a polygamist household, with three houses next to each other. There are other places elsewhere in the city that they also use, changing locations often to keep the secret synagogue safe. By the way, the guards out front are Maccabeus, the Shomer Israel. They're the protectors and guardians of the remaining Jews, the remnants of Israel, in the country. And they're seriously armed."

Joseph noticed the compact semi-automatic rifle slung over the man's shoulder and the heavy pistol in a holster on his belt.

Inside, they were greeted with happy cries of, "Shabbat Shalom," as they gathered with a small group of two dozens, some young, but mostly older Jews. All the men were wearing small caps or hats, most beautifully embroidered. The women and girls were wearing sheer silk shawls over their heads. Rachel covered her hair and handed Joseph a multi-colored woven cap to wear. "We cover our heads to honor Adoni, God, in humility. But also, in mourning for the ongoing destruction of our people and our exile from our ancient homeland, Israel."

They sang together in Hebrew the prayer for the lighting of the candles, while the women and girls all lit small floating candles on a large dish of water. Following the directions Rachel gave him, Joseph pulled the light with his hands into his eyes, and covered his eyes with his hands, while trying to follow the words of the prayer. "Baruch atah, Adoni..." Joseph sang along as best he could, with his eyes now closed, suddenly seeing in his inner vision a brilliant light that outshone the many candles, and he heard a sweet female voice saying to him over and over again, "Tikkum olam, Tikkum olam, Tikkum olam ..."

"Joseph, what are you saying?" Rachel asked him. He opened his eyes and could see the entire group looking quizzically towards him.

"I...I... what? Tikkum olam. What someone was chanting or singing, I guess. I'm not sure. I heard a woman's voice. I thought it was someone here. I guess it might have been inside my head. I heard it so clearly. It was saying that, so I repeated it. Did I do something wrong? I'm sorry if I did."

My first time as a Jew and I've done something wrong.

An older white-haired woman in a long brightly-colored dress walked across the room to Joseph and said, "You haven't done anything wrong. On the contrary, what you were saying is the essence of our purpose here in this life as Jews. The healing of the worlds. All of the worlds." She reached out her hand to him and said, "My Hebrew name is Miriam. I understand that yours is Joseph ben Daveed?"

"Yes. That's what a letter from my father said. How did you know?"

Miriam. Is she the one who came by our apartment?

"I know many things. I understand that you have just recently found out who you are. That you are a Jew, and that you were, and are, a hidden Jew?"

"Yes, that's all true. How did you know?"

"Well, as I said, I know things. We welcome you to the tribe and our community with open arms. Let us talk more after the Kiddish."

The prayers and songs continued for more time, all lovely sounding but mysterious to Joseph. He followed along with the transliterated Hebrew in the prayer book Rachel had given to him. He especially liked the song-prayer that went, 'Lecha dodi likrat kala, p'nei Shabbat n'kabelah.'

"This is a song welcoming the Shabbat Bride, the 'Shekinah,'" Miriam turned to him and explained after they all had joyfully sung the many verses while another young man played guitar to accompany them.

The service ended with a blessing over the wine and the Challah bread. They all sipped wine from the Kiddish cup and fed each other pieces of bread torn off the twisted loaf.

Miriam fed Joseph a piece of the Challah, and then said, "I understand you have a question for me?"

"Yes," said Rachel. "Joseph, do you have the paper?"

He reached into her pocket and handed the notebook page to Miriam. As he did, the words spilled out of him, feeling that at last there was someone who he could tell everything to "These three letters are carved onto the head of a strange violin I encountered last month. I understand they spell the Hebrew word for truth, and ever since then, unusual things have happened to me. And when I held it, touching the varnish with my bare skin, it took me somewhere else, like it was back in time and far away. Ever since then, I see it, see her, actually, in my inner eye and dreams, when I'm asleep, and now even when I'm awake. And just the other day, I was nowhere near it, and for a moment, I slipped into the same time or place, when fully awake."

"On the head, you say?"

"Yes."

"This is a powerful Kabbalah, young man. I sense that you have encountered a golem. And that you have some deep connection to it."

"A golem," Rachel said. "That could explain a lot."

"What is that?" asked Joseph.

Miriam continued, "A golem is a legendary protector of the Jewish people. I have not heard of one made or existing since the Middle Ages in Eastern Europe. When a golem is created, one needs to write the letters, Aleph, Mem, Tav, which spells Emet in Hebrew and means 'Truth,' on the golem's forehead and then the golem will come alive."

"So that is why these letters are carved on the instrument?"

"Yes, and it means that that violin must also have some dust from a sacred or blessed place in it, or on it somehow, maybe in the varnish, to bring it to life.

Joseph, you need to go and re-connect with this golem to see just what you're supposed to do. It sounds to me, and I can see..." She had her eyes closed as she took slow deep breaths in and out. "I can see that you're being drawn to it, back to it, to her. She will guide you in the use of her power."

Miriam started to sway back and forth now, her head rising and falling as she began to chant in a low voice, "Shekinah. Shekinah. Shekinah. Shekinah. Oh, my." Suddenly, she stumbled and started to fall forwards towards Rachel, who leaped forward to catch her. Two others helped Rachel hold Miriam upright as another woman brought over a chair and helped her to sit. The rest of the group, who had been talking in small groups and eating cookies and fruit, quickly gathered around her in the chair.

"What happened?" asked an older man.

"I don't know," said Joseph.

Rachel said, "She was telling us what a golem is, and then she started to pass out and fall over."

"Miriam can see deeply into all the worlds, seeing our ancestors, and sometimes our future. She is our practical Kabbalah master, who along with our Maccabeus, our Shomers, keep us safe here."

Miriam was looking better, and she opened her eyes and looked directly at Joseph, who was standing in front of her. Pointing at him, she said, "Your name is Davidson? Is that correct?"

"Yes. That is my given name."

"My son, you are in grave danger, and I'm afraid you are perhaps putting all of us here in danger too. Those of the Yetzer hara, those who intend evil, are coming for you now, as we stand here. Our community can offer you help and some protection, but you must continue your quest, and follow your guides as they will direct you to your path forward."

Rachel gasped at this. "Oh, God. And I thought we were safe here for a bit." She turned to him with shock and fear on her face, and taking his hand; she said, "Joseph, we've got to go. We can't endanger these good people any more than we already have."

As the two young people moved towards the door, Miriam continued, "You must go and find your golem. Without you controlling her, she could be very dangerous. She could be very, very powerful. You are of us, and you will help us. You may even save us all. But at this moment, you must leave and not come back here again."

"But what is my path forward? Where do I go? And what do I need to do?"

"You have no path. You have just the eternal oneness of the Light of Adoni. The Light of Eternity."

"But what must I do?"

"You must leap into Eternity." And in a loud, clear voice, the voice Joseph had heard inside his heart, she called out part of the priestly blessing of the Kohanim. "May your angels be with you to guide and protect you on your way. But now, with our help and blessings, you must go."

The next morning at Rachel's apartment, a knock came at the door.

"Who is it?" Joseph called out.

"It's Judy, from next door. Two telegrams were delivered to my apartment by mistake. I thought they were from my family, so I opened them before I saw they were for Rachel. I'm so sorry. Please apologize for me."

"Sure, no problem. Rachel's over at the school doing some Saturday work on her viola. I'll take them to her."

Closing the door, he glanced at the first one, which was half out of its envelope. Reading to himself the brief message, he stopped, rooted to the floor.

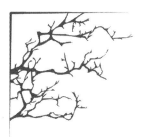

Twenty-Nine

SALT LAKE CITY, UTAH
April 19, 1986

Walking into the nearly empty school workroom, Joseph approached Rachel's workbench. Intensely carving the inside of the top of her latest viola with a long-handled razor-sharp gouge, she didn't notice him at first.

Pausing in her work, she looked up at him with a broad smile. "Hi. Did you come by just to say hello?"

He didn't smile back, and instead of answering her, said, "Rachel, tell me again how you came to be at school here?"

Startled by both his serious expression and the question, she answered, "Why are you asking? I told you. I transferred here for the higher level of instruction, and to have a better chance of seeing more old violins."

"Is that all?" His face was a firm mask, with no smile.

"Yes, of course. What's going on, Joseph? Why are you looking at me that way?"

"Who is Servino?"

With a startled expression, Rachel blurted out, "What? I don't know any Servino."

"You're quite sure? What about Fatima?"

"That's where I was studying to be a nun, in the convent there."

"Tell me again who you were speaking to on the phone in California? You said it was about your grandmother's estate. Was that a lie?"

"What do you mean by that?" she asked, raising her voice and growing angry. "Are you calling me a liar?"

The raised voices caused two more students from the other room to look in while the two were talking.

"Is everything all right here?" asked one of the other students.

"We're fine. Nothing to worry about," Joseph replied in a cold voice, and then more quietly just to Rachel, he said, "Let's take this outside."

Raising her voice even louder, she said, "No. If you're accusing me of something, then say it now and here in front of witnesses. I'm not going anywhere."

The two students quickly backed out of the room, leaving them alone.

"Okay, have it your way. But from this, it looks like you're going somewhere. Back to Fatima." Opening the telegram, he said, "This was opened by mistake by our neighbor upstairs. She brought it over, and I saw what it said. Shall I read it out loud?"

"No. Give it to me." She stood up abruptly, and grabbing for both telegrams, pulled them from his hands.

As she silently read the first one, he grabbed it back and read it out loud, "'This is an order. Return to Fatima immediately, mission terminated. Your status to be determined. Do not alert subject'. I assume I'm the subject? 'Office will apprehend him ASAP. Servino."

Rachel gasped. "You don't know the whole story. They forced me to come here to make friends with you. But I didn't tell them anything. That's why the gunman followed us."

"Yes, some 'friendship.' So, you seduced me at their orders?"

"No! I really, truly love you."

"And, yeah, sure, you don't know any Servino? Liar! How many other poor sorry suckers have you seduced for the Church? I should have known it wasn't for love that you slept with someone like me, a cripple."

"What? How dare you! I made love to you because I love you. I don't care about your scars."

"So, you're a professional seducer for them? And I was just another guy to take to your bed and pump for information?"

"Joseph, I did fall in love with you. What we've shared is so precious."

"So precious that you told those bastards everything about me? Rachel, you opened my heart. But now you've ripped it out and crushed it completely."

"Joseph, please! They have my sister there. She's fourteen, just a baby. They threatened to do terrible things to her!" In a voice wracked with sobs, she said, "Things, things like they did to me. That monster raped me and then blackmailed me, threatening my sisters and mother." Crying and sobbing un-controllably, she broke down completely. "Joseph, please forgive me. As soon as I knew you that first night, knew who you were to me, I... I knew I could never follow through with what they wanted me to do, to tell them every-thing you did and said. I love you so much."

"Well, that's nice to know. So, you've told them nothing, but you've done nothing but lie to me through your teeth? And you call this love?"

Tears streaming down her face, she said, "No, that's not true!"

"Sure, right! And why should I believe you?"

Reaching out to him with her hands, she tried to touch him, saying, "Be-cause I love you more than anyone and anything. Please, don't reject me."

Pushing her hands away, he shouted, "It's too late. My life is in danger, and your boss is ordering you to go back to where you belong, with your damn Church goons. You'll be fine, I guess. Did they pay you enough to se-duce and spy on me?"

Her face wet with tears and her voice cracking, she managed to say, "That's cruel."

"Okay, so tell me the truth. Is all your money from the damn Church?"

With both of her fists clenched, she stamped her foot and said, "It's mine! My family's money. When I started to become a nun, I signed it over to them in trust. When I left, they let me re-access it. But it's mine complete-ly."

Handing both telegrams back to her, he said with a tone of bitter satire, "There is this second one as well. I assume that these are more of your march-ing orders from the Church?"

Reading the second one, Rachel abruptly collapsed to the floor and gasped in alarm. "No. Oh, no! It's from my sister. She's in danger. She wants me to come and get her as soon as I can. She's been pretending to be sick to avoid the cardinal. He's the monster who raped and blackmailed me when they found out I was Jewish. They discovered my entire family are hidden ones, secret Jews, so they forced me to work for them, or they would arrest my sisters and mother. And, he's going to do the same to her. He'll rape her too, that fucking monster! My sister used a fake name, but they must have found out who she is."

He looked down at the sobbing young woman on the floor before him, tears running down her face. "Rachel, keep the card I had made for you. Use whatever money you need to save your sister. But as for you and me, it's over. We are finished. And keep the ring as well."

"No, Joseph! Come with me. I need your help."

"No, you don't. And I can't say what I might do to you if we were alone together. I have never, been this angry at anyone, ever. You have betrayed me! You are quite literally a lying fucking bitch! A two-bit whore! And I never want to see you again, ever!" He picked up the new small bag he had carried down from their apartment. "I'm headed to Vermillion right now, early. To start the internship at the museum."

Turning his back on the broken, crying woman sitting in a heap on the floor, he walked out the front door of the school and stepped into his car.

The car vanished down the street as Rachel stood up and ran for the door, too late, crying out at the top of her lungs, "Joseph! Wait! Don't go!"

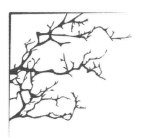

Thirty

SALT LAKE CITY, UTAH
April 19, 1986

Sobbing, Rachel slowly climbed the stairs to her apartment. Her eyes filled with tears, and her mind was racing.

Distracted and half-blinded by her tears, she tripped on a piece of torn carpet just before the second-floor landing, tumbling and rolling down twelve steps to the halfway turn, only stopping when she had smashed into the plaster wall.

"Oh, god." She rubbed her head, where it had hit the wall. "Ouch, that hurts."

"Rachel, are you okay?" asked her friend, Diane, as she opened her apartment door on the landing to see what the loud noise was.

Continuing to rub her head, she said, "I'm all right. I just slipped on that old rug on the top step."

"The school needs to fix that. Do you want me to get some ice for your head?"

With a sad shake of her head, Rachel said, "No, but thanks. I just need to sit here for a moment. Then I should be okay."

It's my heart that's hurting the most. But I've got to make some calls.

Continuing back up the stairs, watching the steps, and where she placed her feet more carefully this time, she made her way to her place on the top floor. The apartment that, until an hour ago, she had shared with Joseph.

Sitting on the beautiful, deep blue soft sofa next to her phone, she began crying again, thinking about him and the love they had shared. As she sobbed and rested, she could feel various places in her body start to ache, where she had landed when she tumbled.

Trying to steady her nerves for what was coming next, she gave herself a pep talk. "Come on, Rachel. Buck up. You're stronger than this. You've got to go save your baby sister."

Dialing the number that she had called to attend the Friday night service, she said in a shaky voice, "Kate, hi. It's me, Rachel."

"Rachel, you sound stressed. Are you okay? Is everything all right?"

"Yes. No. Sorry. I'm not okay. Can I ask you a favor?"

"Sure, what wrong? What can I do for you?"

"Joseph and I fought. He's gone, but he may need some help."

"Okay, what kind of help? You mean...?"

"Yes. You know the other night, who we spoke of? And what?"

"You mean the...?"

"Yes. He's in danger."

"We guessed as much. Don't worry; he's in good hands. Our people have been watching you both since Friday. I was just told that he drove off after you... ah ... they heard some of it from across the street."

"Oh, no. Yeah, we were loud. I think the entire neighborhood heard us."

"What happened?"

"I don't want to... I can't tell you on the phone. But our friends have been watching? Since the gathering?"

"Yes."

"Okay, I will trust you. I think he's headed for Ver..."

Kate cut her off. "Don't say it on the phone, Rachel. I know you're upset, but you must be more careful."

"What? I... Oh, god, I... don't know where he's going. He said something about San Francisco or his hometown in California. I'm not sure."

"We can still help."

"Okay, that's good. But I have to leave too. My sister, I think she's..."

"Rachel, shush. Don't tell me anymore. Your line may be tapped. All right, I will think about this. But you have a plan?"

"Yes."

"Good. Then you know what to do?"

"Yes. I'll be more careful."

"'Do you remember how our ancestors escaped from Pharaoh? And that we believe that we are reenacting this escape from Egypt every year at Passover? That we were all there?"

"Yes, of course. Pharaoh and his army pursued us through the desert to the edge of the sea. The waters parted, our ancestors escaped across the dry land, and Pharaoh's army was drowned."

"And you know Passover starts in four days? And the words that Moshe relayed that God said to our people? 'Just go forward.'"

"But you said the phone might be..."

"It's okay. It's in their Bible too. They already know the story. And the warning to 'let my people go!' I'm reminding them of it now. And of what happened to Pharaoh's troops when they followed."

"I think I understand your meaning."

"Yes, I think you do. May you travel in peace on the wings of the Shekinah. With the protection of the angels."

In a small room at the back of the Cathedral of the Magdalene, three blocks from Rachel's apartment, a man took off his headphones and said to the other one sitting nearby, "Did you get all that on tape?"

Abruptly rising from his chair, the other said, "Yes, Father."

"The kid's running, but we'll chase him down. Send men to the airport to cut him off. Now!"

"Yes, sir. Right away, sir." Picking up the CB radio microphone, he commanded, "Follow him now. Quickly send everyone. Don't let him get away."

"Good. He won't be able to evade us this time. And just in case, I'll position agents ready to fly to California. We need to figure out what Ver refers to. Do you have any idea?"

Pulling down a thick file folder, he started to flip through it. "I'll look at his records, where he's been, to see if anyplace stands out."

"Damn it; I've got to tell the chief the boy knows. She must have tipped him off somehow. I'll call this in. Also, be sure to have a man follow her and make sure they see her get on a flight to Fatima."

"Consider it done, Father." Picking up the microphone again, he said, "Send one agent to watch and follow the girl and make sure she gets on a flight home."

"It's the endgame now. We'll soon have them. Each in their own, nice little cozy cell. Father Servino will be interested in what she said and who she was talking to. And if we can find out who they are, and where the local Jews are meeting, we could arrest them all, despite the Mormon interference."

Rachel dialed another, longer collect number. "Hello? Servino?"

"Why, darling, it's so nice to hear your sweet little voice again. It's been a while since we last chatted..."

Abruptly cutting him off, she said, "Take your attitude and stick it somewhere, you..."

"Now, now, sweetheart. Watch your dirty little mouth when you speak to your superiors. You had better learn some respect. Remember, I'm a priest."

"I'll speak to you any way I want to. Respect, my ass. And you're no fucking priest; you're just a hatchet-man. Tell your icky boss I'm on my way. I got your telegram. I will get there as soon as I can."

"That's good to hear. But I don't like your attitude. You're a mouthy little bitch."

"Get used to it. It's part of my complete package."

"Yes, we know. And the boy? Does he know anything? You didn't fill him in, did you?"

"No. He knows nothing."

"That had better be true. All right, since you're behaving yourself now, I'll release funds for your travel."

"I don't need your damn money. Or should I say, my money from you."

"Independently wealthy, are we now? How'd you manage that?"

"Just stuff it. But, yeah, release the money. I'll fly first class. And I'll be there tomorrow."

"That's good. It's your money, so fly any way you like. By then, your boy will be here too. We'll have him in our hands quite soon. And then you two can have a nice little reunion. I will inform His Grace of your groveling surrender and your new-found complete and utter abject obedience."

"Screw you."

"Sweetie, in time that could be arranged. I'm licking my lips just thinking of it."

"Bastard."

Slamming the phone down so hard it fell to the floor and off the hook, she collapsed, sobbing.

She suddenly remembered her sister's plight and, jumping up, dashed to her closet, picking up a small bag. With tears streaming down her face, she quickly packed a few essentials. With a sad backward glance through tear-filled eyes at her precious cello she loved to play, the viola she had been building, and her richly furnished apartment, she closed the door and ran down the stairs.

Joseph headed west on North Temple Ave towards the airport, driving as fast as he could. Gripping the steering wheel tightly and still possessed by his overwhelming anger, he did not notice the black Sedan gaining on him in the heavy traffic.

As the Sedan grew closer, another car behind it sped up alongside it, changed lanes and cut it off. The black Sedan's driver leaned on his horn and slammed on his brakes, causing his car to leave the pavement and spin out on the gravel median, finally coming to rest after scraping against the guardrail.

As Joseph sped onward towards the airport, he did not see four shaken men stumble out of their car. He also did not notice the blue car that was now following him carefully until it pulled up next to him in the long-term parking. As Joseph stepped out of his car, a young man with a military bearing got out of the blue car, followed by another. Startled, Joseph realized he recognized both men from the Friday night gathering. The Maccabeus.

"You need to get on a private jet now, and get out of here," the first man said in a commanding voice.

"What the...?"

"You were followed. They are now in hot pursuit and will do anything to seize you. We don't know why and we don't need to know. Hand me your keys so we can hide your car somewhere safe."

Joseph, still reeling from what he had found out about Rachel, stood open-mouthed at this news. Finally realizing that he was in even graver danger than he had thought, he handed over his keys. The first man handed Joseph his small bag, and with no delay, drove the car away.

Then the second man said, "Now, quickly, walk with me to the private terminal. I have something important to share with you." They walked towards the terminal. "Do you know the story of our people? Of Passover?"

Joseph stopped for a second. "Yes. Rachel told me about it. Why?"

"Keep walking. Right now, you cannot stop for anything." Joseph resumed his quick steps with the man by his side who kept looking around as they got closer to the building, and then said, "You need to cross the Sea of Reeds before the waters return. We have stopped Pharaoh's soldier for the moment. But now you have to go far from here, leaving no trace if possible. Do you understand? You need to go where Adoni guides you. To your Promised Land. But you don't have forty years to find safety; you have only an hour or less to leave no trace."

Shaken by this, Joseph brought his attention to the moment, the full reality of the danger he was in and said, "Thank you." He rapidly continued into the private terminal.

I have to get to the violin, to try to figure out just what it is to me.

Now entirely focused on escape, Joseph chartered a private jet that, with enough cash handed over, allowed him a changeable flight plan. He reflected that Rachel was correct about money being able to buy him complete discretion and safety.

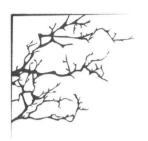

Thirty-One

SHRINE TO MUSIC MUSEUM, Vermillion, South Dakota
April 19-20, 1986

Joseph had previously arranged with the director of his school to become an unpaid intern along with Rachel at the Shrine to Music Museum in South Dakota. It had turned out the museum had needed to have trained repair persons do minor work on the instruments in the collection and were eager to have qualified students from the Salt Lake City school do the job.

The museum had expected two students, but with Rachel on her way to Portugal, only one would have to do. Thinking about her gave him a deep pain in his heart. It was made up of the love he had felt for her combined with profound sorrow for the betrayal she had committed against him. That pain and loss, combined with the most potent hatred he had ever felt for another person, made up a disturbing combination.

The experience he had with the violin had come back to him in dreams and was still quite vivid in his mind, though now with a bit of a distance, was not as frightening. Or was it somehow all just his imagination?

When Joseph arrived at the museum and settled into a room at the nearby university, he tried to keep a hold of his feelings of apprehension and fearful excitement. He did know that awaiting him was that violin, with some charge of energy surrounding it. He wondered if anyone else had ever experienced what he had.

Many people in the last five hundred years must have touched the varnish, and played it, or had they?

Maybe no one else has ever touched it. Was it hidden and lost for years? But was it just me? Am I crazy? Should I worry that I am mentally unstable or worse? A brain tumor, or some other deadly thing wrong with my brain? Or maybe some unknown mental illness in my family?

189

He knew next to nothing about his family history or ancestry, except for what Rachel had helped him discover.

Jewish, yeah, sure. Likely a lie. But the box, and my father's letter? Can I trust anything she told me?

He doubted everything she had said and everything he had experienced in the last short weeks since his first visit there.

It was true that he was now wealthy, with enough money to go anywhere and do anything he wanted. He could have the surgery on his scars and hopefully finally be free from the pain he felt nearly every time he moved.

Settling in at the museum, he examined and did minor work on other instruments, putting off going near that violin for a few hours. But finally, he had to face it. He needed to examine it to see what work was required, and if necessary, to stabilize the wood and structure. Wearing white cotton gloves and being cautious not to touch the varnish with his skin, he carefully removed it from the glass case where it rested on a black velvet cloth-covered violin-shaped cradle. He could now see with a practiced eye that the top plate had some very fine cracks that started at the ebony tailpiece saddle where the spruce tone wood had shrunk. He would need to remove the top to repair the cracks to prevent further damage if they got any deeper.

Carefully inserting the sharp opening knife to be able to remove the top of the violin from the rib structure, he carefully worked the blade around under the edge of the top plate, breaking the glue joint. It resisted here and there, but mostly the old hide glue just crumbled away. At last, with a final pop, the top came free, and he carefully laid it top-face up on a second felt cloth-covered cradle on the wooden workbench. The glue appeared extremely old and brittle, with no evidence of previous repair work.

With the top off and the inside of the maple back-plate fully illuminated, he could now clearly see the strange letters or marks that he had only seen through the 'F' sound holes when he first looked at it. Now they did look like Hebrew, though different from the formal letters carved on the head of the scroll, or in the Jewish prayer book he had read from only a few days before.

Copying them carefully onto a pad of paper on the workbench, he intended to go to the library and try to find a book to tell him what they spelled. In the bright light of the work lamp, he looked at the paper label that had the maker's name written on it. He saw soft brown letters written in an elegant hand that looked to be Italian.

Marcus Antoni... us? Who were you? I wish I could talk to you. That name, Marcus... It's so familiar. Could it be the Marcus of my visions, with Rachel, Rebecca, and the violin? No, that's not possible.

Along with the name, there were numbers, 5280. He recalled that the museum curator had said the numbers translated to be 1525. *But why did the maker use these different numbers for the year?*

He turned over the top plate of the violin to look at the cracks from the inside. When he did so, he was surprised to see many more letters and words, similar to those on the inside of the back. They were scattered all over the surface of the spruce and arranged in a pattern that looked like a grid, or design, almost like a tree in shape. He looked at the puzzle box that he had sitting near him on the back of the workbench.

They're just like the pattern of circles on the puzzle box. It looks the same, or nearly so. It's another Kabbalistic Tree of Life.

Around the tree, he saw a series of three and four letters grouped as if they were words. He also counted twenty-two other single shapes or letters scattered between the groups spaced out through the area of the more extended groups. And he thought he could make out some delicate lines, like silk spider threads, connecting the symbols or letters, crossing over each other in a pattern.

It's just like the interlaced connecting lines on the box.

Other chains of Hebrew letters wrapped entirely around the inside edge of the top plate as if a long inscription was written just inside the rim. He found some clean sheets of paper and carefully copied all the shapes and groups of shapes he could see. When he had finished, he took the sheets of paper with him to the Vermillion University library.

When Joseph showed the sheets of paper to the librarian, she scowled and pointed him toward an obscure area back in the reference section, where she said there was a text on Hebrew. After looking for a bit, he pulled the heavy old book off the shelf and brought it over to a large table. Opening it at random, he started to compare the shapes copied from the violin with the ones in the book. They seemed to match up to much of what he saw.

Indeed, it was Hebrew writing inside the violin. The letters had looked different from the more formal ones he had previously seen. These were all handwritten in a flowing script.

What was an Italian violin maker doing writing Hebrew words inside a violin he had made?

Miriam at the Friday service had told him the violin was likely a golem, with the three letters carved on the head of the scroll.

So, if that's true, then what is all of this inside the instrument?

As he was making astonishing noises, while looking at the letters and the apparent Hebrew words they spelled, Joseph became aware of a well-dressed older man with a short white beard and close-trimmed white hair standing in the aisle between the stacks, looking sharply at him with piercing blue eyes.

"I'm sorry to have disturbed you," Joseph whispered.

"Not at all. What do you have there?" He softly asked as he walked over to where Joseph sat with the open book.

Relieved he hadn't annoyed him, he showed the man the writing and letters, asking, "Would you possibly know what these words or groups of letters mean?"

"Where did you come across this? Vermillion is not the usual location to find Hebrew inscriptions."

Joseph somehow felt utterly safe, telling this total stranger the truth. "I found these letters written inside an old violin I'm working on over at the museum."

The white-haired man looked closely. "What you have here looks like what is known as the Kabbalistic Tree of Life, of the 10 Sephirot. It is the central mystical symbol used in the Kabbalah of esoteric Judaism." He pointed at the tree-like diagram Joseph had copied. "The understanding of the energy centers is used for important spiritual purposes, of the order of Jewish prayer and in healing, and to be in contact with angelic forces. It also has great power to call forth help in mighty ways."

"Do you know what this other writing says?" Joseph pointed to the long series of lettering he had copied from the inside rim of the violin top. "It was just faintly visible, written in a delicate, spidery hand, with letters of the same script."

He looked more closely at what Joseph had copied, squinting his eyes. "Is this the first part? Could you tell? You know it's written and read from right to left?"

"I didn't know that, or anything else about it. To me, it all looks like just squiggles. It's written inside of the top of a rare and very old violin from the museum collection."

Now sitting at the table next to Joseph and holding the paper, the man said, "What I see here that you have copied looks like part of an invocation of the prophet Elijah. And this other section is a blessing and a prayer for future generations, for them to be safe and protected. And that part is a prayer for them to stay connected and not lose their faith, no matter how far they travel or how many generations may pass. To never lose the connection to their people." He turned and looked directly into Joseph's eyes.

"All of that is in those words?" He asked

"And more. There are prayers here ..." He pointed to one part. "Regarding Passover and escaping from Mizraim, Egypt. Young man, did you know Passover is in just four days?"

Joseph answered, "I know about it, but did not realize it was so close. What does Mizraim mean?"

"It means a double narrow place. It is the Hebrew word for Egypt." Turning to look more closely at Joseph, the man continued, "Are you currently in a tight, narrow place, young man?"

He let out a long sigh, "Yes, you could say that."

"Well, you must cross the Sea of Reeds before Pharaoh's armies reach you. I would like to see all of what's written, for it looks like the person who wrote this was writing for his descendants." Pointing at another long passage of letters, he added, "And this part here is what is called Practical Kabbalah, a formula for creating and bringing a golem to life."

"It does?"

"Young man, if you have encountered a golem, then you must be extremely careful, as only the creator of the golem can completely control it." Turning to once again look even more closely at Joseph with his piercing eyes, the old man asked, "Who are you? Do you really know who you are, what you are, and where you are?"

Joseph looked up from the book and seeing the deep blue eyes staring at him, had a sudden recognition of that look. "Me? What do you mean by that? I've heard that before somewhere."

"Of course, you have."

"But what do you mean? I'm just Joseph Davidson."

Joseph looked back down at the book, shaking his head to the question.

What did he mean, do I know who I am? And his eyes, have I seen him before?

"You may be more than you realize, and in time, this will unfold. But for now, I must go. Remember, Tikkum Olam," Joseph heard the old man say, as he continued to concentrate on the book in his hands.

When Joseph startled at what the man had just said, looked up a moment later, the man was gone.

He suddenly remembered where he had seen those eyes before, and heard those same words spoken, in Salt Lake City and San Francisco, and the dream, with the voice calling out, asking who, what, and where he was. Joseph cried out, "Wait! Don't go!" He got up and walked to the end of the aisle. He saw the librarian upfront glaring at him along with several other patrons. Walking to the librarian's desk, Joseph apologized for being so loud and whispered, "Did you see an old man with short white hair and beard leave the library just now?"

In a loud whisper, the librarian answered, "I saw no one like that enter or leave the library today. Are you feeling all right?"

Mystified, and shaking his head at this, Joseph went back to the reference book to photocopy pages that would give him the names and meanings of the letters. He also copied several pages of the prayers written in Hebrew and English with Hebrew transliteration. After he was done and had re-shelved the book, he continued wondering if he was really okay or not.

Puzzled by this latest strange encounter, Joseph headed back to the museum to resume his work on the mysterious violin.

Before he started, his thoughts strayed back to Rachel.

God, I loved her so much. But what a goddamn liar. She betrayed me. After her, I don't think I can ever trust anyone ever again.

Putting his head down on his arms on the table, for the first time since he last saw her, he broke down and cried, sobbing in loud gasps with tears flowing freely. After a time, drying his eyes with his handkerchief, he recovered and re-focused on the job of repairing the violin. So far, nothing unusual had occurred while he was working on it, and he proceeded to fix two hairline cracks with narrow strips of hot hide-glue-soaked linen cloth. When they had dried, he glued the top-plate back on, holding it in place with cork-lined clamps, and left it to dry overnight.

That night, he could hardly sleep as he dreamed of Rachel with her warm skin lying naked in his arms. But in the dream, she kept interchanging with the violin, as he caressed them both. Hearing a chorus of mixed female voices calling his name, he ran down a hot cobbled stone street. He awoke in the middle of the night with a start, crying out in terror as dark figures in black robes waving bloody knives reached out for him.

Shaking off the nightmare the next morning, he returned to his workbench to work on other instruments while the violin had time to dry. Later that day, he removed the padded clamps that had held the top of the violin in place while the glue dried. Deciding it was ready, he reinstalled the sound post and proceeded with the set-up and installation of the missing strings, and the newly carved bridge, all the while still keeping the white cotton gloves on his hands.

Rachel would have loved to see the inside of this fiddle, but what I am I thinking? I've got to forget her.

Distracted by his thoughts, he decided to take a break from the intense work. But as he stepped away from the instrument to go take a walk outside, he thought he heard a female voice calling to him, *"Come back. Don't leave me alone. Come to me. Come to me."*

Stunned by what he had just heard, his heartbeat raced.

What am I hearing? Am I going mad?

He had to sit in front of the violin for a time to finally calm his heart and breathing.

When Joseph had finished installing the strings and tuning the violin, he admired his work, seeing the formerly unplayable violin now ready to sound once more. Looking at the brilliant golden-colored body in his hands, he found himself staring into the varnish, at the light that was captured by the layer of melted amber that covered the iridescent fiddle-back maple and narrow-grained spruce. Feeling relaxed, he started to take off his gloves. All the time he had been working on the violin, nothing unusual had happened, except for the dreams, and so he decided to pick it up and try playing it. He felt that he had to hear it, to know what it sounded like. His hands were quite clean, so it should have been okay.

He picked it up by the bare unvarnished area of the neck and held it ready to play. Taking a bow and tightening it to playing tension, he adjusted the instrument under his chin with a clean handkerchief to pad and protect it against his chest. As he moved it into place, he barely touched the varnish on the top surface with one finger and he was suddenly falling with full, sickening vertigo, feeling his hand and arm disappearing into the violin, his shoulder following, then his head in a long spinning, rushing descent into a black and golden spiral pool of roaring sound.

And he was gone.

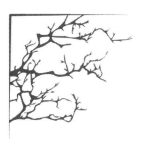

Thirty-two

CIRCLE OF FATIMA, FATIMA, Portugal
   April 20-21, 1986

She gazed at the vast stone plaza illuminated in the cloud-shrouded moonlight, thinking out loud, "It's so beautiful. It was so beautiful." Tears half-blinded her as they rolled down her cheeks. Sparkling light caught in each teardrop as it fell, only to be changed into dark spots as they landed on the white cloth of her nightgown. Now speaking in a whisper to the night sky, she said, "I'm so sorry, Rachel. I'm so ashamed. I can't ..."

If anyone had witnessed it, they might have thought they had seen an angel take flight, as a small white figure with outstretched wings launched itself into space from the eighth level of the Basilica tower.

Rachel drove her rental car from Lisbon at breakneck speed, covering the 122 km in less than an hour, with her rate reaching 150 km at times. It was past eleven pm when she pulled into the parking lot behind the convent. Quietly closing the car door and grabbing the bag of street clothes she had brought for her sister, she dashed to the back of the building. She remembered that, at one time, there had been a secret back door key hidden nearby. It was copied and placed there by one of the wilder sisters, who loved to sneak out in disguise to go dancing at clubs in town.

She searched for possible hiding spots, at last finding the key under a pot of half-alive geraniums. The key looked a bit rusty as if no one had used it for a while, though this was not surprising since Sister Boniface had been expelled for immorality years before.

Quietly turning the rusty key, which resisted her efforts at first, she opened the door and silently crept into the convent kitchen. Remembering the instructions her sister had given her in the telegram, she whispered to herself, "Okay, third floor, cell A, at the end of the hall."

Finding the stairs in the darkened building, she quietly climbed up to the third floor. Walking softly on the carpet that ran the length of the hall, she found the door she was seeking. Rachel quietly turned the knob and stepped into the darkroom. Barely seeing a sleeping body curled up under a blanket on one of the two narrow beds, she softly moved to the bedside, and gently placing her hand on the slight shoulder, whispered, "Debra. Debra, it's me, Rachel. Wake up, I've..."

The young woman woke up with a start, and in a loud, groggy voice said, "What? Who are you?"

Rachel, at once understood her mistake and placed her steady hand firmly across the girl's mouth. "It's okay. Please be quiet. I'm Debra's sister, Rachel. Do you know where she is? I thought this was her room. I'll move my hand if you can be quiet."

The young girl nodded, and Rachel removed her hand. The girl replied, "I, I'm not sure what I can tell you. Did Mother Superior contact you? You must have heard."

"Heard what? What do you mean?"

"She's gone, since yesterday."

Rachel sat down on the foot of the small bed. "Is Debra alright? Where did she go? Where did they send her?"

"I... I don't think I can... "

"Is she okay?"

"I'm so sorry. We don't know what happened... They didn't tell us much."

"What do you mean?" Rachel sharply asked, her eyes looking at the wooden crucifix on the unpainted rough plaster wall.

"For some reason, she was up in the bell tower of the Basilica, and she..."

Rachel placed her hands over her mouth to stem the scream that was welling up into her throat but couldn't entirely stop it. "Oh, no. No." Abruptly standing up, she dropped the bag she had been carrying and screamed out, "That monster! I'll kill him! But first I'm going to cut him so bad!"

The young girl had pushed herself into the corner of the bed, away from this suddenly transformed apparition before her. The soft-spoken and gentle woman who had entered her room a moment before had suddenly turned into a fierce warrior intent on a deadly revenge.

Seeing the impact, her words had upon the girl, Rachel said, "I'm sorry. I didn't mean to scare you. But that monster, DeSilva, he must have hurt my sister."

With a shocked look on her face, the girl asked, "His Grace? Are you saying he did something to her? How can you say that?"

At that moment, voices were heard out in the hall, as Rachel's scream had echoed through the entire floor. A loud knocking came at the door, accompanied by a voice with a Spanish accent. "Novice Margret? Are you all right?" Without an answer, the door opened, and there stood a tall, stern-looking woman in a housecoat and nightgown, who, upon seeing Rachel, asked in a commanding voice, "Who are you and what are you doing here?"

"Reverend Mother, she is Debra's sister, Rachel. She was asking..."

The older woman cut her off and sternly admonished the young novice, "We do not speak the name of one who is a lost soul. Suicides are destined to burn in the fires of Hell forever."

Rachel pounced on the woman. "What the hell? My sister killed herself because of that monster DeSilva you call a Cardinal! She was hiding from him! She telegrammed me, and now she is dead. What did he do to her?"

"Young woman, you need to leave here now. You do not belong here. Your sister was too weak to cope with the demands of our Lady of Fatima and our Order."

Rachel raised her voice into her full righteous anger. "I'm not going anywhere until you tell me what happened to my sister! Too weak..." Her rage was overwhelmed by the unbearable grief she was feeling, as anguished sobs burst from her. She sat back down on the bed, burying her face in her hands, while her tears splashed onto the legs of her blue jeans.

The Mother Superior assumed a slightly more compassionate tone. "I am sorry for your loss. We are saying prayers for her soul every day now, but she is lost in Damnation."

"I don't want your worthless fucking prayers, and my dead sister doesn't need them either! You may not recognize me, but I was at one time a novice here in this very convent."

"Your foul mouth certainly would not allow you to stay here very long."

"That okay, I'm out of here now. Where does the so-called Cardinal De-Silva hang his hat these days? I need to see him."

"Just who do you think you are? You can't just expect to see His Grace in the middle of the night, or anytime, for that matter."

Rachel's voice became as hard as steel. "I know who I am! I'm a special agent of the Holy Office. And if you know what is good for you, you will step out of that doorway so I can report to Father Servino, my handler."

At that, the older woman with a stunned expression stepped aside, as the young novice sat on her bed, her eyes wide and her mouth hanging open.

As she stepped through the door, Rachel asked in an icy, controlled tone, "And may I ask where my baby sister is buried?"

Now in a bit more of a respectful and fearful tone, the woman answered, "Outside the walls, in unconsecrated ground."

"You fuckers! You couldn't even give my baby sister a decent grave! Where do I find this midden heap where you threw her body?'

"It's not a midden heap. It's a beautiful little grove of trees, behind the back-parking lot. It is where the lost and unbaptized souls are buried. You will see her grave in the back. It's the fresh one."

In a burst of increased anger, Rachel rudely pushed the older woman aside and strode rapidly down the long hallway. No longer seeking to be quiet, she passed open doors and a number of both young and older women in nightclothes, their voices falling silent. They stared at her as she stormed by. The convent was now completely lit up, with many of the sisters awakened by the uproar on the third floor. They all stepped back from her, afraid of what they saw as she passed them. Her face set in a grim mask, Rachel pointedly ignored them as she made her way down the stairs and back out the kitchen door, heading for the small grove of scrubby trees beyond the parking lot. Entering the little woods, she could now see that it was a serene spot, with flowering bulbs and some statues of the Virgin and Saint Francis. Tears were flowing down her cheeks, as Rachel looked among the older graves, all just marked with simple wooden crosses, for Debra's, at last finding it. Someone had placed flowers in a jar of water by the unmarked cross and the fresh mound of dirt. She cried out to the night sky as she fell to her knees and threw her arms across the pitifully small grave. Sobbing, her lungs gasping for air between bursts of tears, she lay there for a long while as her tears soaked into the raw, fresh soil. Gradually, her sobs died down, and she dug her hands into the moist dirt as she spoke loudly to the cold, dark night. "DeSilva, you evil bastard. I'm going to kill you."

"But, Your Grace, you want to see her alone? Do you think that is wise? Do you think you can trust her?"

"Yes, Servino. I think I can handle this little girl, just as I have in the past. I'm looking forward to tasting her again, as it's been a long time since I had her."

Servino hesitated. "But you haven't heard her speak on the phone with me. She has become a venomous little bitch. Your Grace, I would not trust her at all."

"Servino, Servino... you worry too much. And I know your background is a bit rough, with your being from Sicily and the 'Family' there. But now, with my new position, I will ask you to watch your language. Please leave me now, and I will prepare a warm welcome home for her."

"As you wish, Your Grace. But if you need me, I will be just next door."

"No. Please wait farther away, as Rachel and I wish to have a private re-union. We have much in common and much to catch up on."

With this, Servino, his face showing deep unhappiness, turned and left the room.

Just past midnight, Rachel made her way across the enormous stone plaza, heading straight for the Bishop's palace on the far side. Approaching the side door that led onto the colonnade that circled the vast plaza, she tried the door and found it unlocked.

Inside, a blue-uniformed guard carrying an automatic weapon stepped forward and blocked her way. He lifted the gun and pointed it at her chest. "Stop. Who are you, and what are you doing here?"

Her resolve steeled, Rachel firmly answered, "I am a special agent of the Holy Office. I have top-level access." She handed the guard a small folder that contained her papers. "Here are my credentials. I have a report of utmost importance for His Grace."

The guard did not move from the doorway as he examined the folder. Seeing the level of access that they gave her, he stepped aside and snapped to attention, his firearm at his side and pointing at the ceiling as he saluted and let her pass.

Without a word, she proceeded down the long marble hallway towards the cardinal's office.

Approaching the large gilded double doors, she thought, *He sure has polished up the place with a lot more gold since my last visit.*

Not bothering to knock, she pushed open one of the large doors, which soundlessly moved at her lightest touch. Now gazing into the vast, richly-decorated space, she saw the object of her hatred standing before a brightly burning fireplace; DeSilva, with his back, turned to her, robed in silken nightclothes of scarlet.

Without turning to face her, he said, "Good evening, Rachel. It's so good of you to come to see me. It has been a while since you last graced us with your beauty." He continued to warm his belly by the brightly burning fire. "Why don't you come join me here? We have much to discuss."

In the sincerest voice, she could muster, while using all of her training to contain the murderous rage filling her very core, she replied, "Yes, Your Grace. Thank you for your kindness. I am, as always, your loyal and humble servant."

Still, with his back to her, his voice now softened markedly, he chuckled at her words. "That's so much better now, isn't it? Servino has told me that sometimes lately on the phone you have been rather, shall we say, rude?"

Still speaking from a well-trained point, with her anger a tightly coiled spring inside her, she said, "I have no idea why he would say such a thing. My communications have always been completely professional with him."

Laughing softly at her cheek, he replied, "Well, Servino has a bit of a rough background. Perhaps it is just a misunderstanding between you two."

Approaching the cardinal by passing close to his large carved desk, Rachel palmed a sharply pointed gold letter opener and slipped it into a back pocket of her jeans. "Your Grace, there is something I do wish to ask you."

"Yes, my child. How can I be of assistance? I am so glad you're back home, and we can resume our work together." As he said this, he turned to face her.

She approached him more closely, saying, "That fire feels good. May I join you?"

"Yes, of course, my dear. Please come here, and stand next to me. Now, what did you wish to ask me?"

"Your Grace, do you still find me sexy and attractive?" She closed the distance between them.

"Oh, Rachel. Yes, of course, I do. And I'm looking forward to your confession. I have so enjoyed them in the past." He licked his lips and looked closely at her soft curves. "You have filled out nicely, my dear, with all the right curves in all the right places."

Rachel reached out to stroke the man's face as she softened her body and pressed it up against his, allowing him to reach out to eagerly squeeze and caress her breasts and hips.

The bastard. He so deserves this.

His excitement rising, he reached to her waist and slipped his hands under her sweatshirt to grasp her breasts. Lifted it and finding no bra in his way, he eagerly fondled her.

"Oh, Rachel. You have always been one of my favorites, so much like Mother." With his heat rising, he opened and dropped his red silk robe, exposing his naked body before her. In his lusty haste to impale her, he did not see her reach for the blade in her back pocket. His moist, greedy lips suckled on her neck and went for her right breast as his hands began to reach into her jeans and between her legs. The last thing he saw with his left eye was the flash of the golden blade as she swiftly stabbed at the pale blue orb. The sharp knife slashed into his face next to the eye, glancing off the bone around it, tearing out his eyeball.

Screaming at the top of his lungs, he pulled away and held his hands up to what was left of his eye as it dangled from its socket, yellow matter and blood splashing over both of them, and onto his carpet of Paradise.

With all the practiced sweetness in her voice now completely gone and replaced with an icy unbridled rage, she said, "That's for my childhood you took from me, you monster. Now you really are one."

DeSilva continued screaming as he stumbled back away from her.

Hearing footsteps approaching, Rachel said, "And this is for my baby sister, who you raped and murdered." She stepped forward and lunged at the wounded, naked man, aiming for his heart. But with his erratic movements, she missed, stabbing him instead in his lower side, close to his now deflated penis.

With blood spurting forth in two places, blinded in one eye, in agony, he fled from the enraged woman before him, screaming, "Guards! Servino! Help! Help me! Servino, where are you? Mother, help me..." He collapsed onto the carpet, writhing in debilitating pain, continuing to scream out.

She ran past the bloody, flailing form on the floor to the large French windows, just as the massive doors to the office burst open. Servino appeared and stood for a moment with a shocked expression before leaping to DeSilva's side, shouting at Rachel, "Stop, you bloody bitch!" Pulling a pistol from his jacket, he fired a rapid series of shots at the swiftly moving figure, only hitting and shattering several of the window panes.

Not slowing her headlong rush to freedom, despite flying bullets and the shower of shattered glass, she crossed her arms in front of her face and burst through the doors, breaking the wood and the rest of the glass, cutting her arms in the process. Large shards of glass fell from her body, and bleeding from numerous small cuts; she dashed out into the enclosed garden courtyard. Using a bench by the back wall, she climbed up the connected trellis to scale it. As she reached the top, more bullets hit close by, cutting her back with shattered fragments of brick. Once over the wall, she was outside the garden, and like a spirit of the night, was gone.

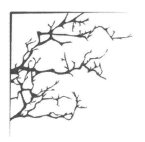

Thirty-three

LISBON, PORTUGAL
 April 20, 1522
 Vermillion, South Dakota
 April 20, 1986

My love ... My master... You have brought your servant back to life. I am complete. I am yours, and I will sing for you alone. I will embrace you with all my warmth, holding you close, protecting you with all of my power...

Blinded by the bright, hot sunlight glaring from the white plaster-covered walls, Joseph caught his right sandal on the edge of a cobblestone, stumbled, and tripped on the long robe he was wearing. Falling outstretched on the rough paving stones, he caught himself painfully with his arms and hands.

Where am I? God, my hands are bleeding.

He looked at his bloody palms and suddenly remembered, the violin.

No, not again.

The second voice in his mind then rose up and wrestled with his for control. But the second voice spoke out loud for all on the street to hear.

"Who are you? Why are you back? What do you want from me? Be gone. Leave me alone. Get out, you devil."

Other citizens of Lisbon walking on the street had stopped at the sight of the priest suddenly falling to the stones before them. Several had moved towards him as if to help him up, but now they stepped back with horrified expressions at the sound of his words.

Joseph could hear Marcus' thoughts in his mind.

Why are you plaguing me? What have I done to deserve this? Be gone. Get out. Get out of me.

I don't know what's happening, why I'm in your mind, in your body. I'm Joseph.

Joseph? You are not me. I am Father Marcus. Who are you? What do you want, and what do you mean, in my body?

I think I'm from another time. Another place. Not here. Somehow, I've slipped into you ... It's happened in dreams, and when I'm making love to Rachel, and now twice with that damn violin.

Dreams? Who is Rachel? Making love... Do you mean sex? But I am a celibate priest, and you are a devil trying to tempt me.

No, I'm not. I'm a man like you.

How can that be? And what is a violin? Do you mean a viol?

Yes, it's like a viol.

You are a devil. Get thee behind me, Satan.

I'm not a devil; I'm a man. I'm Joseph Davidson.

I do not believe you. The Church has warned us of demons like you.

I am not a demon.

If you are a man or a soul, how can I be conversing with you in my mind?

I don't know, but we, you, need to pay attention. Right now. Look around you. You need to try to act normal. We're being watched.

You are a dark spirit, a demon trying to snare me. I will pray to Mary to expel you from my body.

No. No, don't say that out loud. Don't do it.

Among the passersby who now stood in a wide semi-circle around Marcus, a priest dressed in the black robes of the Portuguese Inquisition had stepped closer to Marcus, who was now on his knees with his bloody palms facing upwards. At this, the passersby had moved farther away, and some quietly slipped away up or down the street. The priest could see that Marcus' eyes had partially rolled back into their sockets, showing their whites. He was visibly trembling as well.

"Father, are you ill? Do you need assistance?"

Marcus again cried out, rising to his feet while waving his arms and bloody hands wildly in front of his face. "Mother Mary, protect me. Mary, my Heavenly Mother, intercede with the holy angels and saints for me." He then seemed to speak directly to the dark-clad figure before him. "Leave me alone. Do not plague me with these lies. Be gone. Be gone. Be gone, you dark spirit."

With firm hands, the black-clad priest roughly grabbed Marcus and called out to two armed soldiers-priests who had been walking behind him. "Guards, take this madman to the prison. We will examine him in the morning for possible heresy."

The argument in the young man's mind between Joseph and Marcus continued.

No. What did you do? I'm not a demon. I must be you. I am your soul.

How can you be my soul? It is a lie.

I don't know, but I'm... somehow you, and you are me...

Joseph then felt the stable cobblestones losing form and melting beneath his feet as the bright sunlight faded, and a black and golden spiraling swirl of roaring light and darkness swept him away.

There was a crash, the sound of something wooden hitting wood, and he could see the room at the museum before him coming into focus as he was roughly grabbed by unseen hands, and a voice that said, "I have you now. Resist, and it will be painful. Come quietly, and the pain will be less."

The man had pulled Joseph's arms behind his back and started to rapidly tie his wrists together with rough cord, hurting him as he jerked it to knot it tightly.

Joseph could see that the violin and bow had slipped from his hands, and the violin was now face down on the workbench where he had dropped it. To his relief, it looked intact, with the strings and bridge still in place.

What's happening to me? I was in that place, in danger, being grabbed, and I'm still being caught here and now in reality. But what is real? I don't know anymore.

Struggling against his captor with his arms jerked back behind him, the scars on his back burning like fire under the strain, he said, "That hurts! Who are you, and what do you want with me?" He half-turned his head to try to see the man's face.

Slapping Joseph's head forward with one hand, he said, "Don't look at me, boy. You don't need to know who I am, except that I'm about to become the worst nightmare you can ever imagine."

Starting from the slap, as well as the pain from the burn scars on his neck, he said, "But I'm nobody. I don't know anything."

"You well know who you are, and why Fatima wants you, so don't play any stupid games with me. You're a problem I'm solving. We've chased you down and caught you. And we have your little girlfriend too."

"What? Who do you mean?"

"That's right; try to pretend. We've got your girl, Rachel. It's over."

They've got her? No. But how did they find me here? No one knew where I was going. Except for Rachel. Oh, God, no ...

"Rachel? Is she okay? Please don't hurt her. You didn't hurt her?"

"That's up to the chief, boy. Who knows what he's done to her? He likes 'em young, so maybe she's all right, as she's an older bitch now. But maybe he's bored with her. So, maybe she's not okay."

"Leave her alone. She hasn't done anything, and neither have I. I'm nobody, just a student working as an intern here for the museum. Please, just let me go. I don't know anything."

Pointing at the violin, which lay upside down in front of Joseph, the man said, "Is this the piece of crap that all this goddamn fucking mess is all about? This stupid fiddle? And you, boy? You look like a piece of crap to me too. So much trouble for a shitty piece of wood and a cripple."

"I'm not a cripple, and it's not a shitty piece of wood, you asshole. It's a violin. Have some respect."

Reaching around with his free hand, the stranger again slapped Joseph hard on the face, causing his entire head to snap back violently. "Watch your mouth, boy. You're speaking to a priest of the Holy Office."

His eyes watering and his face smarting from the blow, he could see the instrument was somehow responding. It started to glow in the pale light, seeming to pulse ominously, the varnish beginning to swirl, and he could hear it too.

Despite the pain in his face, his back, and his wrists, Joseph tried to keep a straight face. *Holy Office, my ass. You bastard.* "No. It's just an old violin I was repairing. It's nothing special."

"Oh, yeah. I'm sure. I was told to collect you and a golden fiddle, and bring you both back to His Grace." He reached for the violin. "So, that's what I'm going to do."

"I wouldn't do that if I were you. I wouldn't touch it."

"What do you mean? Is this stupid fiddle going to bite me or something?"

"It won't bite you, but I can't say for sure just what it might do."

"Boy, I'm not scared of you, or this piece of wooden garbage. It's just a piece of wood His Grace wants to collect." Reaching for the violin while keeping a tight grip of the rope holding Joseph's arms behind him, he continued, "Some crap about a prophecy or something." As he roughly grabbed the violin by its unvarnished neck, Joseph was disappointed though half relieved that nothing unusual happened. "Like I said, it's just a trinket for the chief."

Now sliding his hand down the neck to hold it by the upper bout, he suddenly screamed out in pain. "Goddammit, it's burning my hand. Make it stop! Stop it!" He backed away in agony with the violin stuck to his hand, dropping the rope that had been holding Joseph secure.

Joseph stood up, turned, and looked in horror at the screaming man holding the now strangely altered instrument. It had become like a burning ember in the shape of a violin. There was a strong smell of melted amber and molten resin in the air mixed with that of burnt flesh. The beautiful varnish was glowing red-golden hot as if it had turned into some kind of liquid fire in the man's hand, which now looked to be sinking into the surface of the varnish. The tormented man tried to use his other hand to free the first one, but now both of his hands were stuck fast, being burned and charred by the incandescent red-hot violin.

Joseph pulled his hands free from the rope as the man stumbled about the room, waving the melting-hot instrument this way and that. He continued to scream in agony, seemingly unable to let go of the fiery violin attached to his burning hands. The stench of burned flesh filled the small room, almost choking Joseph, making a sickly-sweet combination with the melted amber smell.

"Give it to me! I tried to warn you," said Joseph, as he reached out with both his hands covered in rags.

The terrified man turned to Joseph, shrieking, "Take it! Take it, please. I can't stand it."

The man's hands were burnt and blackened with his skin starting to peel in places like a barbecued chicken on a white-hot grill.

Joseph was able, with some difficulty, to pry the instrument from the man's flailing grasp, with his screams now turned into anguished, rasping gasps for air as his chest heaved in labored agony. Released from the instrument, at last, he collapsed, breathless, to the floor. Holding up his blackened hands with tears flowing down his face, he panted rapidly. "Help me! My hands... Water. Do you have water?"

Joseph, still holding the violin, stepped back farther from the man and pointed to the sink at the side of the workroom. "There. Run them under cold water; it'll help cool the burns."

The man crawled over, and with more shrieks of pain, unsteadily rose up to the sink, managed to turn on the faucet with his elbow, and ran both hands in the cold water. As he did so, he let loose gasps of relief as the chilled water removed some of the remaining heat in his flesh.

Joseph, taking care to avoid touching the suddenly cool and solid varnish, gently placed the violin back in its case. Still keeping his distance from the distressed man, he reached out and said, "Here are some clean rags you can wrap your hands with."

"No! Stay away from me!" The stranger looked in terror back towards the violin now safely in its case. "You're a devil. He's right about you and that fiddle. It's a tool of the devil. You fucking Jews. All of your kind are of Satan."

Joseph, in horror at what had just happened and the man's hateful words, said, "I'm sorry, but not completely, that you got burned by your own hatred." He reached out again with the pieces of white cotton.

In response, the stranger with wild eyes grabbed the rags and jumped back away from Joseph. Using the cloths, he managed to open the door and ran in panicked flight from the building. Joseph stood for a moment, stunned by what had just occurred, hearing the man's cries and screams fade into the night.

Joseph turned back to his workbench and picked up the violin case. Looking around quickly for the treasure box, he stuffed it into its leather bag, headed in the opposite direction from the stranger to a different door, and stepped outside.

Standing quietly and letting his eyes adjust, he looked for any movement on the museum grounds. There was nothing except for the faint, distant cries of the wounded stranger. After a few minutes, Joseph quietly slipped away into the dark.

Adrenalin still pumping fast in her veins, Rachel ran as fast she could across the parking lot and jumped into her car. Starting the engine, she pulled out into the dark, quiet city of Fatima and made her way towards the outskirts, headed east towards Spain. In the distance, she thought she could hear the wail of an ambulance, as well as multiple police sirens.

Taking a narrow back road, she climbed into the hills, following a small river gorge. Realizing she was still clutching the bloody letter opener in one hand, she slowed for a moment, opened the window, and threw it as far as she could out into the fast-flowing water.

After she had driven for hours deep into the mountains, she pulled over off the road out of sight into a small grove of pines. Stopping the car, her face fell onto her arms on the steering wheel as she cried, full-on tears of despair.

Joseph, Debra... I've lost you both. I have nothing left... nothing at all. What can I do? Where can I go?

Sobbing herself to sleep, utterly exhausted, she dozed for a while on the steering wheel, but suddenly awoke with a start, knowing what she needed to do.

Joseph. He'll go to the villa. That's it. I'll go to Italy to search for him at the Villa. I'll search every villa there until I find him. I'll ask him to forgive me. Joseph, I love you. Can you hear me now? I love you. I love you. I'll love you forever.

Blue and amber blinking strobe lights illuminated the dark night around him as he was loaded into the ambulance. Cardinal DeSilva, his voice and mind dulled by morphine, his face and belly heavily bandaged, called Servino to his side. Speaking in a hoarse, gasping whisper, he said, "Find her and kill her. Now!"

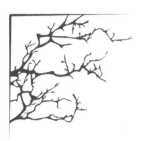

Thirty-four

SOMEWHERE IN PORTUGAL
April 21, 1986

Rachel drove for hours into the night before she dared to stop at a small hotel in a high mountain town. She pulled into the gravel parking lot behind the rough stone buildings and opened the car door. Stepping out, she heard the tiny clinks and tinkles of small shards of glass falling off of her torn and bloody sweatshirt and jeans.

With the realization that some of the blood was likely DeSilva's, her stomach heaved in disgust at the thought. Unable to stop it, nature emptied what little was in her belly onto the ground. Spitting out the acid taste of vomit in her mouth, she stopped to shake and carefully brush off her clothes as more glass pieces fell to the gravel. Turning to look at herself by dim, cloudy moonlight in the side mirror, she was shocked at the sight. "Hell. I look and feel like a used-up extra in a zombie movie."

Nearby, she could hear the soothing sound of a small mountain stream tumbling over a waterfall into a pool at the back of the gravel lot. After picking more glass off the car seat, she moved her car close to the water and, in the darkness, washed her face and mouth in the cascade while standing on a small patch of soft green grass. Gingerly taking off her shoes, pants, and shirt, she prepared to change into clean ones that were not torn and bloody.

Small cuts and abrasions on her arms and legs crying out with various levels of pain drew her attention as she changed.

Oh god. I've got cuts all over me. I just threw myself through French doors and was shot at twice. What a mess I'm in.

Standing nearly naked in the cold night air, she dabbed at the cuts with a clean piece of clothing dipped into the icy water. After a lot of careful wiping with the cold, wet cloth, she was starting to feel somewhat refreshed though thoroughly chilled. Examining her skin by cloud-covered full moonlight, she was relieved to see that none of the blood-covered places on her skin seemed too severely cut. Shaking out her shoes to make sure all the glass shards were gone, she finished dressing in several clean, warm layers. Some of the clothes were a tight fit since she had brought them for her younger sister to wear.

Debra, my sweet sister, gone forever. I couldn't save you. I'm so sorry, my little girl. I'll never be the same without you.

Her pain quickly turned to anger.

If I only could have had a bit more time to finish that bastard off. Stabbing him in the heart would have been perfect!

Sitting by the small waterfall, she let the sound soothe her agitated mind and broken heart. After a while, feeling quite chilled, she finally got up off the grass and braced herself to check into the hotel and get some badly needed rest.

But first, she needed to dispose of the blood-splattered clothing. Seeing a small trash dumpster nearby, she opened the lid and carefully, to avoid any remaining glass shards, stuffed the items deep into the back.

With her small suitcase in hand and a more relaxed expression on her face, she stepped into the small lobby. A sleepy-eyed young woman, awakened by the front desk bell, asked few questions as she took the fake passport Rachel handed her in exchange for a key. Up in her room, with a sigh of relief, she collapsed into the bed fully clothed, with only her tennis shoes remaining on the floor.

Closing the doors to the ambulance after one last look at his mutilated and possibly dying boss, Servino turned to the group of guards gathered around him. "Have you had the national police put out an alert with her photo and description?"

"Yes, Father... pardon me, Monsignor."

"You may address me as Father. I am in charge with the cardinal indisposed, but I am still just a simple priest."

"As you wish, Father. All agencies have been alerted and supplied with a full description of the car along with the plate number and a photo of her."

"Good, she could not have gotten far. And they know this is a Church matter?"

"Yes, as you requested."

In a deadly cold voice, Servino replied, "The witch will not live long to regret her actions, and it will not be a pleasant time for her. She attempted to murder the cardinal who will be our next pope. She will pay for that."

"Yes, Father. Shall we eliminate her when she is found?"

"No. Before we send her to hell where she belongs, we need to use her to find the boy. Be sure to track her credit card. Keep it open and funded so she will leave us and the police a trail to follow."

"When we find her, should we bring her to you here in Fatima?"

"No. Pass the word to all authorities, branches of the Office, and agents in the Church to track and locate her, but request that they do not show themselves or scare her with their presence. We need her to lead us to the boy and the other subject of our search. We have agents everywhere, each with two eyes. She cannot elude us."

Rachel awoke after a restless and short night's sleep. It seemed every time she had closed her eyes, she had the same nightmare, recalling DeSilva and Servino sexually abusing her as a girl of only fourteen. She dreamed that they had her again, still having their way with her, and Joseph was there standing apart, watching in disgust, as he then turned and walked away, leaving her in their greasy hands. She tried to call out to him, begging him not to leave her, but she had no voice. In the dream, his name caught in her throat. Waking with a start, she realized she was saying his name out loud.

Shaking from the dream, she sat up with her back against the plastered stone wall, trying to wake up.

Quickly showering, dressing, and packing her small bag, she hurried down to the front desk.

"Is there a place to fill up with petrol here in town?" Rachel asked the hotel clerk, an older woman this time.

"Si, Senora. Just down the road and up the first side street, there is an auto repair shop that sells petrol. But, Senora, do you know where it is you are going?"

"What? Yes, you just told me."

"No, I mean, where you are *really* going. Your destination."

Puzzled, Rachel looked more closely at the white-haired woman and saw piercing blue eyes that seemed to be looking right through her. Eyes that seemed so familiar. *Who is she?* "What do you mean, where am I going?"

Rachel stood stunned as she could feel the woman answering her without words.

"What you are seeking is the Villa of the Forever View, of Portofino."

Letting this strange experience wash over her, she continued looking into those eyes, and said, "Who are you and how do you know this?"

Silently, from within Rachel's mind, the woman answered. *"You know who I am, Rachel. Go and find him. He needs your love and your help."*

Still standing at the counter, stunned by this inner exchange, all Rachel could say was, "Thank you." The name formed in her mind. *Miriam.* Startled by this, she stared intently at the woman as she handed over cash for the room and breakfast.

"Yes, you do indeed know," the woman said, adding silently inside Rachel's mind, *"Tikkum Olam, Rachel. Go now. Quickly. They are coming after you. Shalom."*

As she walked to her car, Rachel attempted to digest this exchange, stunned at what had just transpired. But now re-energized and feeling hopeful once more, she set out to find her lover.

Driving by the auto shop, she saw they had a few used cars for sale, and a solution occurred to her. Instead of buying gas, she followed another side road up into the hills and found a thick grove of trees with a faint track leading into them, and drove the rental car deep into the woods and stripped anything from it that identified the rental agency. Pulling some small pine branches off nearby trees, she covered the light blue car to hide it from the lower road.

Finally, using a blade from her pocket knife, she unscrewed both license plates from the car and threw them far off into the woods. Carrying her bag, she set off back down the road to the shop, stopping at the start of the faint road, she looked back to see if the car was visible. Satisfied that she had obscured any causal view of it, she walked back downhill and along the main road to the repair shop.

She had used the church credit card to fly to Lisbon and rent the car. But now to help her disappear, she could no longer use it, even though the money backing it was hers. With cash she had drawn from the account at the airport in Lisbon, Rachel bought a small used car and headed deeper into the mountains towards the border with Spain.

"Father Servino, our agent we sent to South Dakota to apprehend the boy is in a hospital burn ward with his hands almost destroyed by some kind of infernal fire."

"How was he burned? And how did the boy elude him?"

"He claims the violin caught fire in his hands, but only his hands burned. The violin appeared unharmed. We believe the boy still has it, but he is gone. We have no idea where he is."

"How dare you report such news to me? Both the girl and boy are gone, and no one can find them. Our future pope is barely clinging to life, disfigured and damaged. One of my agents claims he is burned by satanic fire from some ungodly Jewish magic fiddle. Go. Get out of my sight! And do not come back until you have found those two and that damn fiddle as well!"

As Joseph flew across the Atlantic Ocean, comfortably seated in a first-class seat with no one next to him, his nerves that had been so frayed by the horror of his near escape finally started to relax. The violin was safely resting in its case in the overhead bin. But despite the physical separation between it and him, or because of it, he could feel its energy, and hear it in his mind, calling out to him.

"I am here. I am yours; you are mine. I am ready for the journey, our journey, ready to take you with me ..."

Shaking his head back and forth, he tried to clear away the sounds that were echoing in his mind. Whispering to himself, he said, as if to calm the haunting call, "Not yet. Not here. Be patient. Not yet. But what? What journey?"

The ethereal female voice continued for a while, pleading with him and pulling on his heart and mind.

"Come with me. Follow me. You, your hands, made me..."

What? My hands? I didn't... It's like the first time I was near it, feeling like I'm being pulled towards a sweet, enticing danger that is both intoxicating and perilous. I feel like there's a vast space beneath me, that I'm about to fall into it. I need to meditate...

After a time of deep, slow breaths and soft-focused attention, the voice finally quieted to a low, insistent whisper that allowed him to concentrate on what he needed to do next.

He thought he knew where he was headed, where he needed to go. To the location revealed in the puzzle box the last time he had examined it. He had been turning it about in his hands with the lid off and running his fingers around the inside when he had apparently triggered another secret compartment to open.

Portofino, Italy, I've never even heard of the place. I don't know what I will find there if there is anything to see. How did my family ever get a place like this?

He looked at the small photo of the multi-storied red-roofed building clinging to a cliff face overlooking the Mediterranean Sea. The picture had been hidden in an additional secret chamber in the box, inside and under the bottom panel.

The letter from his father that had been under the diamonds and gold coins had mentioned a villa in Italy as part of Joseph's inheritance. The letter did not say where it was located or how to find it, but this new discovery provided that missing information.

On the back of the photo was an address with directions from Genoa, Italy, and the transliterated Hebrew words, Tikkun O`lam.

Healing of the worlds. I have now seen and heard these words so many times in the last few months, but I'm still not sure of what they really are, and just what they mean for me. What am I supposed to do? Maybe at the villa, I will find some answers.

The writing on the back of the photo had continued in English. *'The answers you need to seek, the mystery that calls to you, are within the walls of our home, Villa of the Forever View, at the heart of our innermost sanctuary. Seek, and you will find that which is beyond your imagination and deeper than your dreams. Kadosh, Kadosh, Kadosh.'*

The last three words were in what he realized was transliterated Hebrew that he remembered seeing in the prayer book at the Friday night service in

Salt Lake City. *It means, Holy, Holy, Holy... Where Rachel had introduced me to my heritage.*

Rachel, his body tensed at the thought of her. God, he'd loved that girl. She changed his life, but he hated her for her betrayal. He could blame her for all this, for everything that'd happened to him, but maybe it was all going to happen anyway.

I hate her and love her. But how can I hate and love at the same time?

Thinking of all this, his heart and mind tormented, he finally fell asleep for some hours, only waking when the descent to London was announced.

Opening and gazing at his picture in the very official-looking passport he had just acquired, he once again appreciated what Rachel had said to him that, 'money could buy discretion, privacy, and comfort.'

Looking at the name on the passport, he knew that even as Joseph Sutherland he could still access all of his funds anywhere in the world, thanks to the 'complete service' offered by his private bank. And now with his hair dyed jet-black and cut very short, dressed in his new Italian suit, he wondered if even Rachel would recognize him.

Leaving the small town near the top of the mountains in a hurry to cover more ground, Rachel drove by an old crumbling convent and chapel complex on the outskirts. She saw the old nun standing by the still intact chapel door. But she did not see the nun comparing the written description in her hand to Rachel's appearance, as she wrote down the number of her car's backplate.

"Father Servino, we have a report from La Rabaza village near the Spanish border of a woman matching her description driving through."

"Did the agent get the plate number?"

"Yes, Father. Should we intercept her?"

"No, let her go on. Have agents positioned to spot her as she enters Spain. She will lead us to the boy in due time."

After driving from the airport at Genoa in his new Italian sports car, Joseph checked the map once more in the attractive—despite the cloudy, wet weather—village of Portofino. The faded pastel-colored buildings lightened his heart a bit before he set out once more on the narrow two-lane road that followed the small inlets and bays of the craggy coast. The violin was in its case on the front seat next to him. It was still calling out to him as it had the entire trip, in a continuous chanting and haunting voice. But now, as he drew closer to the villa, the voice was so present in his mind that he almost couldn't tell the difference between its, *her* voice, and his thoughts. *We are one. We are one body. Together, we are Tikkum Olam.*

The narrow curving road he had driven from Portofino followed the hillsides and cliff faces above several small bays. The slopes were covered with the lush greenery of grapevines, olive, palms, and pines, with tall cypresses sending their spiky branches into the sky. He passed many colorfully painted villas perched high on the hillsides or on the narrow spaces between the road and the sea. Ascending back up from one larger bay, he came upon a tight curve where the road cut through a hillside extending to form a peninsula reaching out into the sea. As he rounded the curve, there before him was the address from the back of the photo. *16039 Villa Vista Per Sempre.* Thinking of his father's letter, he knew precisely what this Italian name meant. "Villa of the Forever View."

I'm home. My family home... at last. Safe. But with so many questions. And maybe, some answers.

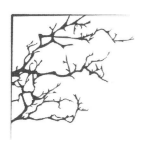

Thirty-five

VILLA VISTA PER SEMPRE, Portofino, Italy
April 22, 1986

When he saw the sign for the villa, Joseph stopped his car and parked next to a tall curving wall of stone. The rough wall was not long across the narrow peninsula, but reached high over his head, blocking any view of what lay beyond. He rolled down his windows despite the cool air, and he could smell the refreshing scent of salt rising from the sea. Listening, he heard the gentle lapping of small waves against the rocky shores in the two bays that embraced the narrow point of land.

He sat in the car for a moment, dazzled at how far his life had come in such a short time, wondering if any of this was truly real, or if somehow, he could be dreaming it all. These last two months were a blur. So much to digest, so much that had happened.

As he thought, he looked over at the violin in its case on the front seat next to him. Looking away from it but quickly looking back, he felt he could almost see a glow of some kind around it. It seemed as if some sort of energy was emanating from the violin, coming through the case that enclosed it.

Tearing his gaze from it, he closed his eyes for a moment to rest his vision, thinking his eyes were just tired. But he immediately opened them again, startled by what he had seen. With his eyes closed, he had seen the violin floating in a dark space in front of his eyes, looking like it had when the Office agent had grabbed it, with flames emanating from and around it, as a glowing hot, red-golden halo.

Joseph, now losing control and finding he could not stop himself, closed his eyes once more and saw the same vision again.

The glowing vision before him answered, *"We are home. We are here. I am in you. You are in me, my master. Ready... ready to serve you now. My power is your power. Nothing can stop us."*

Then, seeing the transparent face of Rachel floating in front of the violin, he heard it say, "*You need her. She completes you. Call out to her now.*"

Responding within his mind, he replied, *Take it easy. Give me a chance to catch up... Who, me, your master?*

"*Yes. You know who you are. She is your ...*"

Rachel. She betrayed me, almost got me killed.

"*She is your beshert. The other half of your soul.*"

My soul? She broke my heart. She hurt me too much.

"*You need her help. You cannot live without her. Call out to her. Draw her to you.*"

I can't do that. I can't forgive her. I won't.

"*You must. You have no choice. Now your teachers await.*"

With that, the vision abruptly vanished into darkness, and the voice was silent. For the first time in as many days since he had returned to the violin and finished repairing it, a vast, quiet emptiness filled him.

Joseph, feeling the loss of that interior presence, the stark sudden quiet, opened his eyes and let out a gasp, tears forming in his eyes. "Oh, God."

With tears running down his face and looking again at the violin case beside him on the car seat, seeing and hearing nothing, he felt complete emptiness. Like he was a blank slate ready to be written on. Breathing deeply, he gradually calmed and found himself surprisingly at peace. Somehow, he now felt okay.

After sitting in his car for a while, as occasional other cars drove past him while breathing deeply to settle his mind, he brought his attention back to where he was.

Stirring from the car seat, he spoke out loud as if to admonish his inertia. "I have to get going and see just who or what is here at this villa, waiting for me."

He looked out the car window and could see in the wall that some of the stones appeared to be marble and were carved with half-visible, battered shapes of human or animal figures. Other pieces and fragments were cut into intricate regular patterns and curved flowing shapes. They looked like broken-off carved leaves and foliage, like perhaps parts of ancient buildings, like he had seen in archaeology books. Examining the stones seemed to give him a physical anchor point, bringing his awareness back to his body, grounding him. To what was real, or what seemed real.

Stepping out of the car, he looked more closely at the jigsaw puzzle wall with its mixture of carved stones, rough, raw stones, and large patches of ancient-looking battered brickwork.

I've read about stuff like this. They must be from Roman times when the coastline here had villas overlooking the sea. I remember reading about one of them they've excavated somewhere near here. I wonder if this villa was one of them. Could it be that ancient?

He walked from one length of the wall to the other and could see the ends were part of sheer cliffs falling to the sea below. Over the top, in places, he could see thick trees that reached even higher into the gray, cloudy sky. Tearing his gaze from the beautiful, though damaged, marble blocks, he walked up to the wide, tall metal gateway in the middle of the wall.

The gate was set into a high curved stone archway decorated with sharper and somewhat newer carving, framing the sides and top. Intertwining leafy vines with bunches of grapes could be seen on the raised relief fluted stone pillars on either side. And on the top, he saw what looked to be a coat of arms of some sort. Standing before it and looking closely, he could make out at the top above, the figure of a rearing lion wearing a crown, and what seemed to be a large carved candle holder with eight candles on it. On each side of the lions' heads, he could see two groups of what looked to be carved Hebrew letters.

Noticing two other shapes, one on each side, he stood still, gazing at them high above.

Are those violins carved into the stone?

"Father Servino, our agents are following her at a distance, so as not to alert her."

"Very good. We need to track her as we must find the boy and what he is carrying with him before it is too late."

"Yes, Father."

"You are dismissed."

The young priest turned to leave, walking towards the carved doors of the cardinal's office, but upon reaching them, he stopped and added, "There is one more minor item to follow up on, Father. Did you have any further instructions regarding the file I left on your desk yesterday?"

"What file? Where did you leave it?"

"On the back of your desk, Father."

"I did not see it yet. What does it say?"

"One of our operatives at the Swiss bank Credit Suisse noted some unusual activity on a long-dormant account. It is one of many that date back to before the war. It is a very old account."

"What do you mean? What kind of activity, and why are you only telling me this now? Is it one of the possible hidden Jewish accounts?" Servino asked sharply.

"We did not think it could have any relation to this case. But yes, it might be a Jewish one."

"You 'think' it might be one of the Jewish accounts? I do not expect you to think, but to just report to me, and then do as I so order."

"Your pardon, Father Servino. Yes, of course."

"So, is this true?"

"The agent did not realize that there might be a connection, as the account in question has shown no activity since 1967."

"Since when? Did you say 1967?" *That is when the operation was conducted to first eliminate this threat.* "Is there more information, like a name connected to the account, a physical location, or any identifier?"

"Father, as you know, that information is closely guarded by the Swiss. Our agent will need to be very careful, so they do not lose their job at the bank."

"I don't give a Holy Hell if he gets fired or not! I need to know that information. Now. That account may be the source of the funds allowing the boy to escape our agents."

"I will so order the agent."

"No. Give me the contact information. I will call him myself at the bank and require him to extract the name or names associated with that account. If I need to, I will threaten him with the full power of the Holy Office."

Somewhat shaken, the young priest replied, "Yes, Father. As you wish."

"And are there any newer reports on the boy?"

"As I reported in the written report previously, he was possibly seen at London Heathrow airport..."

"And when did you submit this report to me?"

"Ah, let me think. I believe it was two days ago, Father."

"Two days ago, you believe it was? And you did not report this to me in person?"

"No. You were with the cardinal, and we did not wish to disturb your bedside vigil. It was also placed on your desk."

"Where?"

The young priest walked to the desk and handed Servino the reports. "Here you are, Father, and here is the one regarding the Swiss account. But to continue, he was in a private part of the terminal, and our agents could not pursue him there to find out his next move."

"A private part of the terminal? They could not use their credentials to follow him?"

"No. The British authorities stopped them from entering." As Servino read both reports, the priest continued. "The Brits are not too keen on the Holy Office. Most of them are atheists or Church of England, and are not very cooperative."

"Well, that will change in time. All of them everywhere will bow down to Our Lady of Fatima when Her Rule covers the entire Earth. But in the meantime, our agents must not be so timid to let that boy slip through their fingers like that."

Holding the paper in his hands, Servino stalked up to the priest, standing just six inches from the young man's face, his voice rising sharply in volume. "From now on, you or your replacement will bring all reports on this operation directly to my hands, no matter where I am, or what time of the day or night!" Finally, shouting directly into the priest's face, he added, "Is that understood?"

The young priest backed away from this frontal assault and managed to mumble, "Well, we still... we thought he could not go far, or not much farther, with no money to spend."

"You fool! You thought? Father, do not think. That is not your job. To travel like that, he must be tapping into some serious funds."

"Yes, Father. Of course, you are right."

"I think that perhaps you need to be transferred, Father? To somewhere far away from here. Now, get out of my sight."

The now severely frightened priest half bowed and made a hasty retreat, backing out through the ornate office doors.

Driving down the Spanish mountains towards Madrid, Rachel had started to notice two similar-looking black cars that occasionally passed her, but now and then, appeared by the side of the roadway stopped, and then afterward, overtook and went by her again. The training she had received to become an Office agent had alerted her to watch for patterns like this type of odd driver behavior.

Realizing she was somehow being tracked, she abruptly turned south onto the sizable circular freeway interchange south of Plasencia just as one of the black cars passed her. As she did, the black vehicle pulled over, backed up and turned onto the large freeway roundabout to follow her. Now she had no doubt she was being followed.

Increasing her speed, she drove around the large circle many times, moving faster each time. Coaching herself out loud, she said, "Stay calm. Stay calm. You can do this. You can find a way out of this."

Other drivers, used to seeing fast cars on this roadway, were nevertheless startled at her speed, and at times had to dodge out of her way as she repeatedly whipped around the large circle.

The gloomy last remaining daylight had faded entirely by then, with the sky now fully dark. With the waning full moon not yet up to illuminate the clouds, she had an idea and suddenly turned off her headlights as she headed halfway around to the north side once more, and at high speed, peeled off onto the northbound lanes. Continuing on the highway for a few miles with no lights at all, being careful of other cars, she first turned on her parking lights, and after a few more miles, the headlights once more. As she approached a side road leading towards Plasencia, she turned off and drove into the city, apparently having lost her tails back at the roundabout.

Driving into the old town, she found a half-hidden side street where she could leave her car with the keys in the ignition as an open invitation to anyone who would like to 'adopt' it. Looking around her at the somewhat shabby workaday city, she thought it would disappear quite soon.

With her small bag in hand, she made her way past the young men of the town who decorated the various street corners, frankly gazing at her with appreciation, and the other young women who were strolling the streets in small groups. Boys watching the girls, and the girls eyeing the boys. *Ah, for the simple pleasures of life.* She longed for once to just be, and maybe join in the evening fun of the Paseo. *But that's not for me. Not now and perhaps never again.*

Reaching the main square, she spotted what looked to be one of the nicer hotels in town. Ducking inside, she registered with one of her emergency passports, a Canadian one this time, and paid for the night. Upstairs in her room, she stepped out onto the balcony overlooking the plaza. Pulling a chair from inside, she sat back almost inside the room, out of sight from the street below, and watched the men and women of the town as they walked around the stone-paved square and small park. They circled the square where a lively fountain was spraying up a shower of water added sound and refreshing moisture to the otherwise mostly dry, stone streets. A half-hour of watching and seeing no one who looked out of place caused her to feel secure and relaxed that she had lost her pursuers.

Now daring to step out onto the street, she bought some new clothes and essentials, followed by a delicious meal in the hotel restaurant. Finally, at a tourist agency on the plaza, she bought a bus ticket to leave early in the morning for Madrid. Turning in for the night, Rachel lay on the bed, wide awake, softly crying to herself for a long time. She was thinking about Joseph, how much she missed and loved him, and called out to him in her mind. *"Joseph, please. Please forgive me. I love you so much. Please, please forgive me. Please let me back into your life."* With these last thought before slipping into dreams or nightmares, she blew him a kiss, thanking him for the bank account he created for her that allowed her to escape from Fatima, before falling into a deep, exhausted sleep.

After seeing what she thought might be agents outside her hotel the next morning, the relaxation Rachel had started to feel, now was quickly lost. She had seen two men in the crowd, having a morning stroll, who, to her trained eyes, looked just a bit out of place.

Oh god. I was sure I'd lost them at the roundabout, but somehow, they followed me.

Leaving the hotel via the back-delivery door, she quickly made her way to the bus station. She had tied up her long hair into a bun and covered it, and half of her face, with a black scarf. Carefully watching for any likely agents, she got onto the bus to Madrid.

Later, boarding her flight to Genoa, Rachel was feeling a bit more refreshed and rested as she settled into her large, soft, first-class seat. She had slept well in the comfortable bus seat on the three-hour ride to Madrid and then booked a ticket for the short flight to Genoa. She had not spotted anyone who looked like an office agent on the bus or at the Madrid airport. Her self-confidence was starting to return, and with the help of the complimentary champagne, she was looking forward to seeing Joseph again. Not without apprehension, but feeling more hopeful that their love could be healed and rekindled.

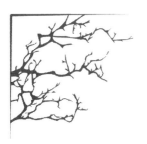

Thirty-six

GENOA, ITALY
   April 22, 1986

Rachel rapidly walked up the long sloping tunnel from her plane into the Genoa airport concourse. She carefully peeked over her shoulder every so often to check the faces of her fellow travelers. None seemed familiar, like they could be Office agents, or like the two she had seen that morning, but she was gaining a new respect for Servino's other agents.

They're damn good. A lot better than I thought. I guess I'm not the only one who was skillfully trained to follow a target.

Her pride in being one of Servino's top agents had taken a blow.

Outside, she hailed a taxi, to quickly get going and try to leave any invisible tails behind her.

"Portofino, perfavore, Signore."

"Si, si, bella Signora. You are, ah, English? Speak Italiano?"

"American. Si, a little, but yes, please. English is easier for me."

"Okay. Mota expensive to Portofino? A-okay?"

Rachel pulled out a roll of crisp high-value Lira bills, holding them up for the driver to see. "Can you be quick?"

"Ah, si, si, Signora. No problem. Pronto," replied the driver as he quickly swerved out into the airport traffic, dodging between other taxis, causing several to sound their horns and slam on their brakes to avoid hitting them.

As they sped away from the airport and out onto the coast roadway, she thought about Joseph.

I don't know if he will scream at me or even speak to me. But I need to see him. I've got to try to heal our love, our bond. We are connected over space and time. I've never felt this way about anyone. I'm so much in love with him. What I feel for him... is beyond anything I ever ... Adonai, Shekhinah, bless me. Help me.

Joseph stood before the tall rusty-red double gate, looking for a way to open it. There were short open bars set close together high up at the top, but most of the metal of the gate was flat and roughly covered with rust. There was not even a keyhole showing. Taking hold of one side, he rattled it to see if it just might break open on its own. The only result was a shower of red dust and flakes smelling of salt and iron falling all over him. Coughing and spitting at the bitter iron taste in his mouth, he stepped back a few feet to consider his options.

Stepping back farther, he gazed along the wall, again walking from one end to the other, looking for another way over or around. But even though the surface was rough and uneven, it seemed too steep to climb.

Coming back to the gate, he noticed near the middle edge of the right half of the gate, where a large amount of rust had fallen loose, that there appeared to be an additional irregular area of metal. Looking more closely, he could see the piece seemed to be a sculpted or shaped form. Scraping at it with his fingernails and car key, more of the rust fell away until he could make out that it was a rearing lion wearing a crown. Near the top part, at the lion's neck, it was fixed with a corroded pin embedded into the gate.

He pushed on it in one direction and then the opposite, trying to slide it against the surrounding flat surface. Finding it to be rusted solid, he looked around and picked up a fist-sized rock laying near the wall, using it to strike the edge of the overlaid metal. With each blow, more rust fell off the shape, and from between it and the gate. Finally, after pushing it back and forth many times, he was able to move the lion piece just enough to see an old-fashioned keyhole hidden behind it. Looking into the key-hole, the metal looked clean, almost new-looking.

Picking more loose rust from the lion and looking at the keyhole, Joseph remembered that his father had mentioned a key in the inheritance letter. He didn't realize it might be referring to a literal key to the front door when he and Rachel first read it. He recalled some words that sounded like poetry when he first saw them, something like, *'Find the key... the heart of all things. The warmth of your love... doors open.'*

Speaking his thoughts out-loud, he struggled to understand. "All things. Heart of all things? The warmth of love? Doors open? Is there a key hidden somewhere? Here? The letter. I've got to re-read it. I've got it here in the box."

He walked back to his car from the gate but first stopped and turned to gaze up again at the carved coat of arms high above it. He saw there what he had seen when he first looked at it; two violins, one on either side and in the middle, a rearing lion with a crown. And now he saw the lion was clutching a large old-style key to its breast.

The only thing I can think of is the treasure box. Could it contain another secret? A hidden key?

Walking back to his car, he reached into the leather bag and lifted out the beautifully carved and inlaid box. Moving the violin case to the back seat, and sitting down on the front passenger seat with the box on his lap, he tried to remember the correct combination to unlock it, the right order of pushing on the series of linked circles of wood and brass. The last time he had opened it, at the bank in San Francisco, Rachel had reminded him then of the correct combination.

Looking at the box with its arrangement of circles and lines, he remembered what she had told him about it. That it resembled a tree in shape, showing the form of the inner Tree of Life of mystical energy centers, the Ten Sephirot within the human body. He looked at them carefully and began to push them in one at a time, in what he thought was the right order. Nothing happened when he finished.

Starting again, he tried different combinations with the same result. Frustrated, he sat, trying to recall the exact sequence she had used.

Giving himself a pep talk, he tried to focus. "Okay, calm down. What did she teach me about my body... how to channel energy in my spine?" Remembering her lessons, he settled down and tried to meditate, quietly sitting as he held the box in his hands, inhaling deeply and slowly. He visualized the colors of each Sephirot, starting with seeing a glowing red light at the base of his spine. Then orange at his belly, yellow-gold at his heart on both sides, and green at his throat. Then blue on both sides of his shoulders, violet on both sides of his eyes at his forehead, and finally, white at the crown of his head.

After a while when his mind had grown calmer as he breathed in and out, moving light and energy up and down the spine, he found he could see Rachel doing the correct sequence to open the box.

Trying it once more, he recalled that she had zigzagged through the circles. Closing his eyes, he could hear her voice as she went through the Sephirot on the tree, and he could see her pushing the correct combination.

So, first, push Keter, the crown, then push Chochmah, wisdom, to the right. Then back to Binah, understanding, on the left. Then zag down to Chesed, kindness, then straight across to Gevurah, power, then what was it? Oh, yes, right in the middle. Tiferet, beauty, just like Rachel. Then zagging down to the right to Netzach, eternity, and straight across to Hod, adornment. Pushing each circle in turn and hearing the clicks of each one and the parts of the lock disengaging, he knew he was almost there. *Now the foundation, Yesod, and finally at the far bottom end of the box, Malchut, grounding.*

With the last louder click, he knew he had finally gotten it right with the opening of the box. Lifting off the lid, he looked inside.

He felt with his fingers and looked under the parchment letter and purple and red velvet, but didn't find a key.

Now, with the box open, he turned it around in his hands, tipping out the letter and cloth on the seat next to him, and felt the edges of the underside of the lid.

There must be another hidden catch here somewhere, like how we found the Swiss bank account number and the picture of this villa.

Pressing on each part of the lid and lower part of the box, he could not find any feature that might be a hidden lever or button. The wood joints that made up the box were so tight and perfect that he wondered how there could be anything more than what he had previously found.

Then, remembering his father's letter again, he unfolded and read it through once more. He noticed that a small piece of the parchment, with some of the Hebrew writing that Rachel had said, spelled his name, was missing. Not seeing the fragment, he went on to read the entire letter once more.

'December 21, 1966, Vina, California.

To my son, Yosef ben Daveed, on this, your twenty-first birthday.

I am so proud of you and the man you have become today, and of all that you have, I am sure, accomplished in your life so far.

As I am writing this to you when you are only two years old for you to read this day when you have turned twenty-one, I can only dream of your future growth.

All these long years, I hope we have enjoyed our loving father-son relationship with your mother helping both of us along our way. But in case you are reading this when we are no longer here with you to guide and protect you, if Adoni has seen fit to take us, or our enemies have found us, then I can only hope that those we have arranged to care for you will have guided and protected you well.'

As he had when he first read those words, Joseph stopped with tears running down his face. He had to move the letter farther from him to avoid the teardrops hitting the stiff parchment.

"I never knew them. Why? Why did they have to die and leave me when I was so young? I was just a baby."

After all that had happened, he knew that it must have been the Church who were 'our enemies.'

Now surrendering to his overwhelming grief and loss, he no longer noticed that his tears were falling freely onto the letter. As when he had read it before, there was a large blank space in the message before his father's final words and signature at the bottom, except for this time, where his tears had hit the parchment, bits, and pieces of letters were appearing.

He started rubbing the tears around and touched his wet eyes to add more to his fingertips. As he did so, the writing gradually began to be readable as pink letters and words.

'I will have taught you by now most all of our family secrets, though there are more you will discover on your own. Most importantly, the special heritage that you have inherited from my father and me, going back in an unbroken line to the founder of our family. To our, to your, direct forefather, David, the shepherd boy....'

King David. No way. That can't be true.

But there it was, written in invisible ink, in a sealed letter written by his father.

So, I'm supposed to be a direct descendant of King David? I wish Rachel were here, to see this. Could I even trust her not to tell those goons? Inside his heart, he knew he could trust her with this, with anything Jewish.

He closed his eyes and decided to try to call out to her, concentrating with all of his focus and intention.

Rachel, I'm sorry. So sorry. I miss you. Hear me. Come to me now. Find me. I love you. I need you. I miss you so much.

He kept up this call for many minutes, picturing her face, her smile, how she felt when they made love together. Pulling on that mysterious place of connection they had felt with each other, reaching out as far as he could, he called out to his lover, to try to draw her to him.

Not sure what he would feel or expect after doing this, he suddenly felt drained, as if a part of himself had shot deeply into space, leaving him exhausted. After a while, recovering his energy with his tears still falling on the letter, he kept on reading the newly revealed writing.

'...who soothed the troubled soul of King Saul with his harp playing.

My son, as you can see, I have hidden this part of my letter so no one can read it but you.'

At this, he reached the part he and Rachel had read before. *'Here is our family's precious Sperot puzzle box, which you will find has layers of mysteries. When you have solved them, one by one, you will discover some of your inheritance. The rest is in the Swiss account I have told you of, and at our villa in Portofino. I trust that by now, you will have spent many happy summers there with your mother and me.*

But now, with your coming of age according to secular society, the villa is yours along with all of its secrets that I will have shown you, and others that you will need to solve on your own. Your mother and I will continue to enjoy it with you as long as we both shall live.

You will find the key to unlock everything at the heart of our family, the center of all things. With the warmth of our love that you hold in your hands, all doors will open to you.

Your loving father, Daveed ben Yosef David Davidson'

Finally, at a loss as to what to try next, he once more sat, holding the empty box with his eyes closed and again slowed his breath into a meditative pace. The box sat between his knees on the car seat with his hands resting on either side of the open lid. For about ten minutes, he continued the slow breathing through the rainbow colors in his spine. As he sat with the box lid in his hands, he thought he could feel the wood inside the top of the cover gradually warming up in response to his touch as an aroma like beeswax tickled his nose. It almost felt like the inside of the lid was wax, or was coated with it. Distracted by the sensations, he looked more closely at the inside of the top and saw a shape emerging from the previously flat wooden surface. Tracing the form with his finger and eye, he realized it was heart-shaped.

Continuing to hold the lid and pressing on it tightly as the warmth in the surface increased, he soon saw the heart-shaped piece of wood, cut from precisely the same wood grain as its surroundings, rise up and emerge from the inside of the lid. Excitedly, he used a fingernail to pry the piece up and out of its wax bedding, and reaching into the softened wax underneath, pried out a key.

Setting the box back into its bag along with the letter next to the violin case, Joseph almost ran to the rusty gate to see if the key might fit. Inserting it into the hole, it fitted smoothly. Turning the key, with a click, it came unlocked. Reaching between the two halves of the gate, he pulled at the edge of one side. At first it would not move, but finally, with all of his strength, came loose with loud creaking and swung open just wide enough for him to start to slip his slim body inside.

As he squeezed into the narrow gap, he stopped suddenly as the burn scars on his back scraped against the edge of the opening. Stopping himself due to the pain, he carefully backed out of the opening. But then he thought he heard a sound, a soft cry of some kind. He turned to look around to see if anyone was there but then realized the voice was inside his mind.

"Wait. Don't... don't leave me..."

The violin had been quiet since he arrived at the villa, but now he remembered it, as it, *she*, called out to him. He walked back to the car and grabbed the bag with the treasure box and the violin in its case then headed back to the gate. Setting them down and stopping to look inside, he could see what seemed to be the beginning of a tunnel carved out of the rock of the hillside. Pushing once more with all of his strength, he managed to open the gate a bit wider.

Joseph stepped through the now wider gap into the cool semi-darkness and walked through into the dimly lit tunnel. It looked wide enough to drive a horse and carriage or a small car through.

He could smell the scent of damp, musty stone mixed with the ever-present salt air of the sea, overlaid with the smell of the soft moss that covered parts of the walls and roof of the rough stone tunnel where the pale sunlight reached. After walking for some paces into the tunnel and finding himself in deep darkness, he stopped to get his bearings. In the quiet, without the sound of his shoes scuffing the sand-covered rocky floor, the soft, distant sounds of small waves hitting the rocky shore could be heard, encouraging him to keep going. Finally, he started to see more light coming from his left, and there was a bend in the tunnel with brighter light showing.

Approaching the light, he broke through into the welcome but gloomy cloud-obscured sunlight. Taking a deep breath of the clean sea air, he looked about at this place that was apparently his family home. In front of him was a tall stone, brick, and plaster building, with three or more red tile roof lines, and balconies at different levels, with at least four stories; a sight that caused his breath to catch in his throat.

Before him and around the buildings were scattered groups of olive, fig, lemon, and orange trees. The trees all looked to be struggling to ripen their fruit in the low heat and sunlight, but they appeared well cared for and doing much better than the ones back near his California home town.

Amidst the other trees, tall cypresses, stone pines, and ragged palm trees partially surrounded a stone-paved courtyard. To his right and continuing to the edge of the cliff, some of the stonework caught his eye immediately.

"Wow, are those Roman columns and arches?" he said out loud as he looked at a line of fluted white marble pillars. Some were jaggedly broken off halfway up, but others were complete with sculpted blue marble capitals and intricately decorated white marble arches springing from their tops. The columns and arches extended out from the main building and partially surrounded a stone pavement made of multi-colored marble pieces laid in intricate designs. The chipped and damaged marble all glistened in the foggy sea-born humidity.

At the edge of the pavement, a white marble railing only partially protected against falling off the side of the cliff to the rocky shore and gently heaving sea below. Joseph walked over and carefully gazed over this damaged barrier into the misty Mediterranean Sea. Below him, he could see pieces of white, blue and colored marble, where parts of the ancient structure had fallen prey to the waves that rose and fell against a rocky shoreline. The colored marble pavement was sheared off at this edge as well, showing where it had once continued out into what was now empty space. Turning back to look at the large villa, his breath once more caught in his throat as he took in the sight before him.

There was a wide stone and brick terrace that ran around the first floor, with tall, closed, green wooden shutters. On each floor, there were balconies with more shuttered openings, and windows with closed shutters pierced the walls here and there. All the openings were closed tight. The highest roofline looked like it had been built like a castle, with crenelated openings, as if for archers to shoot arrows from behind.

Maybe it was a fortress and also a Roman villa? What a place!

Looking more closely at the gardens and grounds surrounding the villa, and starting to walk around it, he could see that care of the grounds was evident, with the hedges lining the pathways neatly clipped. Around the main building, at the front edge facing out to sea, there was an open courtyard with a beautiful multi-colored tiled fountain with water shooting high in a series of small jets. Amidst the greenery of the hedges, there were ambitious plantings of flowers struggling here and there, but the lack of sunlight was apparently stunting their growth and color.

Joseph had been so distracted by all he had found, but suddenly remembered that he was a hunted man, so he stopped his explorations and headed back out of the tunnel to bring his car into the courtyard to hide it from the road. Walking back, he struggled with the gate until he had forced both sides to open fully. After driving into the tunnel, and pulling the two sides of the gate shut behind the car, he heard the gate lock itself with a sharp click. Now no one would know he was there, and no one else could get in.

Whoever is caring for the grounds must have another way into the gardens. I wonder where it is.

The taxi pulled into Portofino in the evening gloom and stopped at the head of the narrow bay on the stone embankment that partially surrounded it. Rachel paid the driver a generous tip and carried her bag along the waterfront towards the hotels the driver had pointed to. Walking along, she felt the slightly warmer coastal air on her face, while breathing in the refreshing salty scent of the sea mixed with the resinous smell of pine trees.

The harbor was quiet with just small working fishing boats tied to the embankment or floating at buoys on the gentle waves in the narrow bay. On either side of the bay and reaching up to the hilltops on three sides were multi-colored houses and many villas, some large and some smaller, interspersed with groves of olive, pine, and tall, ragged palm trees.

The shutters on the buildings were closed on most all the doors and windows, giving the whole village a feeling of having silently suffered through and barely survived the horrible war and long cold years since. Surrounding the harbor edge, the narrow three and four-story houses had at one time been brightly painted, but now most looked faded with areas of plaster that had fallen off.

The two hotels that remained open both showed peeling paint and faded signs that had seen better days. Rachel entered the better looking of the two, the Hotel Moderna, and registered, asking, "The village seems very quiet. Is it early in the season, or...?

"Si, Senora, it is early, but not much sun no more. More cold. No one wants to vacation anymore here. Almost no more season."

"Well, I am grateful that you're open. Grazie."

"Prego. We have for you a molto bella room. Is own bath, grand balcony, to see the village and bay. Is bene, good, si?

"Yes. Si, that will be fine. But before I go up, can you tell me if you know of the Villa Vista Per Sempre? It is somewhere near here; I have been told."

The young woman at the front desk looked startled at this question. "You are English? American?"

"Yes, I am. American. In English, the name is the Villa of The Forever View. Have you heard of it?"

With a strange look on her face, the woman answered, "Si, but... why do you seek this place?"

"I am going to meet a friend there."

"That would-be no-good place you may want to go, Signora. And no place to meet a respectable friend. It is haunted. No one goes there. The fisherman when out to sea, they see lights there, strange lights at that place. They stay far out from when coming to the shore there. They stay away. As should you."

Rachel was a bit nonplussed by this outpouring of caution. She wondered just what was at that villa, and hoped Joseph was okay there.

"Well, thank you for telling me what you know. But can I ask if you know if anyone has lived there for... how many years?"

"No. No one there has lived there, since before I am born. And maybe only when my mother was young? I hear something terrible happens to the family who lived there before, during the war. All dead, gone. After the war ended, family, relatives, some Americans, they come. The villa is alive once more then, very beautiful villa. Lots of light, music, dancing, my mother says. But then they have gone too. They vanish and never return. We hear something terrible happens to these ones too. So many terrible things, lots of ghosts. So better you no go there. Better stay away."

Stunned by these strange, dark stories, she did not have a ready reply, except to say, "Well, perhaps you're right. On second thought, I must have the wrong name. Are there other villas nearby? And any with names anything like this one?"

The young woman relaxed her tightly wrought face, saying brightly, "Si, Signora. Many bella villas along the road by the sea. Many bella names, some like this one in ways. But, oh yes, you must have wrong. Many beautiful villas, many closed up now, but with no ghosts. Taxi man here, he will be good to help you to find the one you seek."

Rachel thanked the woman for her information and help, and after a change of clothes and a hot shower, strolled along the harbor looking for a likely spot for dinner. Still watching for any possible Office agents, she saw no one who looked out of place here. Finding a simple cafe on the waterfront serving freshly caught fish, she settled into a booth tucked in the back and sat facing the front door.

She put the strange stories she had just heard out of her mind for a time and settled in for a dinner of fresh Italian seafood. Feeling full and comfortable after the delicious meal and enjoying a small espresso with tiramisu for dessert, she once again thought about Joseph and reflected on her biggest fears. *Will he listen to me? Will he ever forgive me? Can he love me again?*

As she held her head in her hands over the table and the half-eaten dessert, tears fell from her eyes into the espresso, causing small rings of salty foam to ornament the surface.

Later, climbing up the stairs to her room, she washed her face of the tears and then opened the glass doors of the balcony. Taking in the breathtaking view of the bay and villa-covered hills, she let the fresh salty sea air pour over her.

Donning the new sexy lace sleepwear, she had bought to hopefully share with Joseph, she sat on the bed and thought of him, and his touch, longing to feel it once more. She touched the engagement ring he had given her, that now hung on a chain around her neck, and cried some more. Sitting and squeezing herself with her arms crossed over her breasts and hands resting on her shoulders, she imagined it to be Joseph holding her so tight until she cried out, "Oh, God! Joseph, I love you. I miss you so much." Comforting herself this way left a momentary glow. But soon her loneliness and despair came back and grew as she realized that she would never feel complete without him. She now burrowed into the warm covers of the soft bed and cried some more. She cried for Debra, for herself, and for Joseph, while trying to somehow find sleep despite her anxiety, fear, and excitement at perhaps seeing him in the morning.

Driving carefully through the tunnel, which was evidently made more for horses and carriages than cars, he made his way to the stone courtyard and pulled the car back to the side of what looked like the old carriage house and stable.

Now feeling safer with the car hidden, he approached the front door, climbing up a flight of broad stone steps and fitted the key into a hole on one of the pairs of large front doors. This lock was rusty, and with some effort, he was able to push open the massive door. Resisting his efforts every inch, it moved with horrible screeching sounds, at last enough to allow him to enter.

As his eyes adjusted to the interior gloom, Joseph could make out all kinds of shapes covered with white cloths scattered about him inside an ample high ceiling space. The inside air smelled like a mixture of wood polish, salt, and oddly enough, lavender; a not unpleasant mix, but somewhat stale.

Walking carefully and feeling his way through pieces of cloth-draped furniture, he made his way to his left to a set of large French doors. Feeling in the dim light for the latches, he opened them up and then reached for the shutter clasps, unlatching them as well. Almost desperate now for air and light, he pushed open the two large shutters, suddenly flooding the room with the sound of the sea, a breath of cold, fresh air, and soft light.

Now able to see the room more clearly and almost in desperation, he dodged between the hidden objects dotted around the place and proceeded to open up every door and window he could find until the enormous room filled with soft, cloudy, midday sunlight, and the sound and scent of the sea.

Stunned by the enormous space, he saw large painted portraits hung on the walls and high over his head, a vast arched and fresco ceiling.

"Oh my," he said as he gazed up at an expansive painted sky that covered the entire ceiling. It was filled with angels playing various musical instruments, harps and viola, and other ones he was not sure of. There were various figures of what looked like pagan gods and other male and female figures, all intertwined with multi-colored clouds, shot through with beams of light streaming through and between them. Pulling a white sheet off a chair, he sat down on the embroidered seat to contemplate the magnitude of his inheritance.

Turning, he could see a large marble staircase that arched across the back of the enormous space, splitting into two branches as it rose up to the next level and beyond. The treads were covered with colorful Persian carpet that ascended with the staircase.

After a bit, he walked over to one side of the room, where there was a long, waist-high sideboard hidden by a white dust cloth. Objects were standing up under the fabric, so he was cautious as he pulled off the cloth. A long row of groups of photos appeared in gold and silver gilded frames.

He was almost sure that he was face to face with his lost family. He walked along in front of the rows of framed photos to one end, looking at the pictures of what must be his parents. He tried to imagine them standing or sitting before him, as they would have when they lived. Then he gazed at the older ones, of generations past, and up at the old portraits hung on the walls, finally sitting down on a still covered settee couch. Joseph broke out in great sobs. He cried for all that he had missed, had lost, and now seemingly had found once more. His family.

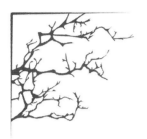

Thirty-seven

PORTOFINO, ITALY
April 23, 1986 - Eve of Passover

Rachel packed her bag, went downstairs, and checked out. Stopping at the doorway, she looked out to see if anyone was watching. Seeing no one that looked out of place to her, she stepped out of the hotel onto the paved area edging the harbor. The morning desk clerk had told her that the one taxi still working this time of year would be found at the bar near where the narrow coast road entered the small town.

Stepping into the dark, smoky bar, she was greeted with several appreciative whistles from the patrons, as her shapely form was outlined and illuminated by the soft cloudy daylight streaming in behind her. She called out, "Signore Carnegie? Is he here? Taxi man?'

"Si, Signorina. I am here at your service. Do not mind my friends here, as they are expressing great artistic appreciative of a beautiful Signorina."

"I understand. Very proper gentlemen indeed. But Signore, can you meet with me outside? I require you and your taxi."

"Si. Pronto."

Rachel sat at a table outside and waited for the driver. After five minutes, she was at the door again, this time shouting, "Signore, taxi! Pronto?"

Stepping out of the bar, the driver apologized as he walked. "So sorry, Signorina. We, these days, have not many people come here. Poor Portofino is poor, indeed."

She replied with an impatient smile, "Well if you were quick to respond, you might make more lira."

"Well, si, but I have only taxi now. And it is morning early; maybe too early. I have a game inside. I go back now," he said with his arms out and both palms up. Turning, he started back to the door of the bar.

"Okay. Wait a bit, let me explain. Sorry to be in such a hurry, but I am on my way to meet my lover, who I have not seen for many days now."

Stopping short of the doorway, he turned back and his face filled with a broad smile. "Oh, you should have said so to me. L'amore. L'amore. For love, I will always be ready to pronto assist such a bella Signorina."

"Thank you."

"And where myself, my taxi need to take you to meet your lover?"

"Well, I'm not sure how far it is, but I need to get to the Villa Vista Sempre."

"No. No, Signorina. You must be mistaken. Is a place haunted, maybe cursed? No one lives there no more. No can. No one go."

"Yes, I've heard this. At the hotel, they told me the stories. But can you take me there? And see what is near it? Perhaps there is another villa nearby. I may have the wrong name."

"Si. Yes, this I can do for you. And yes, you must have wrong. There is no-a-way into cursed villa anyway. It is locked, closed uptight. But nearby, is a small villa on the bay down below. People there are my friends for many years. Is where I take you to. Is okay?"

"Si, si. That will be good. Now, we go, pronto? Remember, l'amore?"

He opened the back door of the old green taxi for her. "Per favore. L'amore cannot wait for Signorina. Then let us go."

Pale morning sunlight poured through the opened doors and windows as Joseph awoke with a start, realizing that he must have cried himself to sleep. It was an exhausted one, so deep that he had slept through the night on the sheet-covered settee with no blanket or cover, but he had somehow pulled the sheet over himself in the night. As he opened and rubbed his eyes and tried to unkink his back and legs, he looked around the enormous room again, once more trying to take in the richly appointed space.

Before him on the sideboard, the groups of photos standing up in their gold and silver frames beckoned to him. They ranged from the sometimes-stern looking expressions in the older black and white pictures on the left, to the smiling faces of adults and children at play in the more modern and color shots. He gazed for a long time at the newest ones on the far right. Something told him he was seeing pictures of his mother and father for the very first time. His mother was so elegant-looking, and his father had been such a handsome young man. Looking at them all, he realized everyone in the photos except for a small infant held in the arms of a beautiful woman, his mother, photographed sitting on the Roman marble terrace outside the villa, were now dead.

Standing up to stretch, Joseph realized he was cold, hungry, thirsty, and in urgent need of a bathroom. Crossing the large room to the grand staircase, he walked up the carpeted marble stairs to the second floor, and on down a shadowed but beautifully decorated hallway to find several bedrooms on each side. Picking a bedroom on the end that looked promising, he felt his way into it through the shadows to a set of large French doors with closed outside shutters. Opening the four large glass doors and then the shutters that were paired between stone pillars with carved capitals and arches, the sound of the sea and soft, cloudy sunlight flooded into the room. The doors opened out to a large tiled balcony with a stone railing facing south, out to sea.

Looking for the facilities, he turned to the connected bathroom he could now see, and finding the water still on though very cold, he utilized the room anyway, including a marble-lined shower-tub for a cold rinse to fully awaken. After finding a clean fluffy towel in a linen closet, he dried off, feeling chilled but revived.

Wrapped in the large white towel as he dried himself and tried to warm up, he now looked more closely at the large decorated bedroom. Walking towards the far side wall, he opened up the two windows and shutters to better illuminate the room. Now with more light, and looking closely at the walls and ceiling, he was in shock upon seeing the place for the first time, and how it was decorated. Pulling the dust sheet off the large bed, he could not believe his eyes at what lay before him.

Oh my, it looks just like the bedroom in my vision... where I was making love to both Rebeca and Rachel. It was so real with both of them. And it's like Rachel's dreams as well. How did she describe it?

He tried hard to recall the details of what she had related to him from her dreams, of a room like this and of what he had seen in his vision.

She had said something like, "A beautiful bedroom, with a large bed, frescoes and tapestries on the walls, and a gilded ceiling. And just outside, a balcony overlooking the sea, high above the waves."

As he looked up at the carved, gilded ceiling, and then up behind the head of the large bed, and on either side wall at the hanging tapestries and fresco paintings between them, a strange feeling of being untethered, as if almost being able to float through solid objects, space and time, came over him. The room seemed to spin before him for a while, and then gradually stopped.

Wow. It was how I felt when I was making love with both of them. It looks like the same bedroom with these same tapestries; the one between the two windows of the woodland scene, with the cupids all playing different musical instruments. It's all the same... or almost.

As this all came back to him, he was staring at the same tapestry hanging on the same wall between the same two windows.

The colors are softer, faded from how bright and new they looked when I was somehow here before. But still, the room is nearly the same as what I saw and what Rachel described to me from her dreams. Oh my god, it's real. It's overwhelming. Just what is happening? My lost family, the violin, this place, this villa, my visions, her dreams. Rachel. Oh, Rachel, I wish you were here now, in my arms, and to see this. I'm so sorry. I was so angry. But you hurt me, betrayed me. But I didn't give you a chance to explain. I thought I was alone before, but now I really am. And it's my own fault. My anger has left me all alone.

His body was chilling, and that plus his empty stomach combined to bring him back to the reality of this strangely familiar room. To how hungry he was, as well as the need to stay warm in the cold sea air. Looking around some more, he opened up some free-standing closets and drawers in the various pieces of furniture, finding both men's and women's clothing.

He realized that he was perhaps seeing his father's suits and casual wear, along with his mother's colorful silk dresses. Looking at one of the more elegant dresses, and a suit of his father's, he again broke down in tears at his loss. He had to stop himself though and quickly got dressed in his own clothing with one of his father's warm woolen coats over the top, to seek his next priority; where he could find some food. As this thought pressed upon him, he suddenly smelled something startling and frightening.

Is that coffee? Who could be here? And what do they want?

"Yes, Father. She has left the hotel and taken a taxi heading east on the road along the shore. And yes, we have a man following her now."

"Find out where she is headed, but make no move until we arrive."

"Understood, Father."

The taxi drove the narrow winding coast road for several miles eastwards from the village, and as they rounded one tight curve that cut through a high headland, the driver pointed out, "There, out on the end, is the haunted villa. Bad place. Terrible things happen to people there. You no go. You promise?'

"Signore, I understand. You are concerned about my safety, yes?"

"Yes. I take you to my old friends, Elias and Marie. They are a very long time here. No one remembers when they not here."

After cutting through the tall headland, the road curved down to a small bay, with more villas perched along the edge of the road, and high up on the hills above. As far as Rachel could see, they all had their shutters closed. "Are all the villas here closed up these days?"

"Si, many shuts for years. Some open in summer, just July and August, but summer not what it was before the war. Since the war, since the big bombs, cold, and now colder. So not-so much-a summer villas nowadays. Very sad, Portofino. Sad Italians. Life now is hard."

"It's so sad to see all of this beauty closed up, with no one to enjoy it. Our world now is so wet and cloudy all the time, and getting colder every year. They say it should stop getting so cold soon, and start to warm up. I pray that it does."

As he pulled up to a small two-story villa set back from the road at the level of the bay, he replied, "Phew. Ah, prayer, no lot a good it does. The priests now say Blessed Virgin Mary of Fatima, that she will bring back warm sun if we send all lira to Fatima. And if we go there as pilgrims and give our self to them. Bah, I keep my lira for my family and me. Fatima is Portugal. They know nothing. New Fatima priest say Jews did all this, make long winter. I no think so. When a boy, I have friends who were Jews. Good people, never did anything to hurt me or anyone. But all gone now. Fascists, phew. Mussolini, phew. Nazis very bad, kill them all. All gone now."

Even here, the lies of Fatima keep trying to spread.

Pushing the thought from her mind, she asked him, "Are we here?"

"Si, Signorina. Here we are. My friends will take good care of you, and help you to find your lover. L'amore is ruling all. Now, love is, how you say it? Is Love worth everything to find? Si?"

"Grazie, signore. L'amore. True love is worth whatever the price. Thank you for your help and advice."

As he opened her door, he offered, "Please, Signorina, let me introduce you to my friends."

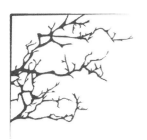

Thirty-eight

   April 23, 1986

Rachel walked behind Alberto to the front door of the modest orange-gold colored single-story villa, but before the man could knock, the carved wooden door opened. Stepping out onto the front porch, a man addressed them both. "Welcome, Alberto. Welcome, young lady, to our humble abode. I saw my old friend here pull up in his taxi. My name is Elias. May I know the name of the lady I'm addressing?" The old man with the long white beard bowed low with the limber flexibility of youth, sweeping his right arm in an elegant motion to the front and right as he did so.

"I'm Rachel Green. And I must say that your English is superb. Thank you for welcoming me to your home."

"Why, thank you. I spent many years in England, and some time in America as well. So, I have had quite a bit of practice. Now, what brings you to my home? And how may I be of service to you?"

"Elias, please take good care of my new friend here. I must be going back to Portofino." And then in a lower conspiratorial voice, he added, "She is seeking her lost love. I trust that you can help her?"

"Yes, yes. Until later, Alberto." As Alberto turned to go back to his car, Elias added, "Now, Ms. Green, come. We must get out of sight into the house here. This dark world has many eyes that watch, and we do not want them to watch us now." At this, he stepped aside to allow her to enter, then closed the heavy door behind her.

Once inside, standing on the tile floor, she said, "I'm hoping that you might be of help to me in finding the Villa of the Forever View. Is it nearby? Is that it up above us, on the peninsula, as Alberto told me?"

As the tall old man looked into her eyes, he asked, "May I inquire as to what business you might have at such a villa, if indeed it was to exist?'

His eyes are so blue like they can see right into my soul. I trust him. Somehow, I do not feel any danger from this man.

She carefully said, "Well, I'm looking for my boyfriend, who was headed there, I believe." Then surprising herself, she blurted out, "He's just found out he's inherited it."

"Oh, I see. And do you know this young man's full name?"

"Yes, of course, I do. Joseph Davidson."

"No, I mean his real, full name?"

Rachel paused at this as she looked into those deep blue eyes. Despite the danger she could be in, she couldn't stop herself from saying, "Yosef ben Daveed..." Frightened, she blurted out, "Oh, what have I done? I've got to get out of here." She turned back towards the front door, preparing to flee.

"Wait. Please don't be afraid, as that is indeed his name. And I see you are worried by saying his true name? Please rest easy in Shalom, here in our home."

Relief flooding her face, she released a deep breath she had been holding in. "You're Jewish? And is Joseph here?"

"To answer your first question, yes, I am."

"But the taxi driver said you had been here for a long time. How have you...?"

"We are well hidden. And as for Joseph, my wife, Marie, is with him now. She is about to feed him a delicious breakfast as we speak. Are you hungry? Follow me. I will take you to him shortly."

"Father, go ahead. You are connected now."

"Thank you, operator. Hello? Where are you?"

"Portofino, Father Servino."

"You were careful not to alert her?"

"Yes, Father. She has no idea she was followed."

"Good. Keep it that way."

"The local priest is part of the Fatima Circle. He was most helpful. He told us the word had spread of the American girl arriving, and of where exactly she had gone."

"You have her in sight now?"

"No, but we have watchers making sure she doesn't leave."

"She had better not leave. And you and your men had better not lose her now. We need her to lead us to the boy and the object we seek. Cardinal De-Silva will arrive in the morning. We will await his orders."

"He's coming? But isn't he still in the hospital? I heard he had lost an..."

"You will not speak of his injuries. That is strictly confidential. Do you understand?"

"Yes, Father. I understand. I will say nothing."

"A wise choice."

"But back to the girl, Father. She has been seen going into a small villa on the edge of the far bay. Our men will keep watch for any further movement. They have all the exit points covered."

"At sea as well?"

Yes, Father. We have a motorboat at our disposal. We are keeping watch offshore."

"And the boy?"

"We're guessing that she came to find him. Somehow, he's already here, but we haven't sighted him, nor a car that could be his. The priest had no intelligence of his location. But we believe he may be inside the large villa above the bay."

"For your sake, I hope you're right."

"The address matches the one from the Swiss account that had just become active in March."

"We must have them both cornered, ready for His Grace. He has plans for these two. Until tomorrow then."

JOSEPH TRIED TO SHAKE off the crazy notion that he smelled fresh coffee and made his way back down the stairs, intending to look for the kitchen and other service areas of the massive structure in a search for something to eat. At the bottom of the stairs, he headed to the left, away from the grand room where he had spent the night. Opening a carved wooden door with a curved top, his breath caught in his throat at what he saw before him.

He had stepped into an extensive library with three walls lined with two-story high bookcases. Looking around the room, his eyes scanned over many thousands of books in all sizes and colors. There was a small keyboard instrument in one corner, maybe a harpsichord, as well as a large harp, and various cases that contained a range of string musical instruments. There was even sheet music arrayed on three music stands as if the musicians had just left the room to take a break from playing. A balcony made from lacy cast iron crafted to look like lush interwoven flowers and leaves circled the room on three sides, with a spiral stair of the same material leading up to it.

Seeing the fourth wall, he stopped and stared. In the center of a wood-paneled wall, there was a full-length painting of a life-like regal figure. The man depicted in the picture was gazing slightly off to one side and was dressed as a king, robed in golden and purple cloth, gem-studded golden chains draped around his neck and shoulders, with a finely painted golden crown studded with colored gemstones. Walking closer and staring up into the figure's face and eyes, he thought he could almost recognize the man. The king in the painting looked a lot like the photos in the other room, including those of his father.

Looking more closely at the painting, he could make out what looked like initials. A. V. D. Who could that be? Stunned by the image and looking again at everything in the room, he saw a carved, inlaid reading table with matching chairs. Sitting down in the chair that faced the painting, he gazed longingly at the face that seemed so alive, and who looked so much like his father.

Looking more closely, he could see that the entire wall around the painting, was covered in marquetry made up of interlaced and interconnected patterns of wood and golden metal. The design made a complex spider web of intricate shapes that framed and embraced the painting with a large Tree of Life shape on each side that reached from the parquetry wood floor to the coffered wood ceiling high overhead.

It's just like the puzzle box, but so much larger. Is it a puzzle of its own? But what treasures does it hold?

He was then distracted from all of this by a different sensual experience.

What do I smell now? It's like someone is cooking breakfast. I do smell coffee. How could that be?

His hunger getting the best of him, he tore himself from the chair and kept walking through another doorway into what looked to be the dining room, with a long table and many chairs.

Entering the kitchen, with the smells intensifying as he got closer, he heard movement in a nearby room which appeared to be a pantry, as a woman's voice called out, "Joseph, are you hungry? I have espresso, eggs, and toast, with freshly made cheese for you."

Stopping short, startled and remembering he was a hunted man, he called out, "Who are you and how do you know my name? And what are you doing here?"

A short, round-faced, white-haired woman of indeterminate age, dressed simply in a checkered apron, white blouse, and dark skirt, stepped into view from the next room. "I am Marie, your mother's housekeeper. I'm guessing that you are Joseph?"

"Yes, but how did you know?"

"We have been expecting you to arrive any day now."

"Who is we?"

"My husband, Elias, and I. We are the caretakers of the Villa of the Forever View."

"Do you live here?"

"No. We live down by the bay, next door. But tell me, you just turned twenty-one, am I right?"

"Yes, in late March. But how did you get in here?"

"We have a passageway from our home to access the villa. But, back to you. You received a letter regarding your inheritance?"

"Yes, but how do you know this?"

"It would seem, as the child of your parents, that you have solved some of the puzzles they left for you."

"How do you know that? And what do you mean?"

"Well, you are the first person other than us, the caretakers, to gain entry to this villa since your parents were last here. Let me see; it's nearly twenty years now? And since you're here in your family's home, then you must be

Joseph, their son. You could only be here if you had solved the puzzles and found the key. Am I correct?"

"It was an accident that I could read that part of my father's letter. My tears, the salt, I guess...? And the key was in the puzzle box."

"Yes, I know. Elias helped your father hide the key to the gate there."

"You have been here ever since then? Since my parents were here... with me?"

"Yes. We have been watching for your return. You were very small when you were here the last time. I will guess you have seen the photos of you with your mother?"

"Those are the first pictures I have ever seen of my parents. The older woman who raised me said that there were no pictures every time I asked her to see some. I could never understand why."

"It was to protect you. You may have noticed that there are some in this world who would do you harm. They are seeking you and what you carry with you as well."

"You mean the..."

"Yes, the violin."

"You know of it?"

"Of course, we do. How do you think it was placed into your path?"

"You. You did that. That violin has tormented me. I can't describe what it's done to me. It's... it`s nearly driven me insane."

"It was Elias who uncovered it from its hiding place in the cellar."

Raising his voice, he replied, "But why did you do it? You said you placed it in my path?"

"We arranged for it to be loaned to the museum, anticipating that you would encounter it there."

"But how could you do that to me?" Now shouting at her, he said, "Do you know I've been shot at? And chased halfway across the world by some very evil people? And not to mention the strange things it's done to me! It's caused me to experience hallucinations when I've touched it, of me somehow being some other person, somewhere else! It's been making me crazy. And all because of that violin. That damn fiddle!"

She replied gently but firmly, "I will ask you to please not shout at me, Joseph. And to not insult your companion like that."

Calming down a bit, he replied, "My companion? What are you talking about?"

"The violin you carry with you is much more than just a violin. She was created four hundred and fifty-five years ago, in fifteen twenty-five. She was given life. And a power of her own by a Master of the Kabbalah. By the one who made her."

"A life and power of her own? But how could someone do that? How can it? That is Jewish, isn't it, the Kabbalah? And wait a minute... the violin was not invented until about fifteen fifty-five by Andrea Amati. That would make this violin the earliest one ever built by thirty years. How can she be...?"

"Joseph, she drew you to her and drew you here to your home. She is a golem, crafted, and empowered to protect you and your people. And the reasons you are being chased are deeper and more ancient than you know at this point. Your father's letter tells you part of the reasons. All of this is more involved than just because you carry the violin."

"But... but..."

"For now, please sit down and eat. I'm sure you're starving. We can talk more about this rather special violin you have inherited along with this villa after you eat."

"Inherited?"

"Yes, the violin is yours. Now eat."

His attention was firmly brought back to his empty belly by a deep, rumbling growl echoing from within the hollow space inside him. As his mind wondered at these new revelations, he sat at the simple white painted kitchen table and proceeded to eat everything Marie placed in front of him.

When his hunger had been satisfied, and the strong espresso had cleared the cobwebs in his mind, he reflected on the morning's discoveries. "So, this place, this villa is mine now? Along with the violin that has been tormenting me these last two months?"

"Yes, this villa is your home, and it has been your family's home for hundreds of years."

"I never had any idea of such a place, or of the wealth my family had. I lived with almost nothing for so many years. I was barely surviving. Why couldn't I know all this earlier?"

"I can tell you some things, but other subjects like why you had to wait until you were twenty-one for your inheritance, I can only guess at. But to clarify what I said about the violin, in some ways, she is yours, but in other ways, she is her own master. But to say she has been 'tormenting' you. That is a pretty strong word, don't you think?"

"Actually, no. Not at all."

"Well, since we are speaking of her, why don't you go get her from the salon?"

"How did you...? No, never mind. Marie, I think I know you. In fact, I think I have seen you now a few times, or am I crazy?"

Laughing, she replied, "I don't think you're crazy, and I can guess that you have had some unusual experiences on your journey here, but we have never met before now. Except that is, when you were born upstairs in your mother's room. The one facing the sea, with the cherubs playing their musical instruments. I was there as your mother's midwife to greet you when you arrived."

"I was born here? And up in that room, that same room ... and you were here then? With my mother and me?"

Marie stood looking out the kitchen windows for a long moment. She looked to Joseph like she was gazing far out into the cloudy sky, or perhaps far back in time. He could not tell which.

Turning back to him, she said, "Please bring me the violin. There is something important I need to show you now."

Getting up from the table, he went back into the main room on the ground floor, and picking up the violin case, carried it back into the kitchen. Marie had cleared the table by the time he had returned and was waiting for him there.

Placing the case on the table, he opened it with trepidation and, keeping a distance as if the violin might somehow move towards him, once again, cautiously looked at the gorgeous instrument.

"Pick it up, Joseph."

"Ah, no. I don't think so. You don't understand..."

"Yes, I do. Pick her up. She won't bite you."

"But then you know...?"

"Yes, I do know. We have been her caretakers here for many, many years now."

As he reached carefully for the neck, the unvarnished part of the violin, Marie said, "Pick up the bow too, and follow me."

She walked out of the kitchen and into the library. Continuing up to the wall, she stopped and began pressing different sections of the carved wood in a long sequence. He stood just inside the library, watching what she was doing.

At last, a silent door slid open directly under the portrait of King David. A dark tunnel had appeared in the wall, and with quick steps that belied her age, Marie vanished into the darkness.

A sudden wave of nausea enveloped him as the room started to spin before his eyes. Trying to walk towards the door that had opened, he stumbled, as his feet seemed not to be touching the floor in front of him.

"Wait, where did you go?" he desperately called out as everything in his field of vision reeled all around him.

"I'm here. Come after me. You're almost home, Joseph. Follow my voice."

"What do you mean, almost home? Marie, I'm dizzy. Something is wrong. I thought I was home. But where are you? I don't see anything."

Stepping and half stumbling into the dark opening as he said this, a brilliant white light pierced his vision as if another door had opened up, but this time on the face of the sun. "God, that's bright." He shielded his eyes, holding the violin up in front of his face. As his eyes adjusted to the brightness, he could see a brightly lit figure standing in front of the light, framed by a doorway that had opened up in the short tunnel.

He could see that the tall, slim figure in the light was female, with flowing, bright golden-white hair, and she was dressed in some kind of long white floating gossamer material that was brightly illuminated. But she looked nothing like Marie.

The figure turned and cried out to him in a high clear voice that pierced him to his very soul, "Kadosh, Kadosh, Kadosh. Tikkum Olam, Joseph. This you must do. You must heal all the worlds. Remember, Tikkum Olam. There is nothing else."

"But how? What should...? How can I...? What is my path forward?"

"There is no path forward, only returning." Then in a haunting, chanting voice, she said, "Return again. Return again. Return to the land of your soul. Return to who you are, what you are, and where you are..."

Joseph found his vision clearing as he stood in the library, holding the violin and bow in his hand. To his surprise, he was holding the violin by the varnished back and side, and nothing was occurring like what had happened in the past. The varnished wood seemed not to affect him now. To his side was a music stand with violin sheet music laid out on it.

Marie was standing in front of him, looking just as she had in the kitchen earlier. "Joseph, why don't you play something on it?"

Startled by this, he looked at her closely, seeing only the short older woman who had fed him breakfast. Shaking his head, he said, "What just happened, Marie?"

"I'm not sure what you mean. We were talking about the violin, and of how she is your companion. But why don't you play something on her? There in front of you is a lovely piece."

He picked up the bow, sat down on the chair, and looked at the music before him; the violin part of Bach's *Air on the G String* arranged for violin and cello. As the notes flowed, he could feel the vibrations passing through his body, the air, and into the wooden floor and walls of the library. The sound continued to build in layers until the entire villa was vibrating with the warm, crystalline cascade of notes.

As Elias led Rachel through the curving stone-lined tunnel that led from the basement of their small villa, up many steps into the cellars of the villa on the headland above, she heard violin music in the distance.

"Elias, can you hear that?"

"Yes. I believe your friend is making himself at home with his violin here."

"Do you know about that violin?"

"Well, of course, I do. This is its home, and I will guess he's playing it now."

Rachel started to move even faster, but the seemingly frail old man stayed right behind her. With the sound of the music getting louder with every step up and turn of the stairs, at last, they entered the villa kitchen, passing on into the dining room.

They both looked into the library and saw Joseph's back as he sat facing the wooden puzzle wall, intensely playing the haunting music, while Marie walked up behind them to watch.

Elias turned and gently stopped her onwards steps with his finger to his lips. He pointed to a cello leaning against a chair with a music stand in front of it, whispering, "For you, Rachel. Play him back into your heart."

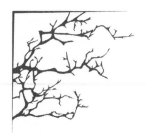

Thirty-nine

VILLA OF THE FOREVER View, Portofino, Italy
April 23, 1986 - Eve of Passover

Elias turned to Marie as they watched Rachel enter the library and whispered, "Shall we open and freshen the house while they heal their hearts?"

"Yes. It's time."

Rachel quietly tiptoed into the library and sat down at the cello. She saw Joseph sitting on the far side with his back to her, intensely focused on his playing. Picking up the bow, she looked at the music and started to play her part of the beautifully haunting duet.

As the sound of both instruments intertwined and flowed together, she closed her eyes and remembered a happier time when they had played this piece together in a recital at ASVM. It seemed so long ago, but it was less than a month. Just before he read that damned telegram.

Playing the last three minutes of it with him, she made her final slow pass of the bow as the music from both instruments faded away into silence, only broken by the distant muffled sound of waves gently breaking on the rocky shore. Looking at his back, with the golden violin now laying on his lap, the bow hanging down near the floor, she once again closed her eyes, awaiting the storm.

Silently, he stood up and placed the violin and bow on his chair as he walked across the room to where Rachel sat. Standing in front of her for several minutes, he finally said with a blank face in a cool-sounding voice, "That was beautiful. Can we play some more?"

Opening her eyes, with tears starting to flow, she answered, "Yes, I would like that."

Walking to the table, he picked up another, longer piece of music, also for the same instruments. With the same serious face, he said, "Now, for something completely different." Handing her the cello part, he took the violin sheets, turned his chair to face her, and sat back down. He set up his music on the stand, his face still a mask as he seemed to await her reaction to his choice.

Ravel's Sonata for violin and cello. This is wild music I've never played before. Did he pick this one to torment me?

Starting with a deep breath, Rachel focused sharply with her full concentration as they began the first movement together. Their instruments' voices alternately clashed and interwove, intensely rising and falling together, playing notes first in harmony and then suddenly with shocking dissonance, finally falling into a deep silence at the end of the movement.

This music feels almost like us, together in love and then hatred, back and forth, rhythm and dissonance. God, I can't stand this separation.

Facing each other across the room, Rachel suddenly stood up and moved her chair, music stand, and cello to three feet in front of him. Sitting back down, so close to him, she looked into his eyes for a moment, showed a small, tentative smile, and set up her music. With her cello ready, she looked up at him again, wiped her tears, and joined him digging into the intensely rapid pizzicato and vigorous alternative bowing of the second movement.

The music was so intense that she could only catch a quick glimpse of him now and then, as she tried to gauge his heart by his blank facial expression. At the end of the second movement, catching her breath after the vigorous workout the playing required and wiping sweat from her forehead, she rested for a moment as he looked at her. But looking down from his gaze, and without words, she embarked with him into the third slower movement, while sometimes gazing back at him. After the third movement ended, she stopped playing and burst into sobbing tears, her wet face, resting against the cello's spruce top. Seeing her tears flowing across the wood, she set the cello down on the carpet with the bow. Bowing her head almost to her lap, she reached out with both her hands, saying, "Joseph, I can't stand this anymore. Please forgive me. I'm so sorry I put you in so much danger."

He retorted, "Are you? I thought you enjoyed your work?"

"Please don't be angry. It wasn't my choice. My... what I was doing... What I felt, that first night with you, everything changed for me, but I didn't know what to do. I was trapped. My sister, they had her, and then they murdered her..."

His face changed as he carefully set the violin down on a stool with its bow. Reaching to her, he said, "She's gone? Oh, Rachel. I'm so sorry. I didn't know. What happened?"

"That monster DeSilva raped her, and then she jumped off the tower of the cathedral. Oh, God. I didn't know what to do, how to deal with it ..."

Hearing this news, he slumped down into this seat and said, "How did you find out?"

"I went to her room to get her out of there, but she was already dead. So, I went to see the son of a bitch himself, offering myself to him to get close. Then I stabbed him in the eye and the belly."

Startled, he sat up abruptly, stared at her, and said, "My god, did you kill him?"

"I don't know." Then with a small, grim smile, she added, "I hope so, but I didn't stick around to find out. Servino, his henchman, shot at me as I got out of there, but missed. I ran and ran and kept on running."

Reaching towards her again with both arms and a concerned expression on his face, he asked, "Shot at you? And you got away?"

"Yes. I can move pretty fast. He missed me three times. I have some small cuts from the glass door; I crashed through, but they`re starting to heal up now."

"Wow, I'm so glad you're all right, and I'm so sorry about Debra." With this, his expression had settled back to the blank cool one he had greeted her with. "But how did you find this place?"

"Well, I got up into the mountains and an old white-haired woman I met told me where to go."

"What? Who? How did she know, or ...?"

"Somehow, she spoke to me in my mind, naming this place. Telling me to come here to find you."

With a stunned look on his face, he stood up and said as he started to walk in a small circle, "Oh my ... Well, considering everything else we've experienced, it fits. Somehow, we seem to be bit players in a story that keeps unfolding all around us. A story that's bigger than we can imagine or dream of."

"I agree, but I don't know what our next step is. Do you?" She wiped tears from her eyes.

Sitting back down, he slumped in his chair and sadly said, "I don't know what to do. How we can heal this. If it's even possible after everything that's happened." He lowered his head.

"Joseph, can we please just start over again? Can we somehow try that? Please?"

Sighing, he lifted his head back up to face her. Looking at her, he wiped his right hand over his face from top to bottom, brushing the tears that had started flowing from his eyes, and as his hand passed, he changed his expression to an open, friendly one. "Hi, I'm Joseph Davidson. I love your playing, especially that Sonata. It's pretty wild, don't you think?"

"Yes. It's sort of like our relationship."

Now slightly smiling, he answered, "Actually we're just meeting for the first time, so I'm not sure of what relationship you could be referring to. What's your name, by the way?"

"Well, of course, I need to introduce myself. I'm Rachel. Rachel Greenbaum." Holding her hand out to him, she added, "Pleased to meet you, Joseph. You are a fine violin player."

"Well, thank you, Rachel. You play the cello beautifully. Nice to meet you too. This violin is a rather special one, and I certainly cannot take credit for it. I've been told that a Master Kabbalist created it five hundred years ago."

Suddenly flinging herself into his arms, she cried out, tears streaming down her face, "I can't stand this. I've missed you so much." Her weight threw him off balance, so they both tumbled to the floor of the library, landing on one of the large, intricate Persian rugs that lay there.

"Ouch, shit, my back!"

Turning him slightly in her arms, she gently rubbed his back with her hand. "I'm so sorry. Are you okay?" Suddenly regretting her impulsive move, she tried to free herself from his arms, struggling to stand up. Her tears poured down her face, and she tried as hard as she could to twist free from his embrace.

Holding her tightly in his arms with a strength that surprised her, he said, "Wait, Rachel. Just relax. I'm fine. It was just when we hit the carpet and slid. It hurt a bit. I think you gave me rug burn." Now laughing deeply, he added, "But for someone I've just met, you're quite friendly, I must say."

Freeing her fists from under him, she hit him in the arms and shoulders, crying out, "

I thought I had hurt you! You chose that music on purpose, to torment me. You jerk. Just shut up and kiss me." As he continued to laugh, he turned to her, suddenly kissing her deeply, stopping the next words she tried to say.

Kissing each other's wet faces, their hungry lips softly caressed each other for many minutes. At last, taking a breath just between her lips, he whispered, "There's a bedroom upstairs that is so familiar. Can I show it to you now? I think you'll recognize it. It's from our dreams."

"Yes, we have the boat exploring offshore looking for a place to land. I already told you that, but there is none. The rocks are too sharp and the waves too rough to allow it. And the gate in front is solid and locked, with no way over it."

"What about going over the top of the headland? Is there any way to do that?"

"No, Father. It's too steep, with crumbling rock faces. It's unsafe. We could lose men."

"All right, let's not lose anyone in this operation if we can avoid it. But what else? Where did the girl go? Is she in the small villa by the beach?"

"Yes, as far as we know. We haven't seen her at all since she went in, and that villa is locked uptight."

"Well, you had better come up with a way in. Break into the place on the beach if you have to. See if there is anyone there, we can force to talk. Is our interrogator with you?"

"Yes, with all his tools. We have to catch them before he can do his job."

"Well, damn it, catch them and make them talk. There must be another way into that villa. The cardinal is coming himself tomorrow to supervise, and he does not like being disappointed. His Grace expects results, above all."

"His Grace is coming here? Isn't he still in the hospital?"

"Not anymore. He checked himself out today."

"Holy crap."

"My thoughts exactly."

"Father, I do have an idea. I think I know how we can gain access and surprise them at the same time. I will get back to you shortly if we can find what I'm thinking of."

Embracing Rachel gently in the warm bed, Joseph's fingers traced the length of her, from her delicate dancer's feet up to her legs and her thighs. And further, to her firm, flat belly, and on to each softly rounded breast, touching the engagement ring that hung between them. Here and there he could feel where a small cut from the glass shards was scabbed over. "I can feel your battle scars. Are they healing okay now? Do you want me not to stroke you like this?"

"Oh, they're fine." Then she added, laughing, "Don't worry, you can touch me anywhere you want to. You won't break me." Hearing this, he continued his gentle stroking.

Running her fingers through his short black hair, she said, "I missed you so much, but tell me, what happened to your hair?" Rachel purred as he caressed her warm curves.

"Well, with a new passport, as Joseph Sutherland, I decided I needed a new look to match."

Clasping his hand to hold it in place as he once again stroked her, she said, "Oh, lover. It feels like it's been so long, and you do look good with short black hair." Laughing lightly, she added, "Though it doesn't match your other hair, in ... other places." She guided him to her.

"Rachel, I love you, so much," he said as he embraced her.

Waking later in the night, with one soft golden-brown arm tucked behind his head and the other arm and her breasts pressed against his chest, Joseph looked around the room, illuminated by full cloudy moonlight and the fading embers of the fire Elias had laid in the fireplace for them. Rachel's warm, soft breathing on his neck was lightly caressing his skin as the faint sound of her breath tickled his ears.

Outside, the restless sea crashed back and forth, beating on the rocky cliffs. He could see that Marie and Elias had brought up both of their bags along with his treasure box, and freshened the room while they had been playing their music in the library. The clean sheets and pillowcases smelled like lavender, as did his lover's soft dark brown hair. Breathing deeply of the flower scent, he felt fully relaxed in this, the bed he was born in, his parents' bed before him. And maybe in the same bedroom where he and Rachel, in other bodies, had made love as well.

The entire room and the bed were steeped in the love of his family and the romance between him and Rachel that seemingly transcended time and space. Gazing at her left hand, he saw the little diamond engagement ring he had given her, that was now in its rightful place, on her ring finger.

Stirring in his arms, she asked in a husky, sleep-filled voice, "Are you hungry? I think we forgot to eat anything since breakfast."

"You're right. Do you want me to go fix something for you?"

Yawning, she replied, "Aww... how about if I go with you? I want to see more of this little place of yours anyway."

"Little? You jest. This place is mind-blowing to me. Marie told me I was born in this room, in this bed, twenty-one years ago."

"Wow, that's incredible. What an amazing thing to have found your family's home and where you were born."

"I just wish I could have had my parents all my life. I would trade all of this for having known them even for a little while. I was so young, just a baby when I lost them and was scarred in the fire."

"I'm so sorry that you never knew them, and for your scars."

Changing the subject, he said, "Okay, let me find you something warm to put on, and I'll get up and feed the fire too. Then, when we warm up, we can go look for a midnight snack." As he got up from under the thick, soft down quilts Marie had placed on the bed for them, the cold night air hit his naked skin, raising goosebumps all over his body. Dashing to the fireplace, he stirred the coals and placed several more thick olive-wood logs on the fire. Back in the bed now, he wound himself around her naked form once more, eliciting a shriek from her as his cold feet rubbed against her legs.

"You're freezing. Keep those ice cube feet of yours on your side until they warm up." Looking around the room, she noticed the fresco of the cherubs playing musical instruments and the deeply carved and gilded ceiling. "Joseph. Did you see the ceiling and the walls here? This room, it's... it's the one I've dreamed about for years. You told me about it downstairs, but seeing it now, for real ..."

"It's so strange, but it seems to be true that we've been here before. And maybe will be here again, someday, somehow. When we were making love tonight, did you see anything unusual?"

"No, I didn't. Did you?"

"No, I didn't either. Do you think maybe it's because we're here, in the same room as our visions and your dreams this time?"

"There's a song-prayer we sing at High Holiday services that goes like this; Return again, return again, return to the land of your soul. Return to who you are, return to what you are, return to where you are, born and re-born again.' So, Joseph, born and reborn again... Think about it. We Jews believe in reincarnation. Maybe we have been together in the past, and in this room."

"Yes, maybe. Rachel, I've heard those words before, and recently. I'm trying to remember where it was."

"I find it so completely haunting, returning to who you are, what you are, and where you are."

"Me too," he mumbled to himself. "I know it was Marie, but not Marie. It was today, down in the library, or someplace near it. She was different, so completely different. She was standing in a brilliant bright white light. She said something like Kodosh or Kadosh..."

"Kadosh means Holy. And she also sang the Returning chant?"

"Yes. She told me that I needed to heal all the worlds, and when I asked her how, what my path forward was, she just said I needed to return, and then she chanted those words."

"This was Marie? The little old woman? The housekeeper?"

"It was her, but it wasn't her at all. She was pushing parts of that wooden wall in the library. Did you notice it, how it looks just like the treasure box, but so much larger?"

"I didn't notice it. I was distracted by..." She gave a broad smile, a little chuckle, and a caress of his hair with her soft hand. "...Other things, like you."

"Well, she was doing that, and then the wall opened up, and all I saw was darkness. Then I started to get dizzy and thought I would faint, but then a blinding light filled the doorway, and I heard and saw this tall illuminated female presence standing there who was not Marie."

"Wow. I don't know what it all means, but let's take the treasure box and go downstairs to look at that wall. Maybe I can figure out how to open it."

"There is also the portrait hanging on the wall, and it's so strange because it looks like the photos of my father in the other room."

Getting out of the warm bed, he went to one of the large wardrobes and found two warm robes for them to wear. Finding warm slippers took a bit longer, but soon they were both covered enough to venture along the hall to the stairs. Their path was illuminated by the moonlight coming in the windows in the many bedrooms since Marie and Elias had opened all of the shutters in the house.

They carefully passed down the carpeted marble stairs, through the richly decorated rooms to the kitchen. Joseph was amazed at all that Marie and Elias had done to the house since his arrival. All of the large cloths on the furniture were removed, and all of the outside shutters were open, letting soft light from the cloud obscured night sky into the rooms of the house. In the kitchen, they found prepared food waiting for them in the refrigerator. Taking sandwiches and glasses of milk into the library and sitting at the table and chairs there, both faced the puzzle wall and portrait, eating their snacks in silence.

Rachel was looking intensely at the various parts of the wall as she ate, and after finishing her food, she finally said, "It looks like two huge Trees of Life, with the spheroid patterns interlaced back and forth, from side to side, passing underneath the portrait several times." She stood up and walked closer to the portrait. "Did you see the writing here on the blue ribbon that's falling from the king's lap? And the initials here? I think this painting is by Van Dyke. Joseph, it must be worth a fortune!"

"I did see the initials but didn't know what they meant. The other I couldn't read, but guessed it's Hebrew."

"Yes. It translates to say, King David, beloved of God. This is a portrait of King David. And you told me that it looks almost like the photos of your father?" Turning to look at him, she added, "Joseph, do you realize it looks like you too? The face could almost be you."

"Oh, Rachel, that reminds me. There's something I've got to tell you, something important. It slipped my mind. You remember that letter from my father?"

"Yes, of course. In it, he spoke of this villa and your inheritance. Is there something else?"

"Oh, wow, is there more. There was a part of the letter that was hidden."

"Hidden?"

"He wrote part of it in invisible ink. I guess to keep it secret. It was only when I was crying while holding it that my tears splashed on it and revealed the writing."

"Can you tell me what it said?"

"Something about how my father and I are in the father and son line of David, the shepherd boy..."

"Joseph, your father is saying you're a direct descendant of King David?" She stared at him with her mouth wide open in astonishment. "Joseph, no wonder they've been after you."

"Why?"

"You may be the only remaining direct male descendant of King David alive."

"So, I'm not only Jewish but Jewish royalty? Descended from King David? What on Earth does this all mean?"

"It means that you and I are in even worse danger than I ever thought. Deadly danger. No wonder you've been spied on and followed from Salt Lake to California and across the globe. And, oh god, maybe even here."

"But how would they know of this place?"

"The Church wants you very badly. If there is a way, they may have found out about your family home. Their resources and network are extensive, and I would not underestimate them."

"But what do they want?"

"Well, I don't think they want to honor you and your family, that's for sure."

"Is that who did it? Who killed my family and left me a burned cripple?"

"Remember what else your father wrote to you. 'In case our enemies have found us.' Pretty ominous, I would say, and I think it was Fatima or someone from there who intentionally murdered your parents and tried to kill you."

Joseph, agitated by all this, stood up and walked to one side of the library as if scanning the book titles. Turning to look at her, with new tears flowing from his eyes, he said, "They took away everything essential to me. Everything important." Turning his back to the wall of books, he waved an arm at them and said, "I don't care about the money and this place. I just wish I still had my parents with me."

"I'm sure of it. It must have been the Circle of Fatima that did this to your family, and no wonder they wanted me to spy on you and report everything you did and said."

Joseph, reminded of her role in possibly betraying him, glared at her, raising his voice, "You would have to mention that." He turned his back on her and pretended to look at the book titles.

With tears falling, and agony in her voice, she replied, "But I didn't do it. Like I told you, I tried to protect you in every way I could. It was just that they had my sister, my sweet baby sister, and they raped and murdered her anyway."

Turning to face her once more, his face softened in sympathy for her pain. "Rachel, I'm so sorry. I wish you could have gotten there in time, and rescued her, or if, somehow, I could have rescued her for you." Sighing deeply, he slowly shook his head from side to side. "If I could have done something, anything to change what happened... I would have even turned myself into them if it could have saved Debra."

"No, this is so much bigger than just our lives. There is some greater power at work here, both for good and for evil. Sacrificing yourself to save Debra would not have worked. They would have still killed her or caused her to take her own life. And they would have killed me, and you. And whatever you are supposed to do or be doing would not have a chance then."

"But what am I supposed to do? What is the answer to all of this?"

"Well, when I was at Fatima as a novice nun, there were whispered rumors of a secret prophecy, a hidden part of the 'Third Secret of Fatima' that supposedly spoke of a descendant of the House of David bringing cataclysmic change to the Church. You're a threat to them somehow just because of who you are, and who your family is. Though I have no exact idea of how you could be."

He ran his fingers through his short-clipped hair, trying to think of an answer. "What danger could I be to the Catholic Church? That's crazy. I just don't get it at all."

Stepping back to the puzzle wall, Rachel started to push the circles in an order that he couldn't follow. She moved from one side to the other, running up and down the two trees when, finally, she said, "This is it. That should do it." And with the last push of a circle, the door slid open under the painting, revealing a dark opening. Eagerly stepping into the darkness and striking a match from the box sitting on a ledge, she lit a candle that was visible just inside. She turned the corner with the candle, lighting up the room that lay beyond, and cried out, "Joseph, come quick! It's a secret synagogue. And there's a Torah scroll here as well."

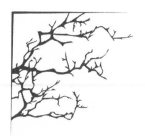

Forty

VILLA OF THE FOREVER View
  April 23, 1986 – Eve of Passover

Lighting several more candles in the hidden space, Rachel exclaimed, "Joseph, I had almost forgotten, but today is the 23rd of April, and so tonight is the Eve of Passover. It started tonight at sundown." She lit two additional candles at the end of the room on either side of an ancient-looking but beautifully inlaid wooden cabinet.

Walking farther into the small space, Joseph was struck by the floor to ceiling bookshelves on either side filled with books. Some appeared to be in English, others Italian, but many of them had Hebrew lettering on their spines. Above the open cabinet at the end of the small room, there was a curved archway with raised relief carved gilded writing that he could tell was also Hebrew.

"What does that say?"

Singing the words, she said, "It says, 'Shomer, Shomer Yisrael. Shimor Shearit, Yisrael. V'al Yovad Yisrael. Haomrim, Shema Yisrael.'"

"My, that is beautiful, but can you translate it for me?"

"'O Guardian of Israel, guard the remnant of Israel, and let not Israel disappear, the ones who chant, Shema Israel.' It appears to be a blessing placed especially over this Torah. How intriguing, but I've never seen this prayer used that way, to mark a space for worship. Though it makes sense since we Jews are in so much danger, and there are so few of us left living now." She gave a long sad sigh, and continued, "This is a prayer used throughout our history, whenever Jews were threatened with death and destruction. It is a prayer to God, to protect even 'the remnant' of our people from vanishing entirely."

Looking up at the writing, he said, "I guess my parents felt that way and were right to do so. I'm sure now they were murdered for being Jews."

"Yes, I think you're right."

"But what is 'Shema Israel'? What does that mean?"

"You may not remember it, but we chanted it on Friday night at the service in Salt Lake. Here, I`ll show you." Picking up a folded silk prayer shawl that was resting on one of the two chair backs, she placed it over her head and draped the rest over both of her shoulders. Reaching out to him, she handed to him the other shawl that was wrapped over the second chair. "Here, let me help you." As she arranged his shawl in the same way, she said, "Now, repeat after me, with your right hand over your eyes

"Shema."

"Israel."

"Adoni."

"Eloheinu."

"Adonai Echad"

Joseph followed her, repeating the words, as she chanted the prayer. She then moved the silk shawl from her head back onto her shoulders and reached over to him to do the same with his.

"Rachel, that was wonderful as well. It's so mysterious sounding. What does it mean?"

"It translates as, 'Hear, oh Israel, the Lord your God. The Lord your God, is one. 'Israel' translates as those who 'Wrestle with God.'"

Approaching the cabinet, he reached out to an embroidered purple velvet cloth that was covering a large double rounded shape on the top of it. As he lifted the fabric, revealing the lines of black inked lettering that ran across the golden sheepskin, he asked, "What is this?"

"That is the Book of our people. She is our Torah."

Reaching out his hand, Joseph was drawn to caress the letters with his bare fingers.

"No. Joseph, you don't touch..."

He traced a line of text before she could stop him. A sudden brilliant flash of light blinded them both as it filled the small room, and a bright, high voice boomed out, echoing and saying, over and over again, "Kadosh, Kadosh, Kadosh, ..."

With their eyes squeezed shut against the piercing light, and their hands covering their ears to deflect the reverberations of the overwhelming voice, the two young people opened their eyes at last to see a transformed Marie.

She was, as Joseph had seen her previously, a tall, young-looking but ageless woman, clad in an illuminated white gossamer gown, with flowing, golden-white hair framing a warm, loving face.

"Joseph, Rachel... I am Miriam. They are coming! Now!"

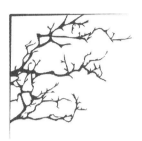

Forty-one

VILLA OF THE FOREVER View
April 24, 1986, Passover

"What? Who? Do you mean...?" They both overlapped their voices in confusion, and Rachel asked, "Do you mean Fatima?"

"Yes, you know who. You have little time."

"But, here? Now? It's the middle of the night. What can we do? We need to get dressed at least."

"It is almost dawn now, and you have no time to get dressed. And no need. As the sun rises behind the mountains and the clouds, you must call out to your ancestors, Joseph. Use your companion."

"What? Rachel? But how?"

"The violin, Joseph. The violin. Just as she called out to you to bring you home, here where she was created, you must now access and unleash her full power. She will guide your return. On the journey, you must take to liberate your people."

As Miriam handed him a set of sheet music, she said, "You must play this music. The Kol Nidre. Three times. Now, out on the terrace facing the sea and the rising sun."

"But, Rachel, who is...? This is happening too fast. We were just upstairs in bed a little while ago, and now we're in danger."

"Rachel is safe with me. Now, you must go. Go and play the Kol Nidre, the music of return, to defeat the enemy, Pharaoh and his army, and launch the liberation of our people into the sunrise and for all time. You must complete playing this piece three times."

"Joseph, I love you. Go. Do what Miriam is asking."

"But our people? Miriam, you're Jewish too?"

She laughed in a sweet, clear musical voice. "I am the sister of Moshe; you may know him as Moses. So, of course, I am a God wrestler too! Now, Joseph, you must go. Play with all of your passion and all of her power."

The large helicopter rose high in the air from the paved harborside in Portofino to soar out over the long narrow bay, heading east along the coast.

DeSilva turned his partially bandaged head, with his one remaining eye, towards the young priest who had talked the Italian military into supplying the aircraft. "Well done. You convinced the authorities criminals were hiding from the Inquisition?"

Servino answered for the priest. "Yes, Your Grace. It was not difficult. The respect for your authority here is quite strong."

"Good. We should have no problem capturing these two and obtaining that violin." DeSilva looked over the dozen grim-faced armed agents, sitting ready to obey his orders.

Joseph had picked up a folding music stand from the library as he headed out the French doors to the south terrace. Despite only wearing slippers and a robe over his naked skin, for some reason, he was not cold.

With the violin and bow in his left hand, he walked out into the pre-dawn foggy light and set up the stand with his right hand. Opening the music, he could see that it was titled in Hebrew, with printing in English letters that said, *'Solo Violin, Kol Nidre, for Bnei Anusim.'*

Checking his tuning, he played the first haunting bars of the music as he gradually allowed the music to deeply swirl and enfold the space around him in wave after wave of alternatively sinking and soaring minor key notes and phrases.

I see the sun rising. I don't know what I'm doing, but I trust Miriam completely. Rachel, I hope you're okay. I love you so much.

He noticed that he had now played the sequence two full times, and was beginning the third time. Miriam had said three times, and then what?

Rachel stood in the secret synagogue in front of the open Torah, as if unsure of what she should do.

Miriam looked at her. "Are you wondering what you should do next?"

"Yes, I am. What can I do to help him?"

"We are about to receive guests at the front door. Perhaps you could greet them? If you wish."

"Do you mean, delay them?"

"Yes, that is one option. It is entirely up to you, Rachel. What does your heart tell you? What, or how much, are you willing to sacrifice for your love, and your people?"

"Everything for my people, and everything that I am and ever will be for his love."

"Well, then follow your heart and never stop."

"I ..." The sound of an increasing roar from out front of the villa interrupted her words.

Rachel looked towards Miriam; a questioning look on her face.

"Yes. Go slow them down. And now would be a good time."

Turning, Rachel ran with her robe threatening to fly open and her slippers flapping on the floor until she kicked them off, towards the front of the house.

As she opened the front door, she saw a large gray helicopter descending through the treetops, preparing to land. When it did so, it would almost fill the front courtyard.

I hope this works. Joseph, I love you so much.

Running barefoot down the front steps, she waved up at the faces she saw on board, and with a broad smile on her face, suddenly stretched out her arms and opened her robe, flapping it back to reveal her naked form underneath it.

Seeing this startling sight out the window with the copter blades still in motion, DeSilva sputtered, "What the fuck? What is that bitch doing?" He looked over and saw his agents and Servino were all staring, mesmerized at the sight of the near-naked woman who was standing just out of range of the spinning blades. Even the pilot was staring, and losing his concentration, as the still airborne copter started to dangerously and steeply lean to one side.

The spinning blades started clipping parts of the nearby trees as the aircraft continued to sharply angle, towards the on-rushing pavement.

DeSilva stood up in the sharply leaning aircraft, shouting so loudly that the strain caused the stitches in his side to open up, "Pilot, dammit! Pay attention and get us down."

With a great effort and at the last second, the pilot managed to get the chopper leveled out, and finally touched down. With the blades still spinning, blowing a cloud of dust and shredded greenery all over the front of the villa, the massive gray machine finally came to rest on the paving stones.

Clutching the bandaged and bleeding wound on his side with one hand, DeSilva shouted once more, "What are you fools waiting for? Jump out and grab her. But be careful, the bitch has claws."

Seeing the door sliding open, Rachel re-tied the belt on her robe and ran off into the gardens on the northeast side of the villa, away from where Joseph was playing the Kol Nidre music.

"Get her!" DeSilva shouted as the men piled off and started chasing the young woman into the gardens.

As Joseph slowed down his bowing to play the last few haunting notes, he saw Elias approach him, saying, "Joseph, you are on your way now. On your journey, you will receive guidance from Miriam and me. By the way, I am Elijah, as you may have suspected for a time."

"Elijah, the prophet? It was you in the snowstorm, and San Francisco, and the library," Joseph said as he played the last slowly fading note.

"Yes. We both Miriam and I, have been guiding your way. Now journey in Shalom, Joseph."

Elias reached out to catch the violin and bow as Joseph's hands started to turn transparent before his eyes, and the violin began to fall to the ground. Joseph, his body slowly fading from view, now heard the sound of loud voices getting closer to him.

With a rush of many footsteps around the corner of the villa, the large group of armed agents stormed onto the terrace. Leading the group was Servino, his face bloody from numerous scratches, with a barefoot struggling Rachel being pushed along in front of him, her arms tied behind her back.

Her robe was muddy, torn, and halfway off her body. When she saw Elijah, she cried out, "Joseph, where is he?" Elijah pointed at the gradually fading form of Joseph.

Crying out to him, "Joseph, wait for me!" She violently jerked her tied hands behind her back, down towards the stones, causing Servino to fall to the pavement, releasing the rope he had been holding. As the rope unwound from her hands, in two quick steps, she was able to reach the now almost transparent form of her lover, wrapping her arms around him. In a swirl of brilliant sparks of light Rachel also started to fade from view while she gazed with love into his eyes. "Joseph, I love you so much. I`m never letting you go, ever again."

DeSilva, struggling with his wounded body and trailing behind his men and Servino, came around the corner of the villa. Seeing his henchman laying on the ground, he yelled, "Servino, get up, you fool, and grab that violin."

Joseph's vision had contracted to just Rachel in front of him, his lips finding hers, as a sea of deep purple light spun in a spiral, surrounded them both.

Seeing Rachel and Joseph in each other's arms slowly fading from view, DeSilva looked at the old man holding the violin. "Give me that damn fiddle."

"No. You're too late," Elias calmly replied.

"Too late? No, I'm not! Hand me that violin or the girl and boy will die!"

"No. You do not understand. You're really out of time."

"What do you mean, out of time?" DeSilva roared, almost spitting out the words. "Servino, shoot them both. Now!"

Servino answered, pointing his automatic pistol at the two and said, "Gladly." But as he squeezed off two quick shots aimed at their heads, Rachel and Joseph both faded from view and vanished.

The sea of brilliant purple light that had surrounded the lovers had quickly expanded into a vast swirling sea of colors, sparks of fiery light, and finally into a deep golden cloud that collapsed beneath them. And they were both gone

DeSilva was suddenly blinded in his remaining eye by the morning sun rising, piercing him with the brightest light he had ever seen, as the thick clouds and fog completely melted away and the sky turned a deep, bright blue. Blinded by the intense sunlight, not seeing the two lovers vanish, and

Servino and his agents fall to the ground and blow away as dust, he lunged for the violin that Elias still held, just managing to touch it with one finger as his hand began to lose its shape and form. With that finger leading him, he fell into a headlong, sickening, spiraling whirlwind of molten black swallowing shadows, and vanished.

Standing together on the villa's south terrace, Marie reached out and took his hand, asking, "Is everything all right, Elias?"

He turned to look at her, and then looked out over the lush gardens in full bloom under the healthy deep green of the trees, some laden with bright colored oranges and lemons, and smelled the fragrant blossoms all around him. Squeezing her hand and turning again to look south out over the calm Mediterranean Sea with a hot summer sun shining in the sapphire blue sky, he smiled broadly, took a deep relaxing breath and said, "Yes, Marie. It is now."

"And is the family coming to stay after their trip to Israel?"

"Yes. All is ready for their summer enjoyment."

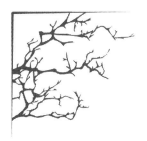

Forty-two
Returning

LISBON, PORTUGAL

April 24, 1522

What is that smell? Barbecued pork? Oh, God, no. It's humans burning. The fires. Oh, no ... DeSilva thought. *Oh, God. I'm about to be burned.*

Screams of the dying filled the air as the condemned man struggled with the strange voice within him. *Who are you? Get out of me. Tempt me not, Devil. I'm about to burn. Be gone...*

"No! No, I am not a Judaizer. I am a good Catholic," DeSilva said out loud as he stumbled and fell to the dirty stones.

"Levante-o espuma. Get up, you scum. Nothing will save you from the fires!" the black-clad priest commanded.

Inside this other body, and mind, DeSilva commanded this other-self. *Listen to me, do you want to burn? You are under my control.*

With a force of will driven by stark terror, combined with his study of Dark Kabbalah, DeSilva bent the other voice to be silent and subservient to his will.

Now taking command of this weaker mind, he took charge of his situation. The dirty, ragged prisoner, down on his knees, looked up at the fires and in a voice dripping with piety and remorse said, "Por favor, please, please, forgive me, Father, for my sins and errors. I repent. I repent. Spare me from the fires this time. Spare me, Father, as I can be of great use to you in your holy work."

The black-clad priest replied, "If you truly repent, and can accuse others, then you may yet live."

Her mother called out to her, waking Rebeca from her sleep. "Rebeca, wake up. Wake up! You must get ready to leave for the convent today."

Oh, what a strange dream I just had. I was some other place, someone else, I think. Servino, DeSilva, Joseph. Oh, God. I was about to be shot ...

Startled, sitting upright on her bed, the young woman's thoughts clashed with themselves.

Who are you? What are you? Rachel? But how are you in me?

I am you, somehow. I see you, your thoughts, and they are my thoughts, Rebeca, as you are me... Rachel.

I have felt you before, in me. So, we are one person?

Yes, we are ...

Breathing deeply, Rachel inhaled slowly and calmly for long minutes as her two self's gradually and gently folded into one.

Joseph, where are you? I feel you now. You are here, now, nearby. Come to me. Come to me, my love. Come to your Rachel, now.

The young priest abruptly sat up on the straw-covered floor of his prison cell, aware that the presence that had filled his mind several times was back once again. *You're back. Inside my head. Go away.*

I am here. I am you, Marcus. And we must get you out of this place. Now.

You? Who, what are you? You're making me crazy.

I am you, and I am here, part of you. We are one soul. Be calm. I am Joseph, and I am you, Marcus. And you are not crazy.

Joseph, remembering what Rachel had taught him, followed the golden energy flowing through his body up in his spine and imagined it flowing into and through the body and soul of Marcus. Breathing deeply, he knitted himself to Marcus, one soul gradually becoming one mind, one body. Slowly the other inner voice, relaxed and merged with him.

Rachel, I hear you now. Keep calling to me! Call to your Joseph. Call to your Marcus. I love you, and I will find you, no matter what.

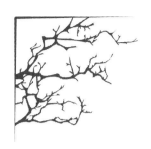

THE END

WHAT DID YOU THINK of The Violin Maker?

First of all, I want thank you for purchasing this book. I know you could have picked any number of books to read, but you picked this book and for that I am extremely grateful.

I hope that you found it entertaining and interesting. If so, it would be wonderful if you could share this book with your friends and family by posting to Facebook and Twitter.

If you enjoyed this book, I'd like to hear from you and hope that you could take some time to post a review on Amazon and/or Good Reads. Your feedback and support will help this author to continue to improve his writing craft for future projects and to make this book and the next ones even better.

I want you, the reader, to know that your review is very important to me. If you'd like to leave a review, all you have to do is follow these links here below, and away you go.

https://www.amazon.com/dp/B07VP92R57

https://www.goodreads.com/book/show/47185313-the-violin-maker?ac=1&from_search=true

I WISH YOU ALL THE BEST!

Follow your Bliss, and live your life in Joy! Glenn J. Hill

Don't miss out!

Visit the website below and you can sign up to receive emails whenever Glenn J Hill publishes a new book. There's no charge and no obligation.

https://books2read.com/r/B-A-GYZH-AJPZ

BOOKS 2 READ

Connecting independent readers to independent writers.

About the Author

I started writing some years ago, when I was studying to become a Certified Jewish Storyteller. At the time I began writing my own original stories to tell to live audiences, along with my own versions of traditional tales.

I had not known my Mother was Jewish when I was younger. I only found out in the last twenty years that she was from a hidden Jewish family who at pain of death, had to flee from persecution and the Inquisition in Spain and Portugal in the 1400`s, 1500`s and 1600`s. And from Russia in abt 1700.

Some of my ancestral Jewish family in Venice claimed to be descended from King David, though there is no sure proof of this. In the 1500`s and later they were court musicians and instrument builders in the Courts of Henry VIII and Queen Elizabeth, where the family continued to play music for the Royal Court and the Globe Theater in London. Eventually their descendants settled in the American colonies, as early as 1609.

I draw upon this once hidden ancestry and my stringed instrument building experiences in my writing. I am a trained classical Italian violin builder, and harp builder, designing, building and carving custom one-of-a-kind harps for forty-one years now.

My creative endeavors over the years include having danced ballet and modern dance with local dance companies, as well as acting, dancing and singing in semi-professional musical and dramatic theater productions.

.

I live and write in Southwest Oregon, with my beautiful wife Laurie, and our two sweet girl dogs, Princess Jasmine, a Shih-tzu, and Bella, a Lhasa Apso.

In my Book Two, "In The Fires of Time", (to be released in August 2020), of this series, "The Music of Time", the story in this novel will be continued back in time in the 1500`s and beyond.

This novel was partially inspired by past life recalls I have had, as well as a near-death experience I experienced on Yom Kippur, before I found out I was Jewish by birth.

Follow your Bliss and Live your Life in Joy.

Glenn J. Hill

https://www.glennhillauthor.com/ https://www.facebook.com/TheViolinMakerANovel/

Read more at https://glennhillauthor.com.

About the Publisher

Mountain Glen Publishing
809 W 1st Street
Phoenix Oregon, USA 97535
glennhillauthor@gmail.com

Made in the USA
Middletown, DE
22 November 2019